WINTER IGNITING

REBECCA ZANETTI

Published by RAZ INK LLC

To contact author:

Website: www.RebeccaZanetti.com

Facebook: www.facebook.com/RebeccaZanetti.books

Newsletter: http://rebeccazanetti.com/rebeccas-newsletter/

Twitter: @RebeccaZanetti

Instagram: RebeccaZanetti

This one's for everyone quietly prepping once in a while for the Apocalypse...just in case. You know who you are.

VANGUARD TERRITORY

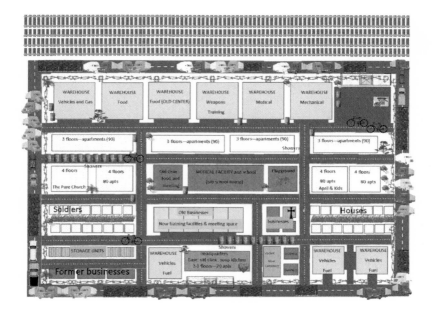

1

I'm the perfect person to take this job. I have nothing to lose.
—April Snyder, Journal

THIS WAS CRAZY. Even in a world already gone to insanity, her going undercover was nutballs. April Snyder kept her face stoic, though her body rioted with a tenseness that made her neck ache with knots. "I can do it," she said quietly, lying her ass off.

Jax Mercury, the leader of Vanguard, sat across from her at the executive-style conference table, his brown eyes soft. Which was incredibly rare. "You don't know the plan yet."

It didn't matter. Whatever the plan, she was in. "I have nothing to lose," she said quietly. Now that was the truth.

Jax sat back and crossed impressive arms. At the early hour, Vanguard headquarters, and especially his war room, was quiet. After Scorpius had infected and killed most of the world, Jax had created this somewhat safe haven in the middle of Los Angeles for survivors. Vanguard territory took up seven complete blocks of old apartment buildings, bankrupted businesses, and a couple of ex-drug houses. Jax ruled them all. "I'm concerned this will be too much for you."

Every once in a while, the guy showed a sweet side that came as a complete shock. But she didn't need sweet.

She blinked and glanced at the empty chairs surrounding a table that must've belonged to a law firm at some point, considering the inlaid design in the middle. This was where Jax and his top lieutenants often strategized how to survive. She didn't belong here, and she knew it. "Nothing is too much for me," she said, meaning it. She'd lost everything. Her husband, her daughter, her friends. The pandemic had killed them all. "You need me."

Jax's gaze narrowed as he studied her. "I'm not looking for somebody to go on a suicide mission."

She barely kept from squirming beneath his regard. Jax's picture should be next to *badass* in the dictionary.

Focus. She had to focus. Taking a deep breath, she settled back in her chair. After her teenage daughter had died, everyone had treated her with a soft touch, including Jax. But he'd never acted as if she'd been destroyed. "I'm not looking to die, Jax. I don't want to. But I don't really care if I do." She owed him that much truth. "I might be able to help some folks before I go, so why not?"

He didn't like her answer. By the tightening of his jaw, he definitely wasn't pleased.

Her stomach ached, but she faced him as bravely as she could. Not blinking helped.

The door opened, and Damon Winter strode inside, munching on a Twinkie. The world might've died, but preserved pastries lived on.

Damon winked at her.

April's breath caught. Damon was everything she was not. Big and tough and dangerous. Even before the world had basically ended, he'd been a cop in Los Angeles. Fighting bad guys. And he had that electric charisma she'd only seen in movie stars before now.

He pulled out a seat at the end of the table, finishing his breakfast. "What's the plan?" His voice was a rich rumble that made her wonder about things she shouldn't.

Jax looked his way. "Did Tace release you medically?"

Damon rolled very deep brown eyes. "Yes. I'm fine. The ribs have already healed, and Tace took stitches out of everywhere he slid the needle in. I'm ready for the op, Mom."

Jax grunted. "You've only been here a week, and I'm already regretting aligning with the Mercs."

Damon grinned. "We are a handful."

The Mercs were military soldiers, all men, who took over Santa Barbara before it had burned to the ground. Now, they were integrating into Vanguard territory, though not very smoothly it appeared.

April cleared her throat. "How's the integration coming?"

"Not well." Damon lost the smile. "It's a bit rocky."

"Good," Jax said.

April's shoulders jerked. "Good? Why is that good?"

"We need internal strife for your mission," Jax said.

Mission. She was actually going to do something that was called a mission. Life had turned into Bizarro World.

Jax looked at her and then at Damon. "The Pure church has been courting April for months, trying to get another woman to join. But Damon's going to be the prize for them."

What? April shook her head.

Damon nodded. "Yep. I'm a prize. It's nice to be appreciated."

Jax rolled his eyes. "They want members, women especially, and we need to find out why. But they're also low on soldiers, and I'm sure they'd love to gather Damon into the ranks since he's trained and hasn't been infected by Scorpius. So, you're going to be the key to him, April."

Okay. She was starting to understand the strategy. The Pure

church had set up inside Vanguard, and Scorpius had not infected the members. Nor had it affected Damon or her. "They've been slow to recruit me," she murmured.

"They're smart," Jax said quietly.

Damon tapped his fingers on the table. "Catch me up to speed about this church. I don't have any details."

Jax scratched the scruff along his jawline. "We don't know much, which is a problem. They've taken over an apartment complex in the western corner of Vanguard territory, and they have food and ammunition. No members have contracted Scorpius, thus, the Pure."

Damon eyed April and then Jax. "What's the problem? The Scorpius bacteria is deadly, and they should be protected from infection if possible."

Jax lifted a shoulder. "Agreed. But we don't know how many kids are in there, or if the members are there willingly. It's too secretive. Creepy, actually. Pastor Zachary King won't let us talk to any of them, and armed guards cover the complex. In my territory."

April leaned forward. "Just the pastor. No name. He said God spoke to him decreed him the Pastor. That names are for other people."

"Jesus," Damon muttered. "Sounds like a cult."

Jax sighed. "That's what I'm afraid of. Okay. I'd prefer to call him Pastor King so we don't get him confused with a prisoner I have locked down named Zach Barter. So far, the name Zach is causing me problems."

April winced. "We know there are at least five pregnant women in the Pure, and we have to find out if they are voluntary members. I want to do this, Jax." What was left of her life had to mean something.

"You're our best option," Jax said, a muscle ticking in his jaw. "They've been slowly making a move on you for a while."

"Only a few meetings and a lot of chance encounters," she said.

"They'll step it up if they think they can get Damon through you," Jax said, wincing and then pulling a knife from the back of his waistband. "Forgot this was there." He plunked it onto the table.

April swallowed, her gaze going to the rough hilt. At least it was in a sheath. "Through me? How?"

"Two ways. First, you're going to assist Damon with integrating the Mercs into Vanguard territory so you have a reason to spend time together," Jax said.

Easy enough. "Okay," she said.

"And, second, he's going to romantically pursue you. Big time," Jax finished. "The church will see and will try to use you to manipulate him since he's about to be so into you."

Her body flushed hot. "Huh?"

"Men falling for women act like morons for a brief time," Jax said simply.

Brief time? Right. April lifted an eyebrow.

Damon smiled, and this time, a dimple showed in his left cheek. "This might be my favorite mission ever."

Warmth spread to her face, no doubt causing her to look like a tomato. Courage. She had to be brave with these guys. "Why don't I pursue him?" she retorted with as much spirit as she could drum up.

"Great plan," Damon said instantly, oozing charm.

Jax cut him a hard glare. "Knock it off." He faced April. "The church knows you and has watched you for months. You're not the type to pursue a guy you barely know. But they don't know Damon. We can make him into anybody we want right now."

Geez. Okay. All right, she wasn't a femme fatale. She'd been with one man her entire life, and then he'd died. So, she truly had no argument. Except the idea of sexy Damon chasing her, a widow from suburbia, was ridiculous. "So, we pretend a romantic...ah...relationship?"

"Why pretend?" Damon asked smoothly.

She gaped. Was he actually flirting with her?

Jax picked up his knife. "I told you to knock it off. I meant it. This is our last-ditch effort before I take the complex by storm, and I'd rather not scare the women and kids there. But I'll do it if necessary." He studied them thoughtfully. "We're going the safe route for now, but we might have a problem."

Damon's gaze narrowed instantly. "Why?"

"Because you're black," Jax said bluntly, turning to look at her, "and she's white. Very white."

April's mouth gaped open. "Jax." Had he just said that?

The Vanguard leader met her gaze head-on. "I don't have time to be politically correct, April. You're white, he's black, and this church has rules we don't know or understand. They're secretive, and my gut tells me something is wrong there. There's bad shit going on, and racism might just be a part of it." He shrugged. "Or not. We just don't know."

"But still," she protested.

"I don't have a racist bone in my body," Jax muttered. "I'm Hispanic, and I have Native American, Korean, Anglo-Saxon, and Texan lieutenants."

She coughed. "*Texan* isn't a race."

"It should be," Jax returned. "Tace is one of a kind. But my point is, even though we're not racist assholes, the Pure church might be. They might not like interracial couples. Or premarital sex. Or brunettes with big boobs. Or LAPD officers. Who the hell knows. I want you to be prepared for that."

Damon looked at her, his gaze warm. "I like that you're offended and surprised by this, by the way."

She shifted in her seat. He was just too much. Dark eyes, rugged jaw, cut cheekbones. His chest was wide and muscled. With a gun strapped to his thigh, and a knife to his calf, he oozed deadliness. That shouldn't be sexy...but it was. But she had no business viewing him like that. This was a mission. A job. "I don't know how to be pursued," she blurted out.

His chin lifted, and a different light entered his eyes. A predatory glint. "Then this should be fun."

Panic engulfed her so she remained quiet.

Jax sighed and shoved away from the table as if bored with the entire conversation. "You two talk and come up with a game plan. April, last time Damon was here, we had him throw a fit about being around people who'd survived Scorpius."

"It wasn't exactly a fit," Damon drawled. "More like a loud objection. A manly one." He winked again.

Was he teasing her now?

Jax grumbled and stood, heading for the door. "Whatever. I'd like to get things into motion tonight. Damon, you're taking point. Figure it out." With the last words, he stomped out the door, slamming it behind him.

Quiet descended.

Her throat clogged. "Um. What does 'taking point' mean?"

Damon studied her, his gaze serious now that Jax had left the room. "I'm in charge of mission parameters."

Considering she'd never been on a mission in her life, she was okay with that. "Which are?"

He leaned toward her, a woodsy, ginger scent wafting her way. Manly and intriguing. "We'll use our real jobs as cover for this mission. Our first meeting will be today at noon, in the park that's been set up middle territory for the kids, to work on integrating the Merc soldiers into Vanguard."

"So we really do our jobs while also doing the other job," she said, blinking. This was confusing.

"Yeah. The more natural we are, the better." He reached out and planted his warm hand over hers.

Heat and electricity zapped through her. She looked at the difference. His hand was big enough to completely engulf hers and had scars across the knuckles. From fighting? She lifted wide eyes to him. "I don't know how to act. To pretend." She'd worked at a dentist's office before Scorpius descended for Pete's sake.

"Just be you, blue eyes," Damon said. "React exactly as you would normally."

She pulled her hand from beneath his and set it in her lap. "Okay." There was no reason for them to hold hands. Why couldn't she breathe? His simple touch had overwhelmed her and forced sensations into her body that she had no business feeling. "We don't need to pretend now."

His eyes glittered with a light she couldn't quite read. "Who's pretending?"

2

Journal entry number one. I haven't kept a journal since my tenth-grade teacher, a very sexy Ms. Dashwood, made us write in one each day. It's an odd requirement at Vanguard, but I guess I understand that history should be preserved. I hope Ms. Dashwood was, too.

—Damon Winter, Journal

DAMON REACHED the weed-riddled front lawn of the former crack house his people were using as a temporary headquarters, sweat rolling down his face from the unrelenting sun.

The second he crossed over the crumbly, brown weeds, a gunshot pierced the silence of the hot-assed day, echoing from inside the house. His head jerked, and his body stilled. He forgot the fact that his best and only friend in the world was inside the house and fell back on training. He kicked in the front door, ducking low, moving fast while smoothly freeing the Sig from his thigh holster.

"Goddamn motherfucker," Greyson Storm bellowed from what used to be the kitchen.

The sound of his voice eased Damon slightly. At least Grey was still standing. Damon put his back to the moldy living room wall and edged closer. "Grey? All clear?" he called out.

"Affirmative," Greyson snapped back.

Damon kept his weapon pointed at the ground and moved into the kitchen, automatically taking mental notes about the scene while preparing to fire if necessary. His shoulders loosened as he found Greyson pressing a boot against the neck of a blond male in his early twenties. He double-checked the far corner for threats and then relaxed. "So, what's up?"

Irritation flashed hot and bright across Grey's hard face as he systematically popped bullets out of the magazine of a small, silver handgun, each one dropping on the back of the guy whimpering on the torn linoleum. The weapon looked ridiculously small in Grey's hand.

"Is that a lady Smith and Wesson?" Damon asked, his eyebrows rising.

"Yep." Grey emptied the magazine of its eighth bullet—hollow-point—and slammed it back home into the barrel chamber. His boot remained on the guy's neck, who still lay flat on his stomach with his palms down. His back visibly spasmed, and he flopped around like a landed trout.

Damon slid his gun back into his tactical leg holster. "Did he point that at you, Grey?" he asked, rather reasonably.

"Yep," Greyson said again, setting the weapon on the folding card table to his right. His grayish eyes were over-bright, his strong features set in pissed lines. "Not only did he point it, the moron accidentally fired." He jerked his head toward the back door. "Ruined the wallpaper."

Damon snorted. Dingy, flowered paper covered the walls, and the damaged floor might've been green at one time. The place was a shithole. Sighing, he angled his neck and partially leaned down to get a better look at the moron on the floor. "Who are you?"

The blond could only cough.

Damon glanced up. "It's hard for him to speak with your foot on his throat."

"So?" Greyson stared down at the prone man.

Damon looked closer. "He's turning kind of blue. If you don't want to kill him, you might want to let up." Though anybody dumb enough to pull a gun on Greyson Storm might as well be dead. Stupid rarely survived an apocalypse.

Grey appeared to think it over while the guy flopped faster, his knees knocking loudly on the filthy floor.

Damon straightened to peer out the one window in the former kitchen, just in case the guy had buddies waiting outside. All he could see was the razor-topped, chain-link fence out the side that surrounded the entire territory. All seven blocks of it in inner-city Los Angeles. "I'd rather interview him before we dig a hole. Any chance?"

Emitting a long-suffering sigh, Grey slowly slid his boot off the guy's neck, leaving a raw imprint of thick tread. "Fine. But make it quick. It'll be too hot outside to dig a grave soon."

Damon grabbed the blond by the neck of his T-shirt and lifted to shove him onto the short stool at the table. The guy wobbled, his eyes wide, his throat a mottled red. "Who are you, and what's with the gun? More importantly, who sent you?" Damon asked.

"Chris," the guy croaked, grasping his neck. He looked about twenty-five with greasy hair and uneven stubble across his face. Blue eyes, slight build, shaking at the moment. "Name is Chris."

Grey looked down from well over six feet of height. "What's up with the death wish?"

Fair question. Damon leaned against the rotting doorframe and crossed his arms. "More importantly, who's working with you and coming next?"

Greyson nodded. "Yeah. That."

Chris looked around frantically, his gaze settling on the back door.

"You won't make it," Damon said, almost gently. He wasn't in the mood to interrogate anybody, but it didn't look like he had a choice. Greyson would just shoot the guy and move on with the day. "Listen, Chris. Start with something easy. Are you a member of Vanguard?"

Chris turned his gaze back to Damon, his eyes wide with the need to make a connection. The desire to be understood and, hopefully, not harmed that all suspects showed. "Yes. Aren't you?"

Grey lifted a dark eyebrow. "No. We're Mercs." While the Mercenaries might currently be taking up residence in Vanguard territory, they certainly weren't losing their identity. "Did somebody send you?"

"No." Chris finally released his neck and rubbed his shaking hands down his jeans-covered thighs. "Nobody sent me, and the Vanguard lieutenants have no idea I'm here." His voice, already hoarse, rose. "Please don't tell them. I'll do anything."

Greyson shifted his weight, his hands loose but no doubt ready to strangle the idiot. "I'm losing patience."

"Like you had any to start with," Damon retorted as Chris crossed his arms and firmed his jaw. Ah. The defensive posturing moment. "If you say anything we don't appreciate right now, like you're a member of Vanguard and are protected, I'm gonna let Grey just kill you."

Grey smiled, the sight feral. "I appreciate that, Damon."

"You're welcome," Damon said as the color slid out of Chris's face.

Chris looked from Damon to Greyson while swallowing rapidly. "I thought you were in charge of the Mercs."

"I am," Grey said easily. "Damon leads the troops. Some might say he's my conscience. He's ex-LAPD and keeps a tight rein on our organization."

Damon nodded, holding on to his patience because Grey

wouldn't. "You should probably understand that we don't bluff. There's no time for it with the pandemic creating an apocalypse and all." What exactly was the threat level here? He'd do what he had to in order to find out.

Chris rolled back bony shoulders. "I watched you training new Vanguard recruits yesterday, and I saw how you were with Jacki. Just wanted to have a man-to-man talk with you, Greyson. Make sure we understood each other, and that she's with me."

Grey snorted. "You don't bring a girl's gun to a man-to-man talk. Jesus." His eyes twinkled, and he turned toward Damon. "I guess he's too dumb to mess with."

Just the opposite. Irritation clawed at Damon's back. While Chris was a jackass, he'd discharged a weapon, which meant that somebody could've been killed. There wasn't time for such stupidity these days. "You can rip his head off if you want, Greyson."

Grey's face lit. "No kidding?"

Chris whimpered and tried to mask the sound with a cough.

"Yeah." Damon slid to the side, knowing Grey well enough to understand that he should get out of the way.

"Cool." Grey moved faster than a jaguar, grabbed Chris by the neck and jeans, and neatly threw him right through the doorway. The kid's boot smashed the doorframe, and wood splintered in several directions. He landed in the middle of the empty living room on gross shag carpet and bounced twice. Maybe three times.

He groaned and pushed to his feet.

"Run," Greyson said helpfully.

Two seconds later, Chris had cleared the front door, letting it bang back into place.

Damon shook his head. "Who's Jacki?"

"Hell if I know." Greyson straddled the chair recently vacated by Chris. "I did Jax Mercury a solid yesterday and showed some new members self-defense moves before they went out on scouting trips. Didn't get names." He coughed. "Haven't looked at another woman since Moe and I hooked up."

Amen to that.

Damon pulled out a chair at the rickety table and took a seat. The smell of old pot and probably mold assaulted his nose. He missed the sea and sand. Merc territory had been a nice stretch of Santa Barbara beachfront, complete with mansions, fresh fish, and clean air. "Just met with Mercury. We're going ahead as planned here."

"I hate this place." Grey scratched his stubbled chin. "I had scouts go look along the entire coast for another stretch for us to call home. Haven't found anything that will work."

Santa Barbara had just burned to the ground from forest fires. Turned out that people, a lot of them, were needed to tame Mother Nature.

She was currently kicking ass on every front. If there were one winner from the Scorpius pandemic and the apocalypse, it was that bitch.

Merc territory, such as it was, no longer existed. "We need to integrate into Vanguard," Damon said quietly. He understood Grey's desire to go back to the simpler days of just being soldiers having to survive the apocalypse, but things had changed. "It's time to start rebuilding. Having relationships and forming families."

Grey lifted an eyebrow. "You want to have a family?"

Heat slammed through Damon, followed by chills. "God, no. But you're getting hitched."

Grey frowned. "I haven't proposed."

Damon didn't bother holding back a snort. "You will." He'd never seen a guy more head over heels than Greyson with Maureen Shadow. "Considering she's shacking up with you, her brother is probably going to cut off your head if you don't make some sort of grand gesture." Maybe they could discover an abandoned jewelry store that hadn't been looted and find a ring.

Yeah, right.

Grey shook his head. "Our men don't want to take orders from Jax Mercury or his lieutenants. I had to break up three fights earlier today, and one of them involved knives. Assholes." Deep lines cut into the sides of the Mercenary leader's mouth. "Any ideas?"

Damon pretended to think it over. Greyson Storm was a phenomenal soldier and a good leader, and he already knew the right answer. He just didn't like it. "We integrate fully, Grey. We become part of Vanguard, and when it's time to head north for resources, we do it as one strong group." Which meant there was a deadline for finding peace within the two factions. They had enough resources to survive about a year, maybe less, before they had to abandon what used to be the city.

"It's not working," Grey muttered, irritation evident in his voice.

Of course, it wasn't working. It had only been a week. "We'll keep assigning folks to different jobs, but what if we had our own force? For our soldiers," Damon asked, his mind clicking security plans into place.

Grey tilted his head. "What do you mean?"

There was a way to keep everyone secure, and it would just take a balancing act of combining skills while keeping egos in check. "Half of our soldiers are at the Bunker providing protection anyway. For now, here in Vanguard territory, how about we have our own squad—or whatever you want to call it—and they answer only to you or me. I can coordinate scouting, defense, and strategy with Jax Mercury so everyone is happy."

Grey slowly nodded. "I'm not aiming for happy, but non-homicidal would be a big plus right now."

Sad but true. "I'll take care of it this week while you and Maureen are at the Bunker." The coordination job would be a good cover for investigating the church. Maybe he could get Vanguard, the Pure, and the Mercs all at peace and working together. Hell. He might as well cure the pandemic while he was at it.

Grey's eyes narrowed. "You can't save everybody, Damon. Forget fixing that church. They're a cult, and they need to be disbanded."

"Maybe. I haven't even gotten inside yet." Unexposed people, the few who still lived, should be protected. Especially since it looked as if Scorpius survivors couldn't procreate. Somebody had to carry on the human race. "I'll take care of it. Don't worry."

"Right." Grey scrubbed both hands down his face. "I wouldn't leave right now, but Moe is dying to get to the archives dealing with food and possible resources at the Century City Bunker."

Damon nodded. The US government had apparently created a series of Bunkers across the country in case of a pandemic, but the survivors only knew of two locations. Vanguard and the Mercs controlled one, and soon, they were going to take the other by force. "No worries."

"I could stay here. Tell Moe she'll have to wait," Greyson said, a slight wince lifting his cheeks.

"Nope. We need food." Frankly, things might go smoother with Greyson at the Bunker. Coordinating an alliance between him and Jax Mercury required a finesse that nobody on Earth still held. "Plus, not having you here might make me seem more approachable to the Pure." He needed to get in there to make sure the members were safe.

"This is a bad idea. You know that, right?" Grey asked.

Damon searched for the right answer. "It's necessary."

"Is it? We could take the church easily."

"Not without casualties. Maybe pregnant ones since there are at least five pregnant women in that small compound," Damon returned. "I want to go in first."

"Maybe." Grey's eyes narrowed. "Or is it just the woman?"

Pretty, sweet, sad April Snyder. She'd drawn Damon since the first moment she'd offered to put herself in danger to help. He had no doubt that she'd infiltrate the church on her own if asked, and he needed to make sure she was all right. That she survived this.

"Damon?" Grey muttered.

Damon looked at his best friend, giving the truth as always. "Of course, it's the woman. How could it not be?"

3

_____

I'm looking forward to going undercover, but I have completely forgotten how to flirt. If I even knew how in the first place.
    —April Snyder, Journal

APRIL FIDGETED on the plastic chair adjacent to a classic picnic table, keeping her face in the shade from a golf umbrella somebody had drilled into the table's center. After an unusually wet spring, summer had blasted in hot and dry as if trying to make up for lost time. Sun beat down mercilessly on the cement, making the heat wave into a mirage.

Several children played on swing sets with plastic slides that had been pounded into the backyard of a tiny bungalow house dead center in Vanguard territory, their laughter oddly out of place in the dismal landscape. Soon, it would be too hot for them to play outside in the afternoons, as there was no way any water could be spared for running through sprinklers.

If they still had sprinklers.

"Sorry I'm late." Damon appeared from around the corner of the house, making her jump.

Her heart fluttered into a faster beat, and she cleared her throat. "You move so quietly."

"It's training, darlin'." He smiled, his white teeth a flash of amusement in his rugged face. "When you're about to kick down a door in a crack house, you like them to be surprised."

Their lives, before Scorpius, were so freaking different. "Have you kicked down a lot of doors?" she asked, trying for flippant but coming across more as if she were *trying* to sound flippant. Why couldn't she act like a normal adult around him?

"I've put my boot to my share." He pulled out the bench on the other side of the table and sat.

"Why?" she whispered. Why would anybody court danger? Was he that heroic at such a basic level?

His deep brown eyes seemed to study her for a moment, and something that looked like acceptance crossed his face before he spoke. "Truth? My dad was a cop, and I wanted to be just like him. Wanted to be the good guy, the one who made a difference." Damon tapped long fingers on the table. "Then, once I was in, I saw so many people who needed help. So many shitheads who'd created situations that required boots to doors."

Man. Her stomach went all tingly in a way she'd all but forgotten. "So nothing about ego, huh?"

He chuckled. "Oh, I've always had plenty of ego. That might be part of it." He leaned a little toward her. "Of course, I'm the humblest of my brothers. By far."

She leaned in as well, her body finally relaxing. "I wonder if they'd agree with you."

"Nope. Not a one of them would've agreed." His smile was a little sad. "Wish you could've met them."

"Scorpius?" she asked.

He nodded. "Scorpius stole two of them. The other one took a bullet about five years ago."

Her heart panged for him. "I'm sorry. He was a cop?"

"No." Damon smiled again. "Not sure where we went wrong, but Alan was a lawyer. Can you believe it? My dad probably turned over in his grave when A was sworn in to the bar. Lost dad to prostate cancer when Alan was still in law school." Pride and love. It was there in every syllable. "Alan was a prosecutor and got shot in the line. Put away a dirtbag and took a bullet afterward."

"Did you find the guy who did it?" she asked softly.

For the first time, his eyes hardened. That quickly, the deadly cop he'd been was present in full force. "You bet your ass we did."

He'd faced as much loss as she had, and some of it before the pandemic. The idea cut into her, causing an odd relief. All of this innuendo and tension around them was okay. There was no way he'd want anything serious or emotional or real any more than she did. The undercover op was just that. Finally, her shoulders went down, the electricity in her hands subsided, and she relaxed, giving him a smile.

He blinked. Once, and then again. "What was that for?" His voice deepened.

"What?" His tone sent up those butterflies inside her again.

"Your smile. The sweet one." His gaze dropped to her lips.

They tingled now, too. "I have different smiles?" she murmured, not letting herself look at his mouth. No. She already thought way too much about the fullness of his lips and that hard-cut jaw.

"Yeah." He reached out and ran his forefinger along her bottom lip.

She jerked. "What are you doing?" Heat flashed into her face, and her dress suddenly felt too confining.

Instead of withdrawing, he cupped her jaw and leaned in some more.

She stopped breathing completely, her eyes widening.

"We're being watched, beautiful," he whispered, his hand

warm. "Just keep talking to me. No—" he said as she tried to turn and look around. "Stay in the moment. You're doing a great job of looking overwhelmed." Amusement filled his voice.

That was the understatement of the century. "How do you know we're being watched?" she asked, her lips barely moving.

He tilted his head and smiled. "Don't you feel it? Just settle yourself and feel the afternoon. Anything off?"

Yeah. The hottest man she'd ever been this close to in real life was freaking touching her as if he were about to kiss her. "I can't feel them," she said.

"That's okay. That's my job." He gently caressed the side of her jaw. "Without looking, tell me how many kids are on the swing sets and what they're doing."

Well, okay. "Five kids. Three are on swings, and two are on the slides, walking up them instead of sliding down." She kept her voice low. "Though I don't know why you'd ask that. I mean, are the kids being watched? Should we take them inside?"

"They're fine," he said softly. "We're the ones being watched. My point was that you knew instantly where the kids were. You have good instincts."

It was part of her job in this new world. She was kind of in charge of the kids. "Okay." Was he going to pretend-kiss her? Could she handle it if he did? She hadn't kissed anybody but Don for decades. A kiss would be too much, right? They didn't want to look too obvious.

"Stop frowning," he said, running his thumb up and across her cheekbone. "You have the smoothest skin."

Ha. Not nearly as smooth as it had been in her twenties. Even so, the touch was unnerving in a way that made her want to both lean into it and run the heck away. "I'm not frowning." She relaxed her brow.

His nod of approval came fast. "Good girl. As I was saying, you have several smiles. The sweet one I just got, the one when you're ticked and don't want to say so, the one when you're being polite, and the one that shows you're genuinely in love with those kids." He finally released her. "I'm looking forward to learning more of them."

Okay. He was flirting with her because of the op. This would get confusing if she didn't keep her mind on that one very salient fact. "You don't need to study me for this job."

One of his dark eyebrows rose. "If you think I'm studying you because of the job, you're getting me wrong."

Her mouth dropped open, and then she pressed her lips together, counting to five. "Do not flirt with me. Not really. I mean, not in a real way instead of the going-undercover way. Okay?"

"What's the difference?" he asked, his gaze way too shrewd.

"You know the difference," she retorted, her temper drumming up energy. Was he trying to keep her off balance because of the mission? That would make sense. If he were really pursuing her, then she'd be thrown off balance, so maybe this was the right way to do it? "Listen. I'm not interested in romance in real life. Just undercover. This is merely a mission." Her first, actually.

"I see." An indefinable light glinted in his eyes.

Her body stilled with an alertness that gave her mind pause. "What does that mean?"

"Apparently, I have more than one mission."

* * *

DAMON KEPT HIS VOICE LOW, and his body relaxed, communicating to the people watching that he had no clue they were in the crumbling, three-story apartment building to the south. The structure was supposed to be empty for safety reasons, but someone was definitely on the top floor—and had binoculars.

He'd seen the sun glint off the lenses. Hopefully, it was binoculars and not the scope of a gun.

April stared him down, her spectacular blue eyes broadcasting so many different emotions it was hard to focus on just one. "Are we still being watched?" Apparently, she'd decided to ignore his warning about missions. Interesting.

"Yes." He flattened his hand on the wooden table, not surprised by the heat that filled his palms. Concrete and old buildings filled the seven blocks of inner-city Los Angeles that made up Vanguard territory. The temperature would get worse before it got better, and they were going to run out of water at some point. "My guess is that somebody will approach you first. They'll feel you out about me."

She shook her head, and her thick mass of hair caught the sun, shining with a multitude of lovely highlights—red and gold. "This is the first time anybody has seen us together. They won't approach yet."

"Time matters," he returned, scouting the area around them with his peripheral vision. Vanguard soldiers were stationed at various points throughout the territory, but right now, the center was empty except for them. It was too hot to be outside if a person didn't have to be. "The Pure pastor knows that Jax is getting impatient to speak to the members and make sure they're okay. He's going to storm the gate soon."

April glanced over her shoulder to make sure the kids were okay. Then she turned back to him. "All right. What's next? I mean, what do we do?"

"Our jobs," he said simply, studying her. Anytime she was near, he couldn't help but try and figure her out. She had the bluest eyes he'd ever seen, set in a fine-boned and rather delicate face. In her early thirties, her skin was smooth enough that she could pass for early twenties. She had strength, or she wouldn't have survived the pandemic and so much loss. But it was the sadness in her that called to him. How screwed up was that? No way could he fix her. Yet he wanted to try. "Are you okay with me kissing you?" he asked.

Her breath visibly caught. "Is that necessary?"

Humor attacked him, and he burst out laughing. A million years ago, he'd had no problem getting a date. In his early twenties, he'd juggled women like a pro until he figured out that he didn't need to be such an asshole. Then he'd dated a lot, but the right woman hadn't come along. Not really. "You know, I'm pretty good at it," he murmured, enjoying the flush that filled her face, turning it a pretty pink.

Her chin lifted. "I've found that when men have to tell you they're good at something, they're actually insecure about whatever it is. Maybe you can't kiss."

Challenge accepted.

He let his gaze drop to her mouth again. Pretty, pink lips, the bottom one surprisingly full. Those lips had fascinated him from the first second they met. She probably tasted like cotton candy—the good kind with real sugar. "When the Pure members approach you, use what you're feeling about me. It's genuine."

She blinked. "What do you mean?"

He sighed. She could be as defensive as she wanted but acting obtuse would get one of them shot in the head. "You're attracted to me, you don't want to be, and I confuse the hell out of you. Yet something in you would love to jump into the fire...just for a short time."

One of her fine eyebrows arched, making her look like a pissed-off teacher. The sexy kind all the guys had crushes on. "Attracted to you? Seriously?"

Well, yeah. He could read people. "I'm attracted to you, too."

Now her brows drew together in an adorable frown. "Why?"

The innocent brilliance in her question slayed him. How could it not? "You're sexy, smart, and definitely sweet. Plus, brave."

She sighed. "Boy, do you have me wrong."

Hmmm. This was going to be even more interesting than he thought. He smiled then, letting his gaze roam over her face.

Her chin lowered this time, firming with obvious stubbornness.

His body heated and flared wide-awake for the first time in way too long. Yeah. Challenge *definitely* accepted.

4

The only real hope I see for this world is in the children. That has to mean something, right?
—April Snyder, Journal

APRIL STOOD in the common area on the first floor of an old apartment building, across from the makeshift playground. Dorms for kids spread out in three directions. The orphans who'd survived the Scorpius pandemic ranged from three years old to seventeen. Around twenty children played board games around her at different tables or on the floor. The days of video games were gone.

Anybody under five years old had been pseudo-adopted by adults, and the teenagers largely took care of themselves, helping out around the territory and learning to scout for necessities. And fight. Everyone learned how to fight.

At some point, it'd be nice to adopt the other kids into new families—if they wanted. If not, they could stay together.

There really wasn't a manual for this kind of thing.

"How are we doing?" Atticus Werner limped in from one of the rooms for boys, wiping his hands on a towel. "Boys are pigs. You wouldn't believe the grime I found under the bunks."

She frowned. "You're supposed to be resting."

"Meh. I'll rest when I'm dead." The eighty-year-old soldier was a sweetheart and a truly phenomenal cook. An enemy had stabbed him just the week before, and a doctor had only taken out his stitches earlier that day. "What am I going to do? Just sit in bed and watch the sun heat the room?"

Fair enough. "All right. But you take it easy." April tried to put command into her voice.

He moved closer, his faded eyes twinkling. "How's the under-cover op coming?"

She breathed out. "Damon wants to kiss me."

Atticus lifted his chin and then threw back his head, letting go of a mighty chuckle. "Oh, sweetheart. Of course, the cop wants to kiss you, and that ain't got nothin' to do with an op." He shook his head and wiped his eyes. "Youth is so wasted on you people."

Youth? Yeah, right. She was in her early thirties and felt about a million years old. "You are not helping."

He shrugged. "Not trying to. If you can find some romance and excitement in this crappy world, why not do it?"

Because she was an ex-suburb softball mom, and Damon was a badass ex-cop with a hard edge he barely kept concealed. She'd never even been naked with any man but her husband. She had stretch marks for Pete's sake. Damon had probably dated models. Or sexy actresses in LA. Or successful and confident lawyers with long legs and toned muscles.

Atticus's bushy, gray eyebrows lifted. "You're spending a lot of time thinking about that question."

Heat slid into her face. She cleared her throat. "I haven't wiped down the room yet today." Scorpius lived on surfaces, and anybody not infected could still catch it. They weren't sure, so she had to be vigilant.

"How many of the kids haven't caught it?" Atticus asked.

She shook her head. "I think all of them have survived, but we don't know for sure. The doctors are trying to find a way to test at the Bunker since they still have machines and electricity there. For now." It'd be nice to know who needed extra protection.

Well over ninety percent of people who contracted Scorpius died. The bacteria localized in the brain and often stopped all function. Or it stripped empathy and created sociopaths.

"It'd be interesting to see if all the folks hiding in the Pure apartment building are actually uninfected," Atticus mused. "Maybe Vanguard should've required mandatory testing before allowing people to settle inside the barbed wire."

April rubbed a bruise on her arm from training the other day. "What test? We don't have one that works in the field."

"Should've come up with one. You know there's probably a good test at the Bunker." He stretched and then winced, placing a hand on his healing stomach wound.

Yeah, but what was done was done.

A little girl of about eight years old ran up, her long, blond hair swinging around her narrow shoulders. She wore a pink shirt with blue flowers dotted across it and faded jeans shorts that were a size or two too big.

April smiled. "Hey, sweetheart. How's the game of Go Fish coming?" She ran a hand down Lena's soft hair. "Is Rory still winning and trying not to?"

The girl's dark eyes twinkled. She snorted, her nose pert and sprinkled with a couple of freckles. April had been working to get her to speak, just once, but so far, she hadn't said a word in Vanguard territory. Nobody knew where she came from or how she'd survived before finding the compound. She reached into her pocket.

April tilted her head, waiting. The girl often gave presents to people, items she found around the territory. It was always interesting. Some folks read meaning into her gifts, but April thought they were working too hard to find a purpose in anything. Sometimes, life was just life, no matter how dismal it became. "What do you have?"

Lena slowly took out a silver cylinder of something and handed it over.

April took the warm gift and slowly twisted the end. "It's lipstick." A muted and very pretty pink. "For me?"

Lena solemnly nodded.

Atticus snorted.

April barely kept from elbowing him. "Well, thank you. I, ah, haven't been looking for makeup." Warmth infused her face. It wasn't as if she were dating Damon for Pete's sake.

Lena rolled her eyes and turned to bounce back to her friends and the cards on the floor. They sat on a newer rug the scouts had found the week before.

"Should've brought you a condom," Atticus muttered.

April jerked, her eyes widening. "You so did not say that."

Atticus was saved from answering by the sound of an explosion outside. The walls rattled, and an odd concussion stormed through the room.

April launched into motion a second before Atticus could, reaching the door to the basement. "Everyone downstairs," she called out, her hands barely shaking this time.

The kids, some groaning, left their games in place and moved a little too slowly toward the door.

"Hurry up," she urged, her heart rate picking up only a little. These moments were coming more and more often. Soon, the kids wouldn't move without crowbars. "Let's go."

A crowd of them grumbled but headed down into the cement-block-fortified basement.

The front door opened, and Damon poked his head in, his gun already in his hand. Cut muscles showed beneath his black T-shirt and down his arms. "Got it?"

April nodded. "Heading down now."

"Good. Stay there until I come back. I have three guys covering your building." He shut the door with a sharp snap.

April made sure the key to the gun locker downstairs was in her pocket and then followed Atticus into the stairwell, turning to shut and lock the door behind her.

"This is happening too frequently," Atticus grumbled.

True. And at some point, an attacker would make it through the Vanguard outside perimeter. Maybe this time. "Let's go." She turned and started jogging down the stairs, the smell of dust and mold assaulting her.

She had to keep the kids safe.

Reaching the area downstairs, she was both grateful and oddly disturbed to see the kids settling easily and grabbing other board games and cards from shelves to start playing new games. Lanterns hung from the ceiling, and the taller kids had already switched them on to illuminate the space.

Blue mats from an old gym covered the floor, and cement blocks lined each wall. Chairs and tables were scattered throughout the space, and two older sofas, both floral though different colors, were pushed against a far wall. It was much cooler down there, and April took a deep breath to center herself.

Frequent attacks shouldn't be routine for the kids.

Atticus limped over to a sofa to sit and then motioned for her to follow. She took another look at the kids, ensuring that each of them was occupied, and then moved to sit next to him.

He sighed. "It's much nicer in here. If it gets any hotter, we might just move the kids down here."

Not a bad idea. Except there were no windows, and it was still a little dark. But heat stroke could become a real possibility.

"The two new kids are settling in all right," Atticus said, nodding his head toward Tina and Rory. They were both around eight, and somehow they'd found each other in the aftermath of Scorpius, eventually getting saved by a couple of Vanguard soldiers. Tina was taller with thick, curly, black hair, dark skin, and the prettiest brown eyes imaginable, while Rory was her opposite with almost white-blond hair, light blue eyes, and a smattering of freckles. The two were inseparable, which was fine. And it looked as if they'd pulled the non-speaking Lena into their makeshift family.

April nodded. "I've been hoping they can draw Lena out so she'll speak, but so far, they seem to be learning her way of sign language." The doctors couldn't find a physical reason for the girl's non-communication, but who knew what she'd endured as the pandemic had swept the world.

"Speaking is overrated." Atticus stretched out his jeans-clad legs, revealing one purple and one yellow sock above his shoes. The guy was seriously color-blind and couldn't care less. "In fact, stop talking to Damon and have some fun. You know. The good kind."

April cut him a look. "Right. We have nothing in common."

"Nothing in common?" Atticus snorted. "You both survived the apocalypse. That's all anybody needs these days. Geez."

She was not making girl-talk with Atticus for Pete's sake.

The faint sound of gunfire punctuated the stillness of the quiet basement.

Not one of the kids even looked up from their game.

"Survival is just temporary," April murmured quietly. Sad but true.

5

I'm better in motion and not standing still. It's a fact, and that will not change. Regardless of the job at hand or the pretty eyes of April Snyder. Though if anybody could make me stop and enjoy the moment, it'd be her.

   —Damon Winter, Journal

DAMON MOVED SWIFTLY PAST the next block of crumbling apartments toward the warehouses at the rear of Vanguard territory, just as Greyson barreled in from the north.

"Visual yet?" Grey snapped into a short-range radio.

"Negative," Jax Mercury said over the comm. "Almost to the basketball court."

"We're right behind you," Grey said as soldiers poured in from every direction. "Is the front entrance covered?"

Damon leaped over a dried-out pothole, his senses narrowing and focusing. Smoke was billowing up from outside the fence. "I put three men on the kids' dorms."

"All points are covered," Jax yelled from in front of them, not bothering with the radio.

The basketball court was located in an empty, concrete lot at the far southeast corner of Vanguard that also held the only other gate—besides the main front entry—where trucks could pass. It was a weak but necessary point for the territory.

Damon slowed next to Greyson and Jax, soldiers fanning out around them. On the other side of the chain-link fence, a semi-trailer truck on its side burned hot and bright, black smoke billowing into the cloudless day. A bomb of some sort had blown out the front window and crumpled the driver's side door, bending it nearly in two.

"See anybody?" Jax asked, ducking and moving for the fence.

Damon scanned the area, which was covered by downed trucks and old tires in front of a bunch of railroad tracks with rapidly rusting train cars set haphazardly along its length. "Negative." The stench of burning rubber filled the hot day. Sweat ran down Damon's chest, and he moved closer to the fence, trying to see beyond the fire and smoke.

Another smell had him stopping cold. It wasn't rubber. He pivoted to put his body between Greyson and the fence until he could see what it was.

Grey paused. Soot was already falling to coat his black hair. "Ah, shit."

"*Mierda.*" Jax's jaw tightened, and he tucked his gun into the back of his jeans. "Cover me." Without waiting for an answer, he unlocked the gate and swung it open. "Mercs go left, I'll go right." He launched smoothly into motion.

Damon kept low and went left, trusting Greyson to have his back. The second he made it around the truck, two bodies came into view. Partially burned, *still* burning, a man and a woman lay face down on the cracked concrete. From their backs, he didn't recognize them.

Jax came around the other side and rushed the bodies, slapping out the flames. He turned the woman over, and her dark, curly hair spread across the scalded concrete. "Fuck."

The woman was in her early thirties with a bullet hole in her forehead. Her brown eyes were still open and staring sightlessly at the sky. Damon gingerly reached out and rolled the guy over to reveal a similar wound. But he was younger. Maybe eighteen. "Jax?" he murmured.

"Scouts. Jennifer and Lewis Washington. Mother and son who somehow survived the pandemic," Jax said, his voice hoarse. "They were out scouting with a larger group early this morning."

"Where?" Greyson asked grimly, his gaze skirting past the overturned trucks and stacks of tires that protected the outside perimeter of Vanguard territory.

Jax shook his head. "Dunno. I'll have to check the records."

Damon crouched down and studied the kid's body. Muscled and strong. His knuckles were split, and his left wrist looked as if it had been broken. "He put up a good fight." Damon looked up at Jax. "How many people are in your scouting parties?"

"Four to six," Jax said, his powerful shoulders down, his accent sharp. In the blazing sun, with the stench of burned flesh all around them, he had gone pale beneath his bronzed skin. "This is the third murder with an explosion around the territory in the last week." Wiping sweat from his brow, he jerked his head. "Check his pocket."

Damon gingerly reached past the burned shirt and tugged out a piece of purple bandana from the dead kid's left pocket. "Twenty gang." He'd fought the gang before the pandemic, and even then, they were deadly. "Weren't you a member?" he asked quietly, reaching up to close the eyes of both victims. They didn't need to watch this world any longer. His chest hurt. Bad.

"Yes," Jax said. "I was a member until I turned seventeen and entered the service. I've been fighting them since creating Vanguard."

Damon stood, the piece of purple bandana oddly soft in his hand.

The hair on his arms rose. He paused, filtering out the sound of the crackling fire. "Wait." Slowly, he turned his head, going on full alert.

A glint from a railroad boxcar caught his eye. "Gun!" he yelled, leaping for Greyson and taking him to the ground. Bullets pinged off the burning truck. He jumped up and ran for the nearest stack of tires, leaning around the edge and firing.

Grey reached him in a second. "What the hell are you doing?"

"My job." Damon reared up and fired again, aiming for the glint he'd seen earlier. He nodded toward Jax and two of his men, all three crouched behind a turned-over SUV, firing in turn.

There was a cleared area of two rows of tracks between them and the old car with the shooter, so heading in that direction would be suicide. "We need to get rid of those old cars," he yelled to Jax.

Jax cut him a look. "No shit," he called back. "You have a tractor handy?"

No, actually. But this was a serious threat to security, and they had to figure it out. "I'll get one to you this week," he muttered. If he were going to concentrate on the inner territory with the crazy church, he had to know the perimeter was secure. "Any ideas?" he gasped quietly to Greyson.

Grey wiped blood off a cut above his left eye. "It'll be a huge waste of fuel, but we'll have to use the trucks. The ones they haven't turned over, of course."

A blur of purple caught Damon's attention. He levered up, aimed, and squeezed the trigger. A cry of pain echoed over the sound of the burning tires. "Got him." Now, it was time to figure out who was out there. "Cover me." With that, he launched into motion.

"Damn it, Winter," Jax bellowed.

Damon crouched and ran in a zigzag pattern, Greyson on his

heels. They both fired toward the offending railway car, even as more gunfire exploded all around them. So, two shooters with automatic weapons.

Fuck.

A gun emerged from the opening of the car, discharging with the shooter's body off to the side. Damon slid left and fired in the direction of the gun.

Blood burst out, and a man screamed in pain.

"Hit the hand," Grey grunted just as they reached the rusting car. Damon jumped inside, fell to his knees on the rough wood, and slid, turning with his gun ready to fire.

Two men in their early twenties sat on the floor, the first dead from a head shot. The second guy held his bloody hand to his chest, rocking back and forth. Tears and snot slid down his face. His gun had fallen to the scrub grass outside.

Damon angled his body and looked out the opening on the other side. More cars and basic quiet. They had to clear this area, damn it. "Two down in here," he called out.

Greyson suddenly filled the doorway. Soot and dirt still covered his black hair, and his eyes looked pissed. "Twenty."

Damon eyed the injured gang member, who hadn't looked up. "We have doctors."

"Good for you," the guy muttered. Dirt matted his dark hair and nearly covered his face. "If you're going to shoot me, just do it."

"Haven't decided yet," Damon said conversationally. "You're obviously a member of Twenty." The purple bandana tied around the guy's left leg was a bit obvious. "Who's giving orders these days?"

The guy finally looked up, his eyes blazing. "President Atherton is giving orders, asshole. He's our Commander in Chief, and Twenty has been subscribed into service as the front line. We're the Marines, 2.0."

Damon cocked his head. "Subscripted? That's not the correct usage of that word, bud."

The guy shrugged. "Whatever."

Yeah. Genius material.

Jax appeared next to Greyson. "How many members in Twenty these days?"

The guy shrugged again.

Damon cut Grey a look. They needed those answers, and no doubt, the Vanguard lieutenants had no problem extracting information. He didn't see the need for torture. Never had. "Listen, buddy. The world has gone to shit, and it's nice to find a place. But are you really a guy who just blows things up, scares people, and then shoots at folks you don't know? What did you do before this?"

The guy looked up. "I was serving ten to twenty for drug distribution." He grinned. "I was a member of Twenty before it became the president's front line."

That was unfortunate.

Jax leaned in. "Must've been after my time with them." He shrugged. "Tell us what we want to know, or we'll take you to the inner territory, and then you'll tell us what we want to know."

Damon stood, his body stiffening. The former cop inside him hated this part of survival. The soldier he'd become understood it. "Listen. These guys aren't kidding, and I'd rather just see you go to the doctor and get that hand fixed. Answer the questions, and we'll even get you medical help." He'd make sure of it.

The guy looked up again. "Fuck you."

"That's a no," Greyson said softly. "Plan B it is, then."

Gravel crunched lightly on the other side of the boxcar. "Unfriendlies," Damon bellowed, leaping for both Grey and Jax, taking them down to the hard railroad ties as gunfire hit right where he'd been sitting. His elbow hit first, and pain ricocheted up his arm. He was up and moving in unison with the two soldiers in a split second. Grey went left, Jax went right, and Damon pivoted to leap back into the car.

Agony pierced his right shoulder, and he rolled, coming up and tackling the newest shooter center mass, Damon's head in the guy's solar plexus. The guy shouted with a shocked "*oof*" as they flew through the heated air and landed on the railroad ties with a hard thump.

Damon swiped the gun out of the guy's hand with one quick punch.

Three shots echoed behind him, and he rolled, coming up on his knees.

Jax had taken down two to the right, and Grey had killed one member wearing a lot of purple to the left.

"Scan the area," Damon muttered as the guy next to him struggled to get up. Enough of this shit. Damon partially turned on the ground and punched the roughly forty-year-old beneath the jaw hard enough to snap his neck back. The guy fell unconscious, his head bouncing twice on a wooden railroad tie.

Damon stood, his gun ready as Jax and Greyson swept the five remaining railroad cars.

Finally, they both called out an "all clear."

Damon ran back to the original car to see the wounded man flat on the floor, the top half of his head missing. Apparently, his buddy hadn't aimed very well.

Nausea rolled in Damon's gut, and he swallowed it down.

Grey jogged up. "You okay?"

Damon glanced down at his bleeding shoulder. "Yeah. Bullet just nicked me." He jerked his head. "I'll help carry that guy."

"No," Jax said, moving their way. "You're bleeding, and he might be bleeding. You have to stay away from fluids."

Man. Sometimes, Damon forgot he was one of the few who hadn't been infected by Scorpius.

Yet.

6

I am so out of my league, it's not even funny. My entire life, I've avoided risk and danger. Those might as well be Damon's middle names.

    ——April Snyder, Journal

APRIL FINISHED SETTLING the kids back at their games on the first level of the apartment building after being given the all clear by one of the soldiers. This guy was a Mercenary, as evidenced by the dark T-shirt and ripped jeans. All the Mercs wore the black shirts on duty. He disappeared back outside.

It was nice to have the new soldiers providing extra protection, but none of them seemed all that happy to be there.

Of course, who *was* happy?

She sat at a beat-up table and read through the notes she'd made on an old legal pad outlining information on the kids and their routines, just in case something happened to her.

The front door opened, and Sharon Matson slipped inside, her face red and sweat dotting her upper lip. Her curly, blond hair was piled high on her head, and somewhere, she'd found mascara to highlight her stunning blue eyes. In her late twenties, probably, she had joined Vanguard three months ago, quickly disappearing into the Pure apartment building. Today, she wore jeans and a long T-shirt, her hands covered by thin gloves.

For goodness sakes. Gloves in this heat? April forced a smile. "I'd offer iced tea, but I don't have any."

"That's all right." Sharon's fake smile outdid April's by a mile and a half. "I wanted to make sure you and the kids were all safe." She strode forward and pulled out the other chair at the table, sitting gracefully.

If that were the case, shouldn't she look around at the kids playing on the floor? "That was nice of you," April murmured, setting down her papers. "A soldier came by and helped us out of the basement." The Merc soldiers weren't known for their conversational skills. Except for Damon. Now there was a guy who could talk. "All I was told was that it was safe to emerge."

Sharon folded her gloved hands in her lap, away from the table. "I heard it was the Twenty gang again. They're stepping up their harassment since that Merc killed the vice president."

"That Merc" had been Greyson Storm, and he was defending pretty much everybody from the psycho president and his sidekick. "The president is crazy, and Grey had no choice." April swallowed, and sweat rolled down her back. Man, she missed air conditioning.

"Maybe." Sharon wrinkled her nose. "Do we really know that for sure? I mean, Scorpius does make some people crazy. Maybe we're being fed lies by Vanguard and now the Mercs."

April shook her head. The president had tried to bomb Vanguard territory. Some Scorpius survivors lost their sanity in one way or another. Some became animals, while others turned into super brilliant serial killer sociopaths. "I believe Jax about the president," she said quietly, tugging out a nearly empty plastic bottle of hand sanitizer to rub over her palms.

Sharon swallowed, her gaze on the gel. "It's not safe here for you."

April finished rubbing and tucked the bottle away. "I'm not sure about that. It has been so long since anybody contracted the bacterial infection from a surface." These days, only the exchange of bodily fluids led to infection.

Sharon shook her head, her cheeks now the color of an overripe red apple. "We're some of the few people left uninfected, and since we're the only ones who can have babies, we have a duty to keep ourselves safe. Right?"

Oh, April was no way ever having another baby. Losing one child was all she could take. "Not really."

Sharon's lips tightened. They were a lush pink. Had she scrounged up lipstick for her outing, too? April squinted and tried to look closer.

"So... I'm here for a reason," Sharon said, her placid smile back in place.

No kidding. "Oh?" April asked.

The front door opened, and Damon walked inside. She partially pivoted toward him. Heat wafted inside, swelling toward her. Though not all of it was from the sun. Her limbs tingled. Why did that happen every time he entered her space? It was just crazy.

Sharon twittered.

April wanted to look at the crazy blonde to see what a twitter looked like, but she couldn't move. Damon was moving in her direction, doing a full body scan of her, head to toe and back up, his deep gaze missing nothing. Now, her knees tingled. Then her breasts.

She should say something, but her throat had gone dry. So she studied him from beneath her lashes. For a big guy, he really did move quietly. There was a sense of grace to him that held an edge of danger. "What exploded?"

He drew out a raggedy velvet chair and dropped into it.

"Another truck. The Twenty gang is conducting a campaign of general harassment at the moment."

"Why?" she whispered. In a time when food was getting scarce, who had the energy to harass anybody?

"They're out for revenge. They work for the president, right?" Sharon blurted, her darkened eyelashes making an impressive fluttering motion as she ran her gaze over the sexy ex-cop.

A hot wave of possessiveness, shocking in its strength, rippled through April. She frowned, her stomach clenching. What was happening?

"You okay?" Damon reached out and brushed a strand of wayward hair away from her cheek.

Electricity zapped through her skin. "Yes." April cleared her throat. "Sharon and I were just chatting. You've met, right?"

Sharon leaned toward Damon, leading with her impressive chest. "I think you nodded at me once."

His grin relaxed the tension around his eyes. "That's how the Mercs say hello. It's nice to meet you."

"You, too." Sharon's voice became slightly husky.

Nobody moved to shake hands. Those days were long gone.

April studied the blonde. She was nearly purring, her gaze running over the very hard planes of Damon's chest. Slapping her would be totally inappropriate. Probably. Should she stake her claim? In a mission, on-op, undercover type of way? She was pretending to date Damon, right? "I, um, missed you," she said quietly.

Amusement sparkled in his brown eyes. "Missed you more." He caressed down her arm to take her hand.

He was so good at this. April tried to smile, but her cheeks hurt. Her lip started to tremble, so she gave up the fight.

Sharon preened. "Our territory is so much safer now that you're here. I heard you just took out the Twenty gang member shooting at Vanguard, Damon."

Well, that was information the blonde hadn't shared earlier.

April's skin cooled. Awareness and a familiar fear slid beneath her anxiety. Was he okay? "You did?"

He lifted one powerful shoulder. "Somebody shot at us, and we shot back. Everyone is fine on this side of the fence, baby."

Even the endearment said in that sexy voice didn't diminish the reality of danger. What was she doing, trying to play a secret agent in this crazy and sucky world? She couldn't even hold his hand without getting all mushy. She tried to free herself, but his fingers tightened around hers. Shock grabbed her at his easy strength, and then an unsettling warmth spread through her lower half. Why did he have to be so sexy? "How many *aren't* fine on the other side of the fence?" she asked.

His expression didn't change but a glint—a hardness—filled his eyes. He turned toward Sharon. "I hope I didn't interrupt your talk."

"No, not at all." Sharon sat back in her chair, the blue of her eyes seeming all for Damon. "I was actually here to invite both you and April to a little get-together at our church tonight. Before the pandemic, did you go to church?"

Now that was an inappropriately personal question. April opened her mouth to answer and then realized Sharon wasn't asking her.

Damon nodded. "Every week. The entire family went every Sunday, and even after we lost Dad and one of my brothers, it was still a tradition. Kept my mom happy."

His mom sounded fascinating. Growing up in a family, an actual unit, was something April had wished for every night while in one of her foster homes. But how could he live, how could he even smile now that he'd lost everybody? The tingles in her body cooled and left her limbs feeling heavy. As usual. "Do you miss church?" she asked, wanting inside his head.

He focused on her again, his eyes softening. How did he do that? "I miss family."

Yeah. That.

Sharon cleared her throat, drawing their attention back to her. "I know you're a Merc, and I'm sure that means a lot to you. But the Pure has a mission, an important one, and you could be a part of that. Neither of you has been infected, and that matters. We're the only ones who can continue the human race." She turned her gaze toward April. "Don't you want to have more children?"

"No," April blurted instantly, her body turning to lava and then ice. "God, no." The room narrowed from the outside in, and her chest compressed with a sharp pain. "Never." She tried to yank away from Damon. Her throat closed. She couldn't breathe.

"April," Damon said, his voice sharp.

She jerked.

"April." The sharpness disappeared and was replaced by a low command. "Look at me."

She swallowed, or tried to, and looked up at his face. Intense, brown eyes. Hard, sculpted features. Raw strength.

He leaned in, both of his hands grasping hers now. "Stay with me. Take a deep breath." The order was said calmly, but it was an order nonetheless. One she instinctively obeyed. "Good," he said. "Another, and let it out slower this time."

She did as he said, and the buzzing between her ears slowly dissipated. The muscles in her chest and shoulders lost some of their tension.

"Better," he said, leaning in and brushing a lock of hair away from her cheek.

The simple touch forced tears to her eyes. What had just happened? Vulnerability rammed through her, making her sway.

"You're okay, baby." He kept coming closer, his lips nearly to hers. "That was a good job. All you have to worry about right now is this minute. There are no obligations. Ever." Then he brushed his mouth against hers in a touch so light it pulled all her focus away from fear and right onto him. "There you go." His lips formed the words right on hers.

She sucked in air.

His smile felt good against her. "Well." He leaned back, giving her space to breathe. "We just found the best cure ever for a panic attack."

She could only stare at him. So many feelings bombarded her that she couldn't actually feel anything. She was numb. In shock. But need? Yes. And intrigued.

Sharon coughed, and April jumped. She'd forgotten the other woman was even there.

Damon didn't look away from April, and he certainly didn't jump. The guy was more aware of his surroundings than anybody she'd ever met. "You okay now?" he asked.

Hell no. "Yes," she murmured. "Sorry about that."

He shook his head. "Nothing to be sorry about. You've been through unimaginable horrors. Panic and fear are normal. We'll deal with them one at a time."

She blinked. Deal with them? "We?"

His smile held more determination than amusement. "Yeah. We. It may take you a while to get settled into it, but you're covered, April. I'm not letting anything happen to you. That's a promise."

Her lips twitched to say something, anything, but what were the right words? Then she looked guiltily over at all the kids playing on the floor. Not one of them was looking her way, and most seemed to be concentrating on different board games. She wasn't doing a very good job of watching them.

Sharon pushed her chair back. "On that note, I should get back to the kids in the church. It's about naptime." She stood. "I'm sorry if I upset you, April. But please come to the dinner tonight and just get to know some of our members. We're actually a pretty nice group."

With armed guards at the entrance to the apartment building.

"We'll try," Damon answered for both of them, his focus remaining on April.

Sharon left quietly.

The kids laughed, and the warmth inside was nearly unbearable. But April could only concentrate on Damon. "I don't know how to pretend," she admitted. "It's all too confusing."

"Because you're attracted to me?" he asked, one eyebrow rising.

She straightened. Had he just said that? Was it arrogance or just...honesty? "Yes." She lifted her chin and forced herself to keep his gaze. "I am, and I'm getting confusing signals from, well, myself."

He didn't laugh at her. Didn't even turn arrogant. "I'm attracted to you, too. So if you're afraid of being embarrassed, of feeling something real while I'm just pretending, then stop being afraid. I think you're beautiful, smart, and kind. Your tits are unreal, and I've wanted to take your mouth from the first time you got sassy with me. Hard and deep."

She freed her hands and threw them up. "Who *says* that? I mean, who in real life actually says that?" A million years ago, she'd read awesome romance novels with something called alpha males, and it had been fun and intriguing. But this guy? He actually sounded like one. A real one.

"I do." His gaze didn't waver. Not even a tiny bit. "I've never been a game player, and since we're at the tail-end of an apocalypse, I don't have time for that crap."

"This—you're...nuts." That's all she had.

"Maybe." Now he did smile. "But here it is. We have a job to do, and we're gonna do it. While we're flirting and touching, I'm feeling it as much as you are. It doesn't have to go anywhere. There's no pressure for you to do anything but just be in the moment. If we take it further—if you want to—then great. If not, we'll have some fun and maybe save some lives."

She shouldn't ask. She really shouldn't. "Do you want to take it further?" Her voice cracked.

He sobered, an intensity swelling from him. "Hell yes. To bed and then to bed again. But I ain't lookin' for ever after, April. Can't."

"Just here and now," she murmured thoughtfully. Was it possible?

He nodded, looking like one of those tough-guy heroes from an action movie. "Think about it."

Like she had a choice. She might not think about anything else. "Okay."

"For now, let's plan for our dinner date tonight. Something tells me it's going to be interesting."

That was probably an understatement. Big time.

7

I like these new guys—the Mercs. Hope I don't have to kill them.
—Jax Mercury, Journal

JAX MERCURY SCRUBBED his wet hair away from his face and settled into his chair in the war room, his gaze on a map of what used to be Los Angeles. His elbow rested on the cool surface of the conference table they'd found at a law office somewhere.

A whisper sounded by the door, and Damon Winter strode in, munching on what looked like fruitcake. A bandage peeked from his superficial wound. "Get the blood off after interrogating that gang member?" he asked, pulling out a chair at the elaborate table to sit. His voice gave nothing away.

Jax glanced sideways. "Yeah." He took in the newest member of his team. The guy could definitely handle himself, but rumor had it he'd been a cop. Even though Jax had been a soldier with the US military, he'd never been a big fan of law enforcement. Of course, he'd been in a gang that had broken laws on a regular basis. Now, he was trying to create law and order. "That bother you?"

"Yeah." Damon took the final bite, his dark eyes sober. "That bothers me."

Jax tugged his fresh T-shirt into place. "Then don't do it."

Damon lifted a dark eyebrow. "I'll do what needs to be done, but we shouldn't like it."

Ah. Jax nodded. "Agreed." He tilted his head. "How's your wound?"

"Just a scratch. Needed a Band-Aid. No big deal."

"What were you just eating?" When was the last time Jax had eaten?

"Fruitcake," Damon said. "Did you know it lasts forever? I mean, forty years from now, the fruitcake we have in storage will still be edible."

That couldn't be good. "Didn't even know we had fruitcake," Jax muttered.

"Scouts found an old factory a day ago and brought as much as they could carry in the van." Damon gave a mock shudder. "It really is as awful as I remember. But it's food."

Yeah. They couldn't turn away sustenance. Not an ounce. "Why you here, Damon?"

"What did you find out?" Damon asked.

All right. The cop would get to his point in his own time. That was fine. This was a man Jax wanted on his team, so he'd play along. For a while. "I have the Twenty's hierarchy, which is pretty damn loose, and I'll make diagrams. Bottom line is that the president is using them to harass us as well as gather supplies and so on. They number about a hundred."

Damon winced. "A hundred gang members who get points for killing us. Wonderful. What does Vanguard number?"

"About six hundred now that the Mercs have joined up," Jax said. If they had. That still seemed to be up in the air. "Do you think you're joining Vanguard?" He studied the cop's face, looking for any clue as to what he was thinking.

Nope. No tells. Damon could probably play poker with the best of them.

Damon turned and studied the map of Los Angeles. "I'll back whatever play Greyson makes."

That was clear as glass. Perfectly, actually. Okay. Jax leaned back, his body relaxing. He liked a guy who played it straight. "What's Grey thinking?"

"Dunno." Damon crossed muscled arms. A small bandage peeked from beneath his T-shirt up high on his left bicep. "But I think we should stay."

Jax went on alert. There was no question Greyson Storm relied on Damon's council. "Why?"

Damon turned slowly, his gaze thoughtful. "For one thing, our entire territory burned down."

Yeah, that did suck. But they could always build somewhere else. Probably. "And?" Jax prompted.

"You have a good group here. People forming connections and families. The Mercs need that as much as the rest." Damon rolled his neck. "And you could use us. Your soldiers are good, but there's strength in numbers, and our soldiers are phenomenal."

"You think they'll be part of Vanguard?" Jax asked, watching carefully.

Damon seemed to think it over. "Yeah, but you'll need to phrase it differently. Have a Mercenary faction within Vanguard that's responsible for security. For fighting. Maybe let some of your Vanguard soldiers, the best of the best, join up and train with the Mercs."

Jax mulled it over. "I don't really see a problem with that." It was all semantics, and he'd never given a shit about that. "What else?" He didn't have all day here.

"April and I were invited to dinner," Damon said, his voice lowering just enough to be noticed.

Jax lifted his head. "You don't think she's up to it."

"How the hell should I know?" Damon asked. "Not that it matters. She's our way in, and I'll cover her. Have you even taught her to fight?"

Jax shook his head. "Barely. She's been busy with organizing the structure for the kids—when she wasn't in mourning. I haven't pushed. There's something just so..."

"Delicate," Damon said. "There's something fragile and delicate about her."

"I was there," Jax said, a ball of fire burning through his chest. "When she buried her daughter. I was there." His throat started to close, so he stopped talking. He wasn't capable of pushing April Snyder to do anything she didn't want, and that was a fact. She needed to be protected at all costs. His head lifted. "I'm allowing her on this mission, but that's all it is. Remember that."

For the first time, emotion filtered into Damon's dark eyes. Amusement and something else. Warning? Yeah. That was a warning. "Mind your own business," he said easily.

"April *is* my business," Jax shot back. If the Merc thought he was going to have a good time and use April, he'd find a bullet instead. "Don't forget it."

Before Damon could retort, Lynne Harmony strode into the room, a ream of papers in her slender hands that she was reading as she moved. She wore a lightweight, white lab coat over a casual peach sundress, and the odd blue of her heart glowed slightly. "I've been reading the newest intel we got from Zach Barter, and I think we need to get into the Reno Bunker as soon as possible— as soon as Tace and Sami get home with information from the Century City Bunker. I may finally have some good news for you." She looked up, and her stunning eyes focused. "Oh. Hi, Damon."

A different heat—the good kind—filtered through Jax. His

woman had her blond hair piled on top of her head in a messy but totally cool way, and her soft lips were pursed as she seemingly thought about a million things at once. "Come here," he said.

She blinked. Once and then twice. A lovely pink filtered into her pale cheeks. "Jax."

"Now."

She faltered, rolled her eyes, and then moved toward him. "I thought we took care of the bossy part of you."

When she was close enough, he grasped her arm and tugged her down onto his lap, as she no doubt knew he would. Considering she snuggled closer while keeping her papers safe from being crumpled, she didn't seem to mind much.

He kissed her forehead. "Damon was just telling me that he and April were invited to dinner with the Pure tonight."

Lynne stiffened just a little.

"Jax was just warning me off April," Damon said easily.

Lynne twisted her head to look at Jax. "Why?"

Why? Because the woman had been through enough. "It's a mission. Not a dating app," Jax returned.

Damon sighed. "You're the only one who can date?" His eyes dropped to Lynne's chest before quickly lifting.

Jax didn't take offense. Lynne had been injected with a cure for Scorpius that had turned her heart blue without curing anything. The organ glowed an aqua shade, as did the veins surrounding it. He didn't mind people being curious, and he appreciated how quickly Damon had looked back up. "April isn't in a state to date. She's vulnerable, and we've already discussed that she's fragile."

Lynne snorted. "You're such a moron."

He tightened his hold on her, not liking the amusement that glowed darker in Damon's eyes. "I'd appreciate if you kept the insults private, baby," he murmured.

Lynne shrugged one slender shoulder against him, obviously unconcerned.

Damon, quite wisely, stood. "I'll check in after this dinner."

Jax nodded. "Do so. Also, we're conducting a raid on a Twenty gang headquarters late tonight. We can't let their attack go unanswered. Figured you had experience raiding gang and drug houses."

Damon lost his smile. "More than I'd like. I'm definitely in."

That's what he'd figured. "I'll have a plan by the time you check in," Jax said, wrapping his fingers around Lynne's ribcage. Was she losing weight? Sometimes, she got so busy with her research and trying to cure Scorpius that she forgot to eat. He hadn't been paying close enough attention.

Damon left and shut the door behind him.

Jax partially turned Lynne. "I'm a moron?" he asked mildly.

Her smile brightened her entire face. "Sometimes."

"When was the last time I spanked you?" he asked, enjoying the darkening of her blush.

Her eyes widened. "Last week during sex. It was pretty good, too." She leaned over and pressed a kiss to his nose. "I'll show you. Next time, I'll spank you."

Humor took him, and he couldn't help the chuckle that rose from his chest. So much for intimidating the beautiful doctor. "I don't think so." He glanced at her papers. "What did Barter's notes give you?" Zach Barter was the fuckwad who'd injected Lynne with the blue drug, and he was only still breathing while sitting in a cell because he had useful information.

She bit her lip, making Jax want to do the same. "There's evidence that the Scorpius bacterium only survives on surfaces for six months. Then it dies and is no longer a threat."

Jax straightened. "Good evidence?"

Her frown drew down her fine eyebrows. "I think so. I'll need the records from the Reno Bunker to know for sure."

The Century City Bunker they controlled had more computer

records and weapons. Apparently, all of the Bunkers had a primary function, and the one in Reno was all about research. Jax started making plans. "I want to get the Mercs integrated a bit more, and then we'll take that facility as soon as Tace and Sami return." They were at the Century City Bunker looking for more intel on Reno before they could attack. It wouldn't be easy. "We also need to find more explosives before launching the attack."

She kissed his nose again. "Has Sami had any luck with the encrypted files?"

"No, but she doesn't think the president has either. She says the encryption is the best of the best." Jax grinned. If Sami couldn't hack into the mysterious file the president had made Greyson Storm steal, then no way could anybody else. For a while anyway.

Lynne fluttered her eyelashes. "You're so handsome."

He couldn't help but roll his eyes. "What do you want, Doc?"

She grinned. "Leave April and Damon alone. If there's a chance for them, stay out of the way."

There was no chance for them. April was barely functional, and Jax didn't know Damon. "It's not going to happen," he muttered. "Stop getting hearts in your eyes and thinking everyone should hook up. Those two are way too different, and she's too fragile."

"Different?" Lynne's lips twitched. "Not like us, huh? I mean, we're so much alike."

Okay. So they were opposites. Completely. "Damon is as dangerous as they come, no matter how mellow he seems," Jax said. He knew a soldier, a predator when he met one. He liked the guy, too. "April has lost everything, and a strong wind could break her. She's not up for a casual fling."

"Maybe Damon isn't either." Lynne sighed. "I think they'd be good together. She's sweet, and he seems like he deserves that. He's tough and protective, and that woman needs to be safe-guarded. I like them together."

How intriguing that a scientist, one of the best in the world, would be so romantic. "You're a sweetheart, Lynne Harmony."

She wiggled a little on his lap, and his dick perked right up and said hello. "You're insatiable," she said, sounding pretty damn happy about it.

"Yeah, I am." He tangled his hand in her hair. "There's a new preacher in Vanguard. Used to preach somewhere near San Diego."

She stilled. "There is?"

"Yeah. How about we plan that wedding you've wanted?" He didn't care about ceremonies, but he definitely wanted to claim her forever as his. "You're everything. You know that, right?"

Her expression softened in a way he'd only seen her do for him. The sight filled something in him that he hadn't known needed filling until he met her. "I do," she murmured.

Then she kissed him.

8

It's not real, it's not real, it's not real. I'm going on a pretend date tonight. It's not real.
———April Snyder, Journal

IN THE SMALL bathroom off her room, April smoothed back her hair and secured it with an elegant clip. A small lantern set on the non-functioning toilet filtered some light into the room so she could see in the square mirror above the useless sink. Running water was a thing of the past.

Her apartment led to the main rec room for the kids and also had an outside entry, which was nice.

It had been so long since she'd worn her hair up, she felt like an imposter. The easy twist had been her favorite for PTA meetings and school functions, and yet, now, it seemed fake.

The lipstick she'd accepted from Lena felt foreign on her lips. She hadn't worn makeup in nearly a year. Survival didn't require looking pretty.

Yet tonight, she had a part to play. It wasn't as if she wanted to look nice for Damon. Nope. Not at all. She rolled her eyes at herself. Guilt, a very familiar feeling, made her chest feel heavy. How could she even think of flirting with another man? With *anybody* in this dangerous world?

A strong rap on the outside door made her jump. Her heart rate kicked into motion, hard and fast, and butterflies flew uninhibited through her abdomen.

For goodness sakes.

She turned on the simple sandals she'd borrowed from Lynne Harmony and walked past her definitional kitchen and bed area to open the door.

Her mouth went dry at the sight of the male standing there.

Damon had somehow found a black, button-down shirt that emphasized the width of his muscular chest. His jeans were dark but not wrinkled, and he wore what looked like black soldier boots. He'd shaven, and to say that his jaw was a hard line would be a serious understatement.

His gaze raked from her hair to her sandals and back again, lingering several times in between. "You look lovely."

She smoothed down the blue skirt of the heat-conscious sundress she'd found in the women's laundry area where clothes from scouting trips were dumped for anybody who wanted them. Spaghetti straps held up the bodice, which led to a waist that flared just slightly at the hips. "Thank you." She leaned in. He smelled good. *Really* good. "You clean up nice, too."

He held out an arm. "You ready?"

"No." She took his arm and walked out into the warm evening with him. The sun was just starting to dip in the sky, and the heat would likely last all night.

"You'll be fine." He seemed so tall walking next to her.

They walked to Main Street and then headed toward the closely guarded apartment building. "I feel like I should be bringing something, but I know they won't eat any food prepared outside of their building," she murmured.

He nodded toward a couple of Merc soldiers patrolling, and they did the nod-thing back. "I filched a bottle of wine from Jax's stash but then figured we wouldn't want to waste it on the Pure folks if this goes south. So you and I can drink it later."

Later. Them. Drinking. Her foot caught on the edge of a pothole, and Damon quickly righted her. "Thanks," she said.

"No problem." They reached the apartment building where two guys with guns flanked the entrance. At one point, the Pure had placed a fence around their building, but Jax had taken it down. The guns were a good deterrent to visitors, however.

"I'm nervous," April whispered.

"Turn that into curiosity," Damon returned. "They're going to ask you about me. All they know is that I'm an ex-cop, a Mercenary, and I pitched a fit about being exposed to Scorpius when the Vanguard medic treated me. Jax set that up, but they don't know it. Use it. Say I'm a bit of a germaphobe."

She nodded. "Let's do this." Before she could move, two men strode out of the entry. The first was Pastor King, who was tall, lanky, and around thirty years old. The second man, Joe Bentley, was a bit older and wore a white golf shirt with trendy, wired glasses. They both approached, donning welcoming smiles.

Pastor King held up a hand. "April. I'm so glad you could join us again." His smile widened on Damon. "And you must be Damon Winter. It's an honor to meet a former police officer. I'm Pastor King, and this is Joe Bentley. Joe runs the practical side of the church, and I'm in charge of the faith." His smile was charming, although his face showed fading bruises.

Damon nodded. "It's nice to meet you both. I've heard concerns about your church."

King chuckled. "Jax Mercury doesn't trust anybody but his own lieutenants. Come inside, you'll see that rumors are unfounded."

"Sounds good. What happened to your face, Zach?" Damon asked as they strode toward the entrance.

"A maniac attacked me awhile back. Nothing to worry about. And please, call me 'Pastor,'" King said. "The folks here have gotten me used to the title, and now I think it sets a nice tone for the entire church. I'd really appreciate it."

"Sure thing," Damon said easily.

If April didn't know better, she'd think he was out for a nice dinner with friends. She kept silent and followed Bentley into a foyer that had been constructed of the same blocks she had in her basement for the kids.

Damon stiffened just slightly next to her.

Pastor nodded. "I know. We have the entire first floor fortified, just in case. Protection of the kids is too important to take for granted." He led the way around the books, down a hallway, and into a large gathering room with tables set comfortably throughout. "This is where we take our meals. The classrooms are on the second level, and all of the living quarters are on the third and fourth floors."

The smell of lemon cleaner and bleach competed with the scent of something delicious. Mouthwatering. April looked around.

The makeshift kitchen was through an open doorway to the right. She caught sight of Sharon working with a couple of other women.

Four men entered through the back door, each carrying what appeared to be supplies. They skirted the tables and headed into the kitchen. Oh, yeah. The Pure had raided a couple of the Vanguard warehouses for food, supplies, and weapons. Jax was still deciding what to do about it.

"Tonight, I thought we could have a more private dinner," King said, gesturing toward a room off the main common area. "Is that all right?"

Damon answered for them. "Sounds good to me. Something smells wonderful."

"It's Sharon's work," King answered easily, escorting them

toward the room he'd indicated. "She was a chef at an exclusive country club in Palm Desert before the pandemic. She can take anything and make it not only edible but phenomenal."

April walked into a room that had probably been the super's apartment way back when. Everything had been taken out, leaving a nice, open room with a heavy and ornate rug covering the floor. A yellow linen tablecloth covered the table, along with what appeared to be pure silver candlesticks, their mint green candles already flickering. The table had been set for six with elaborate nametags. "Fancy," April said.

"We do like to please." Pastor King drew out a chair for her next to the head of the table.

She sat, almost sighing in relief when Damon sat on her other side. Bentley took the spot at the foot of the table, and two women, one of them Sharon, entered to sit across from April and Damon.

Damon read his nametag with its oddly scrawled and perfectly straight penmanship. "Somebody has OCD."

King chuckled. "That's me. I use a ruler and everything. But I wanted this to be kind of formal."

Sharon smiled widely and set down two opened bottles of Cabernet. "I hope you like barbequed steaks."

April's stomach almost growled. They had barbecued steaks in the Pure? Maybe she would just up and join. When was the last time she'd had a steak?

Damon slid an arm over her shoulders as if he'd done it a thousand times before. "Must've been some grill you picked up. Where did you get the steak?"

Darn good question. April stiffened, and then she forced her body to relax. She had to start playing her part and stop being such a complete dork. Going on instinct, she let her body lean a little toward Damon.

Pastor King watched them carefully, his green eyes shrewd. "God does provide."

That was so not an answer. April blinked. "The steaks are beef, right?" She wasn't to the point of eating dog yet. She just wasn't.

Sharon giggled. "Of course. Definitely beef."

There were a couple of farms still working upstate, but when had the Pure group made it out to get food? Or did they have contacts in the outside world? April made a note to ask Jax when she got a minute.

As her mind wandered, people brought in dishes, laughing and joking. Men and women alike, and they all seemed to be having a good time. After setting down the very fragrant food, they quickly disappeared.

The pastor grinned. "We all take turns with the work around here. Whatever you've heard, it isn't true." He poured April some wine and handed the bottle over to Damon.

"Where are the kids?" Damon asked, pouring his wine and then passing the bottle down.

"They ate earlier," Joe Bentley said, passing the wine to the other two women without taking any. Must not be a drinker. "I wish Jax Mercury would stop worrying about the kids and women here. They're fine."

April studied the charismatic leader. He was young but definitely had an energy about him. "Then why not let Jax come in and meet with people?"

"They don't want to meet with him," Pastor King said quietly. "They're terrified of catching Scorpius, all of them. And it's up to us to protect the kids."

She shook her head. "Jax can take serious precautions for a meeting, and you know it."

King smiled. "And then what? Periodic visits? Jax dictating how people should act or live? Even before the pandemic, we had freedom of religion in this country. My congregation is living the way they want. That matters to me." He sipped again and then nodded at Damon. "You're an ex-cop, and you've been checking all of us out since the second you arrived. What do you think?"

Damon shrugged, and his shoulder brushed April. "So far, everything looks fine to me. And this food smells fantastic." He accepted a bowl of salad from Sharon and dished some for April and then himself.

"How long have you two been together?" Sharon asked, her lips just a tad tight.

Damon flashed April a grin. "I think this is our tenth or so date. I want a bigger commitment, and April is thinking about it."

April smiled. That would explain any awkwardness on her part. "I haven't dated since I was a teenager, but Damon can be very persuasive."

"I'm sure," Pastor King murmured, taking a sip of his wine. "I'm sure he'll become protective rather quickly. There isn't much choice these days, now is there?" His voice was calm, almost serene.

"Vanguard seems well protected," Damon said, cutting into his steak. "Don't you think?"

"From the outside, sure," King said. "But my people need shielding from the bacteria."

April took a bite of steak and tried not to moan in pure pleasure. "How many people are in your congregation anyway?"

Sharon finished chewing. "Thirty women, twenty men, and fourteen kids. That's all."

Damon ate some of his salad. "How do you know all of your members haven't been infected?"

"We have the test," Bentley said after swallowing some truly amazing potatoes.

April jerked. "You have the test? Wait a minute. What?" The Vanguard group didn't even have a medical test yet. They were looking for one at the Bunker.

Bentley nodded. "Yeah. One of our members worked for one of the early labs, and when it folded, he took all the tests with him. It's an easy spit test. If the vial turns blue, you've got it. If not, you don't."

April looked at Damon.

His shrug was casual, but the look in his eyes was anything but. "The early tests were spit tests, if I remember right. But then the labs became secured, and testing was moved to certain locations. I hadn't realized anybody still living had access to those easy and early tests."

"We do. Like I said, God provides," Pastor King said, lifting his glass again. "And I should tell you both, I believe He brought you here to us. April, you're fantastic with organization, and we need that. Damon, we need your skills as a police officer to protect us."

The heads around the table all nodded.

Pastor King smiled, displaying his perfect row of teeth. "Welcome home, my friends."

9

There's more to this woman than a pretty face and a kind heart. I want to dive head-first into those depths.
—Damon Winter, Journal

DAMON TOOK April's hand as they walked away from the Pure apartment building and headed east for her place. The once busy LA street was almost dead quiet as darkness had fallen, and only the rhythmic clop of patrolling soldiers' feet could be heard.

A lion roared somewhere in the distance.

"At least that steak wasn't Marvin," April noted. The moon caught the highlights in her auburn hair.

Damon shook his head. He couldn't believe Jax Mercury had named a lion and then set out raw meat for it outside the territory. Too bad the beast hadn't eaten any of the Twenty gang members. "That steak was delicious. I wonder how they got the beef. The old leader of the Pure was seen on video, a while ago, talking to enemies behind their little fence there." The Mercs should set up a soldier right on the other side of the perimeter from the Pure building. Yep.

"I don't know." April's hand felt fragile in his. "But I thought it was interesting the women asked me back tomorrow to get to know me." She looked up at him, her blue eyes shining in the moonlight. "Were you invited back?"

He nodded, his body heating at her nearness. She was a sweetheart, that was for sure, and he didn't like that the Pure group was separating them. "They want my take on the weapons they admittedly stole from Vanguard."

She shook her head, and some of her hair slipped out of its knot. In the heated night, bathed in moonlight, she was a goddess. It had been brave for her to attend the dinner that night, and she'd done a good job of asking questions. The wine had mellowed her out a little, and she didn't seem so jumpy next to him for once.

"Did I mention you look pretty tonight?" he asked, knowing he should back off but needing to say the words anyway.

"You did," she murmured, her face turned up to the moon. "That was kind of you."

He pivoted and put her back against the brick side of her building. Her small gasp only spurred him on. "I wasn't being kind, April. Know that right now. I'm a decent guy, and I do the right thing, but kind isn't on the menu." It was only fair to warn her.

Her delicate snort stopped him short.

He leaned back to study her. "Did you just scoff at me?"

"Yes." She smiled, and the expression transformed her face from pretty to absolutely fucking beautiful. "I've seen you with your friends, I've noticed you talking to the kids, and I've spent a little time with you. You're definitely a kind man."

A kind man who'd put a bullet through an enemy just hours before and then turned another guy over to Mercury to torture. Man, did she have him wrong.

Worse yet, she sounded pleased that she thought he was kind. Had he come on too strong? "You know I'm not looking for happily ever after. Right?"

Her snort wasn't as delicate this time. "There's no such thing, Damon. Don't worry. I'm not seeing hearts in my eyes or rose petals or even old age. Even with the surrounding circumstances, I had a good time tonight. Which should make me feel guilty, but for some reason, doesn't. Maybe because we were mixing work with pleasure."

He'd like to mix a whole lot more pleasure with her, but that was definitely a bad idea. Jax Mercury had been right. Damn it.

Damon gently pulled her away from the wall and tugged her into resuming their walk. "I don't like you going in there alone." He couldn't help but take her hand again.

"Yeah. Like they're a dangerous group. My biggest threat is ruining this mission."

Not true. "The last leader of the Pure kidnapped Lynne Harmony and nearly killed her." Damon's blood chilled at the thought. "You don't even know how to fight."

"The last guy is dead, and the new pastor doesn't seem that crazy." She didn't respond to the other part of his comment.

They had almost reached the outside entrance to her tiny apartment when a Vanguard soldier walked their way, his gaze alert, his body tense, and his gun held by his thigh. "April. I was just checking on you." The guy was blond and stood to about Damon's height of six-four, and spoke in a southern accent. "It's late."

She didn't look surprised by the guy. "Hi, Quincy. Damon and I were out. Have you guys met yet?"

"No." Quincy's jaw hardened.

"Nice to meet you," Damon said, hiding his amusement. Apparently, April had a friend. Just how good of a friend? The guy obviously didn't know about the op with the Pure church.

"Where were you?" Quincy asked, his frown making him look a little too menacing for Damon's taste.

April paused. "We went to dinner at Pastor King's place. Why do you ask?"

Good. She didn't think the guy had the right to know where she'd been. Damon's shoulders relaxed. A tiny bit. But he kept a good grip on her hand.

"Pastor King?" Quincy snapped. "Are you kidding? Those people are nuts." He turned on Damon. "What were you thinking taking her there?"

April tilted her head as if surprised by the outburst.

Jesus, the woman was clueless. This guy was so into her it was sad. "I thought it was a nice place for a first date, considering they had steak and there was no worry of infecting anybody," Damon said easily. "The second date will probably be a picnic, and the third maybe another stroll around the territory. No good movies playing, you know. That good with you, buddy?"

Finally, April caught the undercurrents because she stiffened next to Damon. He'd figure out how he was so in tune with her another time.

Quincy's glare promised a discussion later.

Fine with Damon. After being turned on all night by the sexy brunette next to him, and deciding that he shouldn't do anything about it, beating the shit out of a moron would relieve some tension. "Bye, Quincy," he said, pulling April around the soldier and toward her door.

"Night," April added, keeping up because Damon hadn't really given her a choice.

Damon opened the door for her and didn't wait to be asked inside. He followed her in, for the sole reason that Quincy was still watching. If they were going to pull this off, everyone needed to think they were dating. Yeah. That was the only reason. He shook his head at himself and shut the door at his back. He was staking a claim he shouldn't.

She turned, her movements jerky, and her ocean-blue eyes wide. "Um."

He held up a hand. "Just letting everyone know we're dating. Take a breath."

Her teeth played with her bottom lip, making her look both adorable and sexy. Her uncertainty was beyond cute, but in that dress, her body was all siren.

"You are a contradiction," he muttered, his jeans becoming way too tight.

"So are you," she countered. "All right, then." She moved toward him, bringing the scent of sweet roses with her. "Thank you for a very nice date." Levering up on her tiptoes, she brushed her mouth across his.

His body electrified. From one simple touch.

She moved to step back, but he stopped her by the arm. An expression crossed her face that was all dare. Sexy, aware, desirable challenge.

All right, then. His gaze dropped to her lips, and he started to move in out of pure instinct.

Shouting started outside, and he froze.

* * *

APRIL JERKED. A fight?

"Stay here." Damon set her to the side and opened the door, shutting it instantly behind him.

She ran to the window to peer out.

Four men, including Quincy, faced off in the middle of the deserted street. They were shouting obscenities and threats. One guy wore the standard black T-shirt Merc uniform, while the other three appeared to be Vanguard. She kind of recognized them, but they were all fairly new.

She scrambled to open her window. Should she do something? It wasn't as if she had a cell phone. She hadn't wanted to keep a firearm around because of the kids, but maybe that had been foolish.

One of the Vanguard guys had a gun out.

She couldn't breathe. Damon continued toward the group. Toward the weapon.

It was three against two, if she were reading the situation correctly. Definitely not good. She looked frantically around and then ran outside to help somehow. One of the kids had left a smaller baseball bat near her door, and she grabbed it. The scrub grass scratched her bare legs.

Damon's voice easily carried through the night. "Whatever is going on needs to stop. Now."

The guy with the gun pivoted toward Damon.

April gasped and stopped short. He wouldn't shoot, would he? Her knees trembled. She looked around, but so far, the raised voices hadn't brought any soldiers running. She edged closer, holding the bat so tightly her knuckles protested.

"Either shoot me or put that thing away," Damon said, his back to her, and his voice way too calm.

A shiver wracked April's back. She reached the edge of the burned lawn and stopped. Nobody seemed to pay her any mind.

The guy with the gun smiled. "You Mercs need to leave Vanguard territory. In body bags if necessary. So shooting it is."

Damon moved so quickly, April could only stare. He punched the guy's wrist, and the gun spun through the air to clatter across the pothole-riddled concrete.

Then everyone moved at once.

Quincy and the other Merc started throwing punches, while the other two guys came at Damon. He ducked and threw one man over his shoulder to land hard on the ground and then pivoted, catching sight of her. "Get the fuck back," he snapped, taking a punch to the face. Fury filled his eyes.

She took several steps back before she could even form a thought.

He struck the still-standing soldier in the neck and torso, and then swept his legs out from under him. Damon followed the guy down and hit him rapidly three times in the face until the guy passed out cold.

"Damon!" April yelled just as the other soldier stood and rushed forward with a knife in his hand. He sliced Damon across the shoulder.

Damon swung hard and stood at the same time, knocking the guy back.

April tried to breathe. Blood flowed down Damon's arm. How badly was he cut?

Damon partially turned to check the fight still happening down the road and then pulled a knife from his boot. He circled the other guy. "I'm giving you one chance to put the knife away and go. Think carefully, because if you stay, I'm cutting you."

The statement was made all the more chilling by the calmness of Damon's voice. She truly didn't know him at all. Not the real man. April took another step toward the safety of her apartment.

The Vanguard guy settled into a fighting stance, his knife up. "I'm here, looking for you or Grey. You both need to go."

These guys had been waiting for Damon when they ran into the other Merc?

Damon had apparently reached the same conclusion because his eyes hardened even more. For the first time, April could see the deadly soldier he'd become with the Mercenaries. No mercy and not an ounce of the kindness she'd found in him were present.

Was that benevolence even real? Had she imagined it?

Damon gracefully circled away from the man he'd left on the pavement, his chin down, his blade loose in his hand.

The guy with the knife charged.

Barely moving, Damon sliced across the guy's chest. The

Vanguard soldier gasped, the sound filled with pain. Then he roared, his knife up as he ran at Damon.

Damon pivoted at the last second and cut neatly up the left side of the guy's face.

The guy yelped and jumped back, his free hand going to his wound. Blood instantly coated his fingers and dripped down his neck to his shirt.

Damon cocked his head to the side. "I'm about done." His voice was guttural.

The guy shook it off, spraying blood, and crouched again, watching.

Damon waited.

The guy advanced, more gracefully this time, slicing at Damon. Damon jumped back and then moved in, plunging his knife into the guy's thigh.

The Vanguard man yelled in pain and dropped to the ground, clutching his bleeding leg. Damon easily—almost casually— kicked him in the face, knocking him out. Then he turned to see the other two fighting guys separate from each other, both stumbling in opposite directions.

April leaned back against her door.

Damon turned, his focus solely on her. Moonlight shone down, highlighting the fierce angles of his bleeding face. Violence surrounded him, more than at home.

She couldn't breathe.

He moved toward her then, his brown eyes nearly animalistic. All instinct.

She couldn't move.

He reached her, and his unique scent of ginger, the woods, and man washed over her. Filled her. "You okay?"

She couldn't speak.

So she gulped and nodded. Her entire body felt as if it were on electrical fire. What was happening?

He leaned in, grasped her chin, and kissed her. Not sweet. Not kind. He kissed her hard and deep, sweeping his tongue in and taking what he wanted.

Her knees went weak. Her eyelids closed of their own accord. She swayed toward him, the feeling of him almost too much.

Abruptly, he released her. In one smooth motion, he reached behind her hip and opened the door, setting her inside the apartment. "I'll have somebody clean up the mess on the street." He shut the door and then...he was gone.

10

I like these Vanguard guys and would hate to have to kill them.
—Damon Winter, Journal

IF DAMON WERE any more pissed, his damn head would fly off. He stormed into Jax's war room, fresh stitches in his arm and a bandage above his right eyebrow. Greyson was already sitting next to Raze Shadow, one of Jax's lieutenants. The guy was the silent type—a former sniper—with longish, black hair and sharp, light blue eyes. He looked to be Native American, and rumor had it he was dating the shrink at Vanguard.

Jax sat at the head of the table. "Did Doc Penelope get you stitched up okay?"

Damon nodded. The petite doctor had been quick and efficient. "Yeah. Once your brother let me near her." That Marcus Knight, Jax's half-brother, had some serious issues.

Jax waved a hand. "He's a problem for another day. Right now, it appears Vanguard and the Mercenaries aren't getting along very well. I kicked the two guys out who attacked you."

"What about Quincy?" Damon snapped, taking a seat.

Jax shrugged. "He said he was just at the wrong place, wrong time. I'm giving him the benefit of the doubt this time."

"He was outside April's place on purpose," Damon snarled.

Jax's eyebrows rose. "So?"

So? She was with Damon, damn it. He bit his lip.

Jax sighed. "Listen. I get it. She has that whole nun-slash-whore thing going on. But, no."

Lava poured through Damon's veins. "What did you just say?"

Jax frowned. "What?"

Damon partially rose.

Greyson raised a hand. "Hold it a sec. I don't think Jax meant any insult."

Jax's lips turned down. "Of course, not. I adore April. But you have to admit, she's pretty and kind and great with the kids...and she has a body like Jessica Rabbit."

Damon gave a sharp shake of his head. "What the fuck?"

Greyson's grayish-green eyes twinkled. "That's kind of true."

Damon might have to beat the shit out of both of them. "One of you says a word about her, and I pull out my knife again." It still had blood on it from the last fight.

Jax cut Greyson a look. "He's getting in too deep."

Not deep enough. Damon had had one taste of her, just one, and she was already in his blood. He'd figure out what to do about that later. "Don't talk about me like I'm not here."

"Jesus." Jax shook his head, the motion almost sad. "First, I had to deal with Raze and the shrink while stupid Greyson here kidnapped and seduced Raze's sister."

Grey reared back. "Hey. She seduced me."

Raze calmly reached across the table and punched Grey in the face before settling back down.

Greyson rubbed his chin. "That was hardly necessary, but I get it. She's your sister. But she's carrying my baby, so don't hit me again."

They were a bunch of lunatics. Damon growled low and deep.

Jax continued as if violence hadn't just occurred at his table. "Then Tace and Sami danced around each other for ages, making googly eyes. I had to send them both to our Bunker just to keep from puking. And now? Damon and April. Well, no. I'm just saying no this time. No romance, no fucking, no emotional shit. Got it, Damon?"

Damon finally calmed. "I think you're a complete moron."

"Ha." Jax shook his head again. "It's too late. You're already lost. Damn it." He looked at Greyson. "I'd ask you to take him to the Bunker with you, but I need him on the inside of the Pure. Speaking of which?" He turned back toward Damon.

Damon shoved down the temper that very rarely showed itself. He had to get ahold of himself. "They were nice and made a big show of folks doing their part—men and women. All laughing and having fun. Which was easy to believe because we had some phenomenal steak for dinner."

Greyson leaned back. "Where the hell did they get steak?"

"Now that's a good question," Damon agreed. The Pure obviously had sources on the outside somewhere.

Jax drummed his fingertips on the table. "I'm thinkin' from your word choices that they were trying too hard?"

Damon rubbed his chin. "Maybe. We saw only what they wanted us to see, that was for sure."

"You weren't here when they had five pregnant women come out and tell me to leave them alone. They were acting all subservient and kind of numb." Jax shuddered. "It was like something out of a horror movie. Any chance you saw any of those women?"

"Nope." Damon stretched his aching shoulder. Stupid knife wound. "If there's anything cultish or sexist or whatever going on, I didn't see it. Also didn't see any expecting women." He thought through the problem. "But I've been invited back tomorrow.

What if April and I get in a bit of a fight beforehand, and I handle her?" He tried not to wince at the thought.

Jax studied him. "If the Pure group steps in, they're legit. If they don't..."

Then maybe they'd see him as an ally. Damon wanted this assignment over—and now—so he could figure out his life.

Raze cleared his throat. "Is April that good of an actress?"

Smart. The sniper was definitely sharp. Damon shook his head. "No. She's terrible. If I pick a fight, it needs to be real on her part." Until he could explain later. "It won't be pretty." Especially for him.

"Can you do it?" Grey asked quietly.

The question echoed the thoughts rampaging through Damon's own head. Greyson was a true brother, and he knew how Damon worked. Grey had his back, and that meant everything. He met Grey's gaze and gave him the truth. "Yes. I can do it. Don't want to, but there's a part of me that doesn't think she realizes the danger she's in."

"She lost her daughter," Jax burst out.

Damon shook his head. "I know, but that was Scorpius. This is a nice and charismatic group of people who cook fine food and say the right things. The darkness, if it's there, is hidden well." April was a nester, and that was a fact. She'd settled into this life, and it still wasn't safe. Showing her that might be necessary.

"The thing she fears may become you," Grey said quietly. "Sure you're prepared for that?"

"That's already happened," Damon admitted. The look in her eyes after he'd stabbed the ex-Vanguard member just an hour before would always haunt him. Then he'd kissed her, and he hadn't exactly asked for permission.

"Sorry," Greyson said.

Damon forced a shrug. "It is what it is." It wasn't as if he were looking to make a connection. His job, after this current mission, was to cover Grey's back like always. Since Grey's fiancée was pregnant, he was distracted. Especially since no Scorpius survivor to-date had managed to stay pregnant long enough to give birth, and Maureen had definitely survived the infection. "Let's move on. What's the plan for tonight's raid?"

"We've changed it to tomorrow night," Jax said, reaching for a map under the table. "Here's the plan."

* * *

A SOFT KNOCK on the door nearly stopped April's heart. She looked up from her perch on the old sofa where she was reading a Lexi Blake novel a group had found while scouting the previous week. Oh, she'd already read it a couple of times before the pandemic, but it took her away from this world for a while. She had to find the rest of the series somehow.

Another knock.

Swallowing, she moved on unsteady legs to the outside door. Had Damon come back? Just an hour before, he'd kissed her as if he wanted to eat her alive.

And her body had been all in.

She wasn't ready to face him. The violence he'd shown in such a calm and deliberate way had shaken her. Completely. Then the kiss had rocked her world. None of it made a lick of sense.

"Hello?" came a soft voice. "April? You there?"

Oh. April pulled open the door to see Lynne Harmony and Vinnie Wellington standing in the soft moonlight. Lynne had a bottle in her hand. "Hi?"

"Hi." Vinnie pushed past her with Lynne on her heels. "Came to check on you and maybe get a little drunk." She glanced to her side. "Shh. We won't have too much. Geez. Go away, Lucinda."

April squinted at the shrink, who sometimes hallucinated her dead stepmother. She'd needed a friend, and her friends were here. "Okay."

Lynne quietly shut the door, her heart glowing a bright blue beneath her white T-shirt. She no longer tried to hide the aberration. "I hope it's okay. We heard you and Damon went on that date with the Pure, and we're dying to get the details."

"Good. I wanted to talk to you, Vinnie, about doing some counseling with the kids." April followed them into the small living area after grabbing three plastic cups from the kitchen. What the soldiers did to protect Vanguard was important and vital. But so was taking care of people inside the territory.

"Sure," Vinnie said easily. We can talk about it tomorrow, when we're working. Tonight, let's just relax."

Yeah. Good plan. Both women were brilliant and had doctorates, and sometimes April wasn't sure what to say around them. She hadn't even gone to college. But they were kind, and they'd become her friends. "It was an unsettling night." She flopped onto a cracked leather chair.

Lynne sat next to Vinnie on the worn sofa and poured three glasses of tequila.

April winced. "Seriously?" Why couldn't it be schnapps or something?

"It's all we had." Vinnie took her glass. The shrink had blue eyes, blond hair, and a wicked sense of humor. She ran the deadly serious Raze Shadow in circles, and it was a lot of fun to watch. She was also a former profiler with the FBI. "Go away, Lucinda," she muttered.

Lynne took her glass and handed one to April. They'd bonded while locked in a room hiding from psychos with guns, and Lynne had been there for April after her daughter died. "Have a drink, sister."

April accepted the glass. "Cheers." She tipped her head back and swallowed. The liquid burned her throat and heated her stomach. She coughed, her lungs compressing.

"Did he kiss you?" Vinnie asked after taking her shot.

Lynne nudged her with an elbow. "Vinnie. Come on." Then she looked at April expectantly. "Well?"

How the hell should she answer that? "Yes, he kissed me. But it was after he stabbed a guy and knocked another unconscious by kicking him in the head. It wasn't after our date in a goodbye-at-the-door type of way." April held out her glass for another shot of the healing brew.

Lynne poured. "Wow. That was more than I expected. I need a second to process."

"Not me," Vinnie piped up. "Did you kiss him back?"

Had she? April took just a sip this time, and her lips burned a little. "I'm not sure. It was such a surprise, and he just took over. I may have moved my mouth?" Man. Had she? Or had she acted like a cold fish? While she wasn't sure she wanted to kiss Damon again, she couldn't have him thinking she was a bad kisser. "Oh, I don't know." Her stomach dropped.

Vinnie gulped down another shot. "I'm sure you did. If he was that into it, then he liked it."

"Wait a minute." April waved her hand. The room tilted a little, and her body fuzzed nicely. "It doesn't matter. Come on. I've been with one man my entire life. I have no idea what to do with a tough guy like Damon."

Vinnie snorted. "It's all the same, sister. They all have the same parts."

Lynne tried to cover a laugh with a cough. Her eyes watered. "Yes, and no. I mean, come on. These guys are a little different. The whole survival and deadly soldier thing. It makes the sex, well, intense."

Vinnie giggled.

April's vision blurred, but she studied the two brilliant blondes anyway. "I got pregnant at sixteen with my husband, which was the best accident ever to happen in my entire life. It also got us out of foster care." Sure, things had been tough, but they'd made it. "I worked, and Don went to school and became a dentist. Things were really good then." Until they weren't.

"Wow." Vinnie tapped her glass against her lips. "You never even dated anybody else?" .

April shook her head. "Nope." Then she tried to clear her head. "And I'm not dating anybody now. You guys know that. This is a mission."

Vinnie nodded, her face morphing just a little. "Yeah, I understand. But these days, that's like online dating. Everything is an op."

Humor slaked April, and she chuckled. That wasn't even funny. But, somehow, she laughed.

"I was on a mission when I hooked up with Jax." Lynne's words slurred. "That worked out."

Vinnie giggled. "I *was* a mission with Raze. Remember? He was supposed to turn me over to Greyson Storm."

Lynne nodded vigorously. "Yeah. And Greyson was on a mission with Maureen, who he kidnapped. They're all missions. Everywhere you look, another mission. Why do they all lead to kissing?"

Vinnie half-heartedly swung out to pat Lynne's shoulder. "Great question! Yeah. That's a really good question. Right?"

"Uh-huh." April couldn't feel her feet. Or face. "Is it worth it? Taking the chance again. After everything?" She blinked, trying to keep her eyes open somehow.

"Yes," both women answered in unison.

11

An alpha male is not for me. Probably. Well, maybe. No, definitely.
But he's just so sexy.

    ——April Snyder, Journal

APRIL FINISHED SWIPING on lip-gloss just as Damon knocked on the outside door. Odd. She recognized his knock. Strong and steady. Man, she was losing it.

She moved through the small apartment and tried not to jostle her aching head. What in the world had she been thinking shooting tequila like she was twenty again? Even her teeth ached a little this morning, and it wasn't as if she could just go buy aspirin at the drugstore.

All painkillers were saved for real pain. Not the kind one deserved.

She opened the door to bright sunshine and sexy man. He wore faded jeans and a light T-shirt, his muscles nicely defined. Pleasure caught her, sprinkling out from her chest. It felt as if she were fourteen with her first crush again. Then the sun hit her eyes, and she barely kept from wincing. "Hi."

"Hi." Damon stepped aside so she could walk past and shut the door. His smell of ginger and male soothed her. "Have a nice night?"

"Sure." She kept her head down and moved across the scrub brush with him by her side. He was big enough to nicely block the penetrating sun, which was way too hot, even with her light blue sundress covering her. "How's your arm?"

"Fine." His voice was curt.

She frowned and looked up into his dark eyes. "What's the matter?"

He grasped her hand as they walked down the abandoned street toward the Pure apartment building. The feeling of security his touch gave her made her uneasy and pleased her at the same time. "Last night, I told you to stay inside when the men were fighting, and you completely ignored me. I don't like that."

What the heck? "I don't work for you." She wanted to get angry, but her head was pounding. Her bed sounded so inviting. Why couldn't she go back there for an hour—or five? What if she invited him? What a crazy thought.

"When it comes to my men fighting, you do listen to me." The hold on her hand was firm. A little too firm.

She tried to draw free...and failed. Her brain woke up completely. "What is wrong with you?"

"What's wrong with me is that you're not listening." They turned the corner and walked down another street that had once been busy with cars, hookers, and drug deals. At least, that was how Jax had described the area to April.

She swallowed. "I am listening." Maybe Damon's injury was worse than she'd thought. He was certainly cranky. "I stepped back when you told me to last night." Her little bat wouldn't have done much good anyway.

"I told you to stay inside."

She jerked to a stop, a little surprised when he let her. Heat cascaded off the pavement below her feet, even at this early hour. "Why are you being so grumpy?"

His eyes glimmered for a moment, and his lips twitched. Then the expression was gone completely. Rock was probably softer than his jawline. "Calling me names isn't going to lead to a nice day for you."

She cocked her head to the side. It wasn't like him to threaten her. "What's up with you? Did you hit your head last night?"

He paused as if not quite sure what to say. "We're going to be late." He tugged her back into motion, his strides too long.

She tripped. "Slow down."

"No." He had the momentum, and she had no choice but to lope into a jog. When it came to strength, they were no match. Not even close.

Confusion blanketed her. "Damon? Are you sure you're all right?" When he'd hit the pavement the previous night, he might've gotten a concussion. There was still a cut above his eye from the guy who'd punched him. "Maybe we should see the doctor."

His sigh was full of exasperation. "Do you never get angry?"

Not when she was totally hung-over. This conversation was so odd. "Do you want me mad?"

He slowed his strides. "Of course not. It's just...how can't you see when somebody else is mad?"

They reached the walkway to the Pure building, and April mulled over his question. Movement cast shadows at the doorway. Was Pastor there? "You don't seem mad. You just seem really cranky. Like you have a sliver in your toe or something."

"Wrong." Damon turned to face her, fully blocking out the sun. His hands clamped on her upper arms, holding her in place. "I'm pissed, April. When I tell you to do something, especially if it involves fighting soldiers with guns, you fucking do it. Got it?"

She blinked. Once, and then again. He'd just sworn at her.

She'd faced a snarling tiger once while on a school trip to the zoo, and Damon seemed scarier. Plus, unlike the tiger, there was no fence between them. "I think you need to let go of me. Now."

He leaned down, his expression ominous. A definite threat. "No. Tell me you get me."

She tried to struggle, but he held her tight. Panic filtered through her, followed by a distant anger that actually felt hot. "You're about to get kicked in the balls. Move back. Now."

In a million years, she never would have guessed his next move. He grabbed her neck and pulled her toward him. She gasped. He squeezed just enough to show his strength. His eyes were a sharp brown, and his expression implacable.

Who was this guy?

She tried to swallow, barely able to because of his hold. "What. Are. You. Doing?" she gritted out.

"Trying to get you to take me seriously," he snapped.

Huh. She should be scared. Or super mad. But her anger puttered out like a candle hit with water. Instead, concern filtered through her. "I'm worried about you. We should go see one of the doctors."

He sucked in air, and his nostrils flared. "You are impossible." His voice lowered to a tense whisper. "Would you just fight back a little so I can be an asshole? Please?"

Her mouth gaped open. Ohhhhh. Okay. Wait a minute. He had this whole plan and hadn't bothered to tell her about it? The pastor was watching quietly from the entrance, and Damon needed a scene. Oh, he did, did he? What? He thought she couldn't act, so he pretended to be a big old jerk and just confuse her? That did actually make him a bit of an asshole.

"Today, April," he muttered.

Fine. "You are such a dick." She punched him as hard as she could in the stomach, kind of meaning the words.

He didn't even exhale as her fist bounced off. Ouch. That hurt, damn it. What were his abs made of? She set her stance to punch harder, but with no hint of warning, he moved.

Fast and decisive.

He ducked a shoulder, hit her midsection, and lifted her right off the ground. Her forehead flopped against his upper back, and her legs dangled uselessly—like something out of an old John Wayne movie. Blood roared into her head, increasing her headache.

She reacted instantly. Her kick to his gut this time was real.

Finally, he did exhale with a muffled "*oof.*" She barely had time to smile at that before his hand, his very large and hard palm, landed squarely on her butt with a loud smack.

The sound caught her first and then the sting. It spread across her entire lower back. She squawked and started to struggle.

"Stop it." He smacked her again, striding easily toward the entrance to the Pure building. Heat flared in her lower half, both intriguing and irritating.

Oh, she was going to kill him. Like, dead kill him. Even for playacting, that was so unnecessary. Her abdomen felt all mushy now. His easy strength was yet another intriguing aspect of the guy. Life was confusing enough.

"Is there a problem?" Pastor King's voice filtered through the haze of her rapid fury.

"Not anymore," Damon said easily. "Small disagreement. I think we have things figured out now."

The world spun wildly, and she found herself on her feet inside the Pure foyer. Her stomach lurched. It would serve him right if she puked all over the arrogant ass. He might be acting for the church, but he should've let her in on the plan. "That was unnecessary," she snapped once she'd regained her balance.

He lifted his chin in an oddly threatening way. "There's more where that came from. Go do what you need to do, and I'll meet you here in two hours." He looked over his shoulder at the two guys guarding the door. "She doesn't leave until I'm with her."

Heat lashed her, and the headache disappeared with honest anger. She opened her mouth to let him have it, but he cut her off at the pass. "You don't want to push me, blue eyes. Trust me." His gaze was hard enough that she heeded his warning.

He wasn't kidding. She swallowed. He'd do what was necessary to prove to the Pure that he was an ass. Instinct told her, deep down, that Damon Winter wasn't a guy you pushed. Not even when he was playacting. Fine. She'd let him have it later. Turning on her thin sandal, she moved past the odd configuration of cement blocks and walked into the main meeting area where Sharon was waiting with a stack of papers in her hands, leaning back against one of the tables.

"Hi," April said.

"I'm glad you're here," Sharon said. Her smile widened as Damon obviously moved around the blocks and came into view. "Officer Winter. It's good to see you again."

"Thanks." His voice was now nice and pleasant.

April bit back a snarl.

The pastor cleared his throat. He looked long and lean in casual jeans and a button-down shirt. "Damon, if you'd come with me. I'd sure like your opinion on our armory. To be honest, our soldiers are more homegrown and accustomed to shotguns. A few of these pieces are beyond my knowledge."

"Sure thing." Damon squeezed April's arm. "I'll see you shortly."

Yeah. That sounded like a threat.

She looked at him over her shoulder. "Oh, you can count on that, Winter."

12
───────

*When the woman gets her claws out, she's sexier than I would've ever
thought. I might be getting in over my head with this one.*
      —Damon Winter, Journal

THE WOMAN HAD USED his last name for the first time, her voice
more than a mite spunky. Damon checked his smile and followed
Pastor King down a long hallway to a locked room at the end.
She'd felt way too good hanging down his back. Something told
him she'd never been tossed over a man's shoulder. She sure as
hell hadn't had her ass smacked before.

The surprise and intrigue in her eyes had been genuine. As
had the anger.

She was going to give it to him later. Something in him looked
forward to it.

King opened the door and walked inside.

Damon whistled at the neatly lined-up weapons in lockers
and spread across a huge, wooden table. "Jesus." Shit. He'd just

said that to a pastor. If King really were one. "Um, sorry about the language."

King turned around, his green eyes sparkling. "I think the Lord will give you leeway considering we're in the middle of a pandemic."

The guy really was charismatic. In his jeans and casual wear, he looked like a buddy you'd go to a football game with. The preacher at Damon's old church had been about ninety years old, but a great guy. Ex-cop, actually. "Sorry about the scene earlier."

King shrugged. "Not my business. You've been dating for a while, and if that's your dynamic, do what you have to do. The world is a dangerous place."

Wasn't it, though? "I figured you'd be upset."

King's eyebrows rose. "Why? You didn't really hurt her, and she was more intrigued than angry. I saw no fear in her. Not an ounce."

Damn it. The guy read people perfectly. Isn't that what most cult leaders did? "What if you had seen fear?"

King winced. "Then I would've stepped in and probably got my ass kicked. I heard about the fight last night. You took out some decently trained Vanguard soldiers without much effort. You mask your abilities behind that thoughtful exterior, Damon Winter."

"I accept the violence in me. Have since I took my first oath," Damon murmured, tension forming at the base of his neck. It'd be a mistake to lie to King because he'd see right through it. The balancing act of giving enough truth and doing his job was definitely giving Damon a headache. "It's helpful to know how to fight in this new world."

"Isn't that the truth? I'd appreciate it if you'd train some of my congregation. We need it."

"What's your story, anyway?" Damon concentrated on King but catalogued the weapons with his peripheral vision.

King took a Sig Sauer off the table and examined the weapon. "You wouldn't believe me if I told you."

"Tell me anyway." Might as well act like the cop he used to be. Damon crossed his arms.

"Okay." King set the weapon down, his gaze thoughtful. "I graduated from college with degrees in philosophy and psychology. The philosophy because it was where my heart was, and the psych because it's where my dad said I could make money." He smiled. "Dad was right. I worked for a few years and then returned to get my doctorate in philosophy. Then Scorpius hit."

There were more weapons in the room than had been in Jax's warehouse that had been raided. Damon had seen the manifest. Where had these come from? "Then what?"

King shrugged. "I didn't catch the bacteria. Everyone else I knew did...and died. There had to be a reason, or none of it made sense." His voice increased in strength.

None of this did make sense. Was that a Barrett MRAD sniper rifle in the corner? Where the hell had the Pure found that? No way had Mercury kept one of those in a weapons warehouse so far from headquarters where a couple of real-life snipers lived. "And?" Damon prompted.

"And? I feel like God called me to this. To form this group of people and protect them from the illness. Are you a religious man, Officer Winter?"

The use of his former title conveyed respect. Damon studied the guy. "I used to be."

King's eyes softened. "More than ever before, this is a time for faith. It's all we have."

Damon's mom might've liked this guy. She was all about the faith. Then she'd died in a pandemic. "So you have this big calling?"

"Sure." Pastor King picked up a Glock and rolled it around in his hands. "Don't you feel the same?"

"No." Actually, Damon had been searching for purpose and

meaning. Finding Greyson and the Mercs had seemed a good fit, and he'd provided security and good council during the time it was needed. Yet something in him, something deep, had a restlessness he couldn't tame. He ignored it the best he could. "I'm just doing what I need to do."

"Going through the motions, huh?" King zeroed in.

Damon exhaled. Was that what he was doing?

King stacked some boxes of bullets. "Have you even grieved all the people you lost?" There was curiosity and an odd tone of understanding in his voice.

"Yeah," Damon said softly. He'd been laid flat, and it had taken a lot of time to stand back up. "But you have to make a choice. Give up or go on. So I moved on." This guy was way too easy to talk to.

"Me, too," King said, looking over the myriad handguns across the wide table as if he couldn't believe he was dealing with firearms. He frowned and reached for a snub-nosed pistol to spin on the wood. "This world just doesn't make sense anymore. There has to be a purpose, though. There has to be meaning here."

For the first time, the guy sounded almost lost.

Damon wanted to find reassuring words, but was there a purpose? Bacteria had taken out most of the human population, ending civilization as they'd known it. No internet, no electricity, no laws any longer. How could there be a purpose in any of that? "Sometimes, I think God gave up on us." He'd never admitted that to anybody. Not even Greyson.

King's chin lowered to his chest for a moment. "I really believe that's when faith comes in. It's easy to believe when life is rainbows and sunshine. The true test comes in times like these."

"I guess I haven't had time to worry about believing," Damon admitted. "Survival is first, and I figured I'd worry about faith later."

King nodded. "I get that." He rubbed an almost-gone bruise on his cheekbone.

"What happened there anyway?" Damon had heard rumors, but he hadn't been present.

King sighed. "I met with Mercury and his men, and I was being an ass. Was dealing with terrified folks in my church who wanted to be left alone, and then went to talk to Mercury. He became insistent. I got rude with Sami Steel. There's no excuse. Her boyfriend went nuts on me."

Ah. Tace Justice, the medic for Vanguard. Yeah. The guy was a former soldier. If he wanted to inflict damage, he could. "Sorry about that."

"I deserved it. Plus, Justice had just survived the infection, and he wasn't in his right mind. Rumor has it, he still isn't." King's inflection held no judgment, just fact.

It was true that Scorpius created sociopaths. Some were still decent people, just with a lack of emotion. And some became serial killers. There was no way to know the long-term effects of the illness. "He's better now." Probably. Damon hadn't spent enough time around him to really know.

"Maybe. But we don't know what happens next." King lifted his head, his eyes a piercing green. "So far, anybody infected with Scorpius hasn't been able to carry a child to full term, right?"

"So far," Damon agreed. But the science was out. "There are at least two women in Vanguard who survived the infection, and they're still pregnant." He scratched his head. "There are probably a lot more out there in the world, but our lines of communication aren't great."

King shook his head. "The two in Vanguard are in their first trimesters. They won't make it to the third, and you know it. Nobody has."

"We don't know that." Damon reached for a scratched pistol. The thing looked about a hundred years old. "Where did you get this?"

"We have our own scouts," King said. "Plus, a lot of these were here when the former pastor was. I took over when he was, ah... killed." King leaned forward. "I know he kidnapped one of the Vanguard scientists, and I had nothing to do with that. I'd never do anything to hurt a woman. My calling wouldn't allow for anything like that."

The guy had an answer for everything, didn't he? Maybe it was all the truth. Maybe not. "Your calling?"

"Yes. To lead this church somewhere safe and then look to the future." Frustration drew King's eyebrows down. "There has to be purpose. The future must be it."

Ah. The future. "You think it's your job to continue the human race?"

"Somebody has to," King said. "What if I'm right? What if Scorpius survivors will never be able to carry a child to full term? Don't we have a duty to ensure our survival? Every nationality, every race, every genetic conglomeration there is?"

Damon snorted. "You think I have a duty to procreate because I'm black?"

"I think you have a duty to procreate because you can," King stressed. "Nearly ninety-nine percent of the world's population died from the pandemic. Of the people still living, only about five percent haven't contracted the illness. That's a small percentage on which to rebuild."

There was logic in the statement that Damon couldn't dispute. But he didn't like it. "What if somebody doesn't want to add to the human race?" Where were those pregnant women Jax had seen?

King scoffed. "Then they don't. Honestly. I'm not keeping a stable of women around here to have babies."

Fine. Time to lay it on the table. "Where are the pregnant women? I know there are some."

King sighed. "They're wherever they want to be. For the record, they're scared to death of catching the illness while pregnant, so no way will they meet with Mercury. And I won't force them."

"Then have them meet with me," Damon said. "I'm pure, as you say."

King nodded. "Take the test, and if you pass it, I'll let you meet with anybody you want."

Man, Damon couldn't get a bead on this guy. Everything he said made sense. Yet Damon's instincts still tingled. Was it just the danger of the entire situation? Was it Jax's irritation at having a group not within his control in Vanguard? Or was it something more? "Where's the test? Let's do that now."

13

So far, I haven't found anything wrong with the Pure church. But still...something is bugging me. Maybe it's just that I'm not in charge of it.

  —April Snyder, Journal

APRIL FINISHED TOURING the area for the kids, noting a few younger boys wrestling over on the floor in the younger kids' rec room. She'd met several, and so far, they ranged from three to ten years old. "Where are the teenagers?" she asked Sharon.

"Learning in the classrooms," Sharon said, leading April into the teenagers' rec room complete with beanbags. "This is where they hang out when they're not in class." The empty room was wide and had a pool table and a ping-pong table behind the beanbags and sofa.

Sunlight streamed in through the windows, heating the room. Even so, it was a pleasant space.

"Have a seat." Sharon took a seat in a beanbag, and April

followed suit, laughing as she sank in. She blinked. When was the last time she'd laughed?

Sharon settled, and the beans in her bag shuffled. "Isn't it nice not to worry about being infected? Just for an afternoon?"

April swallowed. She didn't have the right answer to that question.

Pastor King suddenly filled the doorway. "I don't think April has cared about being infected or even surviving for quite some time."

April's breath caught.

He smiled, his gaze gentle. "Have you?"

"No." Her chin lifted. She'd lost everything. Why lie?

"I don't blame you." King moved inside gracefully, looking more like a drummer in a band than a preacher. With his ripped jeans and dark shirt, he was more approachable than he'd appeared the night before at the somewhat fancy dinner. "I felt the same way when my fiancée died."

"Oh." April looked behind him, but the doorway remained empty. "I'm sorry."

"So was I." He sat on the couch, his hands clasped between his knees. This close, calluses were obvious. He'd worked with his hands at some point.

She frowned.

He glanced down at his hands. "Before Scorpius, I used to rebuild engines for fun." His voice deepened, and his smile slid away. "My dad and I...it was our thing."

April's chest ached. "Scorpius?"

King shook himself out of it and looked up. "Yeah." His smile was rueful and tinged with sadness. "The bacteria took everyone, right?"

She nodded. That was the sad truth. Even though she was probably a couple of years the pastor's senior, he seemed older than her somehow. That could be part of his charisma, or maybe he did have something going on religion-wise. Who knew? That was way out of her experience. "Where's Damon?"

Now King rolled his green eyes. "Going through every storage locker and room I have containing either weapons or defense equipment. I thought he was going to kiss me when he found a cache of bulletproof vests."

Kiss him? More likely punch him. "You stole those from Jax," April said.

"Actually,"—King smiled wider—"the last guy who ran this church stole from Jax. I'm giving the vests back. It's only fair."

Well. April studied the handsome man, trying to get inside his head. Was he actually a decent guy? Or was he just that smooth? Intelligence shone from his green eyes, and he filled out the T-shirt like he worked out daily. "I'm not a real fan of God right now," she murmured.

His chuckle was both surprised and genuine. "I don't imagine many people are. Were you before Scorpius?"

She shrugged. "Didn't know much about Him. Grew up in foster care and then formed a family. Didn't really go to church regularly." Would that make the pastor dislike her?

He nodded. "Growing up, my family went to church on Christmas and Easter." His shrug moved very nice muscles. "I didn't find God until I lost everything else." He stretched out his long legs. "The funny thing was that Annie, my fiancée, was trying to get me to attend church with her all the time, and I never did." His chest moved with his heavy exhale. "I wish I had."

April looked for the door again.

"We want you to join us here," King said easily. "You know that already, but I thought I should say it out loud. You and Damon."

Her and Damon. She couldn't leave the kids she cared for, even if she wanted to. They needed her. But this was a mission, and she had to play it cool. "We know," she murmured. "There aren't many uninfected people in Vanguard. That we know about anyway." She tried to find fault with anything he'd said so far. "What's your plan? Just stay in Vanguard, isolated? For how long?"

"Until we all leave," he said, drawing in his legs and leaning toward her. "We're all going to have to move north soon, and when we do, I'm hoping to find a nice place for our people. For the uninfected people to keep us safe."

"Why not leave now?" she asked, meeting his gaze.

He shook his head, and the sunlight glimmered across the fading bruises on his face. "The Twenty gang is out there, as well as numerous other predators, and we don't have the soldiers we need. If Damon came on board, it'd help a lot. But still, we'd require Vanguard security to get safely out of the city."

Maybe. The president was still gunning for Vanguard, so maybe not. "I'm not the key to Damon," April said softly, feeling out the pastor. Just how hard would he push?

"You might be," King said simply. "He wants you safe, and he's obviously staked a claim." He held up a hand. "I don't mean that in a bad way."

Her ass still tingled from Damon's two slaps. "I'd think a pastor would have a problem with the way Damon carried me in here." She looked from King to Sharon and back again. "Yet neither of you have said anything."

Sharon shrugged. "To each his own. I don't know your relationship."

King scratched his head. "I don't want to interfere. But if you're in danger or need help, all you have to do is ask. Is he a threat to you?"

A threat? Hell, yes. Not in the physical sense, though. Not really. But Damon Winter took everything about her and tilted it. He tempted her in a way that just wasn't all right in the crappy world these days. "He wouldn't hurt me," she said.

"That's what I thought, but I needed to make sure," King said, his eyes sharp.

"Would you forgo having him as security if I had said yes?" April asked, tilting her head.

King nodded. "In a heartbeat. There's right, and there's wrong. I can't lead this church if I don't know the difference."

Man, he was good. Was he being honest?

"April?" Damon suddenly filled the doorway, much more than the pastor had earlier. "How's it going?" He loped gracefully into the room, his eyebrows rising at the blue beanbag next to her.

She couldn't help the chuckle that let loose. The idea of somebody with Damon's muscled size dropping into a beanbag gave her the first light moment of the entire day. "What? Too far down for you?"

He frowned. "It's not the drop, it's the ascension. Not sure I could get out of it." He strode over to the sofa and sat next to King. "Cute room."

"It keeps the teenagers somewhat happy," Sharon said, brightening suddenly.

April bit her tongue to keep from snapping. The woman was way too flirty with Damon. Sure, he and April were just playing a part—maybe—but Sharon thought they'd been dating for a while. She purposefully brought his attention back to her. "How was the armory? Lots of guns to play with?"

"A surprising amount." Damon studied her. "You still mad at me?"

Heat infused her face. "We can talk about it later."

He sighed. "I'd prefer now." Without warning, he ducked and lifted her right out of the beanbag chair and settled her on his lap.

What the heck? Her eyes widened as she struggled to find her balance on his hard thighs. Was this a show for the pastor and Sharon? Damon didn't do a thing without reason, but it'd be nice if he let her in on what that was. Should she struggle? Put up a fight so Damon could act like a jerk? Or maybe to see if the pastor would step in?

"There," Damon said. "I like this room much better now that you're where you're supposed to be."

Okay. She totally didn't know how to play this. And the easy strength with which he'd lifted her had her heart beating a little too fast. On his lap, she felt small and feminine. Protected. "I'm still mad at you." It was the only thing she could think of to say.

"But not afraid," King murmured, amusement in his voice.

Was she supposed to be afraid of Damon? She'd forgotten that part. Okay. So she did suck as an actress. "The day is early," she said. It was true. Damon had scared the crap out of her the night before with the controlled violence he'd used in the street with those other guys. And yet, a part of her had warmed to that. She was discovering a dark side to herself that she hadn't known before. Maybe the pandemic had brought that out in her. Maybe it had always been there.

Damon jostled her into position. "You're awfully quiet. Thinking hard?"

She recovered quickly. "Yes. This is a nice place, Damon. It's bright and clean, and so far, everyone seems happy." It was true, and saying it out loud would give King and Sharon openings to talk. Maybe she could get better at this undercover stuff. The kiss Damon had given her the other night had felt real, though. Geez. This was too much. She was way out of her depth. "Don't you think?" She gave in to temptation and pressed her hand against his slate-hard chest.

"I do." He eyed King over her shoulder. "Though I would like a better explanation about some of the weaponry I just saw. Where did it come from? More importantly, how did it get here? No way would you be able to get some of that in here without Mercury taking notice."

King nodded, his gaze sober. "I know. I'm still investigating part of it since I wasn't involved."

It was hard to imagine that somebody had just walked up to the outside fence and tossed weapons over without any of the

Vanguard soldiers noticing. Sure, the patrols were on a set schedule, and April had seen it posted in the main headquarters. But still. "Who are your contacts out in the world?" she asked, trying to sound merely curious.

King blinked. "Just some organic farmers up north. We've sent scouts out to trade."

"So you haven't traded for weapons. At least since you've been in charge?" she asked, instinctively pressing him.

"Nope." He scratched his slightly whiskered chin. Without the clean-shaven look, he seemed a lot more approachable. "I don't have any contacts with guns out there. Unfortunately."

April might not be a genius, but come on. Of course, she wasn't a member of the congregation either. Pastor King didn't owe her an explanation or even the truth. At the moment, he didn't owe her anything. Yet he seemed somewhat willing to share. Maybe. Then Damon started playing with her hair, and she forgot how to think.

Movement at the door stole her attention away from the hot guy holding her.

"Pastor King?" A woman in her mid-twenties hovered just inside by a table, holding several board games. She had long, black hair, dark eyes, and pretty Asian features—as well as a very rounded and pregnant belly. "I have the test."

"Tomo." Pleasure crossed King's face, and he stood, walking toward the pregnant woman. "Thank you for bringing this." He grasped her hands and looked down. "How are you feeling?"

"Like a beach ball is bouncing in my stomach," the woman said, her smile rueful. She rubbed her belly beneath a lightweight cream-colored sundress. "The kid likes to kick."

April straightened on Damon's lap, craning her head to see. He set her next to him, sliding an arm around her waist and drawing her into his side. The natural motion felt way too right. She placed her hand on his thigh as if she'd sat with him like this a million times.

Her body flushed warm, and sparks zipped across her nerves. She shook her head to concentrate. "Hi."

Pastor King drew the woman into the room. "Tomo, this is April and Damon." He grinned. "Tomo is our resident medic. She was a practitioner in Century City before Scorpius."

"Nice to meet you," Tomo said, her smile soft.

"You, too," Damon answered before April could. "It must be nice to have a doctor in-house."

King nodded. "She's invaluable."

Man, April wanted to ask who the father of the baby was. Was there a right way to inquire about that? What if something bad had happened to Tomo before she found shelter with Vanguard? The story was all too familiar. So there wasn't a good way to ask.

"Is the baby's father still living?" Damon asked bluntly.

April barely kept a wince off her face. "Damon."

He didn't move.

Tomo's eyebrows lifted, but no other expression crossed her face. "Here's the test." She handed over a small, wrapped package to King and then smiled at April. "It was very nice to meet you." Turning on a tennis shoe, she disappeared.

King opened the package while returning to the couch, and drew out a cotton swab on a stick to hand over to April. She took it and swabbed the inside of her mouth and then watched, curious. She'd seen the test months ago, but then the world had pretty much ended.

King took the swab and inserted it into a small vial filled with liquid. It remained clear. "It looks like both you and Damon are pure." He smiled. "No infection."

April already knew that.

Damon turned his head. "Tomo didn't answer my question. Where's the father?"

King's smile lacked charm this time. "That's absolutely none of your business. And I think you know that."

14

My focus can't be split right now. I have to watch Greyson's back...too much is happening.
    —Damon Winter, Journal

DAMON TUGGED down the very nice bulletproof vest he'd taken from the Pure church while leaning against a crumbling wooden house in east central Los Angles. The moon shone down, illuminating the garbage strewn over what used to be a backyard. The stench even smelled hot.

"Nice vests," Greyson whispered, settling his own into place. "Where the hell did the pastor get these?"

"Couldn't get an answer to that," Damon said, stretching his leg to make sure he could get to his knife when needed. After his visit to the Pure building, he'd left a still-ticked-off April to her job so he could get to his. It had taken the rest of the day to prepare for tonight's raid, and he was more than ready. In fact, he was itching for a good fight.

"You gave just the facts in your debriefing with Jax," Grey said, double-checking a VP9 and then putting the gun into his thigh holster.

"I had just the facts." Damon tightened the Velcro around his own thigh holster, securing it more firmly in place. "My gut feeling is that something is off, but I couldn't find an ounce of proof. Even the pregnant woman I spoke with seemed okay. Closed off but not scared. That I could see anyway."

A lion roared blocks away.

Damon stilled and then forced his body to relax again. He took a deep breath to control his breathing.

"Mercury here." Jax's voice came clearly over the radio at Damon's waist. "Five minutes, and we'll be in place. Following your op, Winter."

Damon had the most experience with the drug houses in LA, so he'd taken lead on this one. It showed something that the Vanguard squad was okay with that.

He drew the radio to his mouth and pressed the button. "Acknowledged." He looked around the backyard. A wooden fence enclosed the burned area, the middle bowed, having given in to heat and time. Some sort of wire cage stood in the right corner, filled with leaves and more garbage. Had the previous owners kept chickens? Weird. He closed his eyes to listen.

"I can't hear anything," Grey said.

Damon nodded. They were a block away from the supposed Twenty gang holding, so it wasn't surprising. "Jax will call in with an update." Mercury and Shadow had both been Special Forces, so they were the logical team to send in for surveillance. Damon was more of a boot to the door type of guy.

Greyson shook out his hands. "How's it going with April?"

Damon's head snapped toward his best friend before he could think. "You want to talk about that *now*?"

Grey shrugged, his shoulders impacting the old house and sending shards of wood down to the brown weeds. "Why not? Mercury is five minutes out and will need at least another five to get a good survey of the property. We never talk anymore, Damon. It's just work all the time."

Damon snorted. Only Greyson Storm would be making jokes at a time like this. The guy had nerves of absolute steel. "Everything's a jumble right now."

Grey's light eyes pierced through the night. "Ah. So you and April are both undercover and maybe starting something. And you are investigating the Pure church, but they might be okay, and you don't know where you stand." He reached down and double-checked the knife in his boot. "And I might be heading to the Century City Bunker and leaving your back unprotected."

Damon shook his head. "No."

"Yes. For the record, I've put off the Bunker assignment." Grey straightened and tightened his vest.

Damon paused. "You did not. Why?"

"Because of you," Greyson said easily. He kicked off the dirt on his boots.

"Me?" Damon shook his head. "What are you talking about? You have to go to the Bunker."

Greyson rolled his eyes, the moonlight allowing his irritation to be seen. "You're my brother, Damon. I know you had biological brothers before, and I never had that, so I understand if it's different for you. But I ain't leaving you on your own during this op. My gut? It says it's more dangerous than we've found."

Damon's throat closed. He missed his brothers every day. Every damn day. "It's not different," he murmured. "They were good guys, and they'd welcome you into the family in a heartbeat. You're my brother, too." They'd fought and almost died together. That mattered. His gut warmed that Greyson would stay for him. "But you have to go. Maureen needs to do research, and since she's pregnant, the Bunker is probably a better place for her to be."

"I can keep her safe in Vanguard territory for now." Grey's jaw hardened. "I'm not leaving you."

"I have the entire Vanguard organization as backup." Damon had to get through to him.

Grey knocked his head back against the house, and paint chips fell to the ground. "Do you? We might have backup from Jax and his lieutenants, but there's still a divide between Vanguard and the Mercs. You should know that from your fight last night."

"I can handle myself."

"I know, but we all need backup." Grey shook himself loose again. "Not arguing about this any longer."

Jax came over the radio as if on cue. "In place, it's a go on location. Two guards front door, two on the back, and at least six members inside. We're ready to breach the rear."

Adrenaline flooded Damon's system. "We'll come from the east and hit the front door. Hold steady." He grasped his HK416 where it had been leaning against the side of the house. The assault rifle was more than at home in his hands.

He moved into a quiet jog with Greyson by his side.

They kept close to the deserted and ramshackle homes until they reached the house in question. Damon halted and peered around the closest building. Two men in Twenty purple guarded the front door, each with an assault rifle in their hands.

Damon gave Greyson the signal and then lifted his gun, firing once. The guy to the left dropped silently.

Greyson fired, the sound a soft ping. The soldier to the right fell against the door.

Damon held his breath and waited. Music wafted in the air. Hard rock. The Twenty gang didn't care much about preserving batteries, did they?

He gave the signal, ducked low, and hustled to the front door to push both bodies out of the way. Then he whispered into the radio. "Breach on the count of three." Tucking the device away, he slowly counted.

At three, he put his boot right near the crappy old lock and kicked.

Greyson went in first, firing before he'd crossed the threshold. Two guys instantly went down. Damon followed, sweeping to the right.

A Twenty member lifted a gun, and Damon fired. A guy came at him from the side, knife sweeping across Damon's upper left arm. Pain cut through him, and blood squirted. Damn it. He turned and fired twice, hitting the asshole center mass.

Two others remained in place on a ragtag sofa, one obviously going through music discs, and the other right in the middle of snorting what looked like coke. They didn't move.

Gunfire came from the next room that was supposed to be the kitchen, and then silence. Finally, "All clear," came from Jax.

The nearest hallway was closest to Damon, so he went in as Greyson covered the guys on the sofa. He cleared two bedrooms, a bathroom, and then reached a closed and locked door. He kicked it open and waited.

Nothing.

Darkness was inside. He reached for a flashlight in his cargo pants just as a body rushed him, impacting his still bleeding arm. He ducked and threw the attacker over his shoulder to land in the hallway behind him, dropping his weapon in the process. Another guy rushed out, this one with his teeth snapping wildly.

Shit. Rippers.

He pivoted and kicked the Ripper in front of him, sending it spiraling back into the dark room. Rippers were Scorpius survivors whose brains hadn't healed from the bacteria and had instead turned from sociopathic to animalistic. They were still human and still alive, but they were monsters that lived to kill. Two more rushed out.

He backpedaled down the hallway, nearly tripping over the guy on the floor. "Rippers," he bellowed, reaching the entrance to the living area. He ducked and yanked out his knife.

A Ripper, his eyes bloodshot, and his fingernails way too long ran at him. His teeth were bared, and spittle covered his lips. The guy had been blond at one time and was at least six feet tall. Damon eyed the dangerous teeth.

The bastard charged.

Greyson unexpectedly hit Damon from the side, smashing him into the far wall. The Ripper latched on to Grey's neck, and he bellowed in pain, swinging wildly.

Damon jumped up and slashed his knife down into the Ripper's neck, shoving him away from Grey. "What the fuck was that?"

Without waiting for an answer, Greyson turned and shoved Damon into the living room. Another Ripper smashed into him. Damon tried to jump back inside the hallway, but Jax Mercury grabbed him in a chokehold and pulled him away just as Raze Shadow leaped in to help Greyson, already firing down the corridor.

Damon struggled. "Let me go," he snapped.

The guys on the sofa just watched, neither going for a weapon.

"Then stay still," Jax hissed back, slowly loosening his hold.

Damon shrugged him off, his hand already curling into a fist to punch the Vanguard leader's face.

"All clear," Raze muttered, moving back into the room, blood sprayed across his face.

"Ouch." Greyson walked behind him, his hand against a bleeding wound in his neck. Blood dripped down to his shirt. "Bastard bit into me like I was a steak."

"What were you doing?" Damon exploded.

Grey paused. His brows lowered. "Huh?" He winced and pressed his hand harder to his neck.

Damon shook his head. No way should Grey have taken that bite. "You heard me." He turned a glare on Jax. "You, too. What the hell?" He was in charge of this op.

Raze tossed Greyson a bandana from his back pocket. "Use this."

"Thanks." Grey caught it and held it to the bleeding neck wound.

Damon saw red. Not a light crimson, not even a pink, but a deep and dark claret. "What the fuck?" he yelled.

Grey reared back, and both Vanguard guys looked at him with surprise on their faces.

"You never yell," Mercury said, tilting his head.

Raze nodded. "Yeah. You're the calm and in-control one. This is weird."

Oh, he was going to kill them. Just end them right now. He glanced down at the knife still in his hand.

"Damon," Greyson said, his voice hoarse. "You haven't been infected. We all have. Don't be a dipshit."

That was not how this worked. "Greyson." Damon tried to hold on to his already rare and loose temper with both hands. "I cover your back. You are the leader of the Mercs, and you now have a pregnant fiancée. You do not, *fucking ever,* jump between me and an attacker." He focused on Raze and Jax. "You either. Got it?"

Raze shook his head. "We can take a bite without facing nearly certain death. You can't. Deal with it."

Damon had never been this pissed. "Then I guess I should just get infected and get it over with now." He'd always figured it would happen at some point anyway. "Then we'll know."

"You can't," Greyson said simply.

"Why not?" Damon growled, his ears actually feeling hot.

Grey grinned, the expression pained. "You won't be able to fuck April. Now that's a reason to stay healthy."

Damon's mouth gaped open. Grey had not just said that. "I am not going to fuck April."

Grey rolled his eyes.

Jax nodded a little too vigorously. "That's right. He's definitely not going to sleep with April. They're just pretending."

Damon's temper turned to irritation, which relaxed his neck muscles slightly. "That's not any of your business, Mercury. If I decide to sleep with April, I'm going to. In fact, if she ever gives me an opening, I'm jumping right in. So butt out." He wasn't sure he meant the words right now, but enough was enough. Who did these guys think they were?

Raze sighed and shook his head. "Can we have lady gossip time back at headquarters?"

Jax pulled his radio out of his pocket. "Good point." He lifted it to his mouth. "House is clear, all scouts move in to scavenge this place down to the bones."

Damon jerked his head at the two guys on the sofa. "Them?"

Jax smiled, the sight making one of the guys gasp. "Oh. They're coming with us. Right, fellas?"

15

Sometimes this life just becomes too hard. Somehow, having Damon with me makes it easier. He's quickly becoming part of my life, and yet, he's always in danger. How does this make sense?
        —April Snyder, Journal

APRIL FINISHED her cup of tea, but the mellow brew failed to calm her like usual. Perhaps it was the double shot of bourbon she'd put in it. Lynne had dropped off the bottle earlier after hearing about April's time at the Pure church. Or rather, the time before it when Damon had treated her like a sack of potatoes and a piñata at the same time.

She had left word at headquarters that he was to stop by after the raid.

It wasn't because she was worried about him and needed to see for herself that he was all right. Nope. Not at all.

She sighed. Yeah, she was a dork.

Moonlight filtered in through the shadeless window in her kitchen. It had to be about midnight. That was good. She straightened her shoulders. It was too late for Damon to come by. That was a good thing. Yeah. Her mind was fuzzy now, and her body way too relaxed. She'd deal with him in the morning when she was at a hundred percent.

Rapid knocking on her interior door had her biting back a yelp.

"April? April, wake up," came an urgent voice.

April ran for the door and opened it to see two teenage girls. "Julie? Molly? What are you doing? Curfew was an hour ago."

Molly, a short brunette of about sixteen, grabbed her arm. "There's something wrong with Freda."

Panic choked off April's breath.

Freda was a sweet seventeen-year-old who had somehow made her way from Texas by herself. April hustled into the main rec room and ran up the stairs toward the teenage girls' floor. Reaching it, she ran into Freda's room and stopped cold.

The girl thrashed on her bed, sweat rolling down her face. Her long, blond hair went in every direction, and her slim body convulsed with the fever.

Oh, God.

April looked around for restraints and ran for a belt. Her hands shook violently. "I thought she'd survived the bacteria?"

Molly nodded.

Julie shook her head. "No," she whispered. "She lied. She wanted to stay here with us, so she told the intake folks that she'd survived the fever."

April secured Freda's left arm to the bedpost. During the fever, sometimes the victim tried to gouge out their own eyes because of the agonizing headache. Restraint was protocol. "Why would she lie? She'd still be on this floor, just down in the safer rooms." They'd tried to keep the uninfected as safe as possible. Maybe the Pure did have the right answer.

Tears rolled down Julie's face. "She wanted to stay right here and be one of us. I should've said something."

April secured the girl's other hand and looked over her shoulder. "Go get a doctor. I think Tace is at the Bunker, so bring Doc Penelope. Run. Now."

The girls turned and ran out of sight.

April sat and smoothed the girl's hair back from her face. Flashbacks of losing her own daughter caught her and squeezed the air out of her lungs. She shook her head. *Stay in the moment.* She had to stay right here. "It's okay, Freda. Hold on, sweetheart," she murmured.

Freda arched her back in the throes of the pain.

April's entire body hurt for the girl. While she hadn't experienced the onslaught of the bacteria, she'd witnessed it several times, and the pain was palpable.

A ruckus sounded on the stairs, and Doc Penelope hurried into the room, already filling a syringe with a complex mixture of Vitamin B complex. Nobody knew exactly why or how, but the Bs helped new victims survive, and then also assisted survivors in staying sane. She reached the bed and injected the girl.

Freda continued to struggle, kicking out her legs. The bedclothes fell to the floor, leaving her in only shorts and a tank top. Even so, sweat soaked through the material.

Doc Penelope sat on the bed and felt the girl's head. "Not good," she murmured, looking over her slim shoulder at April. The doctor was petite with very dark eyes and long, black hair. Her features were Korean, and her skin tone darker than average. "Any idea when she was infected?"

April shook her head and looked toward the doorway where Marcus Knight blocked the exit. Jax's brother stood about six and a half feet tall with pure, raw muscle and a whole lot of anger. Or insanity. His eyes were more green than brown, and his features more hard-cut than chiseled. "Marcus? Let the girls by," April murmured.

He didn't move.

Doc Penelope sighed. "I'm fine here, Marcus. Please, let the girls in."

He instantly pivoted to the side.

The girls carefully skirted Marcus and hustled inside, their eyes wide and trained on their thrashing friend.

"I remember this part," Julie said, wincing. Her face was incredibly pale against her long, red hair. "It's awful."

"How did she get infected?" Doc Penelope asked, running her hands down Freda's arms. "There are no bite marks."

The girls shrugged.

Shit. This could be really bad. April patted down Freda's leg. "We don't have any cold water, do we?"

"Maybe in the basement of headquarters," Penelope said quietly. "We have water down there, and it's semi-cool." She looked at Marcus. "Would you please go and get rags and a bucket of the coldest water we have?"

The man faltered.

"Please, Marcus," Penelope urged. "I'll be fine."

He gave her a look and turned, his large footsteps eerily silent on the stairs down the way.

April exhaled. "Is he getting any better?"

"Yes," Penelope said. "Believe it or not, he is."

April wanted to talk about anything but the ill girl in front of her. Another sick child. "I've watched him with you, but nobody has told me the story. I've meant to ask." Penelope and Marcus had only been with Vanguard for a couple of weeks, and April hadn't had much time to get to know either of them.

Penelope took Freda's wrist and silently counted. Then she shook her head. "I worked at the Bunker that Jax now controls, but I didn't know what was happening in the underground labs. They were experimenting on Scorpius survivors, seeing what they could handle in terms of torture and such. Marcus was one of their subjects."

April's stomach lurched. "You're kidding."

"No. The Bunker scientists, at least the ones at *that* Bunker, were evil." Penelope shuddered, her gaze on the now moaning girl. "I got called in to treat Marcus and saw what was happening. I promised I'd get him out."

"And you did?"

Penelope nodded. "Yeah. When Jax took the facility, I was injured, but I went to help Marcus. He was bleeding, but I didn't care. His blood hit my wound, and I contracted the Scorpius fever."

Whoa. So the doctor had risked her life to save Marcus. No wonder he was so dedicated to her. Even so, it was a lot. Obsession was often a side effect of surviving the bacteria, but Marcus seemed to take it to a whole new level.

"I've heard he doesn't remember life before Scorpius," April said softly, moving over for the girls to sit on the bed, too.

Penelope nodded. "Yeah. Whatever the doctors did to him messed with his memory. Sometimes I think he remembers his brother, but he's just not ready to reach out, you know? We'll see."

It had to be a lot of responsibility on Penelope, trying to keep Marcus sane.

Suddenly, Marcus stood inside the room, a bucket of cold water in his hands. He wasn't breathing heavily, but he must've run like crazy. He handed over some cold washcloths.

"Thank you," Penelope said, drawing another syringe out of her lab coat pocket. "I can give her morphine now. The B should be taking effect." She quickly gave the girl the painkiller.

Freda subsided into small and snuffling whimpers.

Penelope dipped a rag into the water and pressed it to the girl's head. "It's better than nothing," she said.

April did the same with Freda's legs and feet, trying to cool them. "Girls? She wasn't bitten. So we have to figure out how she contracted the illness." If bacteria were still living on surfaces after all this time and all the numerous cleanings, then they were in trouble. Without question. "Where has she been, and what has she been doing?"

The girls exchanged a look.

April's instincts rose along with the hair on her arms while Doc Penelope busied herself with trying to cool Freda. "Girls? Nobody is in trouble, but this is a big deal. How did this happen?" April asked.

Julie bit her lip. "I don't know. Not really."

Okay. Tread lightly. "Give me your best guess," April said softly. "It doesn't matter how crazy. Was she somewhere she could've easily gotten infected?" Where would that be? The girl wasn't a scout or a soldier. She remained and worked inside Vanguard. "Did she leave?"

"No," Molly said. "She hasn't left." She ran more water down Freda's arms.

April bit back impatience. They had all night—if Freda kept fighting. "Talk. Now." She used her best mom voice.

Julie broke first. "She's been dating one of the Vanguard soldiers, and this was their first night together. You know, their first night. She came in late from curfew."

Nausea dropped into April's stomach. "Scorpius lives in bodily fluids. She knows that. You all know that." She shook her head. How had this happened? "Who the hell is this soldier?" The soldiers were all over eighteen, and this was a seventeen-year-old girl. "Give me his name."

"Monty Jones," Molly whispered. "He's only eighteen, and I don't think he knew she hadn't been infected. If she didn't tell me, she probably didn't tell him."

"They used a condom," Julie snapped. "I know they did. I gave her a couple before she left this afternoon."

April's head ached. The whole room spun. The girls were right. The boy probably hadn't known that Freda wasn't infected with the bacteria. Even so, if they used a condom, they should be all right.

Julie winced. "She wanted to try giving a blowjob."

Oh, God. April hung her head. Kids should be allowed to have stupid moments without facing the fear of death. Even so, what had Freda been thinking?

"I don't know if she did," Julie rushed out to say. "Just that she was thinking about it. Just doing that wouldn't transfer the bacteria, would it?"

Nobody knew exactly what transferred it besides fluid. It was still possible that Freda had touched a surface with the still-living spores on it. Or that the condom had broken, and since it was probably Freda's first time, there might've been blood. Who the hell knew? "We have to find out if the bacteria still survives on surfaces," April muttered.

"We are. There's definite intel at the newly discovered Bunker," Penelope murmured. "I think Jax is planning to take it soon."

If that were possible. Those places were seriously protected. Right now, April had to get this kid through the night. That was all that mattered.

Freda stiffened and cried out. Then she went limp.

"No." April grabbed her arms.

Doc Penelope levered up on her knees and started CPR, calmly counting. Then she breathed into Freda's mouth. For minutes. Then more minutes.

Julie gave a low sob and put her arm around Molly.

Tears pooled in April's eyes. "Wake up, Freda. Right now. You wake up." The room narrowed from the outside in.

Penelope grew frantic, her movements stronger. The girl remained unresponsive beneath her hands. "Come on, Freda. Let's go."

Julie and Molly started crying harder. This wasn't happening. It couldn't be.

Finally, Marcus moved forward and touched Penelope on the shoulder. "Penny. Let her go," he said, his voice a low rumble.

Penelope's head dropped, and she gave a low sob. "We have to examine her at the office. See if we can find the infection." Her hair covered her face.

Marcus lifted her away from the bed and then covered Freda with a blanket, picking her up against his chest in a surprisingly gentle move. He looked down at the girl, his expression stark. "I've got her," he said quietly.

April turned to see Jax Mercury and Lynne Harmony in the doorway. When had they arrived? Lynne was crying, and Jax looked like he wanted to murder somebody.

Lynne reached for her to hug. "Go on. We've got the girls."

April nodded. She couldn't talk right now. Everything was too fresh and too painful. And there was an entire bottle of bourbon with her name on in it her apartment. She turned and walked blindly down the stairs.

16

My sense of control has never been shaken on the job. It won't be this time either. No matter how sweet and soft April Snyder is.

—Damon Winter, Journal

DAMON TRIED to sit still as Greyson finished digging into his wound with a needle in the Mercenary headquarter house. He sat at the table in what used to be the kitchen, his shirt off and his shoulder on fire. Now, both shoulders had wounds, damn it. "You are the worst at this," he muttered, reaching for another shot of Jack Daniels and taking it quickly.

"You told me not to get the doctor," Grey reminded him, finishing with a bandage.

Maureen sat on another chair, watching her hands in her lap instead of the minor surgery. "Are you guys done yet?"

"Yes," Greyson said. "He's good as new. You can look and probably won't puke now."

Moe looked up, her blue eyes sparkling. "You have matching bandages. How symmetrical."

Damon grinned. The spunky food expert was one of his favorite people in the world. The fact that she made Greyson Storm actually smile and laugh once in a while was just a bonus. "It is important to match."

Moe pushed her dark hair away from her face. "What's up with you and April?"

"We're just working together," Damon said, taking another shot of Jack to dull the pain. "After tonight, I realized that trying for anything else is crazy." He paused. "Though not for you two. I mean, you're fine."

Grey snorted. "Smooth. Very smooth."

Well, they were having a baby, so they had no choice but to be fine. Damon poured both himself and Greyson another shot of booze. "My job is always going to be kicking down the door, and as we just found out, Rippers are going to be waiting. At some point, I'm getting the bacteria." And if his family's survival rate of zero were any indication, he wouldn't survive. He couldn't do that to April, even if she were game. Which she probably wasn't. "So, this is what it is."

Maureen rolled her eyes. "You're kind of a moron."

Grey lifted his glass. "To morons."

"I'll drink to that." Damon tipped back another shot. The pain was finally numbing in his body, and his head was getting a bit cloudy. Shit, it was hot in the old house. "When is summer over?"

"We're mid-July, buddy," Greyson said.

Damon shook his head and tried to concentrate. "We should have a meeting about resources. We have to be getting down there, considering we didn't arrive with very much." They'd only been able to save a small amount of supplies before the fires took everything. It had been fairly decent of Jax Mercury to let them in the Vanguard gates.

"That's on the agenda," Greyson said, pouring more shots. He winked at Maureen and then turned back to Damon. "The pain any better?"

It was a hell of a lot better, actually. "Yeah." Damon took the final drink and stood, not needing a bigger hint. The two definitely wanted to be alone. Maybe he'd go and check on April— just to make sure her day went all right. And since he no longer felt any pain, maybe it'd be a good time to fight about the smack to her ass earlier. Just in case she kicked him in the balls. "See you guys later."

They were already making kissing noises by the time he cleared the front door.

The night was unbearably hot, and he missed the beach. The sound of the ocean had become almost necessary to sleep, and the cool breeze off the Pacific at night hadn't hurt. He nodded to patrolling soldiers and kept walking, thinking about the fight at the house.

A Ripper had nearly bitten him. Should he tell April about that or not?

He reached her apartment and saw a light on in the kitchen. Since it was well after midnight, he'd expected darkness. He moved to the door and knocked lightly.

She opened it, dressed in tiny shorts and a tank top.

His body flared wide-awake and alive a second before he caught her expression. "What happened?" he moved toward her, and she met him halfway, her face against his chest.

"Lost a teenage girl," she said, her voice muffled and her tears wetting his skin. "Scorpius."

He closed his eyes and let the hurt settle in his gut. "Ah, baby. I'm so sorry." He ran a hand through her long hair, surprised again by its softness. "Was she bitten while scouting?"

"No." April shook her head and leaned back enough to see his face. "We think it was sex. Probably. Doc Penelope has the girl back at the trauma center."

Sex? Ah, man. "The kids know better," he muttered. "No condom?"

"We don't know yet," she said, wiping her cheek with one hand. "Jax went to talk to the boy."

Damon winced. That talk would be terrible. He focused on the pretty brunette in his arms. "I'm sorry."

She swallowed. "Me, too."

He wiped the rest of her tears away and gave her a gentle kiss on her pert nose. She stilled. He kissed her cheeks, offering comfort. Man, her skin was soft and cool. For some reason, he was still burning up from the fight earlier. Damn adrenaline.

She made a sound, one of acceptance, and planted her hands on his upper chest.

Whoa. His body burned hotter, and her scent of woman and sweet roses sank beneath his skin. The alcohol in his bloodstream spurred him to act. No. Definitely no. *Slow down.* This was for comfort only. His cock perked right up. Bastard. This was not a time for sex.

She stretched up on her toes and pressed her mouth to his. She tasted like sweetness and bourbon.

He stopped breathing. A Ripper could come through the door, and he probably wouldn't move. Tension cascaded down his arms, tightening each muscle. The need to grab her and deepen the kiss nearly killed him.

But this was for comfort.

When he regained control, he caressed her back, trying to offer reassurance. His hand dipped in, and he spanned her entire lower back. "It's okay," he whispered.

She bit his bottom lip.

He sucked in air. His dick shot to full awareness against her softness. "What are you doing?"

She looked up, her eyes a deep midnight hue with pain and need. "Kissing you. This night, Damon. Let's feel something good."

Jesus. Saying no was going to destroy him. But she was hurting, and he was buzzed, and the adrenaline heating him wouldn't calm. "Not a good idea." Yet he couldn't push her away.

"One kiss." Her gaze, stark and unguarded, dropped to his mouth. "One real kiss."

His head was moving down before his brain had even registered what was happening.

Finally, he kissed her. Maybe it was because of the soft way she'd asked. Or perhaps it was from the adrenaline cutting him. Or maybe it was because of the lust he was tired of hiding from her.

Finally, the iron grip on his control snapped. He took her mouth hard, finally tasting those full lips. His tongue thrust inside, and the taste of her—the real taste of woman and bourbon—nearly drove him to his knees.

* * *

WHEN DAMON'S mouth finally took hers, the entire world settled. Finally. The desire in his kiss, the promise of more took her out of the pain to just feel something good. To escape reality and delve into passion.

His tongue stroked inside her mouth, and his hand pressed against her lower back. So much strength and power in one small move. She lifted up on her toes, kissing him back with everything she had. The need between them exploded with an electricity she hadn't imagined.

He backed her up, and her butt hit the edge of the table. She didn't care. Closer. She needed to get closer to him. Her abdomen cushioned the impossibly hard ridge of his penis, and at the thought, she gave up any pretense of doubt.

She wanted this. And she wanted him. If just to get away from the world for a while. Just to feel.

He grasped the hem of her tank top, his long fingers brushing against the bare skin of her abdomen. Her stomach rippled, and heat exploded through her nerves. "Please, Damon," she murmured against his lips before he kissed her harder, making speech impossible.

His body shuddered, and the fight within him played out against her skin.

She slid her hands beneath his shirt and moaned at the feeling of ripped muscle. How was he even possible? She traced the ridges of his abdomen and frantically caressed up to the hard planes of his chest. Really hard.

"Wait." He tore his mouth away. "How much have you had to drink?" The words sounded strained.

"Not much," she lied. He tasted like whiskey, too. Who the hell cared? "I want this." Which was the absolute truth. Then she tugged, and he had to drop his head to let her yank off his shirt. Twin bandages covered both his shoulders.

A bullet hole scar marred his right pec. She traced it and then looked closer. Smaller scars, many old, showed in various places on his dark skin. Her cop had led a dangerous life. She leaned in and kissed the healed bullet wound.

He sucked in a breath.

Then he lost the fight.

Grabbing her hair, he lifted her up to his mouth again. He yanked off her tank top and tossed it somewhere. Then his talented fingers found her bare breasts. He bent his head, and his mouth closed over a nipple.

Ecstasy took her, and her knees gave out.

He caught her with an arm around her waist. His tongue stroked her. With an abrupt movement, he lifted her against him, and his mouth crashed down on hers. It took her a second to realize that they were moving toward the bedroom. When they reached the bed, he paused and looked down at her. "You're sure?"

"Yes."

He set her down and tugged off her shorts. "You want fast or slow?" The tone of his voice was low and guttural.

The sound washed over her skin, and she shivered. "Fast." God, fast. And hard and deep.

He shoved down his jeans, giving her the first look at his erect penis. The guy was huge...and ready to go.

She gingerly reached out and ran her finger along the impressive length of him.

"Later." He shuddered and pushed her back, a condom in his hand.

Later worked for her. She scooted up on the bed, enjoying the graceful way he climbed up her. He was so big above her, he blocked out the moonlight streaming through the window. "Damon." Her hand shook, and she cupped his angled cheekbone. His five o'clock shadow scratched her palm.

He paused, his dark eyes boring into her. "I want to taste you."

She shivered. He didn't mean her mouth. "Later." She repeated his word, a small smile playing on her face. She had to know what he felt like inside her. What it felt like to be that close to him. Something in her, a part she'd never known, needed to be a part of him. Just for a moment. He'd drawn her from the beginning, and she had to know.

He reached between them, his fingers circling her clit.

She arched against him and shut her eyes. It felt so amazingly good. Sparks flew through her lower half, turning her need into a devastating ache.

He rubbed lower, murmuring in approval.

Yeah. She was good and wet and ready. His fingers were killing her. She moved restlessly against him, needing to be filled. Just for a while. Just to get away.

He rolled on the condom and moved closer, pausing at her entrance. "April. Look at me."

She opened his eyes to stare into his dark ones. Then he

started pushing inside her. Slowly and gently, taking his time, he entered her.

Pain flashed, and she bit her lip. Her body shook. The confusing contrast between her need and the hurt caught her up short.

He paused. "You're okay," he murmured. Halfway inside her, he shifted to the side just a little, and his fingers stroked across her hip. Those long and talented fingers, slightly callused, moved across her clit.

She gasped as fire lanced through her.

"There you go." He caressed over her, keeping his weight on one arm, his muscles straining.

Pleasure cut through her. She whimpered and moved against his hand. He pressed hard against her clit and sent her into a shocking orgasm. Clamping her hands on his arms, she held on tight, riding the waves.

Then she came down, still gasping. Her body softened onto the bed, her thighs naturally opening wider. She was wetter than before. More relaxed.

He slid farther inside her.

That quickly, her heart rate picked up again. She lifted her knees on either side of his hard hips. A quick thought came out of nowhere to question what the hell she was doing. She threw it away into the abyss.

He pushed harder, finally shoving all the way inside her.

She gasped and settled, feeling him all around her. Inside her. Everywhere. Her body wound tighter than before, and she moved before he could.

Then he was thrusting inside her. Hard and fast. Close. She was already so close.

The moment took her away, and she stopped thinking. This wasn't gentle, and it wasn't a promise. It was intense and devastating.

She grabbed his arms again, digging in, trying to reach that pinnacle. Her hips lifted to meet his powerful thrusts.

Only his hands on her kept her from flying up into the headboard.

She clenched his hips with her thighs, and then she was spiraling. Her climax threw her away from the moment, consuming and taking everything she had. She rode the waves, her eyes closed, the release so intense she couldn't breathe.

He was right there with her.

With a powerful shudder, he came against her, his mouth gentle on her neck. Then he moved inside her a few more times, sending tingles throughout her lower half. Finally, he withdrew and disposed of the condom.

Returning to the bed, he piled the covers on top of them and curled her into his side. "That was a nice start," he murmured, his hand already at her breast.

Her eyes opened wide. "Start?" Her breath quickened.

"Oh, yeah. Hold on, baby. We're just getting started."

17

Scorpius will probably always be a risk. I've known that from the beginning.
—Damon Winter, Journal

DAMON WOKE, sweating through the sheet. He opened his eyes to see early morning light coming through the window blinds. His head felt as if he'd taken a hammer to the temple, and every muscle in his body ached as if he'd been through a cement mixer.

Something soft brushed his upper arm.

He turned his head to see April sprawled across the bed, her head on her pillow and her hair everywhere. The woman was a bed hog.

His smile made his teeth hurt. What was wrong with him? He blinked. Oh God.

His eye caught on the bandage on his upper arm. He'd been cut, and a Ripper had sprayed blood. Panic grabbed him, and he slid from the bed, careful not to wake April.

Was he infected?

The room spun dizzily around him.

He swallowed, and his throat protested. He'd kissed April last night. Full on and a lot. They'd sweated against each other. He swayed and nearly fell on his face. Wait a minute. Just hold on. He quietly yanked on his jeans and shirt before hustling for the door, pulling on his boots as he went.

If he were infected, he'd go crazy and want to bite her. Or he could just hurt her without meaning to by thrashing around. She was safer with him figuring this out at headquarters.

He had to see the doctor.

The sun nearly blinded him, even though it was weak at this hour. He rushed through the streets, ignoring soldiers, and reached the main headquarters for Vanguard territory. His stomach lurched, and he had to take several deep breaths before sliding open the back door to the main dining area for the lieutenants. The top Vanguard soldiers lived at headquarters. The bottom floor held a medical area, a dining room, and then Jax's war room and weapons lockers.

Upstairs were apartments.

Trying not to puke, Damon moved into the somewhat cooler dining room and skirted plastic and wooden tables to reach the stairs.

The room tilted around him again, and he grabbed the wall for support. Then he inched his way upstairs to a narrow and dingy hallway with metal doors every few yards. Reaching one toward the end, he knocked as softly as he could.

The apartment across from him opened immediately.

Damon partially turned to see Marcus Knight step out, wearing only shorts. His bare chest had so many healed scars that Damon wanted to puke again. "Get away from Penny's door," Marcus said, one long line of threat.

The door opened. "Hello?"

Damon turned to see the petite doctor, her hair up on her head, her eyes unfocused. "I think I was infected last night," he said, pressing a hand to the doorframe to keep from falling over.

Marcus moved in, setting him to the side and away from Doc Penelope. "You look like shit."

"Feel like it, too." Damon's throat felt like it was on fire. "I had sex with April last night. If I'm infected, was there time to get her infected?" There couldn't have been. His main goal was to keep her safe. She had to be all right.

Doc Penelope leaned up and felt his forehead. "You are burning up." She glanced down at her thin shorts and T-shirt. "Let me get dressed, and Marcus will take you down to the infirmary. I'll be right there."

"Want me to secure him?" Marcus asked, his hoarse voice harsh in the early morning.

Penelope frowned. "Not yet. He seems to still be in control. If he starts to fight or thrash, then we'll tie him down." She looked closer at Damon's eyes. "How long have you felt like this?"

He shrugged, trying to keep his legs locked in place. "I'm not sure. I was hot last night, but it's always hot around here these days." Sweat rolled down his back, somehow chilling him. "If one of the Rippers got to me, it would've been last night. Then I went and kissed April."

Penelope felt his head again. "Let's take a look down in the infirmary. I'll meet you two there in just a few moments."

Damon's vision fuzzed. "No. Need to get to April. She's what matters." He tried to move toward the doctor.

Marcus shoved him up against the wall, and for the first time, Damon couldn't fight back well enough. The darkness got closer, and then took him over. His last thought as he dropped to the ground was that when he awoke, he would kick Marcus's ass.

* * *

APRIL SLOWLY ROLLED over in the sunlight, almost waking up.

Aches and pains flared alive on her body in new places. Her eyelids flashed open. Damon. She'd slept with Damon.

She turned to face him...and he wasn't there.

What the hell?

She partially sat up and listened to the rest of the apartment. Nothing. No way. Slipping from the bed, she padded into the empty living room and former kitchen. He was gone.

There had to be a note. Right?

She looked around, her stomach starting to drop. No word. He'd just left?

Biting her lip, she returned to the bed and snuggled down, smashing a pillow over her face. Guilt bombarded her so quickly, her muscles trembled.

She'd slept with another man. Long ago, she'd been happy with the fact that Don would be her one and only. He was sweet and kind. Even as a kid, he'd looked like the boy next door with his blond hair and green eyes. And he'd been good in bed. Very.

Damon was devastating. Beyond so. She hadn't realized her body could feel like it had the previous night. Maybe it was Damon, or maybe it was just being in her early thirties and having more experience. Or perhaps it was because the world had ended, so why not forget insecurities and just feel good?

Something told her it was Damon. Damn it.

He hadn't even left a note. In the movies, the guy always left a cute note folded in a cool way.

Had she sucked in bed? She groaned. Damon had done all the heavy lifting. She'd just flopped there, grabbed his arms, and orgasmed until her head had almost blown off.

Oddly enough, she wished that Don were there to talk to. He'd always been her sounding board. Of course, if he were there, she wouldn't have slept with Damon.

Obviously, she couldn't talk to the sexy ex-cop. He'd taken off and left her.

Her cheeks burned. Yeah, she'd had too much to drink last

night. After they'd had sex—three times—she'd pretty much passed out.

Had she farted in her sleep?

God. She rolled over and buried her face. What if she had?

This was why people did not have one-night stands with people they would see again. One night meant one night and goodbye. Probably. What did she know? She'd never had one. Apparently, she sucked at it. How could he just leave without saying a word?

Was she snoring when he left? She wasn't a snorer as far as she knew, but she had been drinking the night before. That changed things.

Shaking her head, she slowly stretched out. Her body felt like she'd run a marathon or two, and her thighs were sore. As were her hips...and her personal areas. A good pain, kind of sexy but achy nonetheless.

Damon had pretty much explored her entire body. There wasn't a dip or crevice he hadn't touched, licked, or kissed. He'd been a bit rough, too. She'd liked it.

She'd heard the expression *attentive lover* before, but she hadn't truly put the words together. He'd attended to pretty much everything. He'd come a couple of times, too. So he hadn't been unaffected.

Between the guilt and doubt, she was going to drown.

So, enough of that. Enough of all of it. Considering that the apocalypse was upon them, and she was going undercover into a possible cult, there wasn't time to worry about whether she was good in bed or not.

Yeah, right.

She groaned and pressed her palms against her eyes. Okay. Enough with the wallowing. Rolling over, she ignored the delicious aches and pains before standing and tossing on a sundress. Her sandals were in the former kitchen, and she slid them on before walking outside toward the outhouses and outdoor showers set up on the side of the building. Individual partitions created some privacy along with dark shower curtains.

Her shower was quick, and at the early hour, she was the only one tipping back the already heated water from buckets tied above.

She had slight love marks across her body. A hickey—definitely a hickey—stood out on her hip. Her face flamed, and she hustled to redress and brush her teeth. After putting up her hair, she moved outside and hurried back to her apartment and then went to awaken the younger kids.

Lena was waiting at her kitchen table, already eating a granola bar.

April smiled at the girl's lopsided braids. "You did your hair yourself."

Lena grinned and nodded, her dark eyes sparkling. She'd dressed in light blue overall shorts with a bright pink top, and her feet were bare.

"Did you brush your teeth?"

The kids had water and buckets to spit in in their makeshift bathroom.

She nodded and continued eating, studying her.

April pushed wet hair away from her face. Did she look different somehow? Of course, not. That was crazy. "Do you want to try to talk today?"

Lena tilted her head. She never nodded or shook her head at the question, yet she understood it.

April sat at the table and studied the pretty little girl. "I know you understand me, and I think you can talk. How about just one word?"

Lena just looked at her.

"You can say *any* word." April leaned in, lowering her voice. "Even poop."

Lena laughed, her young cheeks creasing. But she didn't attempt to speak.

April sighed. "When you're ready, you'll talk. But I wish it would be soon." Her heart hurt for the little girl.

Lena reached into her pocket and drew out a present.

April caught her breath, wondering what it would be. Would it have a significance? She'd given Jax Mercury blue rocks, blue glass, blue...everything before Lynne Harmony, the woman with the blue heart had entered his life.

Of course, it could all be coincidence. People were looking for any meaning these days.

Lena pushed something silver across the table. It was a star. A sheriff's type star, probably from a kid's Halloween costume. The badge was dented and rusty, and it was missing two of the prongs. But it was definitely for a cop.

April's breath caught. "Is this for Damon?"

Lena slowly shook her head and pointed at April.

"For me," April said, taking the warm metal. "You brought me a police badge." She rubbed her neck, which had a little bit of whisker burn from Damon the previous night.

Lena smiled.

18

There's way too much testosterone around here. And I grew up in a house with several brothers.
— Damon Winter, Journal

DAMON CAME to at the sound of raised voices and bunched, reacting to the danger.

"You're fine." Doc Penelope's soothing voice calmed him before he could move.

He opened his eyes to find himself in the infirmary off the main room in Vanguard territory. A quick and rather frantic check confirmed that he was lying on an examination bed but wasn't tied down. His head felt as if it might blow off.

Penelope stood next to him, a cold cloth in her hands. She pressed it to his forehead. A cracked orange counter ran along the wall behind her, holding bandages and not much else.

Suddenly, the door banged open, and Marcus flew past the bed to hit the opposite wall. Who had thrown him? His eyes turned a startling and deep green. He instantly regrouped and bunched his muscles to attack.

Damon shoved to sit. What the hell was happening?

"Marcus," Penelope said sharply.

Marcus stilled in place as if every nerve in his body had responded to her voice.

Greyson Storm shoved the door out of his way and stomped inside, cutting Marcus a hard look before focusing on Damon. Worry darkened Grey's eyes almost as much as fury tightened his lips. "I told you to get the hell out of my way," he snapped at Marcus while studying Damon.

Marcus growled low like a panther. Or a psychotic wolf.

Damon's eyebrows rose, making his head hurt even worse. Grey had attacked the attack dog? "I'm okay," he croaked.

"Bullshit." Greyson moved in and placed his large hand over Damon's sweating forehead.

"Jesus." Damon knocked his hand away. "I'm fine, Mom." He wasn't. Not even close.

Greyson rounded on Penelope. "Was he infected? Damn it. Those fucking Rippers." He shook his head, his back a line of raw tension. "I pushed him out of the way, but he had a wound. Blood must've gotten into it. Shit. Do you have B in him?"

Penelope gingerly stepped around Greyson to place a cloth on Damon's forehead. It cooled him somewhat, but not a whole lot. "He doesn't need B."

Greyson jerked back. "The hell he doesn't." He started scrambling through the drawers.

Marcus moved for him.

Greyson turned, settling into a fighting stance.

If Damon didn't feel as if he were about to die, he might've laughed. "Stop," he croaked.

Penelope clapped her hands together as if she were dealing with toddlers. "Everyone knock it off. Right now. There will be no fighting."

Marcus straightened but didn't lose his threatening look.

Greyson didn't move an inch.

Damon swallowed and winced. "Doc? Why aren't I thrashing around and trying to bite people?" It was the oddest part of the infection.

She looked down at him, appearing unflappable in her white lab coat with her hair up in a twist. "You haven't been infected by Scorpius." Then she shrugged. "I'm pretty sure. Well, almost positive."

He tried to focus on her words.

Greyson pivoted and leaned toward him. "What do you mean? He's sick."

Penelope nodded. "His eyes are clear, and he's way too in control right now for Scorpius. I think he has the flu."

Damon reared back, oddly insulted. "The flu? You think I have the flu."

Her pink lips twitched. "Yes. I've had several cases over the last week. It's definitely going around. You're dehydrated, you have several injuries, and you haven't slept well in what, months? It's a wonder you're not comatose right now."

He couldn't have the flu. That was just so...wimpy.

"The flu?" Greyson said incredulously. "There's no flu after a pandemic."

Penelope chuckled. "We've had new people moving in, and the flu definitely exists now. Always will, probably."

Greyson looked at Damon. "You have the flu?" If anything, Grey looked chagrined for him.

Even more heat filled Damon's cheeks.

"He passed out," Marcus said helpfully from his corner. "Had to carry him down here. Guy weighs a ton."

Grey shot Damon a sympathetic look. That was even worse than the surprise.

"I do not have the flu." Damon tried to swing his legs over the bed, and the entire room spun around him.

"Whoa." Penelope put a cool hand on his shoulder. "Think of the good news. There's no way you infected April last night while having intercourse."

Grey pivoted. "You slept with April?"

Marcus shook his head. "Not cool, man."

What the hell? The silent Neanderthal was suddenly speaking? "You don't get an opinion," Damon muttered.

Marcus snorted. "Jax is gonna kill you."

Penelope started and looked at Marcus. "You remember Jax? What he's like?" Her voice softened.

Marcus's expression smoothed out to nothing. "No. Sorry. Just heard Jax say the other day that if Damon fucked with April, he was going to hang him up by his toes and use him for target practice."

That sounded like Jax.

Greyson scrubbed both hands down his face. "If you slept with her last night, why isn't she here?" His eyes cleared. "Oh. I get it. You told her to wait there because you thought it was Scorpius." When Damon didn't answer, his chin lowered. "Tell me you talked to her."

Penelope pressed a hand to her upper chest. "You did not just leave this morning without a word."

Damon winced. "I panicked." He needed to throw up.

"You left a note?" Penelope asked, her voice rising with what sounded like hope.

Damon heaved.

Marcus and Greyson leaped away from him and ran for the door, colliding and then somehow making it through to the hallway. Penelope calmly grabbed an old classroom-type garbage can off the floor and handed it to him. "In here, if you have to vomit."

Damon slapped both hands against the side of the cool metal and glared toward the hallway. He gulped several times to keep from emptying his stomach. If the Scorpius bacteria hadn't gotten him, there was no way a flu bug would take him down. "You guys are assholes."

Greyson poked his head back in. "Can you give him anything, Doc?"

Doc Penelope nodded. "I can spare some over-the-counter pain relievers, but I don't have any flu medication."

Damon shook his head and instantly regretted it. He stared at the garbage can for a minute until his stomach was back under control. "We have to save those for sick kids. I don't need an aspirin."

Penelope shrugged. "That's your choice. The fever is high because your body is fighting the virus, but it's not high enough that I'm worried. So far, with the cases I've seen this week, it's a twenty-four-hour bug. You should be feeling much better by tomorrow morning."

He tried to move off the bed again, and his body fought him. "I have to go talk to April."

Doc Penelope all put pushed him down into a prone position. "You should probably give her a little space. I'll talk to her and make sure she hasn't contracted the flu. You sleep, and I'll be back to check on you a little later." She headed for the door, her movements brisk and efficient like always. Marcus followed her down the hallway. Also like always.

Grey grimaced. "Not even a note?"

* * *

APRIL SAT in the shade of the umbrella bored into the middle of the wooden table while the younger kids played on the swings and slides. A couple of girls threw a baseball back and forth, their movements slower than usual because of the heat. It was still morning, but April would have to take them inside soon. She caught sight of Doc Penelope and Marcus Knight down the block, heading her way.

Doc Penelope often checked in on the kids, so the sight was nothing new. April watched them approach. Penelope walked calmly and with a quick stride for somebody so petite, while Marcus kept right behind her, his gaze scouting the entire area around them at once.

He looked like a bodyguard—one of the deadly and threatening ones—to a movie star.

There was such a contrast in their body movements and size that it was interesting to watch. He had to be at least a foot taller than the doctor, and while she was definitely small of build, Marcus was all size and muscle.

Had he been like that before he was infected with Scorpius? The bacterium was known to change not only the brains of people but also their bodies. Many survivors became bigger and stronger.

"Good morning." Doc Penelope reached April first and gestured toward the empty seat at the table. "May I?"

"Of course." April looked around for another chair for Marcus.

He shook his head. "I'll go sit." Without waiting for an acknowledgement, he walked over to the house next to the playground and sat on the burned grass, his back to a short and crumbling stone fence some homeowner must've tried to build himself.

From Marcus's position, he could see anybody coming for Penelope or the kids.

April tilted her head. "You have quite the bodyguard."

Penelope's eyes softened. "I know. He's getting much better, though. He won't admit it, but I think he's beginning to remember his life before Scorpius."

"That's great." Would it make a difference in anything, though? April flattened her hands on the rough and heated wood. "You here to see the kids?"

"No. Damon wanted me to pop by."

At the mention of his name, April's ears started to heat. "Is that a fact?"

Penelope winced, her dark eyes sympathetic. She shrugged out of her white lab coat and straightened a slim, gray sundress. "He woke up with symptoms of Scorpius, panicked, and wanted to get away from you before he became dangerous or infected you if he hadn't already."

The words smacked April in the face. Fear roared through her. "He was infected?" Oh, God. She partially stood. She had to get to him. No wonder his skin had been so hot last night.

"No." Penelope held up a hand. "He thought he was, but it's the flu. More than likely."

April paused, halfway from her chair. "The flu?"

Penelope smiled. "Yes. He's quite embarrassed about the whole thing, to be honest. It's kind of cute."

One of the teenagers had been sick the week before, so the flu was definitely going around. "He had to have known it wasn't Scorpius." April sat back down.

Penelope looked thoughtful. "Not necessarily. Those soldiers push themselves too hard. He's been in several fights over the last months, and their home burned to the ground. I heard he went into burning homes to pull out survivors."

April had heard that, as well. "True."

"He's been wounded, and I know he sleeps only an hour or so a night to keep up with the patrols and protecting Greyson's back. It's a wonder they're not all sicker than dogs right now." Penelope tugged a loose string on her dress and neatly broke it off. "Plus, he hasn't had Scorpius, so he doesn't have the added immunity we think it might give to survivors."

That was all conjecture. Wait a minute. "He told you he left me this morning?"

"Without a note." Penelope nudged her arm. "How was he? I mean, he's all tough and silent and somehow sweet. I bet he was a power machine in bed."

April's mouth gaped open. The prim and proper doctor had just said 'power machine?' "Um."

Penelope laughed. "I had three sisters, twenty-eight cousins, and about a million other relatives. You think we didn't girl-talk all the time? Man, I miss that. Don't you?"

April forced her shoulders to relax. "I didn't have that. Not really. Grew up in foster care, which was actually pretty nice. Good people and safe places. But you were always moving, and getting close to anybody didn't make sense. Until Don. My husband." Who she'd cheated on last night. Guilt made her flush.

Penelope sobered. "Scorpius took him?"

April nodded. "Yeah. He's long-gone, but I still feel like I was unfaithful." She looked down at her left ring finger, which had been bare for quite some time. She'd had to barter the ring early on during Scorpius, when people thought gold still mattered.

Penelope placed a hand over April's. "You know that's not true, but feelings are different than logic. If you want to talk, I'm here."

They were talking. April smiled. It felt good to have a friend again. She turned to check on the kids and caught her breath.

Lena was sitting next to Marcus, her back to the stone fence and her little legs extended on the weeds, mimicking his pose. She was showing him a series of what looked like playing cards, and he seemed to be watching intently.

April moved to get up.

"No." Penelope stopped her. "They're fine. He'd never hurt a child."

"Are you sure about that?" The urge to run over and grab the girl away nearly choked April's voice away.

Penelope nodded. "Yes."

April remained sitting but watched carefully for any indication of danger.

Lena handed over a card.

Marcus took it and studied it. Then he handed it back. Lena grinned, slapped his knee, and gave him another card.

It was an odd game, but the two seemed to understand the rules.

"See?" Penelope asked.

Maybe. Lena did have a way with people.

April glanced at the sun. "Damon and I were supposed to go to the Pure church for dinner to meet more people tonight."

Penelope studied the other kids for a moment and then seemed to decide they were fine. "Guess that's off, huh?"

"No." April smoothed her hair back away from her face. She'd lost a teenager the night before, and there might be kids in trouble in the church's apartment building. She needed to get in there and talk to more people. "He might be out of commission, but I still have a job to do."

No matter what.

19

One time with April is definitely not enough.
—Damon Winter, Journal

DAMON RELAXED on the bed in his room in the crappy Merc headquarters, his head still hurting but his stomach settling. He'd
slept most of the day away and was feeling marginally better. A
look at the sun behind the cheap blinds showed it had to be late
afternoon.

A soft knock drew him up short. "Come in." Greyson never
knocked. The guy always barged in wherever he wanted.

April opened the door.

Damon sat up in the bed and tried to look tough. Or at least
not half-dead. "Hey."

"Hi." She faltered and nodded at a Vanguard soldier who'd
obviously escorted her.

A hot wave of possessiveness gripped Damon. He cut the guy
a look, and the young soldier scrambled away. Then he smoothed

out his expression for April. "Come on in, beautiful." His voice was returning, thank goodness.

She walked into the small room, looking around. She had on a pretty pink sundress, and her thick hair was in a ponytail. "This is...nice."

He snorted. He had a bed, an end table, and a basket of clothes in the corner. That was it. Anything he'd owned had been burned up in Santa Barbara. "I'm sorry I left so abruptly this morning." That was a freaking understatement.

She reached the bed and sat on the end of it, her blue eyes cutting through the hazy day. "I understand why you left." Her fingers plucked nervously at a string on the threadbare comforter.

"Good. I would've rather stayed in bed with you," he said.

She looked at his bare chest and then looked away.

His stomach dropped. Oh, shit. This wasn't going to be good. "April?"

She stiffened her shoulders. "I'm not mad at you, but I realized this morning that I'm just not ready for, well...this." Her hand swept out. "For you."

Oh. Ouch. Well. He rubbed a hand over his very short hair. When he'd worked on the force, he'd shaved his head, and he'd gotten out of the habit. "I understand." It took guts for her to seek him out like this after the previous night, and he could make it easy on her. Now that he'd had a taste of her, he wanted more. "I thought last night was pretty good."

Her head jerked, and her stunning blue eyes widened. "You think?"

Amusement cut into him, and he hid it. "Yeah. Didn't you?"

She nodded vigorously, her ponytail bobbing. "I did. I mean, I've never had a one-night stand before, so I wasn't sure, but the sex was really good."

A one-night stand? The term pierced into him, and he fought

a frown. He didn't like that. Not one little bit. "It was more than that to me, April."

She rolled her eyes. "Okay. Casual sex, then. Forget the number of times."

Well, he didn't much like that either. But she had a point. Neither of them could afford to go all in right now. Life was just too dangerous. "I didn't think it was all that casual," he murmured.

Her pretty blush warmed him throughout. "You know what I mean."

Yeah, and if he felt better, his mind would be working faster to reassure her. In bed, she was just as giving as she was outside of it, just as sweet. Nicely wild, too. He'd wanted to untap that side of her, and now that he had, he didn't want to return to the friend zone. Every new part of her he discovered, he liked even more. She was kind and strong and sexy as hell. "Can we talk about this?"

"Sure." She turned to more fully face him on the bed.

His cock woke right up, forgetting he was getting over the flu. Or just not giving a shit.

She drew air in through her nose and then released it, obviously counting. "Here's the deal. I don't know how to do this. Be with a man who isn't Don. Ever." She shook her head. "Especially somebody like you."

"Like me?" he asked quietly.

"Yes." She looked around and then focused back on him. "You're on the front lines, Damon. You fought with Rippers just last night, and the bandages on your upper arms are from bullets. *Actual bullets.* You're in danger every single day, more than the rest of us."

Well, yeah. He'd dated a waitress once who'd had enough of his life, too. She couldn't take the fear. People who could be with a cop or soldier and not go crazy with worry were incredibly strong. Unique and special. "We're all in danger." That was the absolute truth.

"I know." She sighed, her skin luminous in the daylight made soft by the blinds. "It's just, I don't know how to be...intimate with another man." She winced, her embarrassment palpable.

Man, she was sweet. And adorable. He searched for the right words. "We couldn't get much more intimate than we did last night."

Her blush turned a fiery tomato color.

He watched, fascinated. Wow.

"I know, but since you ran out, we missed the awkward morning-after moments."

His hands clenched with the need to grasp her and draw her near, but he might still be contagious, so he didn't move. "The morning after would've been spent with me inside you. Nothing awkward about that."

"Damon." Exasperation rolled through her words, but her lips tipped into a small smile.

Good. He was relaxing her. His dick still hadn't taken a break, though. This close to her, he was ready to go again. Man. Calm down. Take it easy. He didn't want to spook her. "Listen, April. I like you, I loved being inside you, and I'd give my left arm to be there again."

Her chin dropped. Surprise winged across her pretty face.

There wasn't room in his life for coyness or smoothness. Or even charm. "I can't promise you anything other than a good time, an escape from this crappy world, and protection from harm during the op with the church. They're not right. I can feel it."

Her jaw clenched. "I don't need your protection. You require rest to get over this flu, and I'll take over the investigation. They'll let me see the kids. They trust me."

Irritation clawed at his skin. "Absolutely not. This—"

"Damon—"

"I'm not done." He waited until she'd snapped her lips shut. "I'm protecting you no matter what because that's what it is. I've been there, you've sighed my name, and even if we never speak again, I'm making sure you don't get hurt any more than you have here in Vanguard."

"I'm not your responsibility," she protested.

"You are." He meant every syllable. "Last night guaranteed that." He held up a hand before she could protest. "I'm not asking for anything. You want to be friends? We'll be friends. You want to be lovers? I'm there in a second. It's up to you."

"Everything except you being responsible for me?" Spunk stamped hard on her face.

Man, he wanted to kiss that expression away. Later. Once he felt better. "Yeah." No reason to lie to her. "I'm keeping you safe because I can. Because, last night, I sank deep inside you, and you dug your nails into my ass."

She shook her head, her eyes going wide. "This is not making sense."

Then he wasn't explaining it right. "Let me try again."

"No." This time, she held up a hand. "I think I've got it. Since we had sex for one night, you now have rights where I'm concerned."

"No," he snapped and then quickly calmed himself. "No rights. Nobody has rights to you." Man, she was stubborn. He hadn't noticed that before. It wasn't so much cute as it was fucking intriguing. "No rights. But I will protect you during this op we've created. It's my job." Even if it weren't his job, it'd be his damn job. Nothing was going to hurt her on his watch. Period.

"You're confusing me," she muttered.

"Not my intention," he replied. Hadn't he just laid it out there? This fever was messing with his mind, even though he was feeling better.

Her lips moved as if she were working through words before saying them.

If she got any cuter, he'd just grab her and damn the consequences.

"I'm not into the alpha male, go all Neanderthal experience," she said primly.

The words still didn't compute. "What does that mean?" he asked.

She rolled her eyes, looking about eighteen years old. "This. The whole, I'm protecting you crap." Her voice had lowered to a terrible imitation of a man's voice and now rose again so she could continue. "Yeah, the wild sex was exciting, but that's enough."

"Wild sex?" he murmured, having trouble following.

"Yeah." She blinked, and her face colored again. "Last night. You remember, right?"

His fever wasn't that bad. "The sex was fantastic. But baby, that was an intro." He said the words gently.

Her teeth played with her lower lip. "An intro? Huh?"

His mouth watered. Oh, he needed another night with her. And then several more. If she thought last night was wild, she was sadly misinformed. "Yeah. A first-time-together, kind of gentle exploring."

"Kind of gentle?" she burst out. "I have a hickey on my hip."

"Just one?" he asked. The woman definitely hadn't looked at her backside in the mirror. Indentations from his teeth were more than likely on her left buttock. He hadn't bitten her hard enough to hurt, but he'd definitely left his mark. "Look closer."

She threw up her hands. "I thought it was wild. And my sex life was great before Scorpius. Don't think for a second that it wasn't."

"I don't think that," he said soberly, feeling as if he were walking through a field of landmines. "I'm sure it was fantastic. But the world is a different place, you're a different person, and I'm a different man. Just because this thing between us is different and good, doesn't lessen what you had. Not even a little."

"Stop saying the right thing," she shouted, shoving away from the bed and standing.

Nobody had ever said those words to him. He couldn't think of a reply.

She put her hands on her slim hips, and no woman in the world had ever looked more gorgeous. Having her hair back showcased the sultry angles of her face. Her eyes blazed a startling sapphire, and her chest actually heaved a little against the light cotton of her dress. A closer look confirmed that her nipples were hard.

His mouth watered more.

"Stop looking at my chest," she gritted out.

Fair enough. He focused on her face.

"You are not listening to me," she said quietly.

He was listening, but he sure as shit had no clue what she was saying. Maybe she didn't either. Perhaps last night had thrown her enough that she was scrambling. It had definitely thrown him, but he'd been sick all day and hadn't had time to process. The idea that she didn't want to see him again hurt something deep inside him that he'd figured had died with the pandemic. "I want to listen to you," he said.

"I think...I mean, I just think that we should keep it to business. And friends." She clasped her hands together.

That would be smart, but he hated the idea. There was no question that April Snyder had lost too much in this world already. He couldn't push her. If she wanted to be friends, then he'd be her friend. "That's fine, sweetheart."

She didn't look any happier when he agreed. "Okay."

"But I'm still in charge with the case. No negotiation there." He waited for her to nod. Good. "So you stay away from the Pure church until I'm up and around again." While he was feeling better, he didn't trust his strength or his aim right now. And he needed to clear his head before dealing with Pastor King again.

"I can go in there alone," she said, her face brightening a little.

"In fact, I think they're more likely to show me around without you there. I'm less of a threat to them."

That was entirely the point he was trying to make. "No."

She jerked. "Excuse me?"

"I said, no." He let his voice lower and lose the gentleness he'd been showing her. "You want to be friends, then we're friends. No pressure. But on the op, I'm in charge, and you're not going in until I'm well. Tell me you get me, April."

Her glare could cut marble, and it turned him on even more. "Fine. I totally get you."

Why wasn't he reassured?

20

I am fully capable of going undercover by myself. Right?
——April Snyder, Journal

THE SUN BOUNCED off the cement in heated waves as April strolled down the street toward the Pure church apartment building. Everyone not patrolling had headed indoors, desperately seeking cool air, so the streets were mainly deserted. The smell of weeds and dust made her sneeze.

She recovered and looked around.

Even the bricks in the buildings looked hot.

Vanguard had enough water stored to last for a couple of months, thanks to the oddly wet spring, but at some point, they'd run out.

She swallowed, already thirsty.

The sky above her was a shocking blue with no clouds, but to the south was bright orange and black smoke. The fires were still raging along the coast.

Pastor King was waiting for her at the entryway to the four-story building, looking out of place next to the men with guns. His smile seemed genuine, though. "April. You look lovely."

Sweat rolled down her back beneath the dress, and her hair had certainly frizzed in the heat. But she appreciated his attempt at kindness. "That's very nice of you." Accepting his hand, she let him lead her inside where the temperature had to be at least twenty degrees cooler than outside. She sighed.

"It's too hot out there, I know." King released her hand. "Where's Officer Winter?"

"He got caught up with Vanguard and Mercenary business," she said. Her cheeks were already red from the walk and heat, so he wouldn't be able to tell a lie. It seemed too risky to admit that Damon was sick, even if it were just the flu. King might not believe that. "I hope he can join us later."

"Me, too." King smiled, showing a dimple in his right cheek. "I guess I'll be your escort then. I'm glad. We haven't had much time to talk." He took her arm and escorted her around the partial wall of cement blocks and into the main room. Several people milled around with plates of food in their hands. A few waved, and she waved back. "I have a treat for you."

His enthusiasm was infectious. "A treat? What kind?"

"This way." He walked them past the room and in the other direction from the stairs to the apartments. They reached a hallway, and he pointed at various doorways. "We keep weapons there, extra food there, and clothing in that one." Then he continued walking toward the end of the hall.

One door remained, and he opened it, revealing a wooden staircase that led down. "There's a small basement."

She looked behind them, but nobody was there. "What's down there?"

"It's a surprise." He gestured her. "You have nothing to fear here, April. I give you my word."

She swallowed. What was his word worth? Man, she wished she'd waited for Damon. But she hadn't. So she shook it off and started down the stairs, ignoring the old, peeling, rose-printed wallpaper on either side.

With each step, the air cooled.

Finally, she reached the bottom step and landed on an antique, gold rug. Then she looked around and gasped.

King chuckled and moved in front of her. "It's my office. Isn't it awesome?"

She nodded. The walls were wood paneling, and the desk and table were old and battered, but candles that had been placed strategically provided soft illumination. An oil painting of a mountain range took up one entire wall, and a chintz sofa and chair provided a nice meeting nook. "It's so cool down here." Almost air-conditioned.

"Please. Sit." He motioned toward the sofa.

"This is a nice surprise." Why had she been afraid of him? So far, he'd done nothing but be nice to her.

He shook his head and headed for a cabinet on the side of the desk. "The surprise is in here." Opening it, he drew out a bottle of white wine. "J. Lohr Chardonnay." Grabbing two wine glasses, he brought them over to the sofa and set them on a sofa table. "The good stuff."

She looked at the bottle. Good enough, anyway. "I used to drink this...before."

"Me, too. Well, when I was on a date." He poured some into the slim glasses. "When I was with my buddies, I drank beer. Or vodka." He handed hers over. "Cheers."

"Cheers." She clanked her glass with his and took a swallow. Delicious. She closed her eyes and enjoyed the taste. The wine was even cool, almost slightly chilled. Then she swallowed and focused on the pastor. "All right. Today seems to be my day for speaking frankly. What do you want from me?"

King chuckled. "Man, you're suspicious." Today, he wore more faded jeans and a green T-shirt from a Garth Brooks concert. He still hadn't shaved, and his lighter hair was mussed.

She'd try to flirt, but it was just easier to ask the question directly. "That's not an answer."

"Is it impossible to believe I just want your company?" He took another sip of his wine. "You're a beautiful woman. You and Damon seem to be more buddies than dating, and if I've read that wrong, I apologize."

She arched an eyebrow. "He told you at dinner that we'd been dating for a while."

"He said it like a guy trying to find out why I've been pursuing you," King countered smoothly. "You two didn't act like you were dating. Not really." He rolled very green eyes. "I understand you both have a job to do, and I'm fine with that. But don't insult my intelligence." He grinned. "Yet, anyway."

"You're flirting...with me," she said slowly as realization dawned. "Seriously?"

His dimple appeared again. "Why would that surprise you?"

"I'm older than you," she burst out. This wasn't what she'd been expecting.

"I'm thirty-four. You?" He took another big drink.

She paused. He looked younger than that. "Thirty-two." She'd gotten pregnant with her daughter at a young age, but things had worked out. "You don't look your age."

"Neither do you." If anything, the church leader seemed amused by her. "You really have no clue how pretty you are, do you." He said it as a statement and not a question.

Was this part of the cult's draw? Make her feel special and needed? If so, she was kind of buying it. Was that how they did it? The guy was handsome and smart—definitely kind. If the world hadn't turned upside down, she'd be flattered. As it was, she couldn't quite get into his head. "What do you want from me, Pastor?"

"I want you to join us here and stay safe from the bacteria," he said simply. "That's what I want. Nothing more, and nothing less." He topped off her glass. "If you'd be willing to go on a date with me, I'd love that."

A date? She'd been with the same man most of her life, and now she had two sexy and charismatic men wanting her. Well. It had taken the apocalypse. She chuckled.

"Now that's a nice sound," he said.

She shook her head. "Thank you, but no. My dance card is currently rather full." Even though she'd told Damon they should just be friends, they had slept together the night before.

King gave a rueful smile. "Fair enough. But you and Damon just don't seem to fit each other. You don't look right."

Her hackles rose. "Because he's black and I'm white?" Racism had better not have survived the apocalypse.

King frowned. "Of course not. But he's always looking around for a threat, and you're a nurturer. I've seen you with the kids. The two of you couldn't have different focuses. Damon is seeking danger at all times. It's who he is. You're seeking safety."

Well. There was some truth in that statement, wasn't there? At least the church leader wasn't racist. He was just willing to go after another guy's girlfriend—if she were Damon's girlfriend, which she was not. "Rumor has it that opposites attract." Why was she defending a relationship she didn't have?

"I guess that's true."

She forced herself to shrug. "Or not. You're right in that I don't want any more danger in this life." It was time to start playing his game. If there were a game. The pastor might be a decent guy. She took a big drink of the wine and let it slide coolly down her throat. "Damon is suspicious of you."

"I'm well aware of that fact." King sighed. "It's who he is."

She tilted her head to the side. "Where are the pregnant women who stood at the fence and yelled at Jax before you were in charge?"

King's eyebrows rose. "That's what this is about?"

"It's kind of creepy." Might as well push the guy a little. "You have to know that, right? There's something so cult-like about the entire situation."

He stared thoughtfully into his glass. "I wasn't present that night, so I can't really speak to it. But there's nothing creepy or cult-like about wanting to protect vulnerable and pregnant women from bacteria that will most likely kill either them or their babies or both." He brushed a stray piece of hair away from her face. "You understand that, right?"

"Kind of." His touch hadn't zinged through her like Damon's had when he'd done the same thing. "But it's weird that you won't let Jax or his lieutenants speak to the women."

King swirled the liquid in his glass. "Does nothing terrify you?"

"No," she said, her voice going hoarse. "Nothing."

He looked up, his gaze intense. "What if your child had lived?"

She leaned back. Hurt imploded in her torso.

He held up a hand. "Just listen. Wouldn't you do anything to protect her if you could?"

April's throat closed, so she just nodded.

"You'd be terrified of this bacteria and this world. Imagine being nineteen and pregnant right now and right here without having been infected. Knowing that if you touched the wrong surface, or if the wrong person touched you, you could get the illness and die. Or lose your baby." He grasped her hand.

She pulled away. "We're not even sure the bacteria still lives on surfaces."

"Would 'not sure' be enough for you in that situation?" he asked calmly.

Probably not. She tipped back her head and emptied her glass. "I'm not Jax, and I haven't been infected. Let me speak to each member of your church and report back to him. There's no reason for you to refuse."

"I'm not refusing," King said softly. "In fact, I think we should start first thing day after tomorrow, once I get everybody on board with the plan. You can meet with each member, talk to them as long as you'd like, and then make up your own mind about me. About the church. We could really use your help."

She blinked. The wine rolled through her veins, mellowing her a little. "You'll let me talk to everybody?"

"Sure. Why wouldn't I?" He refilled their glasses. "Now. Let's return to that first date idea."

21

*April dumped me last night, but I'm thinking it's just a temporary
situation. Like any campaign, I'll proceed calmly and deliberately.*
   —Damon Winter, Journal

DAMON WOKE up feeling like himself again. After April had left
the night before, he'd pretty much passed out and slept the night
and most of this day away. The late sunlight pouring inside
showed it had to be around six at night.

The flu was rough but quick. Man, he felt better. After a quick
outside shower where he washed the sweat off himself, he
continued into the Vanguard headquarters, searching for dinner.

The cafeteria for the headquarters sat in the middle of the
building, once a soup kitchen. A wide counter ran along the side
with sandwiches piled high. Men and women sat around at old
tables, eating quietly. Merc soldiers sat on the left side of the
room while Vanguard soldiers sat on the right. Maybe they
should have a mixer or something.

Whistling, he found a PB&J stack and grabbed a couple of

sandwiches before heading toward Jax's war room. A couple of guys nodded at him, and he nodded back.

Jax, Greyson, and Maureen were seated at the table.

"So. You're not dead," Jax said, looking up from what appeared to be a map.

"Nope," Damon said cheerfully, his vision plenty clear. "I feel fine. It sucked, but Doc Penelope was right. Twenty-four-hour flu." He studied the map. "Reno?"

"The other Bunker. We need to take it as soon as we get enough explosives. After Sami and Tace return from Century City," Jax said. "From what we've gleaned, it has more research on the bacteria than we do at our Bunker."

"And hopefully, a line on food production possibilities," Maureen said, gazing at the map. "Or lead us to more Bunkers. They have to be spread across the country."

Jax shrugged. "We'll see. But we need a plan, Winter."

Damon took a seat. "We have to get the Merc and Vanguard soldiers working together."

Greyson nodded. "A common enemy should do it. We'll combine squads in the attack."

"Are we planning this now?" Damon asked.

Jax shook his head. "No. We're waiting for April to report in."

"April?" Just the mention of her name warmed him right up—and it was already hot in there. It was good that he'd see her again on neutral territory. Had she really dumped him? The last day was kind of hazy, but she'd definitely tossed him back into friend territory. "What's she reporting in on? The kids she's working with?"

"No." Greyson frowned. "She met with good ol' Pastor King last night, and he agreed to let her back in tomorrow to interview anybody she wanted—pregnant women and all. So we're here to come up with a plan. I thought you were lead on this investigation?"

The warmth he'd previous felt turned to a chill and then moved right back to lava. "She. Did. What?" Damon snapped.

Grey pushed back from the table. "Uh-oh."

Damon's jaw clenched, bringing back his splitting headache. "She went into the church building by herself last night?"

"Had a bottle of wine with the guy," Jax said cheerfully, his brown eyes glittering. "Down in his comfy and nicely appointed office—in a basement with only one ingress and egress. Definite fire hazard."

Damon sat back, his focus narrowing. He did not have a temper. No. Not him. He did not have a temper.

"You totally have a temper," Greyson said, reading his mind as usual.

Maureen nodded. "I've only seen it once, but it was spectacular."

"I do not," Damon gritted out. "I'm the fucking calm one." He had specifically told April, without question, to stay away from King and his church until Damon could go in with her.

"Thought you were point on this op," Jax reminded him.

Damon lowered his chin. "Enough from you, Mercury."

Jax straightened. "Excuse me?"

"I don't think I will." Damon planted both hands on the table. "My love life is none of your business." Love. He'd just said love. Damn it. "If April is willing, and if I want to fuck her three ways to Sunday and back, then it's none of your business."

"Three ways to Sunday and back," Greyson snorted beneath his breath to Maureen.

She nodded, looking back and forth between Damon and Jax. She bit her lip and seemed to hold her breath.

Damon continued on as if his best friend weren't a jackass. "Jax, if you have a problem with me, or with me and April, then you and I can step outside right now." There was no reason to damage the nice table.

Mercury's eyes narrowed. The guy wasn't challenged very

often—by anybody. "I do appreciate a nice invitation." He began to push back from the table.

"Then consider yourself invited." Damon rose.

"Wait a minute." Greyson stood, right between the two of them. "We're trying to get Vanguard and the Mercs on the same page. If you two go at it, we'll be sending the wrong message."

Maureen stood next to Grey. "I agree. You guys have to bury the hatchet. Come on."

"I'd rather bury my fist in his face," Damon said, meaning every word. He'd had it with the Vanguard leader's interference.

Jax studied him. "Didn't think you'd be the one to declare war."

Grey rounded. "You thought it'd be me?"

"Yeah," Jax said, keeping his gaze on Damon.

Greyson shrugged. "I can see that." He glanced over his shoulder. "The Mercs follow Damon as much as me. They're loyal to him and will take up arms."

"I've noticed," Jax muttered. "I ain't okay with you and April."

"No shit," Damon snapped. "Want to explain why? You have a woman."

Jax's gaze narrowed. "I buried her child. Me, Damon. I'm the one who piled the dirt on the coffin."

Damon swallowed. "I know."

"You weren't there. Didn't see her almost shoot herself just to escape the pain." Jax's eyes darkened. "She's better now. With the kids and herself, she's better. If she loses one more person she loves, I won't be able to save her again. I just know it."

"She doesn't love me," Damon said quietly. The woman had made that more than clear. "And she's stronger than you think."

"Nobody is that strong," Jax countered, pulling back his chair.

Damon did the same and sat. "You're wrong."

Jax lifted a shoulder and slowly folded up the map in front of him. Finally, he looked up at Damon. "I hope we never have to find out. But I still think you and April are a bad idea."

"I don't give a shit," Damon said evenly. "If I want April, I'll have her."

"Is that a fact?" came a spirited voice from the doorway behind him.

Jax's eyes twinkled again as he looked past Damon. "Hello, April."

* * *

APRIL COULDN'T BELIEVE her ears.

Damon partially turned. "You only heard a very small part of that conversation."

"I heard enough." She moved past him to the center of the table to sit across from Greyson and Maureen. She looked around at the assembled group. "Damon and I have decided to just be friends."

Damon exhaled loudly. Jax nodded and smiled. Greyson shook his head, and Maureen just gave her what had to be the most sympathetic look ever.

Jax reached over his shoulder to a pile of boxes and drew out a legal pad. "I would never interfere in your personal life, April. But thank you for keeping us informed. It's good when we work together and have everything out in the open."

Damon's chin lowered threateningly.

April's pulse kicked up a few beats. The undercurrents in the room were making her skin itch. "Um, okay."

Jax nudged the pad over to her to show a list of names. "Here's who we think are members living in the church apartments."

April flipped the top page over to see more names.

Jax slid a pen her way. "Please confirm tomorrow if they are there or not. And if there's any way to get some of the folks to open up about church members who are living *outside* those walls, do so. I know they have people in my ranks."

April nodded.

"She is not going in alone," Damon said, his voice a low growl.

She blinked. "I think I should. I've been perfectly safe each time I've gone, and the members relax more around me." Her adrenaline was flowing. "They like you and want you to join and keep them safe, but we're trying to get sensitive information here. I should go alone just this time."

"No." Damon's jaw set so hard it had to hurt.

"Yes." April crossed her arms.

Raze Shadow appeared in the doorway, seemingly out of nowhere. The guy moved like a ghost. "We have two soldiers back from our Century City Bunker to debrief. They just arrived."

Jax nodded. "Good. They're late, but I figured they'd run into some trouble on the way here. Greyson, you're welcome to stay. Damon and April? Please go figure this out and let me know the plan before it is executed tomorrow."

"You know the plan." April shoved away from the table, grabbed the papers, and headed for the door at full steam.

Raze slid out of her way, his dark eyebrows rising.

She didn't need to turn to know that Damon was on her heels. Even though he moved silently, the guy let off heat like crazy. At the moment, she didn't care.

"April—" he started.

She threw up a hand. "I don't want to hear it."

His hand at her nape jerked her to a halt. She gasped, her heart thundering. He'd stopped her in the middle of the cafeteria area? What the hell? She slowly turned. "What are you doing?"

"We're talking about this."

All around them, soldiers stopped eating and looked up to watch.

"You okay, April?" one of the Vanguard guys asked, setting down his utensils.

"Yes," she said. "I'm just fine." The idea that Damon was perfectly okay with starting a scene shocked her. Fighting was for alone time. This was so far out of her experience, it wasn't funny. "Have you lost your mind?" she whispered.

A Merc soldier stood up in the far corner to get a better look. Tensions rode high in the room, and Damon wasn't doing a thing to stop them.

He stood so much taller than her that he towered without seeming to try. "I said we're talking about this."

It hit her then. The guy didn't bluff. Never had and never would. And the damn man seemed to be in charge of whatever room he was in. Oh, he was the quiet and thoughtful one who watched everything. But people naturally gravitated to him and to his thoughts. "You are a total control freak," she murmured, putting more pieces of him together.

"So I've been told," he said dryly. "Now. Are we going to go somewhere and discuss this rationally, or do you want to do it right here?"

The first soldier stood up. "I say right here."

April waved him off as more chairs scraped back. Her mind spun, and her temper finally exploded. "Everyone, knock it off. This is not a Vanguard vs. Mercenaries issue. This is a Damon is being an ass issue because we slept together last night." Oh, God. Did she just say that?

"You slept with her?" The Vanguard soldier charged.

A Merc soldier intercepted him, and they crashed onto a plastic table that cracked right down the middle.

Then all hell broke loose.

April yelped and ducked as a body flew over her head.

"Damn it." Damon put a shoulder to her stomach and tossed her over, manacling her legs with one strong arm. Dodging and weaving, he kept both of them from getting punched and ran for the back door.

Within seconds, they were outside in the warm night.

He shut the door and slowed his pace, walking down the

street. The sounds of the fight filled the night behind them. Something large crashed through the glass door.

"That's gotta hurt," Damon said, not pausing in his stride.

April came back to reality, her hair hanging down his legs. She started to struggle. "Put me down, you jackass."

"No." His hold on her legs kept her pretty much immobile.

She punched his back from her awkward angle, no doubt inflicting absolutely no damage. Her shoulder protested the odd move.

"You want to get spanked again?" He sounded as if he were asking about the time. He was so casual.

"No." She balanced herself on his broad back to ease the pain in her shoulder following her ineffective attack. Even though he moved smoothly, her stomach took a few bumps as they made it through Vanguard territory.

"Winter," another soldier said casually, walking by.

"Hey, Henry," Damon said congenially. "Doing the rounds tonight?"

Was he actually having a conversation right now? April snarled.

Henry hustled away. "See ya. Good luck."

Damon kept walking to her apartment and opened the door, carrying her inside. He walked several steps and then set her on the worn Formica counter. His hands landed on either side of her legs, his arms caging her. "All right. Now, we talk."

22

There's a lot in this world I can handle. Damon Winter is not on that list. Not even close.

   —April Snyder, Journal

APRIL STOPPED BREATHING. Damon's arms caged her, and he'd lowered his face to a few inches from hers. His eyes were a deep brown, and his gaze was direct. She totally didn't know what to do. Her legs were spread, her knees on either side of his hips. Desire slammed into her, and she fought it. "I can't believe you let a fight start back in the cafeteria," she whispered. If all else fails, deflect.

"It had to happen at some point," he said. "And I don't care about them. They all know how to fight and defend themselves. It's a good way to blow off some steam. You and I, apparently, have things to talk about."

"Like what?" she snapped, lifting her chin. His warmth cascaded over her.

He just studied her with his intense gaze. Within a minute,

she found herself squirming on the counter. Man, she wanted to be so tough and say the right and snappy thing. But her mind went blank.

Finally, he breathed in as if taking in her scent. "You ready to talk now?"

A part of her she didn't much like wanted to nod and agree with him. "Nope. I'm all talked out." Yeah. Not the snappiest response, but it wasn't entirely obedient either. If he didn't move back, she was going to run her hands over those very fine abs. What was *wrong* with her? "So time for you to leave. Nighty night, Damon."

He smiled then, the sight a clear warning.

She blinked, bemused. So that's what a deer felt like stuck in headlights. She felt small and trapped...but not afraid. Interesting. He'd never hurt her, and she was comfortable in that assessment. She was not happy with the way her body electrified at being so close to his. She had to get a grip. "Either talk or get out," she said, testing the waters.

"You ever been really spanked?"

Her body stilled. Her mind fuzzed like a bunch of clouds covered it.

"April?" His voice rolled right over her like warm whiskey.

"N-no." Her skin started to tingle. *Everywhere.*

His expression told her nothing. "I didn't think so."

Sure, she'd read all those sexy books way back when. But she'd never explored. "Is that a threat?"

"More like a promise." He leaned in closer. "On the force, if somebody disobeyed me on a job, they got fired. In the Mercs, they get kicked out, which is as good as a death sentence. But on this mission, I can't fire you or kick you out. So what recourse does that leave me?"

She stiffened, totally intrigued and not wanting to be. Her nerves jumped, and her sex softened. She had to hide her reaction. "This is inappropriate."

"What is?" he asked softly.

"You, ah, threatening to spank me." She tried to drum up more outrage and not stare at his too kissable lips.

He cocked his head ever so slightly. "I didn't threaten you. Just asked you a question."

She rolled her eyes, and her nipples tightened against her thin bra. "Give me a break, Damon."

"Did I, or did I not, tell you to stay away from Pastor King and the Pure church until I recovered from the flu?" The authoritative tone of his voice was even more of a turn-on.

Her body was totally betraying her right now. "You did," she muttered.

He nodded. "And did you, or did you not, go have a nice bottle of wine with the good pastor—alone—in his basement office?"

She fidgeted as much as his arms would allow. "You know I did." She sounded like a petulant teenager, so she snapped her head back. "But I was doing my job, and you know it."

"You were defying me, and *you* know it." His voice was so soft it was almost deadly. "Right?"

She swallowed. That was all true. Admitting it seemed like a bad idea, however. There had to be a way out of this mess without giving him total control. Yeah, right. Like he didn't have the upper hand the second he'd decided to take the mission. "I wanted to help those people."

"Maybe," he allowed. "You also wanted to disobey my orders."

All right, he might have a point. She did want to prove something to both of them. He was so insightful, it was scary. And another turn-on. "Maybe I did want to show that I could handle an actual mission," she allowed.

His low chuckle warmed her face. "Ah, baby. You wanted to challenge me."

She could only stare at him. Could he be any more arrogant? The sun started to go down outside, and the pinks and golds of the sunset splayed across the strong lines of his handsome face, not softening him in the slightest. "What are you talking about?" Her voice rose just enough to show that she knew exactly what he was saying.

His gaze bore into her. "You sure you want to play it that way?"

She didn't want to play it any way. Nope. Not at all. She didn't know how to do this, and if *playing* connoted a game, then she probably wasn't winning. "Wh-why would I want to challenge you?" She rolled her eyes and blew out air as if saying "whatever."

His knuckles caressed the side of her face, and she jumped. "To prove you could and see what I'd do?"

"You're crazy." Yep. Now that she was really thinking about it, that's exactly why. Well, plus, she really did want to help the folks in Pure if they were in trouble. The jury was still out on that.

"I like this stubbornness of yours," he said abruptly.

She sat up straighter. "You do?" Bubbles popped through her abdomen.

He nodded. "I do."

"Nobody has ever said that to me," she said, softly surprised.

"I have no doubt." He leaned in closer, and one of his big hands tangled in her hair. The feeling of his strong fingers at her nape streaked heat down her body. He slowly twisted until he had a good grip, and she couldn't move. "You don't want to be stubborn on an op involving danger."

Op? What op? Forget the damn op. Her breasts strained against her thin bra, wanting free. Wanting *him*. The night before, she'd had the warm mellowness of alcohol to lower her inhibitions. Tonight, it was all Damon. If his hands were on her, then turnabout was fair play. She palmed his twelve-pack.

His eyes darkened even more. "April. I'm trying to make a point here."

She snorted. "You have me against the cupboards with my legs spread and your hand in my hair. Just what kind of point are you trying to make?" If he could call her on her baloney, she could do the same.

"That you're in a precarious position and need to think clearly," he ground out.

Thinking clearly had gone out the window the second he touched her. "All right. I get it." She slid her hands down to get under his shirt. It was a travesty that he even wore one. "Danger... bad. Damon's orders...good." Now she sounded snappy and flippant. Yay, her.

"I thought you just wanted to be friends." His tone dropped to guttural.

Yep, his abs were amazing. Ridges and hard lines and raw strength. "I don't like you very much right now. Doubt we're friends." If she tried to take off his shirt, would he help?

His hold tightened, and he twisted his fingers in her hair until she had no choice but to lift her head and meet his gaze. "What. Are. You. Doing?"

Tingles exploded along her scalp. The shiver that took her had nothing to do with fear. Man, he was hot. "I'm tired of talking." She shoved his shirt up to see those glorious muscles. Humming, she planted her hands on his tight abdomen. Her skin looked so pale compared to his. There was such a contrast between not only the color but also the feeling of their skin. Hers was soft in comparison.

There was nothing soft about Damon Winter.

"You're sending very mixed messages," he murmured.

"Don't care." She really didn't. Not right now. Tomorrow, she'd worry about it. Right now, she was turned on and not hating life. And she was tired of talking about ops, missions, and the Pure. It felt good to feel. Sometimes, things were that simple. "So. I was thinking fast and hard." She met his gaze evenly. "You?"

* * *

THE LUST RAGING through Damon's body exploded, going wide and hot. The woman was going to kill him. He was trying to give her a gentle lesson, and she'd turned the whole thing around on him.

The feeling of her soft hands against his skin was driving him mad, and he was quickly losing the fight to go the friend route. "Hard and fast?" he repeated, his blood heating.

She nodded and pulled up his shirt. "Yeah."

He had to duck or get strangled. She yanked off the material and tossed it onto the floor. Her smile was cat-like as she started exploring his chest. "If you're fucking with me, I really am going to spank you." His voice came out hoarse.

"I'd rather you just fuck me." She reached for his belt.

His dick shoved hard against his zipper. "Wait a minute." He jerked her head back hard enough that her eyes widened and her hands stilled. "You're not playing this game. Have sex, regret it, say it's over. I'm not doing that cycle. We're either friends, lovers, or co-workers on an op. That's it."

Her blue eyes softened. "You're right."

Damn it. He hated being right. He could've just taken what she offered and dealt with the fallout later. But, no. He had to get things straight. What the hell was wrong with him? "I know," he sighed.

Her teeth played with her bottom lip. "When I first heard you were sick yesterday, I thought you'd been infected by Scorpius."

He blinked. "Yeah. Me, too."

"I was sad." Her voice cracked. "That you were here and gone. It hit me then that this is all we have. Right now, and right here." Her honesty was flaying him open. "I don't want to play games or get stars in my eyes or anything. But I choose all three options."

The blood rushed rapidly between his ears. "Three options?"

"Friends, lovers, and co-workers." She started releasing his belt. "I'm not asking for true love or any promises of tomorrow—

because tomorrow is an illusion these days. Let's find pleasure where we can."

He swallowed, looking for the trap. Her guileless gaze met his. No trap. There wasn't one with this woman. "Are you sure?" He had to ask.

She nodded. "I am. But while you're sleeping with me, you're not sleeping with anybody else."

No shit. "Agreed." There wasn't another woman he wanted like this one. Not even close. He leaned in and took her lips. Those full, generous, smartass lips. He thrust his tongue into her mouth, the taste of her driving him wild.

Lust and need and something else, something deeper he wouldn't explore, filled him. His cock stretched even more against his jeans, wanting inside her.

Now.

She moaned under his mouth and scraped her nails along his chest.

The small bite snapped the chains of his control.

He kissed her harder, the way he wanted to fuck her. Completely and until neither of them could breathe.

They'd just crossed a line, and he knew it. A point of no return. They'd talked about it and made the decision clearly and concisely.

He moved closer to her, using his free hand to pull her forward against him. Her dress moved up her thighs, and he pushed his aching cock against the apex of her legs. Even through his jeans and her panties, he could feel her heat.

Her thighs trembled on either side of his hips.

A knock on the door had him releasing her instantly and jumping around, shielding her. His heart pounded, and his lungs seized.

"Damon?" Atticus yelled. "You're needed at a Vanguard-Merc meeting right now."

God. His dick was going to explode. Damon shook his head,

trying to get his bearings. "Is it crucial?" he growled. The soft sound of April's panting breath behind him was like a beacon in a storm.

"Yes. Right now. Greyson has called everyone in."

Fuck, fuck, fuck. Damon closed his eyes and tried to regain control. Any control. "Merc headquarters or Vanguard headquarters?" His voice sounded like he'd been eating glass and shrapnel all night.

"Neither. The training building. All soldiers are supposed to report in." Atticus's voice grew fainter. "Five minutes." Then he was gone.

Damon turned slowly.

April remained on the counter, her dress pushed up, desire in her eyes.

He groaned.

Her smile was way too sassy. "Told you not to start a fight between the soldiers."

He exhaled to calm his breathing, meeting her gaze directly. "We're not done with this. I'll be back right after the meeting." Yeah, that sounded more like a threat than a promise.

So be it.

23

My temper is usually completely controlled. Not so much lately. I
have to get a grip on this.
　　—Damon Winter, Journal

IF ANYBODY even looked at him the wrong way, Damon was
going to rip his or her head off. He needed to punch something
and now. Leaving April in her house was the hardest thing he'd
ever done.

The night had cooled to nearly bearable, and stripes of pink
and gold covered the still-light sky. The pavement was hot under
his feet, and he kept his head down as he moved briskly down the
street to the training building.

Anybody in his way got quickly *out* of his way—Merc and
Vanguard alike.

He reached the center of the Vanguard territory where an old
school house stood. It was now a medical facility for anybody in
the inner area. A crumbling building to the west was now a
training area because it had been the gym for the school. He

stormed inside, and the smell of moldy socks assailed him. Some things never changed.

A raised dais, wooden and worn, stood at the very end of the space. Probably where the school had held assemblies and plays.

Jax and Greyson stood there with two covered chalkboards. Raze took point next to Jax. Upon seeing him across the wide expanse, Grey motioned him forward.

Not bothering to cover his pissed-off expression, Damon made his way through the crowd of soldiers, appreciating the fact that most people moved right out of his way. Several of the soldiers were bleeding or rubbing what appeared to be bruises already forming.

Even so, Jax and Grey had stopped the fight rather quickly.

Damon jumped up on the dais and moved to flank Greyson.

Grey eyed him. "What happened to you?"

"Nothin'."

"You look...pissed." Greyson checked him out.

Damon's lips tightened. "I was interrupted."

"Oh." Grey coughed it out. "Sorry about that."

So was Damon. He partially turned to study the crowd and look for threats in case anybody was stupid enough to have Greyson in their sights. He recognized about forty Mercenary soldiers and nearly two hundred for Vanguard. The rest of the soldiers were probably either on patrol, scouting for supplies, or covering the Bunker in Century City.

Jax lifted a hand, and everyone quieted, looking on expectantly. His sharp gaze swept the crowd. "The fight that just happened is over. It won't happen again. Anybody caught fighting with each other because of Vanguard or Mercenary alliances will be fed to Marvin for dinner."

A rumbling started in the crowd.

Greyson stepped forward. "Fucking listen to him. The lion is hungry, and I kinda want to feed him."

The soldiers silenced.

Damon fought a grin, and his body finally gave up the lust. For now. All right. He could concentrate.

Jax continued. "Greyson and I have explored several ideas, and we've decided to completely merge the two groups. If you stay—and you certainly don't have to—you're now a member of the Vanguard Mercenaries."

Huh. Not a bad name. Damon nodded. Good move. Keeping the two forces separate had done nothing but cause fights. Well, with his help. He should probably feel guilty about that, but meh. Why?

Jax looked around. "Several of us have either Vanguard tattoos or Merc tattoos. Smiley? Where are you?"

A guy in the far right raised his hand. His arm was covered with a tattoo sleeve of a vivid blue scene.

"That's Smiley from Vegas Tattoos. Some of you might remember his show that was on television. He's coming up with a design that will encompass Vanguard Mercenaries that can be added to the existing tats." Jax raised his hand when a couple of people started to protest. "We don't give a shit if you want to keep what you have. Feel free. Or don't have a tat. Or get the combo. This is a personal choice. We just wanted you to know the option is out there."

Damon craned his neck to see Smiley. His brother had loved that show.

Greyson looked like a badass with twin guns strapped to his thighs. "We're relocating living quarters this week. Several of my team will move into the headquarter building, and we'll have soldiers living in the two rows of houses in the next block and then the apartments at the far end of the territory to cover the entire area. We'll give you your new digs later."

Damon planned to move in with April, but he wouldn't mind having an apartment in the headquarters near Greyson.

Greyson whipped off one of the sheets. "Here's the leadership structure as it is. Jax Mercury is in charge of the territory." He pointed to a box with his name in it. "I'm in charge of the military and all campaigns." Then he pointed at Damon's name by his. "Damon Winter is in charge of planning and executing all military campaigns outside of these fences, and Raze Shadow is in charge of anything having to do with the war with the president."

Damon studied the board. All right. It basically just formalized what was happening behind headquarters doors anyway.

Jax continued. "Samantha Steel, one of my lieutenants, is in charge of all training for soldiers and civilians. She's also our lead computer expert, so she's at the Bunker right now hacking into whatever she can find."

Grey tapped the chalkboard, and white dust flew. "Tace Justice is with her, and he's in charge of all medical issues, as well as personnel problems. Doctors and shrinks report to him."

As an organizational scheme, it didn't suck. But seeing a diagram and living it were two different things.

"Any questions?" Greyson asked, his gray-green eyes sharp.

Nobody said a word.

"Good." Jax whipped off the second sheet and rolled the old chalkboard closer to the edge. "We have three primary missions right now. One, we have to figure out where the president is, what he's planning, and how strong his military is. Raze will form a team to do that."

Damon rolled his shoulders back. Fighting with the president still didn't sit well with him. Maybe if they took the guy out, the next one who stepped up would be decent.

"As part of that objective, we need to find out how strong the Twenty gang is, and we need to attack their holdings," Greyson said. "They're the president's front line, at least with us, and we need to strike back. Now."

Damon made a mental note to meet with the scouts. They had to start looking for trouble for a chance to take down Twenty.

Jax nodded. "Second, we need to take the Reno Bunker and

then find more Bunkers from there. Damon will have a plan in place soon."

So far, Damon was involved in both missions. He cut Grey a look.

Grey smiled. "The third mission is to deal with the integration of the entire territory, and that includes the Pure church." He shook his head as the group started to grumble again. "They're right to protect uninfected people, especially kids. But we need better communication and access."

Jax breathed out. "Any questions?"

The myriad of soldiers looked a little put out, but nobody raised a complaint.

"Good. Dismissed." Jax turned to Damon. "Looks like you're going to be busy."

No shit.

* * *

APRIL WOKE up to find strong hands on her hips. She jerked, and Damon's scent surrounded her. She lay on her stomach, and she stretched her arms and legs, trying to awaken. "What are you doing?" she mumbled sleepily.

"Finishing what we started." He flipped her onto her back, partially straddling her.

She woke right up. Her pulse kicked into a gallop, and her body warmed instantly. "Wh-what time is it?"

"About two in the morning. Maybe later." He palmed her breasts through her thin T-shirt.

She arched against him. "How was the meeting?" Why was she asking stupid questions? She should be taking off his clothes. Wait a minute. His chest was bare, as were his feet. He only wore his jeans. How did that make sense? "Why did you only get partially undressed?"

He pulled on her nipples.

Sparks flashed through her, and she moaned. "Damon?"

He paused. "Because I wanted to double-check that you meant what you said earlier."

The sweetness of that thought, even though he was still caressing her breasts and making it way too hard to think, settled in her heart. "I meant what I said. I want this." More than anything in the world right now. Her body softened for him, more than ready.

"I believe you said hard and fast." He ripped her shirt over her head in one smooth motion.

Her breath caught. "I did say that." She unbuttoned his jeans and released the zipper. His cock almost jumped out at her. Man, he was big. She caressed his long length. It was amazing that this fit inside her.

He swung his leg to the side and stood, shoving his jeans down. Then he grasped her hips and pulled her to the edge of the bed. Two seconds later, her shorts and panties flew over his head.

She laughed, the sound strained with need.

He started to lower his head.

"No." She grabbed his ear. "Up here. I'm ready. Was having a dream about you, actually." He'd been taking her over a desk—an old schoolgirl fantasy she'd always had.

"But I want to taste. Make sure you're prepared." He didn't move.

She wasn't ready for that. Way too intimate. "No. Now." She jerked him up her.

"Hmm." He pushed her up the bed and followed, his mouth right above hers. "Somebody feeling shy?"

Not so much shy as a little freaked out. And turned on. "Hard and fast doesn't include foreplay."

He chuckled and settled between her legs, pressing against her. "Everything includes foreplay, sweetheart." Then he kissed her.

His mouth was firm, and his tongue seeking. Damon Winter

definitely knew how to kiss. She took him in, returning the kiss, allowing her body to move against his. He caressed down her ribcage, and then she felt the rough touch of his fingers on her inner thigh.

More. She needed more.

She tried to angle closer to him, and he rewarded her by brushing her clit. She arched, sparks flying behind her eyes. There was too much pain and fear in the world, and she wanted this. Needed this moment of just them. Just pleasure and touch.

His fingers pushed into her sex.

She groaned, still kissing him, her thighs trembling.

He nipped her bottom lip with his teeth. "You'll have to tell me about that dream you were having. Baby, you're wet." He stroked her clit.

She gasped and moved against his hand. "Maybe." Not in a zillion years.

His free hand tangled in her hair and tipped her head back. He kissed her forehead and then down the side of her face, nipping her earlobe.

She kissed the hard line of his jaw, marveling at its strength. And warmth. Damon was always hot. "Now. Don't make me wait."

He leaned up and balanced himself on his elbows before sliding to the side and unrolling a condom he'd already unwrapped. Then he returned right where she wanted him. He pressed into her, going slow, filling her almost immediately.

Her blood heated, and she wrapped her legs around his hips. He shoved in all the way, and she gasped, her body arching at the invasion. Pain quickly melded into pleasure. She stared up at him. His eyes glowed in the dim light—a burning amber. His jaw was locked.

He pulled out and thrust back in, stretching her wide, making her feel full.

"Faster," she murmured, scraping her nails down his arms.

He withdrew, sliding out, and then hammered back inside

her. Again and then again. Her breasts bounced, and her hair flew across the pillow. She couldn't get enough.

Harder and faster. His powerful thrusts echoed in the room. She held on as tightly as she could.

He shoved harder inside her, and desire had her sex clamping down hard on him. She rose high and crested the waves, climaxing with a sharp cry of pleasure. Her eyelids shut, and she shuddered against him, her entire body on fire.

He jerked hard and erupted inside the condom.

And then he stilled.

She panted against him, kissing his neck and up his jawline. Amazing. Absolutely amazing.

He rolled over and held her tightly, and only then did she realize that she'd never let go of him. Her nails dug even farther into his skin. She held him as tightly as she could...because she didn't want to let him go.

Now, what was she going to do?

24

She keeps trying to keep me at arm's length. For the first time in my life, that's not where I want to be with a woman. This is crazy.
—Damon Winter, Journal

DAMON AWOKE to a very soft hand stroking his chest. April. He'd know her touch and sweet scent anywhere. He opened his eyes to a dimly lit room. It had to be around dawn, and the air was still somewhat cool. He lay on his back with the sheet shoved down to his waist, and she lay on her side, her fingers tapping across his skin. "Morning."

"Morning." She stretched and moaned, the sound lazy and fulfilled. "Sorry to wake you."

If she were going to hit him with the friends speech again, he'd lose his mind. "It's okay. Why are you up?"

"I naturally wake up early." She blinked, her blue eyes focusing. "Was already playing with your hard chest before I fully awakened. It's like you swallowed a plate of iron or something."

Now that was an alarm clock he'd love. "Don't stop now."

She smiled, her cheeks a light pink, and her eyes still drowsy. "Three times last night, remember? I'm a bit sore."

He'd tried to be gentle, but it had been a passionate night. "I can do plenty with you without ramming my cock inside you," he murmured.

"The things you say." The pink turned to a dusty rose. Making her blush was quickly becoming his favorite hobby. It was so easy to do, and she looked almost happy whenever she was trying to hide the reaction. "What's your favorite color?" she asked.

Ah. The getting-to-know-you-even-though-I-really-already-know-you phase. Damon thought about it. "Probably Viking blue. The color of my high school sports jerseys."

She reached a scar along his ribcage. "You've had some dangerous times. Knife?"

Her touch was awakening all parts of him. "Nope. Old Man Tillman's fence. My brother Danny bet me I couldn't filch an apple from the tree in less than a minute." He pushed her hair away from her stunning face, sinking into the soft blue of her eyes. "Your favorite color?"

"Green. Reminds me of Ireland, although I've never been there." She caressed down his arm and found another scar. "This one?"

He glanced down. "My brother Alan's baseball cleat. He slid into home, I blocked, and there you go. That one took five stitches. I think. He hit his head on a rock we'd forgotten to move, and he had seven. Lorded it over me for weeks."

She grinned and moved farther down to the divots on his hand. "Alan or Danny?"

He glanced at the three decent-sized scars. "Robert. Middle brother. We were chopping wood..."

She snorted. "Your mother must've been a saint with nerves of absolute steel."

"She was," he agreed. "She also knew how to deal with four boys. If you weren't bleeding to death or needing stitches, you grabbed a Band-Aid and went back to play or work." God, he missed her. She would've liked April. A lot. "She once asked the doctor at the nearest emergency care unit if they had punch cards for free lattes after ten visits."

April chuckled. "Please tell me the bullet hole in your shoulder was from work and not playing with your brothers."

He rubbed the old wound. "Yep. First year on the job. When the call came in, all three of my brothers beat the ambulance to the scene. Can you believe that? Even Alan, and he wasn't even a cop." Damon sighed. He missed them. Bad.

April tapped along his collarbone and frowned. "There's a divot here. Break it?"

"At least twice. I actually fell out of an apple tree trying to climb higher than Danny one time. Did it before falling." Yeah. He always could climb higher than Dan.

April shook her head, her smile thoughtful this time. "Did you know that the majority of the scars on your body are from living a happy childhood? Not from your job?"

He actually did know that. Without that time and those memories, he'd be insane right now after so much pain and loss. Instead, he kept strong and forged on. His family would insist upon it. "How about you? Any scars?"

"No. My childhood was decent in the foster care system, though. Met some real nice people. Just didn't have a place to call my own." She rubbed her nose. "Then when Don and I had Haylee, we had to grow up fast. I worked to help him through school, and when he opened his dental practice, I helped out there. But mostly, I was a stay-at-home mom."

Damon kissed her nose. He could see her baking cookies and helping with homework. "I bet you were good at it."

Her grin was shy. Sweet. "I was. Was the classroom mom, and softball team mom, and the PTA president."

He rubbed his hand down her arm. "I bet you were a sexy president."

She laughed, the sound relaxed for once. "I was a tyrant. I was the mom other parents ran from as fast as they could when it was time to sign up for volunteering for something. Bake sales, car washes, concession stands. I was brutal."

"I don't believe that," he murmured.

She coughed. "I even had a clipboard with a metal pen I'd tap against it." Her face colored. "I was ruthless."

He could just see her. "Sexy as hell, baby." He'd give anything to see her with a clipboard, demanding that people step up and do a job. "I might have to drum up one of those around here. Would you tap a pencil against it and get all bossy?"

She rolled her eyes. "Every time I try to get bossy with you, I end up over your shoulder."

"Exactly," he said, feeling like a satisfied lion. "I like you there." This was easy. Nice and calm and relaxing. Was it too easy? He'd promised to keep things casual, and this didn't feel like that. This felt like...more. He banished the thoughts. "Favorite ice cream?"

"Peanut butter and chocolate. You?" She traced circles on his chest.

Her touch electrified him, and he shoved down the desire. This mellowness and togetherness was important, too. He wanted to know more about her. Everything. "Strawberry with chocolate chips on it." Was ice cream a thing of the past? That idea sucked. "First crush?"

"Bobby Jacobson in first grade. He had his own frog that he kept in his lunchbox." Her eyes sparkled. "You?"

"Keesha Malben in third grade. She wore dresses and no underwear." He felt along April's jaw. Her skin was unbelievably smooth. Next time he was out scouting, he'd look for lotion. The good kind for faces. His mama always had a different lotion for her face than her body. "Are you okay with our new paradigm?"

She snorted. "That's a big word for saying we're having casual sex."

There wasn't anything casual about the previous night, but if it helped her to keep from freaking out, she could label it any way she chose. "That wasn't an answer."

"Oh. Yes, I'm okay." She looked up to meet his gaze, her eyes the blue of the sky over the Pacific in spring. "I'm trying to keep it casual, but it's easy to let feelings in. I get attached."

Was she warning him? That was beyond sweet. "I'm not going to hurt you, April."

She blinked. Once and then again. "I won't hurt you either."

He hadn't been worried about his own heart. Everything inside of him wanted to gather her close and protect her from this world. Keep her as his own. "I know."

She snuggled closer. "Why weren't you married? You're definitely a keeper."

He smiled and ran a hand through her long hair. "Didn't think it was fair to anybody. With my job and life."

Her breath brushed his neck. "Guess that hasn't changed much."

No. Definitely not. He couldn't ask anybody to be that strong for him. He was the tough one. "I always intended to slow down someday and then settle down." Maybe as a detective. "But not until the far future. I'd just made SWAT when Scorpius started infecting everyone."

"SWAT?" She lifted her head and smiled. "Good for you. That's incredible."

That simple acceptance hit him hard. Sweet and kind, his April. To understand what that had meant to him and to still congratulate him, even though the dream was long in the past... He kissed her nose. "We need to talk about the plan today with the Pure church."

That quickly, her brows drew down. "I already told you. I'm going alone."

Sweet and stubborn. Definitely made just for him. Things might be casual on the surface, but that's not how this was going down. "Not a chance in hell, baby. Trust me."

25

·

It's getting harder and harder to separate my new job from my partner. Damon has a way of taking over even the oxygen around us. Why in the world do I like that so much?

　—April Snyder, Journal

APRIL TRIED to outwalk Damon down the street to the Pure apartment building, adjusting her backpack of notepads on her back. Obviously catching her thought, and not liking it, he took her hand. Or he was just being sweet. No. He seemed to read her mind, and he knew she was ticked, so he was holding her hand.

She bit her lip to keep from snapping at him. Although a part of her was grateful she'd have backup inside. Just in case.

He whistled a tune she didn't recognize. Something upbeat and fun.

She cleared her throat. "I wish you trusted me to do this right."

"I do trust you. It's Pastor King and his flock I don't trust." Damon's hand felt solid around hers. "I won't get in your way, I promise. Would just rather not have to go through armed guards if I need to get to you."

Yeah, she could understand that.

They reached the apartment building, and the guards with guns looked young. Maybe about eighteen.

Damon released her hand and paused. "You two know how to shoot those?"

The kid on the left stood straighter, his legs long but skinny. "Of course." His voice cracked as if he were going through puberty.

"Wonderful," Damon said.

Pastor King appeared at the doorway. "April. I didn't realize you were bringing Damon today."

Damon moved forward. "We're partners, Pastor. If she's here, I'm here." There was something menacing about his posture. A look passed between the men, and King stepped back.

"All right. Come on in," King said, gesturing them.

It was as if they'd had an entire conversation with one look.

Coolness met them inside. April sighed, happy to be out of the heat.

Sharon was waiting for her and handed over a piece of paper. "Here's a list of everyone you'll meet with today. I thought we could start with the teenagers up in the rec room."

King cleared his throat. "You'll intimidate them, Officer Winter."

Damon nodded. "Understood. How about you and I go have a little chat? I'd like to know more about how you're running things here." Without waiting for King to answer, Damon slapped his arm around the pastor's shoulders and herded him around the cement blocks.

Sharon watched them go. "Okay." She shook her head, and her long hair tumbled around her shoulders. Today she wore a lighter peach lipstick with a white sundress and sandals. "This way."

April nodded. Where in the world was the woman getting lipstick? Well, today was a day for asking questions and being a pain in the neck. "If you don't mind my asking, where are you getting makeup?" If she weren't mistaken, Sharon was also wearing eyeshadow.

The woman laughed, climbing the stairs to the next floor. "We have a stash. Somehow, it gets replenished every once in a while. Pastor understands that we like to feel pretty."

Was that creepy or sweet? "Are you and King...ah..."

Sharon looked over her shoulder, her light eyes sparkling. "That's a mite personal. Are you and Damon...ah..."

Fair enough.

A woman of about twenty years old waited at a card table in the older kids' rec room, a book in her hands. She had black hair, blue eyes, and a very pregnant belly. "Hey, Sharon."

"Hi, Jada. This is April. She'll be conducting interviews in here today. You need anything?"

"Nope." Jada set the book down.

April's hands turned clammy. All right. This was no big deal. She put the papers on the table, set down her backpack, and pulled up a chair. "Thank you for meeting with me today."

"Sure."

April took out her own notebooks and made two stacks. She found Jada's name on Jax's list as well as the Pure's list, and she made a notation. "Where are you from?"

The woman looked surprised and then recovered. "Originally from Seattle, but I was in my junior year at Pepperdine when Scorpius infected everybody. Never got a chance to get home."

"I'm sorry," April said, reaching for the woman's hand.

Jada slid her hand off the table and away. "That's okay. My family and I weren't close, so I hadn't intended to go back anyway."

April twirled a pen in her fingers. "I'm not infected."

"So you say. You've been outside, and you might've just

brought the bug back in." Jada's tone remained matter-of-fact and calm. "I'm not taking that chance with my baby."

April nodded. "I understand." She eyed the woman's stomach. Maybe five months along? "I see from the Vanguard list that you joined the group about six months ago?"

"Yes. Right when they started forming. The gangs were taking over Los Angeles, and Rippers were everywhere, so a few of us went looking for some sort of safety." She patted her enlarged belly. "We found Vanguard, and then I found the Pure inside Vanguard." She leaned in. "Isn't 'the Pure' a stupid name? It's so dumb."

April chuckled. "It really is. I take it the old pastor named it?"

"Yeah. He was a religious nutjob, I tell ya." Jada warmed up and leaned forward as if with good gossip. "We're not even a church. Not really. I mean, Pastor King gives sermons once a week, and we're all thanking God that we're not dead or crazy, but it's more like a safe zone than anything religious."

That's what April had observed so far. "Have the members fought the change?"

Jada scoffed. "Not at all. Pastor King was kind of in charge from the beginning, but more from behind the scenes, you know? I think he was trying to find his place, too. He's such a good guy."

"He is very charismatic."

Jada's gaze narrowed. "Isn't he, though? Are you interested?" The mood in the room changed.

"Nope. I'm with Damon Winter." April gave the truth to calm the woman. Plus, why not go with the truth? "It's complicated, though."

"It wouldn't be if you moved in here," Jada said easily.

Huh. Good point. Had the woman been told to say that? To draw April in? She played along. "Yeah, I know. The closer I get to him, the more scared I become that he's going to get killed in a raid with Jax Mercury. Or worse." Whoa. That was actually the truth.

Jada nodded. "You'd be safer here. Both of you would."

"You do have better food," April said.

"We do. Not sure where the pastor gets it, but we have great food. I think he has scouts on the outside. He must have." Jada didn't sound too concerned about it. "Someday, we're going to find a nice organic farm away from any threats, and just live our lives. Once it's safe to move out of the city."

Sounded like a good plan. "Jada, if you don't mind my asking, who's the father of your baby?" April tried to make her voice gentle.

Jada's eyes sparkled. "I do mind you asking."

Oh. Well. April cleared her throat. "I'm sorry to be personal, but one of Jax's concerns is that people are here involuntarily and maybe women are being forced to have babies in some attempt to continue the human race. If I could report the truth back to him, then maybe he won't storm through the front door with a cache of Vanguard Mercenary soldiers." If all else fails, throw a good threat in there.

"We're protected here," Jada said, not losing a beat.

April frowned. "By God?"

Jada snorted. "Yeah, by God. And man. We're not worried about Mercury busting down the door."

What the heck did that mean? "Why not?"

Jada shrugged. "Join us and find out." She stood. "If you'll excuse me, I have work to do." Reaching down, she picked up a slouchy-type bag. Then she stilled. "Oh." She partially leaned over and dropped the bag.

April reached for her arm. "Jada?" Her heartbeat quickened.

Jada exhaled and smiled. "Sorry. Little guy kicked my bladder. He likes to do that."

"Oh." April relaxed and reached for the bag the same time Jada did. It fell over, and pictures slid out, followed by a silver gun. "You're armed." The pictures were of Rippers, their teeth gnashing, their eyes wild. From early newspapers or magazines? "What are these?"

Jada quickly gathered the photographs and gun back into the bag. "I have a lesson with the older teens later. We like them to know what's out there."

April frowned. "Don't you think that's overkill?" The poor kids. To be bombarded with images like that... No wonder they were terrified of the outside world.

"No. That's what's waiting for them if they leave or become infected."

"What about the gun?" April breathed. She didn't even have a weapon.

Jade's mouth tightened. "I'm protecting this baby with everything I have. If that means being armed in this world, then so be it."

Okay, that made sense, but still. Carrying a gun around inside an apartment building protected by armed guards? Why? "Are you trained?" April asked, looking for any information to take back to headquarters.

"Yes. We train daily. Or weekly," Jada allowed.

April studied her. Something was off here, but she couldn't put her finger on what. "Where? You guys don't leave this building. Where do you train?"

Jada moved for the door. "There's a concrete room on the top floor, or we go to the roof where there are blocks set up so we don't hurt anybody. For hand-to-hand, there's a makeshift gym on the first floor with mats from the old schoolhouse."

"Jada," April called.

The woman turned around. "What?"

April studied her. "What aren't you telling me?"

Jada shook her head. "You know everything. Why are you trying to find something that isn't here? Are you that unsure about the path you've chosen?" She waved her arms. "It's safe here. You could have the life you want, with Damon, inside here. There are people who need your help."

April opened her mouth and then closed it again. She breathed in. "If you ever need to talk, I'm here."

"Ditto." As Jada left, another woman walked inside.

"Hi," April said. This woman was in her mid to late thirties with just a few strands of gray peppering her brown hair. She looked to be about, what? Four months pregnant. "I'm April."

"Jessica Daniels." The woman moved inside gracefully, her legs and arms toned and displayed in pregnancy shorts and a pink top. "I'm here voluntarily, don't want to leave, and it's none of your business how or when I got pregnant." She sat, her eyes a sharp brown. "Any other questions?"

April swallowed. It was going to be a long day.

26

I'm feeling anything but casual right now with her. Why pretend otherwise?
  —Damon Winter, Journal

DAMON TOOK April's hand again as they left the Pure apartment building after a truly delicious dinner of a pasta dish with sauces. The noodles had been homemade, or he wasn't a Winter.

The sun hadn't given up the fight of the day yet, and its rays bounced off the brick buildings, turning them a deeper red. Heat wove from every direction—the bombarded pavement, surrounding structures, and the sky itself. Sweat slicked his brow, but he slowed his pace so April didn't have to hurry.

She was uncharacteristically silent at his side, obviously mulling over her day. Her notebooks were tucked neatly in her backpack, and she hadn't protested when he took it from her to carry.

They passed patrolling soldiers, but everyone else was inside on the lowest floor they could find, trying to stay cool.

"Heatstroke is going to be a problem if we don't get a break," she said, eyes squinting in the glare.

He nodded. "Yeah. We've had scouts out looking for new locations, but I think it's going to be a trek north for the entire community. We'll have to come up with a reasonable timeline within the next month or so." After he got them into the Reno Bunker. The information there might give them a different path.

They finally reached headquarters and headed inside where it was slightly cooler. Not much, though. He kept her hand as they moved through the throngs of tables and soldiers before entering Jax's war room.

Jax sat at his table with Greyson on one side and Lynne Harmony on the other.

Damon couldn't help the quick look at her blue heart beneath her peach shirt.

Jax sat back, stretching his neck. His olive-colored T-shirt pulled tightly across his wide chest. "Well? You see the light and find God?"

April snorted and dropped into a sleek, leather chair from the law firm Vanguard had raided. "No, but I've been all but promised a happy and safe life if I get Damon to fall in love with me and join up inside. Bliss and the promised land of an organic farm in the future."

"Organic, huh?" Greyson scrubbed both hands down his face and over his stubble. "Isn't everything organic now?"

Interesting. Good point. Damon set the pack on the ground and sat, wiping sweat off his forehead. "I wasn't promised fifty virgins or anything." He settled his chair closer to April. "I investigated the entire building, top to bottom, and will draw you schematics later. Didn't see much out of place. But something is off. Don't know what."

April nodded. "I agree. Can't put my finger on it, but I'm telling you, they're not a cult. Or even a zealous religious group.

They have a weekly sermon, and King thinks God called him to this, but it's not overt or in your face."

Damon sat back, watching the expressions move across her cheekbones. Her quick mind was fascinating to watch in action. There was such kind gentleness to her that her obvious intelligence was easy to overlook. "We had spectacular homemade pasta for dinner."

Greyson stilled. "I read the manifest from the warehouse the Pure emptied. No flour. Doesn't fresh pasta take flour?" He looked at Lynne.

The scientist shook her head, and a couple of blond strands of hair escaped the clip on top of her head. "Don't ask me. I was never a cook."

"Yes, you need flour," April said. "And this was the good kind with flour and not some alteration to the recipe. The sauce was fresh, as well. That means flour, sugar, and maybe even some ripe tomatoes."

"Damn it," Jax muttered. "Where are they getting supplies?"

Damon drummed his fingers on the luxurious table. "Well, we know they were talking to somebody in the president's camp through the fence not too long ago."

Jax shook his head. "I've had men on the Pure apartment building, inside and outside of Vanguard-Merc territory since. Nobody has passed anything over, through, or under that fence. It has been twenty-four-hour surveillance, and I've rotated soldiers, so even if one is aligned with King, the rest aren't."

Sometimes paranoia just made sense. "Then they had to have the provisions before taking the warehouse," Damon said. Nothing else worked. He looked at April. "What else did you learn?"

She shook out her dress to pull it away from her body. "Only one out of the twelve pregnant women would tell me who the father was, and she is ready to give birth any day. The father was her husband, who died because of Scorpius."

Damon cocked his head. "That's weird, right?"

"Maybe," April said. "Or they're just being stubborn and letting us know we're outsiders and their lives are none of our business. Which is kind of true."

"Anybody seem coerced or scared?" Jax asked.

April shrugged. "Definitely scared, but more of me and Scorpius. Like I had it all over my body or something." She wiped her hands down her legs. "They all said the same thing, pretty much."

"Like they were coached?" Damon asked.

"Maybe." She nodded. "And they show the younger kids scary pictures of the world out there, and of Rippers. I guarantee no teenagers will be sneaking out of the Pure building to have a good time in Vanguard-Merc territory." She winced. "And they're all packing heat."

Did she just say "packing heat?" Damon tamped down a grin. Then what she said registered. "Even the pregnant women are walking around with guns?"

She nodded. "Teenagers, too. It's like they're expecting an attack at any second." She looked at Jax. "But they're not scared of you. Several of them alluded to the fact that they're protected somehow, and it's not just from God."

Greyson cut Damon a look. "Explosives?"

Who the hell knew? "I didn't see any evidence, but that doesn't mean the entrances aren't wired behind all the cement blocks and alterations they've made," Damon said, clicking through mental pictures of the apartment building. "Were there explosives in the warehouse they emptied?"

"No," Jax said shortly. "But, apparently, that doesn't mean much. Even if we have a scout or two bringing them supplies, wouldn't we have noticed it?"

Lynne shrugged. "Maybe not. The scouts return to the front entrance and take their hauls to the warehouses where it's catalogued. I guess a scout or two could drop by the Pure first. But with explosives?"

"Maybe it's time we catalogued everything the second the scouts come in through the front gate." Greyson rolled his shoulders back, wincing. He'd been injured when he killed the vice president, and he still didn't seem a hundred percent. Damon made a mental note to talk to him later.

"We'll have to implement something new," Jax agreed. "What's the next move with the Pure?"

April straightened. "I've been invited to a women's bible study tomorrow night. It sounds more like a social event than a church thing, but maybe I can get more of them to relax around me. I'd like to attend."

"Damon?" Jax asked.

April all but bristled next to him.

Damon didn't want to tick her off, but it was his op. "I don't have a reason to be there, so no."

April turned toward him so suddenly that her chair hit his. "What exactly do you think is going to happen to me in there?"

"I don't know," he said tersely, his back going up. "But I don't want you inside where I can't get to you quickly without shooting a couple of kids who think they're guards."

Greyson studied him.

Damon felt the stare and turned, staring right back at his best friend. Damn it. He was being too overprotective. There wasn't much that could actually happen to April inside, especially at some bible study. And having her in there alone would give her greater freedom. "Shut up," he said to Grey.

Grey shrugged.

April frowned and looked back and forth between them. "He didn't say anything."

"Yeah, he did." Damon's jaw clenched, making his teeth hurt. "All right. You can go in alone. Here's the deal. You go in with a radio as well as a weapon in your pack. I have access to you via the radio at all times. No exception."

He waited until she nodded before he continued. "Tonight, we do some target practice, and you start learning hand-to-hand tomorrow." He'd meant to make that happen anyway. He looked at Jax. "Where's the schedule for that?"

"In the cafeteria," Jax said. "Most training sessions have been moved to early morning or late night because of the heat. Sami's at the Bunker, so other soldiers are filling in." He nodded. "At some point, if you really want skills, we'll get her to train you."

Damon nodded. He'd teach her for now. He didn't like this, but from a professional standpoint, there was no reason to keep her from going in. From a personal one, he didn't have the right.

Jax jerked his head toward April. "Find out where they're getting supplies."

"Okay," she said softly. "I'll try."

Greyson grabbed a map off the nearest table and unfolded it, shoving the paper toward Damon. "The gang members we grabbed gave us the location of three other houses."

Damon studied the map. He didn't want to know how the guys had given up the info. "Anything else?"

"The Twenty gang has taken out most other gangs and competition in California, and they're answering directly to the president," Greyson said soberly. "He has them thinking they're part of the US military, and he's arming them with what he has. He wants us dead. Now."

Killing his vice president had probably guaranteed that. But the guy had been crazy nuts and truly evil. He'd had to go.

Damon looked up. "I like that we have one main enemy and not a hundred. That's good. We can strike surgically."

Lynne leaned forward. "The priority has to be the Reno Bunker. I need that research. Now."

Jax nodded. "Agreed. How much time do you need to plan

once we have enough explosives, Damon? I want to take that place."

April stiffened next to him, and Damon grasped her hand beneath the table. "If somebody else is covering the plan to protect the territory when we're gone, I could have a strategy to you by tomorrow night to execute the following night. I'll need all schematics and notes that we have on the entire block holding the Bunker."

"You've got it," Jax said.

Greyson stood. "Your new apartment is the third from the left on the second floor. We're almost finished with relocating everywhere, and the teams, scouts, and squads have been altered to include both former Vanguard and former Merc members."

"Any problems?" Damon asked.

Greyson lifted a shoulder. "A few bloody noses and split lips, but no deaths. We'll be okay."

Damon stood and assisted April up. "We'll go do some target practice, and then I'll be back for those notes and such." He placed a hand on her lower back, nudging her to the door. Maybe they should break in his new digs first.

"Damon?" Greyson asked.

Damon paused and turned.

"The Twenty gang members... The two that we, ah, interrogated?"

Damon's shoulders felt heavy. "Yeah?"

"We let them go afterward." Greyson's eyes were more green than gray or blue tonight. "Sent them out into the world."

Damon nodded. His brother knew him and had just alleviated a concern that would've stuck. Killing didn't sit well with him, even when necessary in battle. Oh, the gang members were probably as good as dead. They couldn't go back to the Twenty gang because everyone would know they talked. But at least they had a chance to find a safe place. "Thanks."

Greyson stretched his back. "You know it."

Damon turned and grasped April's hand again. Touching her just seemed so damn natural. Arousal sparked through his veins. The more he had her, the more he wanted her.

Keeping it casual was going to kill him.

27

Vanguard is significant, as are the Mercenaries. Research into curing Scorpius is of the utmost importance. But in the end, when the sun sets, it will be Jax Mercury who matters the most to me. Just him.
—Dr. Lynne Harmony, Journal

LYNNE HARMONY WATCHED DAMON, April, and Greyson leave the war room and shut the door behind them. "I like them," she murmured. It was odd to think that the Mercenaries had been their enemy before.

"Me, too." Jax settled his hand on her bare thigh, and his callused fingers caressed her skin. "You think April is up to this?"

"Yes." Lynne turned toward the only man she'd ever loved. In the dimmer light, his face was sharp and strong. Those eyes, those bourbon-colored eyes, startled her every time with their sheer intelligence. "She's falling for him."

"I know," Jax muttered.

Interesting. "Is that why you spoke about the Twenty gang houses as well as the Bunker strike in front of her?" Lynne asked.

Jax nodded. "Yeah. She needs to know what she's getting into with him. I knew guys like Damon in the military. They're solid and strong...and if anybody else is in danger, they're jumping in the way first. It's who he is."

"He's a good guy," Lynne said. Didn't April deserve something good?

Jax studied her. "I know. Even when I wasn't sure about Greyson or the Mercs, I liked Damon and wanted him on board. He's smart and loyal. You can't beat that." Jax tapped farther up her thigh, sending her senses into overdrive. "But if you're on the front line, you're a target. With his size, he's a hell of a target."

"So are you." Lynne leaned over and kissed him. "I've managed to live with that fact."

"You're stronger than any person I've ever met." He took over the kiss, taking her deep, giving her everything.

Nobody was strong enough to lose the one they love. She never said those words out loud, but they were the truth. She leaned back, her body tingling head to toe. How he did that, she'd never know. "I noticed you didn't tell Greyson or Damon what else those Twenty gang members told you."

Jax cut her a look. "Why would I?"

She pursed her lips. "It's information they both need for their jobs."

"No." Jax shook his head. "Just because some low-level gang member said that my brother was trained to work for the psycho president doesn't make it true. Those guys are given misinformation every day."

Yeah, but Marcus was definitely off.

Lynne trod lightly. "I think you should increase his sessions with Vinnie. She's a good shrink, even if she doesn't want to be one."

"Those sessions are useless because Raze won't leave Marcus alone with the shrink." Jax played with her fingers, his touch warm and reassuring. "I'll get through to him. At some point, I'll figure out how."

What if Marcus were working with the president? She couldn't even imagine the experiments that had been conducted on him by the Bunker scientists. And if President Bret Atherton had been leading the charge, it was brutal and inhumane. She shivered.

Jax leaned in. "He is never going to get you."

She swallowed. Before Scorpius, she'd dated Bret. He'd been Speaker of the House. Then he'd been infected, and he'd become brilliantly insane—if he wasn't already. And he wanted her. Was obsessed with her like only a Scorpius survivor could become. "I know," she murmured.

But they'd meet again. At some point, it'd come down to Bret Atherton and her. A fight to the death for one of them.

How she knew that, she couldn't explain.

Some things were just meant to happen.

* * *

PRESIDENT BRET ATHERTON looked out of his office window at the sparkling Lake Tahoe in full summer shimmer. Blue and strong, it glimmered beneath a powerful sun. A fan blew somewhat cool air across his face, and he breathed deeply. At some point, he wouldn't be able to use the generators for something as luxurious as a fan.

Maybe.

He'd taken over a mansion-turned-federal-park as his new headquarters, and the place suited him fine. After a recent attack, he'd shored up all of his defenses.

For now, he needed to think. He looked down at a drawing he'd finished the night before of Dr. Lynne Harmony, his soul mate. Her green eyes glimmered with desire, and her smooth, pink lips were pursed, waiting for him.

He really didn't want to kill her. Oh, she'd pay for her betrayal. But she was strong and would survive what he had planned. Then they'd live the life he'd always wanted.

"Sir?" Dr. Ramirez stood in the doorway, his white lab coat wrinkled.

"Yes?" Bret focused on his head scientist. The guy had run the Century City Bunker before escaping when Vanguard had taken the facility. He had then, quite wisely, sought out the president. "I've finished gathering what intel there is on the other Bunkers. Besides the one in Reno, we have some evidence of a Bunker in Portland. May I send scouts to the city to start searching?"

Bret nodded. "Do it now." He'd arisen to the office of president so quickly that many of the protocols hadn't been followed. Namely, that of information. He didn't even know where the Bunkers were located or how many existed.

He couldn't even get into the Reno facility until now.

The people living in them, if there were any, certainly hadn't sought him out.

Ramirez hovered in the doorway. "I also have that report you requested on my research." He moved inside and slid a bright yellow file folder across the expansive desk.

Research? Human experimentation was a better description. Not that Bret gave a shit. "Do you have the intel on Marcus Knight?" The way to take down Jax Mercury and Vanguard was through Jax's brother. Of course, Bret had other safeguards in place—namely inside Vanguard territory.

"Yes." Ramirez stood to almost five-foot-nine, his back ramrod straight. "He was my strongest subject. No matter what we did to him, he survived."

Bret flipped open the file folder. "He didn't change?"

Ramirez chuckled. "Oh, he changed. He went from fighting us to defying us. He may have lost his ability to speak, and I think his memory was lost. In fact, I turned him into more of an animal than a human."

Was that pride in the doctor's voice?

"You did most of your work in Century City?" Bret asked.

"Yes." Ramirez faltered for a moment and then recovered. "To be honest, Marcus was brought to me from another facility. One that specialized in conducting such research on Scorpius survivors. With the intent to create the ultimate killing machine, of course."

Bret's head snapped up. "Where was the other facility?"

"We weren't told." Ramirez's darker skin paled a little. "The location of the Bunkers was a secret even to those of us in one. The government wanted secrecy on the project, obviously. I tried to get the location out of Marcus, but he didn't know."

He didn't know, or he hadn't broken enough to tell. It was more important than ever that Bret get his hands on Marcus. "How are the experiments going here?"

Ramirez shook his head. "The basement facility isn't close to what I need. I had another subject die earlier this morning."

"All right." Bret smiled. "I have good news for you. We leave in an hour for Reno."

Ramirez's eyes lit up. "I'm being relocated to the Reno Bunker?"

"Yes." It would be under Bret's control by the following morning. While he'd had difficulty infiltrating it before now, after Greyson Storm had gone in, the scientists there must be terrified. It was time for them to rejoin the U.S. of A. "Do you have subjects to bring?"

Ramirez played with his new goatee. "Yes, three. I have two others, but they're useless. I'll take care of them before we go."

"Make preparations." Bret dismissed him. "Blankenship?" he yelled.

Ramirez hustled out of the room just as Jerome Blankenship strode inside. "Sir?"

"I've been reading your military file." What there was of it anyway. Records were a thing of the past.

"Yes, sir?" Blankenship said, his brown eyes sharp and unyielding.

Bret reached for a stack of papers and read out loud. "US Military, Special Forces. Wet work. That you?"

"Yes, sir." Blankenship's posture and expression didn't alter.

He wasn't Vice President Lake, unfortunately. Although Lake had never been infected, he was a true sociopath who had no qualms about killing. Enjoyed it, actually. Oh, Bret was going to make Greyson Storm pay for killing Lake. Someday.

He brought himself back to the moment. "I need a vice president and a head of the military for now. Are you interested?"

Blankenship stood straighter in his black jeans and green T-shirt. "I am, sir."

"Have you survived the bacteria?" It didn't much matter to Bret since he had survived and didn't have to worry about being infected, but he was curious.

"Yes, sir."

Interesting. "Are you different than you were before the bacteria?"

Those piercing eyes focused on Bret, and he fought a shiver. "I feel less and am stronger. My path is more focused and clearer than ever before."

Now that's what Bret wanted to hear. "Do you have the plans to retake our Reno facility tonight?"

"Yes, sir. You're the president, so I'm not expecting much of a resistance considering Greyson Storm already infiltrated them last month when he kidnapped Dr. Barter. Anybody still living there was put in place by the government, and that is you." Blankenship was one long line of muscle, but his movements were graceful and smooth as he handed over a piece of paper. "If not, they will feel the force of our military."

Bret glanced down at the directions. "What about Vanguard? They're planning an attack soon, correct?" His sources were good, but there was a time lag in the flow of information.

"Yes, but they'll have other things to deal with...soon." For the first time, Blankenship smiled, and the sight was chilling.

Bret returned the smile. "All right, then. Let's get you sworn in."

28

I'm good friends with Lynne, Vinnie, Sami, and Maureen. But I look at them, and I wonder. How do they take such a risk by falling in love, knowing the odds these days?
—April Snyder, Journal

DAMON WAS BECOMING a force she didn't want to live without. April settled down in her bed. After another wild bout of love-making, her breath came in pants, her body still stimulated. She snuggled into his side while he lay on his back, like usual.

His breathing had already evened out.

Moonlight filtered through the blinds, caressing his rugged face. She wanted to trace the contours, but they both needed sleep. It had cost him to agree to let her go into the Pure by herself, but there was no choice. Plus, she knew how he felt. Every time he suited up for a mission, her heart stopped.

She drifted into sleep, her body warm and satiated.

An explosion blew the peace apart.

Damon jumped up, already reaching for his jeans to drag on.

Another explosion boomed, this one much closer. The building swayed and jumped.

"Get the kids," Damon ordered, grabbing his gun off the nightstand.

Screams filled the night. Another explosion blasted the air, and an old-fashioned siren ripped through the night.

April pulled on her shirt and shorts, running for the main area.

Damon reached the door before her, the powerful muscles working in his bare back. "It's the building next to us, closer to the fence line. Take the kids down to the basement and stay there until I get you."

Lena and the younger kids were already stumbling out of their rooms.

April grabbed his arm. "What. What are you going to do?"

The smell of smoke started to permeate the space through the opened windows. His lips pulled into a grim line. "I'm going to find out who's attacking us and stop them."

She wanted to grab his arm. Make him stay. Even ask him to protect them when he was needed elsewhere. Instead, she moved toward the kids. "Blue drill, everyone," she called out, giving them the signal to head to the reinforced basement.

Several of the teenagers were already running down, scooping up younger kids as they went.

Damon nodded at two soldiers in black T-shirts who ran inside. "Secure the building."

They went to work, armed with big guns.

Damon pressed a kiss to her nose. "Go, April. Downstairs. It'll be okay."'

There was so much she wanted to say, but none of the words would come. So she grasped Lena's hand and started jogging for the basement door.

Another explosion rocked the building, and a ceiling tile fell down. This blast was a lot closer.

"Damn it." Damon took off at full speed through the doorway and moved out of her sight.

Her body shook and somehow chilled. She handed Lena over to one of the older girls before going to check each room to make sure all the kids had gotten downstairs.

After clearing each room, she ran down the stairs to find all the kids and several of the volunteers huddled on the mats, quietly listening. It had been at least five minutes since the last explosion. That had to be good.

She breathed out, her stomach dropping. Okay. "Great job getting down here, everyone." The door quietly shut upstairs, with two soldiers on the other side prepared to defend them. "The buddy system worked well, but let's do a quick head count just to make sure."

After doing so, she breathed a little easier. All of the kids and volunteers in the building were nice and safe in the fortified basement.

"Julie? Why don't you break the kids into groups and give them games to play?" There was a whole shelf of stuff to entertain the kids during these interludes.

Julie nodded and set to work.

April tried to hide the trembling in her limbs and moved closer to the door, sitting on the mat with her back to the cement blocks.

Lena maneuvered between bodies and approached her, turning at the last minute and sitting on April's lap.

April hugged the girl from behind and pressed a kiss to her head. This was why she couldn't go live inside the Pure apartment building, no matter how much safer it was for her. The kids needed her, and Lena in particular. The girl had survived the illness, no doubt, so the church wouldn't let her in. She inhaled the girl's powder-fresh scent. "It'll be okay, sweetheart. Damon and the other soldiers will figure out what happened."

The explosion had definitely been inside the territory and not outside the fence, where stacks of tires and turned-over trucks offered more protection. Had it been a bomb?

There was one apartment building between April's complex and the fence, so somebody could've fired over the perimeter. It was dark, so the patrolling soldiers might not have seen the attack in time. But there had been...what? Maybe three or four explosions? They all ran together in her mind.

Damon was out there with explosives. Or with enemies who'd used incendiary devices.

She shivered.

Lena patted her hand. Then she reached into her overalls and drew out a small action figure. It was a man with a black vest across his chest. SWAT was clearly emblazoned in gold letters. She slipped it into April's hand.

April looked at the figure. "How do you know things?" she whispered.

Lena sighed and leaned back against her. Her small body barely weighed enough to notice.

"Do you want to talk?" April asked, her mouth close to the girl's ear.

Lena didn't so much as twitch.

April sighed. "What about Marcus Knight—Jax's brother? Most people don't go near him, and you do. Is he your friend?"

The girl paused and then slowly nodded.

Alrighty, then. At least she was communicating again. It had been a few days.

"Would you say one word?" April asked, almost holding her breath.

Lena stayed silent.

Just like the night outside.

* * *

DAMON RAN THROUGH THE SMOKE, reaching the burning building

at the same time as Greyson. Grey was also shirtless with unbuttoned jeans and boots; no doubt having had been in bed when
the explosions started. Maureen was at his side, her eyes wide.

Jax ran up from the other side, looking up.

The detonations had blown several holes in the side of the
building, and fires raged inside.

Fuck. Damon looked up at the clear sky. No clouds, and definitely no rain. "How many barrels of water do we have?" he
asked Jax.

The fire crackled wildly, burning hotly.

Jax shook his head. "Not enough to fight this and still have
enough for people." He looked around. "Where's Quincy?"

Greyson watched the smoke billowing out of the top floor.
"Around the side, taking stock."

Damon and learned more about Quincy and decided he was
a decent guy. Who wouldn't want to protect April? He was a
former explosives expert and firefighter for the military with
experience with forest and structural damage. "Quincy?" he
bellowed.

"Here." Quincy ran around the building, an ax already in his
hands, his southern accent out in full force. "The brick will take a
while to burn, but the roof, interior floors, and walls are all wood.
We're losing this building, gentlemen. Forget about saving it. Are
all the people out?"

Greyson nodded, smoke and soot already staining his face.
"Yes. This was one of the Mercenary buildings, but we moved
everyone into other quarters to assimilate the two groups."

A bad taste filled Damon's mouth. "If somebody didn't know
that, they might've thought they were hitting us." Or what used to
be them.

Greyson's eyes hardened.

Quincy looked around. "All right. Investigate later. This,
tonight, is about saving the building next to it and the houses to
the north."

Heat from the fire burned even through Damon's clothing. He backed away from the boiling mass along with the other men. "Is the territory secured?"

"Just sent five squads per fence line to patrol and protect," Jax said.

Wood popped wildly up in the air, and fire rained down. Damon ducked out of the way. "Let me know the second we should evacuate the kids next door, if necessary."

"Yep." Quincy looked beyond the fence at the turned over trucks. "The first explosion definitely came from a projectile, and I think we'll find a rocket when this thing dies down." The lines deepened at the sides of his mouth. "The second explosion sounded different."

A group of soldiers ran up with shovels in their hands.

Quincy pointed. "Dig a trench between the two buildings. Now." The men took off at a run. He looked at Jax. "How many barrels of water can you spare?"

"None," Jax said tersely, wiping soot off his cheekbone.

"Too bad. I want four barrels on the roof of the adjoining building. If this thing jumps rooftops, we have to be quick." Quincy pointed at six soldiers who'd just rounded the building. "You're with me. Hope you are in shape." He took off at a dead run.

Damon grabbed Grey's arm and dragged him closer to the fence. It was secure if the patrols had taken their places. "Did he just say that one of the explosives might've been from inside?"

"I'm not sure." Greyson pointed toward the street between the building and the row of houses. "We need to water down all of those weeds. If this thing gets out of control, the entire territory will burn like Santa Barbara did."

"There isn't enough water," Jax snapped, grabbing a shovel from one of the passing guys. Another guy threw several shovels down and then continued carrying more around the corner. "Best we can do is dig holes in front of the houses. If the fire jumps to rooftops, we're fucked."

Damon reached down for a shovel. "We need to add snipers to the security plan."

Greyson hefted a shovel over his shoulder. "We have three snipers total. They can't work every night."

The building popped loudly, and lava-hot bricks blew over their heads.

Damon ducked. "Jesus." He moved toward the street along with the other men. "Scouts, then. We need people on rooftops watching for this type of thing. The vantage point will help." Now that it was summer, it was necessary. The rainy spring would've made it difficult. The moonlight helped a lot, but on cloudy nights, they were screwed anyway.

Jax nodded. "Good call."

Greyson nudged Maureen toward Damon. "I want to check something. Give me a second."

Damon paused at the edge of the street as Jax and a couple of soldiers continued on to start digging up the front yards of the old homes.

"Where is he going?" Maureen muttered, wrapping an arm around her stomach.

Damon edged in front of her. It wasn't his place to suggest that she go back to headquarters, but the woman was pregnant for goodness sakes. "If you want to head back, I'll cover Greyson," he said.

She rolled her eyes. "I can dig a hole with the best of them. Pregnancy doesn't change that."

Yeah, but Greyson would. Damon would bet his left arm that there was no way Grey would let her dig holes with a fire roaring behind them. Though Damon had always liked this blue-eyed spitfire.

Grey came around the corner with a couple of pickaxes and Atticus, one of their older soldiers. He pointed out Maureen.

Atticus caught sight of them and nodded, turning their way.

"Guess you're going back to headquarters with Atticus," Damon said quietly. Yeah. That's what he'd figured. When Maureen started to protest, Damon shook his head. "You're pregnant, Moe. Grey can't concentrate with you here, and I need him focused."

Maureen gave him a look but didn't argue.

Atticus reached them. "Hey, girly. I'm supposed to escort you back to safety and away from this blasted heat. It's just too hot. You got any wine or booze for me?" He grasped Moe's arm.

Damon chuckled and started to turn toward the houses.

A shout sounded from behind them. A man ran away from the building, panic on his face. "Bomb!"

The earth rumbled.

Damon acted instantly, throwing his body over Maureen's and trying to cushion her stomach as the building exploded. He hit the ground hard, partially rolling to keep her safe. Something sharp smashed into Damon's head.

He felt heat, then pain, then nothing.

29

*How is it possible this man is still standing? I thought I knew strength
before. Apparently not. Damon Winter is strength. The real kind.*
—April Snyder, Journal

APRIL BARELY KEPT from screaming her head off, the panic inside
her was so great. Instead, she ran next to Atticus toward the infirmary at headquarters. It was dawn, but smoke blanketed the
entire street, so she had to squint to see.

She covered her mouth with her hand, her eyes tearing from
the smoke.

The fire still burned in the adjacent building, and soldiers
with shovels and axes threw dirt across it. One wall of bricks,
scorched black, still stood.

Damon had been hurt. Hours ago. While she sat in the safe
basement with the kids, he'd been unconscious at the infirmary.

They reached the back door to what used to be a free clinic,
and Atticus yanked it open, panting heavily. She shouldn't have
made him run.

She hurried inside and ran smack dab into Marcus Knight. It was like hitting a cement wall. She bounced back and started to go down until he grasped her arms and all but lifted her off her feet, holding her aloft until she stilled.

His greenish-brown eyes were serious as he slowly put her down.

"Um, thanks," she whispered. He'd definitely kept her from falling hard.

He nodded, eyed Atticus, and then stood to the side with his back to the wall. She shook off her panic and looked into the first room where two men were on beds, their skin burned. Both had cloths of some kind covering their arms and shoulders.

She winced and moved past that room for the next one.

Damon was sprawled over an examination table, his knees and legs hanging off the end and his shoulders off each side. His chest was bare and had soot all over it.

Doc Penelope looked up from listening to his heartbeat. She removed the stethoscope. "He's been unconscious for hours."

April's legs trembled, but she forced herself to walk closer to the too-still man. A bandage ran above his right ear, and his head had been shaved, probably for the stitches. It made him look even tougher somehow. "What hit him?"

"A brick," Penelope said, leaning against the orange counter. "I had to take pieces out of his flesh and give him forty stitches. Good news is that his skull is intact. Bad news is that he definitely has a concussion. We need him to awaken."

Marcus appeared in the doorway.

Penelope looked up. "I'm needed in the other room?"

Marcus nodded.

"Talk to him," Penelope said. "I can't find any other injuries, so it's just his head. Though that's bad enough." The petite woman hustled away.

The room spun crazily around April. Her daughter had died in the room next to this. Okay. This was a different time and a different life. She had to tell herself that to survive, and if it was crazy, then too bad. "Damon." Her legs shook, but she levered up by his head and touched his shoulder. "Wake up."

He didn't move.

His shoulders were bare without any of the previous bandages, showing his injuries. More stitches.

"You're almost a pincushion," she whispered, looking around and finding a folded chair by the far wall. Her body feeling a thousand years old, she lugged it over to sit next to him. She took his large hand, marveling at the size. Resting her head on his shoulder, she closed her eyes and said a quick prayer. While she didn't much believe, Damon did, so that had to count for something.

A shadow crossed the door, and Greyson walked silently inside. Black soot marred his entire face, and it looked as if his neck had sustained a burn. He wore filthy jeans and no shirt.

April hadn't gotten much of a chance to know Damon's best friend. "What happened?" she asked, shocked that her voice didn't crack.

Torment filled Grey's eyes as he looked down at Damon. "He protected Maureen and the baby when a bomb blew." As if he couldn't help himself, he took Damon's other hand. "Even turned his body to protect the baby and Moe's stomach, but that exposed his head to flying debris."

A brick to the head? It was a miracle his skull hadn't shattered.

Grey's laugh was almost a growl. "His skull must be made of solid rock."

"That's what I was just thinking," April whispered, keeping her chin on his still-warm skin. "Are Maureen and the baby okay?"

Greyson's eyes darkened. "Yes. Damon took all the impact. He saved them."

"A bomb went off?" she blurted. "Inside the territory?"

"Yes, but we haven't been able to get close enough to check it out. The fire is too hot." Greyson reached for another chair to unfold and then sat. "Thought I'd check on Damon. He's been out too long." He nudged Damon's shoulder. "Wake up. We have work to do."

The unconscious man didn't move.

April kissed Damon's neck, realizing it was wet. From what? She leaned back. Oh. Tears were sliding down her face. She impatiently wiped them away.

"You've been good for him," Greyson murmured.

She jerked. "How so? He's been shot, and now he's taken a brick to the head."

"Yeah, but the in-between times have made him happy. I didn't know the guy could whistle until he met you." Greyson wiped dirt off Damon's arm.

He whistled all the time now. "It's surprising how many songs he knows," she said.

Greyson nodded. "I know, right? It's the jazz songs that throw me. Damon doesn't seem like a jazz type of guy."

"It was the first country song I heard that surprised me." She smiled, trying not to cry. "And it wasn't a tough-guy country song from Garth Brooks or Kenny Chesney."

"Reba McIntire?" Grey asked, his lips twitching.

She nodded. "Yeah. A slow ballad. And he knew every note."

"The guy has unexpected gifts," Greyson snorted. Then he sobered. "Though he needs to wake the hell up. Now."

Marcus Knight poked his head into the room, no doubt on Doc Penelope's orders.

April shook her head. "He hasn't moved, Marcus."

Marcus's frown made him look deadlier than ever. He lifted his chin and then disappeared down the hallway again.

Greyson looked up at her. "Damon ever tell you how we met?"

She rubbed the whiskers on Damon's chin. "No. What happened?"

"He saved my life," Greyson said. "I had just started to establish Mercenary territory in Santa Barbara and was out scouting for guns and medical supplies. A group of Rippers descended upon me."

She stilled. "Rippers working together? Like a pack?" They were just humans who'd gone so insane that they were animalistic. But she'd always heard they worked alone.

Greyson nodded. "Yeah. Like a pack of hyenas. I started fighting them, and I was losing. Damon came out of nowhere and instantly had my back."

"He's a good fighter," she murmured.

"The best. We started talking, and he had some phenomenal ideas for security and enforcement. Before I knew it, we were running the Mercs together." Greyson rubbed soot away from his left eye. "Truth be told, he's been the conscience of the Mercs since he joined. Without him, I'm not sure where or who we'd be."

He was definitely a good man. She had to shake herself as a reminder that he wasn't *her* man. Sure, she cared about him. How could she not? But this was just further evidence that she needed to put the brakes on. Nobody, not even Damon Winter, could tempt fate like this so many times and survive. "I'm glad he has you, Greyson."

Grey pushed dirt off his hard abs. "I'm glad he has you."

April shook her head before she could stop herself. "We're casual. I mean, we like each other, but it's not a *have* type of situation." Did that make sense? She wasn't explaining this very well.

"Uh-huh." Greyson didn't look up from his stomach and, instead, pushed more soot off. "This stuff itches."

April opened her mouth and then closed it. She tried again. "I'm not saying I don't care about him because I do. But we've agreed to no commitment. Life is just too dangerous. Not that we're seeing other people or anything like that. Just that this is, well, casual." Was she babbling now? She felt like she was babbling.

Greyson looked up then, giving her the full force of his odd gray-green-slightly blue gaze. "That's the dumbest fucking thing I've ever heard."

Her mouth gaped open. "Excuse me?"

"You've been dating a short time, and you've blossomed like I've never seen any woman do. And my brother here? He's whistling. Like, for real." Greyson shook his head, and white dust from the ash flew in every direction. "Tell yourself what you want. But don't lie to me."

Irritation clawed through her fear. "You don't know what you're talking about, Storm. Look at him." She swept her hand above Damon's prone body. "He's out cold right now."

"So? He has a tough head," Greyson countered, the worry in his expression contradicting the carefree words. "He could be an inner-territory mechanic, and he'd still be in danger. This world defines danger these days."

April wiped grime off Damon's chin. At least he wasn't burned anywhere. "Wake up," she whispered.

Greyson sat back in his chair. "He's not an undercover type of guy. At all."

She looked up. "What do you mean?"

Grey blew out air. "Damon. He's the first through the door, not a secret agent. His plan would've been to bust open the front wall of Pure and see what was happening inside."

What was the man's point? "Jax wanted an undercover op," April countered, her heart beating faster.

"Exactly. Damon would've been just fine with Jax conducting an undercover operation. He would've rolled his eyes and told Jax to give him a call when it was time for boots to doors." Greyson stretched out his legs, and soot dropped to the cracked tile floor. "Then he would've stayed out of the way until he was needed."

April's mind spun, and her breath quickened. "Damon is a cop. A good one."

"He's SWAT." Greyson waved a burned hand through the air. "Or, at least, he *was*. Briefly. There's one reason, and one only that he agreed to infiltrate the Pure church and play their game."

Her throat closed too much to swallow. "You're wrong." But was he?

Grey's gaze raked her. "I didn't understand it either. When he told me about the plan, I thought he was joking. Then I met you. Saw him near you."

Every second Damon remained unconscious, it hurt her. Somehow. "I already admitted we're attracted to each other." She met Grey's gaze head-on. "And it's totally him to save somebody. To see that a person needs help. He was worried about me."

Grey nodded. "That's true. He did go in to make sure you were covered."

Yes, there had been attraction between them from their first meeting. She had tried to ignore it, but look how well that had worked out. "Why isn't he waking up?"

Greyson sat straighter and nudged Damon's arm. "You're right. Naptime is over. Wake up, buddy."

Damon shifted lightly on the table. "Who can sleep with you two droning on and on?"

30

I'm getting real tired of being attacked. It's time to take out every enemy we have. It's the only way I can keep April safe.
—Damon Winter, Journal

DAMON SLOWLY OPENED his eyes as a jackhammer slammed inside his head. "Is Maureen okay?"

"Yes. I owe you everything, and we'll talk about that later." Greyson leaned over him, his eyes worried. "Maureen and the baby are fine. How do you feel?"

"Like I got smashed in the head. What happened?" The room spun around Damon.

April's sweet lips brushed his forehead. "You got hit in the head by a brick."

Well, then he felt exactly like he should. He pushed himself to sit, and his head nearly blew off. His stomach lurched, and he swallowed rapidly to keep from puking. He had to wait a minute before speaking again. "How long have I been out?"

"Hours," Greyson said soberly. "Doc Penelope gave you forty stitches."

"My skull okay?" Damon asked, not sure he wanted the answer to that.

April nodded, her small hands patting his chest and shoulder. "Yes. She said your skull was completely intact but that your brain was definitely bruised. So no metal plate or anything."

That went in the plus column. He focused on the far wall, waiting until it morphed into something he recognized. "Status of the fire?"

"Burning down to embers last I checked," Grey said. "We lost the entire building but managed to save all of the surrounding structures, including where the kids are housed. Had to dig a bunch of trenches, and we used all four barrels of water, which didn't make Mercury happy."

Damon swung his legs over the edge of the table.

"Whoa." April grabbed both of his shoulders from behind. "What are you doing?"

Dizziness slapped him again. He tried to focus on Greyson, who hadn't moved. "Injuries?"

"A few burn victims, a broken arm, two broken legs, and a concussion," Grey said easily. "Everybody is going to survive."

Good news. Damon sucked in air and gripped the edge of the table.

"Stop." Doc Penelope appeared in the doorway. "You don't move from that position."

April sighed in what sounded like relief. "Thank goodness."

The doctor moved in front of him, easily stepping over Greyson's outstretched legs. She looked into Damon's eyes. "Follow my fingers."

He did so and kept the wince off his face as his eyeballs tried to explode.

"Hmmm." She peered closer. "How bad do you hurt right now?"

"It's okay," he said. "Not my first concussion." Probably wouldn't be his last, either.

She straightened. "All right. I suggest you take it easy for the next several days. I don't have an MRI machine or a CT scanner, so I don't know the extent of the damage. If you feel sick or dizzy or start losing your memory or begin passing out, come back." The doctor turned on her heel and headed for the door where Marcus Knight waited.

"That's all?" April called out.

"Yep," Penelope called back. "Unless you want to tie him to the table, I don't see what else to do."

April grabbed Damon's arm and leaned around to apparently see Greyson. "Do something."

Grey stood. "Okay." He held out an arm. "Let's get you out of here."

This time, April's sigh was more of a growl. "You've been awake for about five minutes. Don't you think you should lie back down and get your bearings?"

Aw, she was worried about him. That warmed him right up. She truly was a sweetheart. "Honey, it really isn't my first concussion." He stood and leaned on Greyson until his balance returned. Mostly returned, anyway. "I can't just rest on this very uncomfortable table for the next several hours until I feel better."

"He did sleep all night," Greyson added helpfully.

Damon shot him a grin, but it felt pained. "True. I've probably had my quota of sleep for the week."

"Maybe the month," Greyson agreed.

"This isn't funny," April exploded. "Stop joking."

Damon released Grey and stood to his full height. His head pounded, his left leg hurt, and his stomach felt as if he'd been repeatedly punched. "If we don't laugh, we'll start worrying." He studied her. She'd been crying, and that was another punch to the gut. "I'm fine, sweetheart. Honest." Though it'd be nice if the drumset in his head would go silent for a few moments.

"You are not fine." Her PTA-president voice was in full effect.

He paused. Man, she was sexy.

Greyson sidled toward the door. "What if we just take in the fire scene for a few minutes, and then he can go rest some more?"

Damon gaped at his friend. Greyson Storm, the leader of the feared Mercenaries and former badass sniper, was negotiating with April like a kid asking for an extra cookie. "What are you doing?" he muttered.

Greyson gave an *aw-shucks* expression that almost knocked Damon into a coma. "Just one lap around the fire scene, and then he's all yours, April."

April tapped her foot. The woman actually tapped her foot. "All right."

Damon didn't know whom to snap at, but since his head was about to fall off his shoulders, he decided wisely not to raise his voice. Instead, he gingerly strode for the doorway. Greyson stood to the side, watching closely, obviously ready to catch him if he fell. "I'm fine," he muttered.

Greyson nodded. "I know." Yet he didn't move away.

April rushed out of the room and slid her arm around his waist. She smelled like baby powder for some reason. "All right. One lap around the fire and then we go rest. You promised."

Actually, he hadn't promised a damn thing.

They reached the end of the hallway, and Marcus stepped out of the office by the door. "You'll want these."

Damon accepted the sunglasses with pure gratitude. "Thank you." Marcus might've just become his second best friend in the entire world. The glasses slid on smoothly, and Damon's eyes were protected from the sun.

His head felt better already. Kind of.

Smoke shrouded the entire street outside. The glasses were tinted, turning the world a deep blueish-gray. He walked through the smoke, April plastered to his left side, and Greyson close to his right. "I'm fine, you two."

"Right." Greyson kept close. "I ain't letting anything happen to you. Ever."

Oh, man. "Grey, it was Moe. I'd never let her be harmed. You don't owe me."

Greyson kept walking through the thick smoke. "I said we'd talk about it later. Once I can figure out what to say."

Soot-covered soldiers scurried around, placing dirt in front of houses and stomping out any remaining embers.

They reached the corner of the burned building. One wall of bricks, crumbling and blackened, still stood past the first story. In the middle, burning wood and other materials formed heated embers that a crew was trying to douse with dirt.

Jax Mercury tossed a shovel to another guy and strode their way, soot covering his face and his shorter hair standing on end. "Damon. How you feeling?"

"Good." Damon coughed and then waited for his head to explode. The pain was nearly unbearable. "What do we have?"

Quincy moved out from behind another stack of downed bricks and headed over. He untied the bandana from around his mouth and spit a couple of times. "It ain't good, my friends." He leaned over and coughed several times before straightening. Ashes covered his thick, black hair and even his eyelashes. He was as tall as Damon with startling green eyes. "I've found two rockets, several broken bottles from a secondary attack of Molotov cocktails, and two bombs."

"Bombs?" April gasped, her hand splayed across Damon's abdomen.

Quincy nodded. "Found the switches. Pretty rudimentary, but they did the job, no?"

Damon's lungs burned. How had these guys worked all night against this fire? "I don't suppose there's any way the bombs were just tossed in here like the rockets?"

"Not a chance," Quincy confirmed.

Jax spit out ashes. "Let me get this straight. We have a coordinated attack that consisted of first two rockets, and then Molotov cocktails thrown from the other side of the fence? And, subsequently, two bombs were set to go off in the building and successfully did so?"

Quincy coughed again and then nodded. "In a nutshell."

Wonderful. "Any sign of the perp?" Damon asked tersely. The gangs in the area liked to leave a calling card.

"Yeah." Jax pulled a purple bandana out of his back pocket. "We found several of these on the red truck outside the fence. They're not trying to hide who they are. Twenty is stepping up their attacks, no doubt at the president's behest."

No doubt. Damon's head rang, but he could think clearly. "We need to strike back and fast. Let them know there are consequences."

Greyson kicked over a burning ember. "We also need to find the traitor inside the territory. Who set the bombs *from inside*? Somebody has to have seen something."

Damon winced. "Maybe. Everyone has been staying indoors as much as possible. It'd be easy to traverse inside the territory without being seen moving if somebody was already here inside." He turned toward Quincy. "Would the materials used be hard to find or put together?"

"No," Quincy said. "We have several storage depots with explosives we've taken from construction sites. Anybody with even limited knowledge of explosives could've rigged these up."

Damon clicked through the facts. "But the bomber in the territory must've met with the Twenty gang outside at some point to coordinate. We're looking at a scout or soldier." Probably. Most likely, anyway.

Jax nodded. "I guess we start interviewing our people. I'll get Vinnie in on this. She's working as our shrink, but she was an FBI profiler before Scorpius. She's good, too." The Vanguard leader looked like his head hurt as bad as Damon's. The guy was definitely being stretched in several directions.

"Jax." Raze Shadow jogged up, wearing ripped and sooty clothing. "I patrolled outside, looking for anything off. This was secured to a post with a Twenty purple bandana." He handed over a folded piece of paper.

Jax unfolded the note to see Marcus Knight's face on some sort of medical form. Jax's face hardened.

"What is it?" Damon leaned closer.

"One sheet of a report from a Bunker where they experimented on Marcus," Jax said, his gaze burning. "Says they broke his bones to see how quickly he would heal."

Smoke filled Damon's nose, and he sneezed. Pain ricocheted through his brain like a buzz saw. His eyes pricked with more pain. He cleared his throat. "Why would the Twenty gang have that and want you to see it?"

"I don't know, but I'm going to find out." Jax shoved the paper into his back pocket. "Nobody say anything to Marcus about this. I'll talk to him when I have more information." He studied Damon. "I want to hit back at Twenty tonight. Then tomorrow night, we'll take the Bunker."

Damon nodded. "I'm ready." If his head stayed on his neck.

Greyson stepped between them before April could move. "You're not on tonight, Winter. We'll see how your head is tomorrow before deciding on the Bunker."

Damon wanted to argue, but as he was at present, he'd be a liability. "Fine, but let me look over the plan for all three houses. There are good exit strategies that we need to examine."

"No problem," Jax said.

April tugged Damon toward her. "Now, we're going to get some real sleep," she said, her voice chock-full of authority.

Nobody argued with her.

In fact, Jax grinned, and Greyson shuffled his feet. Quincy just nodded.

Amusement overtook Damon, and he let her turn him toward her apartment. "You're kind of bossy," he murmured.

"Get used to it," she replied.

Huh. Maybe he would.

31

Wait. Just...wait. I thought I'd seen crazy a few times. Nope. Not even close.

———April Snyder, Journal

APRIL FINISHED TAKING care of the kids and returned to her apartment where Damon was still poring over a map with Jax and Greyson. Lines pinched the sides of his generous mouth, and his eyes were so bloodshot, they might as well be fully red. He was shaking his head, and the movement obviously hurt like hell.

She cleared her throat. "It's supper time. Shouldn't you guys go eat something?"

"Not until we agree on this," Damon said, his voice a low growl. "Jax, you don't have the forces right now to take all three of these houses, especially since we're finishing fighting the fire, and everyone is exhausted. It'd be a mistake to go tonight, and I'm not going to let you do it."

Jax's chin lowered, and he looked like a tiger about to strike. "You were on board earlier before you slept all day."

Damon turned toward him, his back a straight line. "I was on board before I saw the locations of these houses." He poked his finger against a blue dot on the map. "This one sits directly in the scope of five, I said *five*, possible sniper positions. Do you think that's an accident?"

April looked over his shoulder at the map. How did he know that? Intriguing. And he needed to take an aspirin and go back to sleep. She could read the pain on his face.

Jax sighed and leaned back. "I don't want to hit the houses on different nights."

"I understand that, and I know you're pissed," Damon rasped. "But to coordinate a hit on these three particular houses, we need to practice the execution here several times before going. They're prepared for a hit, I promise you. More so than I would've thought before I saw the locations."

April sidled closer. Damon was just so in control and commanding when it came to planning.

Jax scrubbed both hands down his face. "You're right, I know. But we have to move, and fast."

"The Reno Bunker is going to be easier to take than these houses," Damon said quietly. "Or rather, it'll take less preparation because we don't know shit."

"The scouts should be back any minute with intel," Jax said. "So we proceed slowly but with precision." He looked Damon over. "Get some sleep, Winter. I promise I won't go attack anybody tonight." He stood and patted April on the shoulder. "I'll debrief you later."

Debrief. She was working in a business where she'd be debriefed. "Sounds good." She felt like James Bond.

Greyson grinned, his eyes tired. "I'm going to check on Maureen, and I'll talk to you two later. Get some sleep, Damon." He followed Jax out the door.

Damon rested his head back and groaned. "Never take a brick to the head."

"Words to live by." She tugged him out of the chair and pushed him toward the bed. "You need more sleep. Doc Penelope said she'd drop by later tonight to look at your eyes or something."

He grasped her hand and pulled her toward the bed. "Snuggle with me."

It was too hot to snuggle, but she lay down next to him anyway. Within seconds, his breathing evened out against her neck.

She pushed away and stood, looking down at him. He overwhelmed her bed in size and strength. In sleep, the pained lines on his face from earlier were smoothed out, leaving him hard and angled again. He'd taken a brick to the head, but then he'd used reason with a very angry Jax Mercury to prevent disaster.

Smart and strong.

She swallowed. She could be smart and strong, too. They were being attacked from all sides, including from the *inside*. The Pure church had to be figured out and dealt with so the bigger issues could be tackled.

It was her job to infiltrate the Pure church and give Jax the answers he needed. Now wasn't the time to wait. Damon had agreed earlier that she was capable of going on her own, although he probably had wanted to be alert during that time. Her instincts told her this wasn't dangerous—not yet, anyway. Yeah, he'd be ticked she went. But it was time to get answers from that church.

Settling the sheet over Damon, she quickly pinned her hair on top of her head and walked out into the still smoky air.

Anybody outside braving the evening heat was on a mission either with shovels or more dirt. She greeted several people on her way to the southwest corner of Vanguard-Merc territory, but nobody questioned where she was going.

Why would they?

She reached the apartment building and smiled at the two

soldiers guarding the door. Apparently, they'd been told to expect her because they moved aside immediately.

Sharon met her inside, grabbing her hands. "What in the heck is happening out there?" Her eyes were wide. "We heard all the explosions, and a couple of our guards went to help with the fire. Do we know who attacked us?"

April shook her head. "The Twenty gang with the purple colors attacked."

Sharon coughed. "I can't believe it. I mean, why? Why are people attacking others when we're all in so much danger anyway?"

That was such a good question.

"Come on. The study is upstairs." Sharon turned and led her through the stacked blocks.

April hesitated at seeing movement down Pastor King's hall. A man stood at the door to the basement office and turned briefly to look at her.

She blinked. Once, and then again. He was large with very short, brown hair. More importantly, she didn't recognize him. She'd interviewed every member of the Pure, and she hadn't met that man. "Who is that?" She started down the long hallway.

Sharon grabbed her arm. "Just a Pure member. You met him the other day."

April pulled free. "No, I didn't." She continued down the hallway.

The man faced her more fully, waiting until she reached him. "Evening." His voice was a low baritone.

"Hi." The stairway door remained closed. "I'm April Snyder, and I thought I'd met every member of the Pure and Vanguard. You're new to me." Was he one of the Mercenaries she hadn't seen yet? If so, why was he here?

He held out a hand to shake. "Jerome. It's nice to meet you." His eyes warmed, and his touch was light.

She was thrown, and she didn't like it. "I interviewed everyone in the Pure. Why haven't we met?" While she'd have to double-check, she was almost positive his name was not on the Vanguard list, either.

He shrugged. "I've been busy and must've missed the interviews." He leaned against the wall. "Would you like to spend time together now?"

The way he said the words was beyond suggestive. Was he just flirting with her or covering his tracks? "Are you a Mercenary?" That's the only thing that would make sense.

"God, no. Hate violence." He was clean-shaven, and a light scar ran right beneath his jaw. "The world is dangerous enough without joining a group who does nothing but attack and steal supplies."

That was an old rumor about the Mercs that had been mostly debunked. Sharon hovered near April, wringing her hands.

Something smelled so wrong about this. Warning ticked down her spine.

The door opened, and Pastor King stepped out. He jerked at seeing April and then quickly recovered. "April. I'm so glad you weren't injured in the explosions." He moved in and gave her a quick hug. Before she could react, he'd already stepped back. "I thought you were having bible study upstairs?"

April met his gaze evenly. "We were headed that way when I saw Jerome here. Oddly enough, his name wasn't included on the list Sharon gave me of your members. Nor have I ever seen him."

King smiled, the expression not lightening his eyes a bit. "The omission was inadvertent, I assure you. Jerome is often repairing the building and out of sight."

"You're a contractor?" April asked, not buying a word of this.

Jerome smiled again. "Of sorts." He eyed her thin dress. "I really would like to sit and chat with you. I'm sorry I wasn't available when you were here the other day."

While he was definitely good-looking, there was just something too suggestive about the guy. "Who did your intake inter-view?" she asked.

He shrugged. "It was five months ago, and I don't remember the guy's name. Those of us uninfected kind of separated ourselves naturally." He rubbed his buzz-cut hair. "Although I would've been more visible had I known you were looking. You're pure, right?"

"I haven't been infected," she said, her instincts humming.

King reopened his door. "If you'll excuse us, we have work to do."

Jerome winked at her. "We can set up a time for our interview if you like." Then he turned and followed King down the stairs, shutting the door behind himself.

April had no choice but to turn with Sharon. It wasn't as if she could just barge in and make him talk to her. "It's so weird that I've never seen that guy. How many other people here are hidden?" She made her way back down the hallway.

Sharon snorted. "Nobody. That was just a fluke. We forgot his name on the list, and he really is usually somewhere in the facility trying to keep us safe." She kept her head down and walked quickly.

Right. That made a whole lot of sense. Not. But April followed Sharon through the dining area to the stairs, her mind spinning the entire time. They reached the rec room for the older kids, and women sat around, some with bibles and some with what looked like glasses of wine.

The pregnant women drank red punch.

Where in the heck had they gotten the punch? April accepted a glass of wine and took a seat on a blue beanbag, watching carefully.

The mood was jovial as they chatted amongst themselves.

A four-month-pregnant woman named Sheila plunked down next to April in a pink chair. "It's good to see you back here. Decided to move in yet?"

April turned and smiled. While she couldn't exactly say that the outside world was safe, since she hadn't contracted Scorpius from any surface, she was starting to believe that it was no longer possible. "I'm still mulling it over. How are you feeling?"

Sheila was a redhead from Santa Clara if April remembered right. She was young. Maybe nineteen. Her green eyes sparkled. "Wonderful. I think I felt the baby move earlier today. We're going to repopulate the country and do it with good genes."

April stiffened and then tried to act casual. "Well, good genes would be a definite plus."

Sheila nodded. "I know, right? I think the plan is a smart one. Pastor King knows what he's doing."

"Oh, he does." April smoothed her skirt down her legs, searching for the right opening with the girl. She wasn't nearly as guarded as many of the other women. "He has been so open about everything, it's hard not to like him. The man is brilliant."

Sheila sipped her punch. "I didn't know he'd shared with you."

"Why not?" April took a drink of her wine. The crisp Chardonnay cooled her throat. "He wants me to join the Pure, so he's been very open. I just have to decide what I want."

Sheila nodded. The girl was sweet but a little simple. April hated to use that, but what choice did she have? "I wanted to be tier three, but I understand starting with the fifth tier. We have to keep the lines straight."

Lines? What lines? "I don't know," April whispered. "Do you think it's that important? Really?"

"Yes." Sheila's eyes widened. "Just think if two same-tiered ones ended up together in the future. They'd be brother and sister."

Oh, crap. This was starting to make sense. Pastor King had a genetic plan to repopulate the Earth. Like cattle? She remembered something about bovine breeding diagrams from ninth-grade biology class. "He mentioned I might be tier one, but he didn't give me my options," she said quietly.

Sheila's eyes widened. "Oh, I'd choose him. If you're in that tier, why not?"

Yeah. That's what April had figured. She set her glass of wine aside and stood. "Excuse me."

"The bathrooms are outside the left corner and are fully shielded and protected by a brick wall," Sheila said helpfully, and definitely loud enough to be heard by anybody wondering where April was going.

Wonderful. April walked out of the room and jogged down the stairs, hustling down the hallway to the basement. She gingerly opened the door and listened. No sounds. The men weren't down there any longer. Holding her breath, she tiptoed down and stopped cold at seeing Pastor King in his leather chair, facing her.

He tilted his head. "You wanted something, April?"

She looked around. "Where did your buddy, Jerome, go?"

"Back to work." King beckoned her inside. "Why are you sneaking around?"

Spirit slammed into her. "I was looking for your breeding chart." She waited for his reaction.

When it came, it surprised her. He chuckled and rolled his eyes. "Oh, that." He strolled over to one of the paneled walls and grasped a barely visible ring to pull a chart from the ceiling. "Before you lose your mind and kick me in the head, please notice that my name is not on here."

It was a freaking breeding chart. She moved closer, reading the names. "You have got to be kidding me."

He sighed, standing very close to her. "You'll notice the guy at the top is the former pastor and not...me."

She read the names. Joe Bentley was apparently tier two. What a minute. "Where the heck is Bentley? I haven't seen him in a while." In fact, the first night she and Damon joined the Pure for dinner was the last time.

"Around here somewhere, organizing something," King said carelessly. He gestured to the chart. "While this is a mite crazy, you have to realize that folks here, some of them, think they're the only survivors. That they really have to repopulate. The breeding chart prevents incest in the future."

Her stomach rolled over.

King nodded. "Yeah. I'm with you."

His name really was not on there. He pivoted and grasped her arms, turning her toward him. "So. Alone at last."

"Um, no." She extricated herself and moved back.

His smile was rueful. "I've been trying to figure out who you look like since the first time I met you, and Jerome nailed it."

She blinked. "Who?"

"Cherry Valance, the bombshell from the Outsiders. The movie they made us watch in high school?" His grin was beyond charming. "All the guys had crushes on her."

Her face heated. Nobody had ever called her a bombshell before. "I don't think I saw that."

"Well, stay true, Pony Boy." King held out an arm. "Let me escort you back to the party. I'd hate for you to miss out."

32

All my life, I've been a shield. That isn't going to change now.
—Damon Winter, Journal

DAMON WOKE, his throat on fire. He rolled to the edge of April's bed and tugged up his jeans before walking into the kitchen area. A pitcher of water sat on the counter, and he drank directly from it. His head ached dully, which was a vast improvement from the day before.

A quick look outside confirmed that the moon was high in the sky. It was about, what? Midnight? Smoke covered the orb, making it glow an eerie, deep yellow.

He set the pitcher down and looked around. April was often called to check on the kids, so it wasn't a surprise to find her gone at midnight. He was much happier waking up with her in his arms, though.

Sitting at the table, he waited patiently for her.

A scrape sounded at the door to the interior of the building before it slowly swung open. He turned, seeking her face, and had to drop his gaze a couple of feet. A child stood there, softly illuminated by a lamp in the middle of the outside room.

He reached for the lantern on the table and twisted the knob, lighting the space. "Lena?"

The little girl smiled and bounced inside. She wore small pajamas with ducks all over them, and her hair was a wild mess around her shoulders. Within seconds, she'd climbed up to sit on his lap.

He looked down at her. None of his brothers had kids, and he wasn't quite sure what to do with the little girl. In the soft light, she looked imminently breakable and fragile. "You okay?"

She nodded, smiling and showing a gap in her front teeth.

He smiled back. "You lost a tooth." Did kids still believe in the tooth fairy? They should. He needed to find something to have April leave under Lena's pillow. Wasn't there candy in one of the warehouses? It was worth a ton more than cash these days.

Lena looked around the apartment as if searching for somebody. Then she shrugged.

This was odd. Where was April? If she were out with the kids, Lena probably wouldn't be here. Unless April was upstairs with the teenagers again. "Are you looking for April?"

Lena shook her head, and her hair splayed all over. Frowning, she looked up at the newest bandage on his head that covered his stitches. Then she gingerly reached up and traced the edge of it, her small lips pursed in thought.

"I'm fine, darlin'," he said. "Just a bump."

Her eyebrow arched, making her look years wiser. Then she patted the other side of his bald head and smiled, running her hand above her ear to the crest of his skull.

"They had to shave my head. I used to do that anyway. Thought it made me look tough like Shemar Moore," he whispered.

She snorted.

All right. So maybe he didn't resemble the handsome movie

star. But April had seemed to like his head shaved, so he might keep the look if the scar wasn't too bad over his other ear. Doc Penelope had a light touch, so she'd probably done a good job with the stitches.

He focused on the little girl. If he hadn't been in April's apartment, would she have been able to just head out the door? They needed to get better security in place to protect the kids. Somebody this fragile deserved a bigger shield than they were providing. "You know to stay inside unless April or another grown-up is with you, right?"

She solemnly nodded.

Okay. That was good. "Did you hear the explosions earlier?" Maybe those had scared her enough that she couldn't sleep.

Another nod.

"You're safe now. You know that, right?" There had to be a way to reassure her.

She sighed, and her eyelids fluttered. The girl was definitely getting tired. That was good. He smiled. "Should you be going back to bed?"

Her bottom lip stuck out.

"Or not," he hastened to say. If she started crying, he'd be lost. She looked adorable with the pouty lip, too. "I'm sure April will be back soon. Do you want to wait for her?"

Lena just studied him with those dark eyes. Her coloring was interesting. Her hair was so blond it was almost white, and her eyes were a fathomless black. The mystery of where she'd come from and how she'd survived to reach Vanguard was one talked about by the soldiers sometimes. Nobody had a clue.

Damon looked back at her. "How come you don't speak?"

She shrugged, her expression almost bored.

Obviously, the line of questioning didn't spook her, so he pressed on. The girl couldn't remain silent forever. If she were in trouble, she needed to be able to yell for help if possible. "Did you speak before? A long time ago?"

She nodded. Ah. Finally getting somewhere with her. So she had been able to speak. There wasn't a physical reason she didn't speak now, so this was something she needed help with. "You're safe now, Lena. I hope you know that. You can talk, and nothing bad will happen to you." He made a note to ask April how anybody knew the girl's name. Chances were, she'd had it on something with her when she arrived, but now Damon was curious. "Do you want to talk?"

She didn't react at all.

He searched for the right questions to keep her engaged. "Sometimes, it seems like you know things about people, but that's just a coincidence, right?"

She tilted her head.

Maybe she didn't know the word *coincidence*. Or perhaps she just didn't want to share. "Do you know things about people?"

She twisted her little face up like he was crazy.

Humor took him, and he chuckled. "All right. I'll stop asking dumb questions." It was silly to think that the girl was psychic or anything. She liked to give gifts, and people would always search for meaning in things. Especially these days. "Though it'd be nice if you decided to speak at some point."

She looked around, obviously getting tired with the conversation.

Where the hell was April? Damon searched for something to say. "Are Tina and Rory asleep?" The three were rarely seen without each other.

Lena nodded.

"But you're not. Did you have a bad dream?"

She cut him another look, this one letting him know he was done asking questions. He sighed. "All right. I don't know what to ask you anyway." Interrogating known killers was easier than questioning this little bit of a thing.

Lena reached into a pocket on her duck jammie shorts and took something out.

Damon's breath caught. Present time. What in the world could she have brought him? He instinctively held out his hand.

She dropped a rusty silver cross with a smooth chain onto his palm.

He looked down. A cross? "I used to wear one of these all the time." On a necklace his mom had given him. His was gold, but the designs were similar.

Lena jerked her head toward his neck.

Well, all right. He fastened the necklace around his neck, and the cross fell to the center of his chest, just like his old one. It was definitely a man's necklace. The second it was in place, he felt centered. "Why me?" he asked simply.

She tapped the cross.

"Where in the world did you find this?" he murmured. The kids were known to investigate all the old apartments, so it wasn't a shock that she'd discovered a necklace. But again, why give it to him? Maybe she'd found it and since he was almost living in her building now, had wanted to give him a present. Or was it something more?

Her eyelids started to droop.

Ah. "Honey? Why don't you go back to bed?"

She swayed toward him and set her head against his chest. She felt so tiny and vulnerable against him. How in the world had she survived on her own before finding Vanguard?

He stiffened and then relaxed, looking down at her blond head.

She snuggled closer with a soft sigh and fell right asleep. She was small and delicate, and she was seeking some sort of shelter. For some reason, she'd chosen him.

He swallowed, careful not to move and jostle her. He'd never had a child fall asleep on him before, and he wasn't sure what to do.

Where in the world was April?

33

I never realized that a kiss could be devastating before.
—April Snyder, Journal

APRIL WALKED INSIDE to one of the cutest scenes she'd ever seen. Damon was sprawled in a kitchen chair, his head back, while little Lena slept curled into his chest. The lantern was on low, illuminating the entire room. The man looked like a natural holding the sweet girl. April's body flared alive, and she could swear that her ovaries sprang to life.

No. Definitely, no.

He slowly turned his head, and his brows drew down upon seeing her at the outside door.

She quickly stepped inside and shut the door. She liked his head clean-shaven. He looked like a total badass, which he absolutely was. Even with a child trusting him enough to sleep on him. She reached him and carefully lifted the sleeping girl from his arms. "I'll take her back to bed," she whispered.

Damon stood, looked at the outside door, and then focused

back on her. His brown eyes flared. "Where the hell have you been?"

She reared back from the heat in his terse whisper. "I'll talk to you in a minute." She hadn't thought it was a big deal to go back to the Pure, but she had promised to return when he could be on a radio with her, so...hmmm. They might be about to have their first real fight.

She walked out of the room and hurried into the younger girls' room to place Lena back in bed. Then she took a couple of deep breaths and returned to her apartment, taking her time during the walk. If they were going to argue, she didn't need to hurry for him.

Her body hummed, and her heart ticked faster.

He was waiting with arms crossed and a glower across his high cheekbones.

Her abdomen went all tingly. She swallowed and shut the door behind herself. "I had bible study at the Pure, remember?" Though it had been much more socializing than Psalms.

Tension flowed from him in a swell of heat, overtaking the atmosphere. "You had what?"

Well, he'd definitely heard her. So he must be requesting clarification because he didn't quite believe it. Her weight shifted from one foot to the other. "You were sleeping. I figured it was safe, and I knew we needed to discover the status of these people so you could deal with the gang and that Bunker you want to steal." Why in the world was she explaining herself to him?

"You went by yourself with no backup or even a line to the outside world?" He spoke clearly, concisely, and with a hint of heat.

Now she felt like a deer facing a hungry mountain lion. "Well, yes."

"I thought we were clear on the parameters of this." His voice remained low, but there was no doubt that he'd crossed over from surprised to angry. It was etched in the hard line of his firm jaw and the tight press of his lips.

If she had anywhere to go, she'd take a step back. Instead, she decided to grow a pair. "There's no need to be pissed."

His longs legs suddenly brought him to her, his gaze dark and angry.

Shit. She took that step back, but it was too late. Before she could get out another word, he had a hand on her nape and one grasping her hip.

She couldn't move.

Even worse, her hesitation hadn't sliced to anger. Nope. It had cut into full-blown excitement. Her heart thundered, and she could feel the pulse in her neck ticking wildly. Her throat was dry, but she forced words out. "What are you doing?" Yeah, her voice was way too breathy.

His hold was absolute, yet it didn't hurt. The control he kept on himself was just another turn-on. "What do I need to do? You're obviously not taking me seriously."

She was. Oh, definitely. "I didn't think there'd be a problem." Yet she'd seen a guy she'd never noticed, and she'd ended up getting caught snooping in King's office. "I may have acted a bit hastily," she admitted.

"Hastily." Amusement tinged the dark anger coming from him. "You're off the op, April."

The words cut through her haze of arousal. "I'm what? No, I'm not. You can't do that."

"I just did." His face was implacable. "I've tried to reason with you, and I warned you. You're done."

He couldn't. She smashed her hands against his bare chest. "That's not your call."

"Yes, it is." Damn it, he was right. Everybody would listen to him, even the Pure church. Probably. And he was point on the op, at least according to the Vanguard-Merc soldiers. "You're being unreasonable." She struggled slightly against his hold, not expecting to get free. Worse yet, she hated the reasonable control he exhibited.

"Too bad. It's done." He waited patiently.

It'd be better if he yelled or lost his temper, because then she could argue with him. But, no. Perfect Damon Winter kept his voice calm, and his movements controlled. "You are being such a dick."

The amusement deepened. Did anything shake this guy's control? "I'm fine if you want a fight, but my mind is already made up."

"Fine." She shoved him. "I choose fight." What was she saying?

He released her. "All right. Just how do you plan to fight me?" The amusement melded with an arrogance that he had probably earned.

How? The idiot was just asking to get kicked. She'd never engaged in a physical altercation in her life, yet everything inside her wanted to shock him. "You're a moron."

He exhaled. "That the best you've got?"

Oh, he did not. Her temper finally flying free, she cocked back her arm and shot her fist into his gut.

He didn't even breathe out heavily. "Hmm." Grabbing her wrist, he flipped her reddening hand over to study her aching knuckles. "Looks like that might've hurt."

Sparks flew through her. She shook her head, her hair flying. One kick to the balls. Just one to make him drop to the ground and take her seriously. He must've read her intent because he shifted his weight just enough to angle to the side.

"I wouldn't," he advised, his voice like molten lava.

There was no way she'd win a fight with him. Physical or otherwise. "Get out," she hissed.

He lifted his chin. "You sure that's what you want?"

Damn it. He really would leave if she asked. How could he be so reasonable? "You aren't in charge of me."

"Aren't I?" He cut fast toward her, lifting her by the waist and putting her butt against the wall.

Her mouth gaped open. Both of her breasts tightened so hard and fast she stopped breathing. "No?"

"Really?" He leaned in, his breath hot on her mouth. This close, the rim of his iris looked more amber than the darker brown of the rest of it. "If you want me to leave, tell me again. Right now, and I will."

Words would not come. Definitely those words.

"That's what I thought." Then his mouth slammed down on hers. Not soft, but hard and demanding as if he'd finally had enough.

She made a noise in the back of her throat, opening her mouth for him.

His tongue darted out and swept inside, knocking her head back against the wall.

He tasted good. Like whiskey and mint and all Damon.

She curled her fingers over his hard shoulders, her knees going weak even though he held her against the peeling paint.

His mouth plundered hers. Completely, and without hesitation. There was no other word for it. Rough and callused, his fingers shoved her dress up her legs and then found her core.

She gasped and then moaned as he slipped those talented fingers past the edge of her panties and inside her. He fucked her with his fingers like he was kissing her, deep and demanding, not giving her a chance to breathe.

"Damon," she gasped against his mouth, panting, the intensity of her need terrifying her.

He snapped the panties off, and she had a quick thought that she needed those.

Her hands fumbled with his jeans, and he took over, shoving them down to his feet. He must've grabbed a condom from his back pocket first because he ripped the wrapper open with his teeth and rolled it on.

Then he grabbed her bare butt, partially lifted her, and then pulled her down to take him. He shoved in to the hilt, fully implanting himself in her. Pain shot through her, and she bent over, her forehead slapping his chest.

He didn't stop.

Holding her hips with ruthless fingers, he hammered into her while pulling her down with each thrust.

The pain shot right into blinding pleasure, and she arched, her head going back. She dug her nails into his skin, trying to hold on, fighting to keep from just exploding into nothingness.

His thrusts were brutal and overpowering, and she started moving her hips to meet him. Her legs tensed tight, and energy coiled inside her with shocking sparks. His fingers clenched on the sensitive flesh of her butt, digging in, and she detonated.

She cried out his name, her eyes shutting to keep them from blowing out of her head. Her sex clutched tighter around his hard dick, the vibrations starting there and rippling through her entire body.

His thrusts, already savage, somehow increased in strength. Her breasts bounced up and down, enhancing every sensation already overtaking her.

He slid his hands forward and clamped them on her hips, thrusting into her one more time and then staying there. His body jerked with his climax, and his mouth dropped to her neck, where he bit her hard enough to leave a mark.

She blinked, her mouth opening and closing but no sound coming out. Wow. Just wow and then wow again. Her body felt as if she'd run a marathon, but her limbs were as relaxed as humanly possible.

He leaned back, his nostrils flared and a stain across his rugged cheeks. "You okay?" .

She swallowed and slowly nodded. He was still inside her— still partially hard. "Yes."

"Could you retract your nails?" A smile tugged on his full lips.

Oh. Whoops. She straightened her fingers and then tried to smooth the divots away. Nope. Looked like she'd marked him, too. "I think I like fighting with you." Well, the making up part anyway.

He leaned in and kissed her again, this time with a gentleness that stole her breath. "Oh, sweetheart. We're just getting started." Without missing a beat, still holding her aloft, he edged to the side and walked toward the bed, falling down on top of her. Even so, he cushioned her on the landing to protect her.

She laughed, snuggling her butt into the bed. She curled her fingers. "Hey. What's up with your abs being tougher than my fist?"

"I'll teach you how to punch after you no longer want to punch me," he said, rubbing his nose against hers, the movement sweet. "This time, you punched and hurt yourself."

He'd made sure she knew it, too. Then he'd fucked her up against the wall like a wild man.

She smoothed her hand over the side of his head, enjoying the freedom to touch him. From the first second she'd met him, she'd felt drawn. "Your skull is perfectly symmetrical."

"Good thing. I was worried about the brick, but if the skull remains intact, all will turn out just fine." He kissed her, his warm lips firm and devastating.

A brain could still be damaged even with an intact skull. He'd been lucky. "How's your head?" she asked.

His smile moved against her lips. "Everything I have feels pretty damn good right now." He withdrew from her, and she bit back a moan of protest.

"This is the most relaxed I've been in months," she whispered.

He took care of the condom, and when he rolled another one into place, her body perked up. Then he was on top of her again, taking his time sliding inside her. Inch by inch, he took her with a deliberation she felt in every nerve.

More was happening here than casual sex, but she'd worry

about that later. His dark gaze captured her as completely as his body did, and she let herself sink into it.

"This is what's going to happen," he said.

She paused in rubbing her hands down his arms. "Giving orders?"

"So you say." He kissed her harder, leaving her lips wanting more. "We're going to do this again, and then we're both going to get some sleep. After a too-warm shower tomorrow outside out of buckets, I'll go get breakfast, bring it here, and then you'll report on your observations from your visit to the Pure."

That sounded reasonable. She wrapped her legs around his waist. "I'm glad we're on the same page again."

"You've misread me." Before she could question him, his mouth was on her breast.

Within moments, she forgot about everything but how he made her feel.

Morning would come soon enough.

34

Whoa. April really does look like Cherry Valance.
—Damon Winter, Journal

DAMON WHISTLED a hard rock tune as he returned to April's apartment with two bagels and some Pop-Tarts the scouts had found the previous week. The Pop-Tarts, not the bagels. Those were freshly made and actually smelled delicious.

The cooks were using generator power to create, and at some point, they were going to run out of fuel.

Not today, though. Today, he had fresh bagels.

He pushed inside her apartment, and she sat at the table, her hair wet from her shower. It curled around her face and hung down her back. "Morning."

She looked up from a list she'd been making. "Hi." Her smile brightened an already bright day. "Bagels."

"Yes. Atticus already took a bunch to the kids, so you don't need to worry about them." He sat and handed over the fragrant bread before taking a bite of his own. It was soft and warm—and pretty much the most delicious thing he'd ever eaten. "We have to figure out a way to keep the power going."

She took a bite and moaned, her eyelashes fluttering.

The woman looked the same way when she climaxed. He grinned. At least he was as good as a fresh bagel. Then he cleared his throat. "All right. Tell me about your night." The part before he'd fucked her against a wall. His cock jerked at the memory. Yep. Gonna do that again.

"Well, it was an odd one." She started telling the story, and his body tensed one muscle at a time until she was through.

Not only was there a man they didn't know in the apartment building, but King had caught her where she shouldn't be. Damon's mouth had gone dry minutes before.

April finished talking, her gaze narrowing on him. "You okay?"

No. Fucking no, not at all. Was she freaking demented? "Yes. Just a little concerned about the danger you might've been in." It was a miracle his voice remained steady. "If this Jerome is a threat, he might've taken you out before you could report him. Or if King is a threat, same thing since he found you snooping."

She twisted her lip in thought. "I just didn't feel like I was in danger."

All right. Instincts counted, but so did training. And she had none. Zero. Zilch. "What about the breeding chart? Your thoughts?" He had to keep her talking while he calmed himself down. She was here, she was safe, and he'd keep her that way.

She rubbed her chin. "I believed Pastor King. He's not on the chart, and he seems to think it's a little silly. Then he said I look like Cherry Valance."

Damon sat back. Holy crap, she did look like Cherry Valance. Every guy who'd had to watch that movie in senior English class had had a dream or two about Cherry. Oh, he'd had to read the book for a report, too. But the film was what stuck in everyone's mind. The movie and Cherry. "The chart could've been falsified."

"Maybe."

If King wasn't in it to procreate right off the bat, what was his angle? Was it truly just to keep the uninfected safe? It didn't feel right, but Damon was off-center when it came to April. King wanted her. There was no question.

That messed with Damon's reasoning skills.

"You're awfully quiet," she murmured, playing with a wrapped Pop-Tart. "Still mad at me?"

"No," he said instantly. "We dealt with that last night."

Pink infused her face. "Yes, we did."

Amusement filled his chest. "I meant before the sex Olympics." God, she was cute. It was getting hotter outside, but he'd be up for another round if she wanted.

Her frown drew down both finely arched eyebrows. "What do you mean?"

He paused. Even her scowl was endearing. But her words didn't make sense. "I'm not following."

"No. *I'm* not following." She crossed her arms over her black T-shirt that paired way too nicely with her cut-off jeans shorts. "I thought we made up last night."

"We did." Big time with him inside her—where he wanted to be right now.

Her posture relaxed. "All right, then. What's our next move with the Pure? I'm thinking I should go back in and maybe flirt with King a little."

No. Hell to the triple of no. Damon studied her, his mind clicking facts into place. "I said you're off the op."

"Then we made up." Frustration crossed her smooth expression. "Right?"

Huh. All right. "I was mad at you, and we made up. Yes." He rubbed the non-hurting part of his smooth head. "But that doesn't change my decision on the op. You're done." Hadn't he been more than clear the night before?

"And now I'm back in."

"Sex doesn't get you back in. It doesn't get you anywhere, no matter how fucking great it was." He explained gently because she truly wasn't getting him.

Her eyes flashed a shocking blue. "Excuse me?"

Well, that had insulted her. Definitely not his intention. He cleared his throat. "On a personal level, we were fighting and made up. On a professional level, I made a decision with the facts available to me, and that sticks. The two are separate."

"You took me off the op because you were angry," she protested.

"No." He didn't make decisions like that out of emotion. Not really. "You disobeyed orders and put yourself in danger that was unnecessary and unwise. As the point person on this op, I took you right off as I would with anybody working for me. As your boyfriend, I smacked your ass. Something I'm feeling might happen again, and rather soon. There's a difference, and you might want to learn it now." Although this would be the last op she'd be on, at least if he had his way.

Her mouth opened and then snapped shut with enough force that he wanted to wince. She glared at him, expressions crossing her face in rapid succession as she thought it through.

He waited patiently. Even though he was a boot-to-the-door kind of cop, patience dictated that he wait until the right moment to move. He could wait all day for her. She was worth it.

Finally, she shook her head. "I don't want to make you mad, but no. I'm going back in."

Interesting. He liked this spirited side of her. A lot. Keeping her gaze, he reached into his back pocket and drew out one of their few still-working radios to lift to his mouth. "Winter here. All seven squads watching the Pure building, check in."

"Squad one in place," came the first low voice.

"Squad two in position," came over the radio next, followed by the other five squads, each going in order.

Damon counted their positions in his head. An eighth squad

would be overkill, yet he was still tempted. These were both inside and outside the fence, and one was even up high. "Acknowledged," he said. "Additional directive. April Snyder is not to get within ten yards of the Pure apartment building. She should be stopped if seen. A fireman's carry is permissible, if—and only if—absolutely necessary. Please acknowledge."

April's eyes widened, and her chin lowered like a cat about to strike.

"Squad one, acknowledged new directive," came the first voice.

As each squad acknowledged his new orders, April's face flushed. First pink, then crimson, then a deep red.

Finally, he slipped the radio back into place. "Any questions, baby?"

* * *

ANY QUESTIONS? Yeah. How could he be such a complete ass? She tried to find a way out of the box he'd just put her in, but there was no solution. Those soldiers, even the Vanguard ones, would stick to his orders. "I can't believe you just did that." Her throat hurt with the need to scream at him. But if he were staying in control, so was she.

"There are consequences, April." He was so calm he might as well be meditating.

Consequences? What was this? Third grade? "You are such a control freak."

His chuckle was rich and warmed inappropriate places inside her. "Look who's talking."

"Me?" She reared back.

"Oh, yeah. Cute Miss Clipboard has tried to take control of this op from the beginning." He shook his head. "You've ignored orders the entire time, doing what you want."

She swallowed. He wasn't exactly wrong. Those inappropriate

places inside her warmed more. This unmovable side of him was kind of sexy. Okay. Majorly sexy. Most people didn't outsmart her. Ever. The fact that he just did sparked her nerves wide-awake. "I wanted to help people. Those Pure women and kids."

"I know," he said, softly. "Your heart is in the right place, and I like that you want to assist folks who might need it. You're a good person."

She settled down, not quite sure where he was going. "All right."

He smiled. "You also wanted to take control and do whatever you wanted." He leaned back and studied her with freaky hawk-like concentration. "And I think you wanted to push me."

"Push you?" she burst out, her heart racing for some reason. How could that be true? "Why?"

He rubbed the stubble on his chin. "Maybe I've been too gentle with you. Taken it too slow." His words were thoughtful, his gaze piercing.

"Gentle?" she gasped. "I have a hickey on my shoulder and bite marks on my ass."

"You can still walk," he shot back instantly.

She blinked. Her thighs rubbed together, and she barely kept a moan from escaping. This conversation was quickly spiraling way away from where she wanted it to be. She shook her head to clear it. "I don't know what you're talking about."

"Yes, you do." He cocked his head to the side. "I'm in control on the op whether you like it or not. It's up to you if I take control personally."

She made a strangled sound.

"But if you give it over, baby, I ain't giving it back," he said, looking big and powerful in her small kitchen. "So think that one through completely before you throw down another challenge. Especially if you make the colossal mistake of throwing the challenge by doing something dangerous or plain-ass stupid. Again."

She threw her hands out. "How can I do anything stupid? You

just guaranteed that if I try to go near Pure again, some Neanderthal of a soldier will haul me back here as punishment."

His gaze somehow darkened even more. "Oh, sweetheart. The punishment happens when they inform me they had to put hands on you." He didn't move but somehow still took over the entire atmosphere of the kitchen.

She swallowed. "Excuse me?" It didn't come out nearly as forceful as earlier.

"I feel like I haven't been as clear as I'd like when it comes to the op. So, here it is. If one of those guys has to put hands on you because you're trying to go where I told you not to go, we're going to have a very uncomfortable conversation afterward." He leaned forward.

She frowned, heat billowing through her head. "You're kidding."

"No. You disobey orders, there are consequences. The consequences will make it not fun for you to sit for a while."

She couldn't speak. Couldn't find a word. The man was deadly serious.

His voice softened. "In a non-work capacity, just let me know when you want me taking over. That may also involve my hand on your ass and an erotic lesson, but it'll be of the more *personal* nature, and I guarantee you'll enjoy it, if you know what I mean."

Whoa. Way out of her realm of experience. Yet her breasts suddenly ached, and her panties were wet. Thank goodness she was wearing denim shorts. "I don't like this side of you," she said primly.

His grin was all wolf. "Liar."

35

I'm gonna be the first guy kicking in the door. That's a fact.
   —Damon Winter, Journal

"DAMN IT." Through the darkened sunglasses, Damon checked the old stopwatch somebody had drummed up. "The third breach is still too late." He stood on the rooftop of the Vanguard-Merc training facilities, staring down at the three houses currently being infiltrated. "The timing doesn't have to be exact by any means, but we have to get through the door faster than that, or the enemy will have time to target shoot our asses."

Jax Mercury threw down his binoculars. "All right. Should we switch up the teams again?"

"No." Damon wiped sweat off his forehead. He, Jax, and Greyson had been on the roof for hours. The merciless sun didn't give a shit that he'd just had a concussion. "I'll go in with that team."

"No," Greyson said somberly. "You still have a bruise on your brain."

Then what was Damon going to do? Wait in a van some-where? "I'm not a sniper. You, Jax, and Raze are experienced snipers, and we've found three good over-watch positions. I need to be on the ground."

"I need you as my spotter," Grey argued.

Damon sighed. "I'm no spotter. Come on, you know that." Sitting still during an op bugged the crap out of him. "Quincy has volunteered to spot for you, and he has experience."

Jax scratched his elbow, which was becoming sunburned. Sunglasses protected his eyes but apparently he hadn't consid-ered sunscreen. "I thought your job here was to strategize. Not sure your head should be in battle quite yet."

There didn't seem to be much choice.

"All right." Greyson handed over a canteen, his eyes also shielded by glasses. "Let's run it through. You've been in the sun all day and haven't eaten. If you can get the timeline right, one chance, I won't argue against your going."

That was fair. Damon tipped back the water and let his body cool.

Jax kicked rocks across the dusty roof. "Rumor has it you've given clear orders for April to stay away from the Pure. What's going on?"

Damon had been wondering when the questioning would start on that, so he gave a quick lowdown. There hadn't been time as they tried to come up with a plan to attack Twenty.

Jax frowned. "Some guy named Jerome who wasn't listed? That's all we've got?"

"Yeah." Damon took another drink and then handed the canteen over to Jax. "I have Vinnie going through the lists of people who've ever set foot in Vanguard to see how many Jeromes we find. It's odd he wasn't on either of the lists April had, though."

Jax shielded his face from the sun with his hand. "We'll figure it out. One thing at a time. Let's teach Twenty a lesson and hopefully find intel on the president and a Bunker or two. Then I'm about ready just to enter the Pure apartment building through the front with force."

Damon was almost there. "All right. Let's do this." He turned and headed for the stairs. After jogging down the four floors, he felt a little dizzy but nothing bad.

Once on the ground, the air cooled. Marginally.

He reached the team of five, who were all sweating profusely. "We're doing it again. This time, here's the plan." He laid it out, answered questions, and then gave the go-ahead. As usual, he was the first one through the door, sweeping left and taking out staged targets.

Pings sounded in the other room, right on time.

Excellent.

They cleared the house and ran outside. He glanced at his watch and looked up at Greyson.

His buddy didn't look happy, but he still gave the thumbs up. "Okay. Again," Damon ordered.

They practiced five more times until Damon was satisfied. His squad was fairly green, but they caught on quickly. "It's different when they shoot back at you," he told a kid from Oregon who'd grown up hunting. "Get some food and sleep. We go at noon tomorrow."

The kid wiped grime off his upper lip. "Shouldn't we go at night?"

Damon had thought long and hard about that part of his plan. "No. They won't be expecting us in daylight." He needed every advantage he could come up with.

The kid looked around Damon. "Um."

Damon turned to see April storming his way, her sandals clip-clopping on the heated pavement. Her hair was up and off her neck, and he could swear steam was coming out of her ears. Man, she was a sight to see. "Might want to make a run for it, kid."

The kid thought about it and then turned. "You've got this."

Even in the heat after working for hours, he loped into a jog to get away faster.

Damon watched her approach, his dick getting harder with each step. She really did look like Cherry Valance, damn it. Why she was mad this time, he had no clue. But something told him he was about to find out.

She still wore the cut-off shorts and black shirt, which stretched nicely over her tits.

Finally, she reached him.

He waited.

"You are not going on a raid tomorrow," she said, her voice a low snarl that was all the sexier for the way she held it back.

He paused. Not what he'd been expecting. Okay. She apparently had strong feelings about that, and he definitely wanted to hear her out. "Maybe we should go talk about this."

"No." She pressed her hands to her hips and levered up into his face.

A glint from the rooftop caught Damon's eye, and he looked to see Greyson and Jax fighting over the binoculars to watch him get his ass chewed. Idiots. "Honey, if this is a personal matter, and I'm thinkin' it is, let's go into the shade to talk." Where they weren't being watched from all sides.

"Don't you *honey* me," she snapped, her temper looking glorious on her. "I get the lecture from hell about putting myself in danger, and you think you're going on a raid tomorrow in the middle of the day with a fucking *concussion*?" Her voice rose enough at the end that he winced.

He wanted to remind himself that she had a point, and that this rant was coming from a place of concern for him. He really wanted to.

But he was hot, he was tired, and he was done. "Turn your cute behind around, and we'll go discuss this."

Her hands dropped, and she clenched her fists so tightly her knuckles turned white. "I am so finished taking orders from you. This is happening, and it's happening right now."

Well, he had told her to drop the challenge anytime. "Fair enough." Ignoring his pounding head, he ducked a shoulder and tossed her right over it. She'd been correct. Every time she tried to get bossy, he put her right where she was.

"Damn it," she yelled, punching him in the kidney hard enough that his stomach clenched.

A couple of his ribs might've clattered a bit, too. Since she was probably expecting another slap to her butt, he pinched her inner thigh.

She stilled completely, like the quiet before a lightning strike. Then she let loose with a string of expletives that was truly inspired. He wasn't sure how motherfucker and jackass Neanderthal dickhead flowed together so well, but the rhythm was pure music.

He pinched her again for good measure, wanting to whistle but needing to concentrate on his footsteps with the wriggling woman over his shoulder.

And man, did she squirm. He'd caught a flounder on a fishing trip with his Grandpop Jim one time that had moved like this. The little guy had shown so much spirit that Damon had released him back into the lake.

Not this fish. This one, he was keeping.

* * *

April's hair flew every direction when Damon flipped her onto her feet in her apartment. She charged immediately, punching out with all her strength.

He caught her fist with one broad palm, instantly closing his fingers over hers.

She gaped. That was something she'd seen on television once.

He'd actually stopped her punch with one hand, and now he had it. She tried to yank free, but he held tight.

Tears filled her eyes so quickly it shocked her more than him. Maybe. Panic crossed his face. "It's okay." He pulled her closer. "All right. Did I hurt you?"

"No." She snuffled into his T-shirt. The pinch to her thigh had just spurred her on. Her knuckles ached a little bit, but it was kind of her fault for trying to hit him. "I'm not a violent person," she murmured.

He pressed his hands through her hair and gently pulled her head back. "We live in violent times, sweetheart. It's okay. I can take whatever you throw."

Obviously.

How could he even think about going on a raid the next day? He was going to get himself killed. The room tilted. She couldn't breathe. Her lungs compressed, and her chest ached like she'd been hit with a bag of nickels. She leaned over, panting.

"Whoa." He rested a strong hand on her upper back. "April? What's happening?"

"I don't know." She coughed out, her vision narrowing and then fuzzing. It hurt. She started to sink to the floor. Was she having a heart attack? She was too young. God, it hurt. "My chest. I can't breathe."

Damon picked her up and headed for the door, breaking into a full-on run the second he cleared the burned grass.

She closed her eyes and gasped for air, going almost limp. He held her securely. The buildings flew by them, and people jumped out of the way. Tears fell from her eyes, and she planted a hand against her upper chest, trying to stop the pain.

They reached the old free clinic, and Damon burst inside.

Marcus Knight leaped into their way.

"Move, or I'll fucking kill you," Damon growled, his voice scarier than April had ever heard it.

Marcus took one look at her and edged to the side.

"Doc Penelope?" Damon yelled, rushing April into the smaller examination room and setting her on the table.

Penelope ran inside, drawing on her lab coat. "What is going on?" She moved efficiently forward and looked down at April.

"My chest," April gasped. "I can't breathe."

Penelope grabbed a stethoscope and listened intently. Then she took April's wrist and counted, her eyebrows rising. "Damon and Marcus, please leave."

"Not a chance in hell," Damon snapped, his eyes a raw hue. "Is she having a heart attack?"

"No." Penelope shook her head. "I don't think so anyway. Give me a minute." She looked up into Damon's face. "Trust me."

Damon looked at April, his expression fierce.

She nodded. "It's okay." The pain was lessening a little bit.

Marcus tugged him back out into the hallway and closed the door.

Penelope reached into a drawer and pulled out a small peach pill. "Open your mouth. This goes beneath your tongue."

April did as she was told, and the chalky sourness almost made her gag. It melted quickly. "Is this for a heart attack?"

"Nope." Penelope drew up a chair. "That was a Valium. I think you just had the king of all panic attacks." She reached for April's wrist again and apparently counted the beats. "It's getting better already, but you're not leaving until your pulse slows more than this."

A panic attack? "But my chest hurt."

"Yep." Penelope's eyes twinkled. "First one, huh? That's always the worst."

April took her first full breath and let her body relax. She couldn't do this. Could not be this person.

Damon poked his head in. "April?"

Penelope stood and gestured him inside before meeting Marcus in the hallway. "She can't leave until her pulse returns to a normal range."

Damon looked from the doctor to April. "Not a heart attack?" The relief on his face nearly made her cry. Then she realized she was crying. She sniffed and tried to get some air into her lungs.

"Just a panic attack," Doc Penelope said, disappearing down the hallway.

He took Penelope's seat and grasped April's hand. "It's okay. Hold on."

"No. I can't do this. I'm so sorry." Her vision fuzzed again.

He wiped the tears off of her face. "It's okay. Just take a deep breath."

She did so, struggling to get the words out. "I thought I could try with you and pretend to keep it all casual, but I can't. I can't do this, Damon. It's too much." What in the world had she been thinking to even try?

He frowned. "What are you saying?" Even so, his voice remained gentle.

She gulped down some air. "Us. We're over. There is no us." When he let go of her hand, she didn't protest. "I'm sorry." More tears fell down her cheeks. That had seriously felt like a heart attack.

He gently rubbed the tears off her face. "Maybe we should talk about this later, when you're feeling better."

She shook her head. "No. It's done." Now her heart really felt as if it was being attacked. "I mean it. Please leave."

She had to handle this alone. It was too much to be with anybody else.

Let's do this.
 —Damon Winter, Journal

THE BULLETPROOF VEST changed the day from intolerable to pure hell. Damon adjusted the straps, sweat already pouring down his back. It had to be well over a hundred degrees, and the inner-city humidity was a killer. Literally.

They'd already lost one guy to heat stroke. He'd had to head back to Vanguard-Merc territory, puking his guts out on the way.

Damon made a quick change to the attack plan, explaining it to his team until he was sure they had it. The Twenty gang house was in an old, rather affluent neighborhood toward Pacific Palisades with some taller office buildings close by.

He shoved thoughts of April out of his mind. She'd asked him to leave the night before, and he'd done so to sleep alone in his crappy apartment at headquarters. Not that he'd slept. He couldn't blame her for dumping him. There wasn't a chance in this life that he'd stop doing his job, and that was too much for most people. Not to mention a fragile softball mom who'd lost everyone.

She was smart to find somebody else. Didn't mean it didn't hurt like a knife to the balls.

His radio crackled, and he lifted it.

"Over-watch in position," Greyson said calmly. "We have visual on two targets guarding the front of the house. Sort of. They've taken up position beneath the trees in the shade. But they're in my scope."

"Others?" Damon asked.

"Negative," Greyson replied.

So everyone was inside the house. That's what he'd figured. "Take positions," he ordered his team, waiting until everyone had spread out in different directions. Then he took the lead down a side alley that had been made for golf carts until he reached the side stone fence. "Now," he whispered.

Only two slight pings echoed through the air. Damon leaned around the fence to see two Twenty members down, blood coating their purple shirts. "Two down," he whispered into the radio.

Then he started counting down. "Now," he told the two men on his flanks. Ducking low, he ran across the burned yard and past a couple of statues of what looked like gnomes. Reaching the door, he set his weight and kicked hard.

He went in to the left, and the guy to his right went fast.

A bullet winged by his left ear. He turned and fired twice, hitting a Twenty member center mass. Then he swung around. Two gang members rushed out of the nearby hallway, one already firing an AK-47.

Damon dropped to the ground, rolled, and fired three times. The guy spraying bullets flew back to hit the far wall, and then smashed onto the gun on the floor.

The kid next to him shot the other gang member right between the eyes.

Damon stood and pulled the kid who'd shot up from his knees. "Great shot, Byron."

Byron looked around. "I've been practicing." He was the whiz kid amongst them, and Jax had definitely been training him hard. Apparently, the kid had a pregnant girlfriend to protect.

Damon nodded toward the hallway. "Stay behind me." He crept close, leading with his gun. Then he listened.

"Kitchen clear," one of his men called out.

"Rec room and offices clear," another one bellowed.

Damon nodded and headed into the hallway. Last time he'd done this, he'd gotten attacked by Rippers. Staying on full alert, he cleared a master bedroom, bathroom, and two more bedrooms being used as storage for what looked like a lot of weapons and a cache of drugs.

"It's clear," Byron said, his slim body relaxing.

Damon paused, looking around. Something was off, but he wasn't sure what. Maybe it was him. His head hurt, and both of his shoulders were still sore. He looked around again.

"What?" Byron asked.

Damon straightened. "I don't know."

On his last syllable, the air vent in the ceiling crashed down, and a Twenty member dropped, already shooting.

Damon leaped in front of Byron. Pain exploded in his back, propelling both of them into the hallway. He shoved Byron to the right and spun around, firing as accurately as he could. He hit the attacker in the knees, and the guy fell.

Greyson leaped over Damon and punched the gang member in the neck, knocking him out cold. "We need one alive."

Damon gasped and rolled to the side.

Greyson was there immediately, lifting him to sit.

Agony spread through Damon's body, and he groaned. "Fuck."

Greyson gingerly removed the vest and lifted his shirt, turning him. "No broken skin." He pushed against Damon's ribs.

Damon coughed in pain.

"Don't think they're broken, but you're going to have a hell of a bruise." Greyson gently slid the shirt back into place. "You hit anywhere else?"

"No." His head was ringing, and his left leg felt a little numb from crashing to the floor. "Jesus, Grey. I need a drink."

Greyson drew a flask out from beneath his vest and handed it over. "It's supposed to be for medicinal purposes, but this qualifies. Your back is already turning a very cool reddish black with a hint of purple."

Byron shoved his glasses up his nose, his hand shaking. "Thanks for getting me out of there."

Damon tipped back a big swig of what turned out to be Jack Daniels. He handed the flask over to the kid. "It was my pleasure. Drink up, Byron. You've earned it."

Byron's brown eyes twinkled, and he took several swallows of the alcohol before handing it back. "Any news from the other two teams?"

"Negative," Greyson said, tapping his radio. "We're more than fifty miles from either, so not enough range."

Byron sobered. "Okay. Please let me know if you hear from them. They need to come this way to get home, so hopefully they'll be in range soon. I'll go organize the squad to start loading drugs, guns, and any intel." He stood and jogged down the hallway.

Ah, to be young again. Damon made to stand up, and Greyson waved him back down, sitting across from him with his back to the stucco wall and his legs extended. "Take a minute."

Damon drank another couple of gulps, letting the booze dull the pain. "Okay," he gasped.

Greyson studied him. "What's up with you? You seem off."

"I was just shot." Damon handed over the flask.

Grey took a good pull. "Yeah, there's more. Talk."

Damon studied his best friend. They were sitting in the

middle of a gang house with bodies all around them while their team stole everything they could. Seemed liked as good a place as any. "April dumped me. Couldn't take the danger."

* * *

APRIL SNIFFLED SOME MORE, staring out at the over-bright evening. She'd fed the kids dinner but hadn't eaten anything herself. Atticus had finally all but pushed her out of the rec room, telling her to go and get some rest.

How could she relax? Damon and the others were still out, probably getting shot at by the Twenty gang.

A knock sounded on her door, and she yelped. Then she ran for it, yanking it open.

Lynne Harmony stood in shorts and a white-T shirt next to Doc Penelope, Vinnie Wellington, and Samantha Steel.

"Sami." April rushed for a hug. Her friend had been working nonstop at the Century City Bunker for too long. Her curly, brown hair even seemed longer than it had been. "I've missed you."

Sami hugged her back. "Rumor has it I've missed a lot." She moved them inside. "We brought margaritas."

Tears slammed into April's eyes. "Oh, Sami."

Lynne set down a bucket with a sigh. "Where are the glasses?"

"Here." Doc Penelope shrugged off a backpack and drew out five glasses. One had the Flintstones on it. "Maureen would be here, but she's busy throwing up from the whole pregnancy thing she has going on."

Could Penelope sound any less like a doctor? April grinned through her tears.

Lynne reached for the glasses. "I offered to stay and keep her company, but she said she wanted to try and sleep."

"Yeah, right," Sami muttered. "None of us is sleeping until the guys get back."

"Moe might," Vinnie countered. "She sleeps a lot lately, even if she doesn't want to. Fell right asleep the other day when I was telling her about some of my FBI cases." She'd pulled her blond hair back into a ponytail, probably as a way to fight the heat.

"Sometimes your stories do go on for a while." Lynne poured the four glasses.

"Huh." Vinnie rolled her eyes. "My stories are funny."

But, sometimes they did go on a little past their expiration date. April nodded anyway. Vinnie was a lot of fun, and she was their resident shrink. No matter how nutty she became. More importantly, she was a friend. That mattered these days. Big time.

Sami clicked her tongue. "Who made the drinks?"

"I did," Vinnie said, her blue eyes sparkling.

That might not be a good thing. The smell of tequila wafted up. April peered into the bucket. "What exactly is this?"

"Tequila, lime juice, and real lemons scouts took off trees." Lynne handed over a full cup and waited until everyone had one. "To the badass men we love. Man, we're all Wonder Woman. Right?"

April held up her cup and cheered before taking a small sip. Holy crap. She coughed. "I don't love him." There was no reason to pretend that she didn't know why her friends had shown up with so much booze.

Vinnie pulled a chair back and sat gracefully, even in her older shorts and shirt with a bird on it. "You sure about that?"

April gestured everyone into chairs and dragged a folding one over to join the party. "Who cares? Either way, he's never going to give up being the first guy in the door. You know. The one who gets shot right off the bat."

"But he hasn't," Sami said reasonably, taking another deep drink. Her brown eyes widened. "Wow. This is great, Vinnie."

Lynne beamed. "Vinnie makes the best drinks. We all have skills." She sighed and pointed at herself. "In love with the leader of Vanguard, an ex-gang member, ex-Delta Force commander, and a guy who shoots first and asks questions later. Also known as Jax Mercury."

April took a bigger drink of the potent brew, and her stomach heaved but then settled.

Vinnie pointed at herself. "In love with a former sniper, Seal Team Six member who looks as deadly as he is and was aptly named when they called him Raze Shadow."

Okay. There was a theme here. April took another big drink, and this time, her stomach left her alone.

Sami sighed and pointed at herself. "Let me think. In love with an adorable Texan lawman who's also a medic and the first one to dive into anything dangerous. He's been shot a couple of times lately, and he jumped into a hovering helicopter to save me. Tace Justice was also named well."

These women were stronger than she was. Right? April took another drink as the sun started to go down and the air cooled just enough to be unbearable. "What about you?" she asked Penelope.

Penelope looked over her shoulder at the doorway. "I don't think we even want to go there right now. Marcus Knight is out there, and no doubt he can hear everything."

What was there to hear? Curiosity grabbed April.

Penelope took a big drink of the mixture and then started coughing wildly.

Lynne slapped her on the back, unconcerned. "I get why you'd panic, April. But he's coming back tonight. You have to believe that. So do you want to be waiting for him and some probably good loving, or do you want to sleep alone, wondering how it went?"

That was an unfair question. "I can't do it. Can't commit."

Sami looked at her over the rim of her chipped glass. It had a yellow flower on it, but the stem had faded away. "Has he asked you for a commitment?"

April paused. "Well, no."

"Why not?" Vinnie slurred, smacking her on the arm.

"Because we're keeping it casual." April might've slurred a little, too.

Sami sighed. "Then what the heck is your problem?"

What was her problem? There had definitely been one when she'd thought she was having a heart attack, but now, in the haze of the tequila, she couldn't remember what it was. "I'm not sure."

Penelope swayed on her chair. "Should we tell her?"

"No." Lynne hiccupped. "Definitely not. No, no, no."

April frowned at the woman who used be the head of infectious diseases for the CDC. Her blue heart glowed eerily through her shirt. "Why not?"

"Because, sister," Lynne snorted. "You gotta figure it out yourself."

"Yeah," Penelope said, falling right off the chair.

Vinnie gasped. "Penelope."

The door burst open, and Marcus strode inside. He took in the scene. Then he moved over and gingerly lifted Penelope up.

She snorted and laughed before hiccupping.

He sighed and looked around. "Everyone move, now. We're going back to headquarters." Pausing, he pierced April with his green-brown gaze. "You coming or not?"

37

I'm getting in deep this time. Good thing I'm still in control. For now.
—Damon Winter, Journal

IF THERE WAS a part of Damon that didn't hurt, he couldn't find it. He moved down the barely lit hallway to his digs in headquarters, wanting nothing more than to head to the inner territory to see April. But she'd wanted space, and he'd promised.

Plus, it wouldn't do to let her know he'd been shot.

It had taken much longer to clear the gang holding than he'd thought, and the moon was high in the sky now.

He shoved open his door and kicked it back shut, stopping when he realized that a lantern was ignited inside. Shit. Was he in the right room?

He moved past the narrow vestibule and saw April sitting on his bed. She still wore the barely-there shorts, only with a new tank top—this one green with flowers along the neck. Her thick hair was up and off her neck, and her cheeks were a lovely pink.

His body ached, and he'd had way too much to drink. After

the flask, they'd dove into a stash of whiskey the gang had no doubt been saving for something fun.

His place had a defunct kitchen, a living area with one sofa and chair, and a bed. Utilitarian and pretty plain. Moving as deliberately as he could, he set his gun in one of the doorless cupboards before turning to face her. "Hi."

"Hi." She wrung her hands in her lap.

His body jerked to go to her and offer comfort, but she'd obviously come with something to say, and he was going to let her voice it. "Everyone survived the raids, and we ended up with more supplies than we could've imagined as well as intel. We don't know what's in it yet, though."

"I'm so glad," she said, her eyes glowing a deep blue through the dim light.

This close to her, it was almost impossible not to touch. So he stayed on the other side of the too-small studio apartment. "How are you feeling?" he asked.

Her eyes widened. "How am *I* feeling? You just went on a raid with a concussion and got shot in the back."

Damn gossips at Vanguard. The soldiers were worse than the old men on porch steps from his youth. He'd only been back inside the territory for about an hour, so the grapevine had to have been working hard. "The vest took all of the impact. I'm careful, April."

She hiccupped.

He cocked his head. "Have you been drinking?"

"So have you," she burst out. "I heard you guys found Jack Daniels and then Irish whiskey."

Who the hell was getting the woman her information? It was like the CIA was active again. He scrubbed his hands over his face. "I've had plenty to drink, and should probably do this conversation tomorrow." When his head was clear, and his ribs had stopped protesting their existence.

"I want to talk now." Her chin firmed in that stubborn way she had. The way that made him want to take a bite.

He shoved down the impulse and tried to concentrate. "Then talk."

She faltered. Her delicate nose twitched, and the pink fled those delicate cheeks that looked as if they were made of glass. She was all curves and fragility, and the way he was feeling right now, he couldn't protect that. What he wanted after the shitty day he'd had was rough and out of control, and that couldn't happen.

He was always in control.

So he cleared his throat and focused. "You're not talking."

"Sorry." Her head lifted. "That's what I wanted to say. Sorry about freaking out earlier and saying it was over. I didn't mean it."

His heart thumped against his ribcage, and only sheer stubbornness kept him from wincing at the ensuing pain. She didn't mean it? "You're going to have to be a little clearer, sweetheart."

She huffed out what could only be considered an exasperated breath. "I don't want to break up. Or stop seeing you, or whatever label you want to put on it." She rubbed her chest. "I thought I was having a heart attack and I just panicked. Wasn't thinking. I never should've sent you off to danger thinking I didn't care."

Ah, shit. He leaned against the wall, his arms itching to hold her. "I know you care." The woman did nothing *but* care—about everyone around her. "And if I get hurt, it's never your fault." He couldn't let her carry that, no matter what happened.

She nodded. "I can try harder to keep this casual and not freak out. I'm just new to this."

The word *casual* was becoming a burr beneath his skin. It wasn't enough...not anymore.

She blinked. "And I like that you push me. It's exciting and new, and that feels good. I, ah, want to try that control stuff you were talking about. I want to challenge you."

Wh-what? Whoa. Huh. His body went from aching to full-on alive. "April."

She leaned in. "Are you into that BDSM stuff?" she whispered, even though nobody who could hear them was around.

He burst out laughing. "No." God, she was cute. "At least, I'm not into labels. I wouldn't mind binding you and making you beg." Anything more hardcore than a couple of slaps to the ass didn't interest him.

"Oh." Yep. That was relief on her classic face. "Good. I don't think I'm a nipple clamp type of gal."

Nipple clamps? Jesus. He'd never met a woman who could be adorable and sexy as hell at the same time before April. "My fingers work just fine on your nipples," he murmured, his voice naturally lowering.

Her breath caught. She bit her bottom lip. "So. Am I forgiven?"

"For being human, freaking out, and getting scared? You were never *not* forgiven." The alcohol was still flowing through his blood and covering the pain. It was also messing with his mind. "Did you reach these conclusions about us before or after drinking tonight?"

"Both," she said instantly. "This isn't the booze talking. It's me."

Okay. Fair enough. He eyed her, suddenly hungry, and not for food. "Come here, April."

* * *

April's insides turned to jelly. Damon's deep and commanding voice somehow shot through her body to land between her legs. Before she could analyze that, she was already moving to stand in front of him. "How badly are you hurt?" she whispered.

"No more than usual." He dragged her tank top up and over her head and then released her bra in one smooth motion.

She gasped, instinctively moving to cover her bare breasts.

"No." He gently set her arms at her sides. "You're beautiful. Never doubt that."

The reality smacked her in the face right then. She'd asked him for wild sex, and even a good guy like Damon had a healthy ego. His head might be splitting in two, and rumor had it his ribs were broken, but he'd still give her what she wanted. She wasn't taking very good care of him. Not at all.

The man definitely deserved better.

She took a step back. "How about we just snuggle down and get some sleep? It's been a long day and night." Without waiting for his reply, she bent to grab her shirt. Or rather, she tried to.

He stopped her with one hand across her neck. Controlling her easily and way too quickly.

Her eyes bugged, and her body went on full alert. "What are you doing?"

"What are *you* doing?" he asked, his voice like raw glass.

She faltered. "You're hurt."

"You're right." His eyes blazed, and he grabbed her hand with his free one, planting it squarely across the obvious bulge in his jeans.

Oh. Well, then. Desire rippled through her, heating what was already hot from their discussion. Her nipples hardened on their own, and tension coiled in her belly. "I can help you with that." She stroked him and licked her lips. She started to kneel.

He stopped her, and his eyes narrowed. "I don't need a pity blowjob."

Well. Her head jerked. "What do you need?" she snapped.

He leaned in, towering over her, his hand still on her vulnerable neck. "I need to be so deep inside you that you fucking stop thinking."

Mission accomplished. Her mind went blank. Every nerve ending sprang to life beneath her skin, which flushed and sensitized. "Then you should probably make that happen."

His mouth crashed down on hers. Forceful and demanding.

She'd known from the first time their lips touched that Damon Winter could kiss. This was different. He wasn't cajoling or showing her passion. This time, he was taking. Claiming what he wanted and not giving any quarter.

Her eyelids fluttered shut as he held her where he wanted her. He ripped off his shirt, released her mouth for a second to free his head, and then was right back on her. Lifting her by the hips, he had her on the bed in seconds and then ripped off her shorts.

"You'd better be ready." He fell to his knees, and his mouth found her.

She arched and cried out. He gave her no time to think. His fingers tunneled easily into her wetness, and his tongue lashed her clit. A climax hit her out of nowhere, and she clutched her nails into the bedspread, riding out the waves.

This was too much.

She gasped and tried to gain control of her heartbeat when he flipped her over. Landing on her stomach, she stilled.

The sound of his zipper releasing pierced the sudden silence.

God. Her body electrified, and a craving for him barreled through her. "Damon."

"What?" He jerked her up onto her hands and knees.

She liked this side of him. A lot. Her head spun, and her body went liquid. "I don't know. Just wanted to say your name," she gasped.

His chuckle brushed her left ear. "You'll be screaming it in a minute."

She did a full body shiver. Head to toe and everywhere in between. He reached between her legs from behind and stroked her. The sound she made should've embarrassed her, but she was way past that point. He stroked her again, and she pushed into his hand.

"There you go," he murmured, releasing her and then grabbing her hips.

She caught her breath, staring at the torn wallpaper at the

head of the bed. He penetrated her, his movements controlled, not slowing down. She arched as the pleasure edged with pain took her. He didn't slow or give her a breather. He took.

Her breath panted out, and the feeling of him overwhelmed her and almost threw her into another orgasm. Her thighs trembled.

He didn't stop until he was seated fully inside her to the hilt.

Her heart beat rapidly, and she had to balance herself with her arms because he had her legs spread. She'd never felt so vulnerable...or aroused.

He reached around her and palmed a breast before rolling her nipple.

The small pain shot down to her sex, which convulsed.

"See why I don't need clamps?" he whispered into her ear.

She trembled. "Yes."

He pinched.

She gasped and arched against him, somehow taking him even deeper.

"Ah, that's nice. We're going to explore this more later." He released her nipple and dug his fingers into her hips.

He pulled out and hammered back into her. No build-up. Just pure, raw fucking.

Her arms tightened so she wouldn't fall. The slap of his flesh against hers filled the quiet night along with his ragged breathing and her soft moans.

He was everywhere. Behind her, inside her, even over her. Damon Winter. All of him.

And he took everything she had to give.

Time moved faster and faster. Her body wound even tighter, and her lungs just gave up the fight and stopped working.

This wasn't gentle or even wild.

This was raw.

She was so close, but she couldn't quite get there. He wouldn't let her. Instead, he pounded into her, leaving his mark with each thrust.

She was frantic. Hot and desperate. She couldn't take enough of him, couldn't move her hips fast enough to find that relief.

Deeper. Somehow, he went even deeper inside her. She cried out and arched, throwing her head back. This was beyond anything she'd ever felt before. Ever even imagined. An orgasm, *the* orgasm, bore down on her like a freight train.

That tension uncoiled, and pleasure cut through her with a sharp edge. She could only gasp and ride out the storm, her limbs shaking from the intensity of it all. And he was right there with her.

Damon's lips closed over her shoulder, and he tensed. "So fucking good." He shuddered around her.

She gasped, her eyes no longer seeing the wall. Her body went soft. Pliant.

He withdrew from her, and she gave an odd mewling sound. What the hell was that? Then she flopped face-first onto the threadbare bed covers. Wow. Just...wow.

Damon returned from wherever he'd gone and lay down, pulling her into his arms before settling a light sheet over them. He kissed her forehead and held her securely against his broad chest. His heartbeat pounded against her cheek. First rapidly and then slowing to a reassuring thump.

She sighed, her body moving against his as she closed her eyes.

"April," he said drowsily, "I swear to God, if you dump me again tomorrow after you've come to your senses, I really will tan your hide."

She fell asleep with a smile on her face. She could feel it.

38

I'll do what has to be done to make this world safer for April. She doesn't need to know the details.
— Damon Winter, Journal

THE MORNING WAS ALREADY HOT, damn it. Damon's ribs felt as if they had a hammer wedged between them, forcing them apart. He ignored the pain and made his way into the war room, a half-eaten Pop-Tart in his hand. It was the caramel kind. Some asshole had taken all the ones with the colorful sprinkles.

Jax, Greyson, Raze, Sami, and Tace were already seated around the table, looking at notes.

"Hey." Tace Justice looked up, his blue eyes running over Damon's torso. "Heard you took a hit to the ribs. Want me to take a look?" His drawl was in full force this morning.

"No." Damon pulled out a chair and sat. "But, thanks." He'd bonded with the Vanguard medic already on a mission and had no problem being direct. "Welcome back, and it's good to see you. How's the Century City Bunker?"

Tace nodded. "Good. Much better food than here." He nodded at the Pop-Tart. "Where are the ones with sprinkles?"

Exactly. Damon shared a look with the guy and then glanced at the intel. "What do we have?"

Tace shoved papers and surveillance photos his way. "These are of the president and his Elite Force, still located in Lake Tahoe. Can't tell yet who's been picked for VP, though my guess is it's that guy." He pointed at a man with short, brown, buzz-cut hair. "He's been in the main office with the president a lot."

Damon studied the guy. "No name yet?"

"Nope. We don't have sound surveillance anymore. Just pictures taken by one of our guys in a tree," Jax said soberly.

Damon smiled at Sami. "Find anything in the computers?"

The woman was the best hacker still alive—most likely. She nodded, her brown eyes sparkling. "Yeah. We have proof of four more Bunkers, but I haven't narrowed down locations yet. Just Reno. And no, I haven't decrypted that copy of the computer file the president has yet." Then she sobered. "Also found Marcus Knight's medical records. Some of them, anyway."

Jax's face hardened. "It ain't good. And it looks like he was moved around a lot, so if we could crack open that head of his, we might find the other Bunkers sooner."

Damon shook his head. "He doesn't seem to remember anything from before."

Emotion flared hot and bright in Jax's eyes. "I know." He cleared his throat. "For now, we have all the intel we're going to get on the Reno Bunker, and it's in that file. We have to assume the president and his Elite Force have taken it over by now, which is fine. I still want it."

Damon took the yellow folder. "You want an infiltration plan?"

"I do." Jax studied him. "And since our intel says that the president headed that way earlier today, I want to go fast and hard before they get settled. I like that he'll be there. In fact, I've been waiting for it."

So Jax had decided to kidnap Atherton. Fair enough. Damon breathed out. "We can travel tonight and execute tomorrow."

Jax nodded. "That's what I wanted to hear. Also, excellent job on the three gang holdings yesterday. We didn't lose a soldier, and we gained reams of data to go through, a ton of drugs, and even more weapons, including some explosives."

"What kind of drugs?" Tace asked.

"Illegal and legal," Jax confirmed. "Some good pain meds, which we totally need. And a bunch of antibiotics as well as ten boxes of the Vitamin Bs."

That was a damn relief. Everyone was due for a shot. They'd determined that after the initial infection, a survivor needed a shot every week for a month. Then every month for three months. Finally, every six months.

There was supposed to be research about making the B permanent in the body, but it was at one of the Bunkers. If it existed at all. Damon shifted his weight in the chair and bit back a groan at the pain.

Jax tossed over an aspirin. "I grabbed this for you."

Damon started to shake his head when Greyson snapped, "Take it, or I swear to God I'll shove it down your throat."

Damon turned toward his best friend. "What crawled up your ass?"

Greyson's lips firmed, but he didn't speak. What the hell was going on there? Damon studied him. Lines fanned out from his eyes, which were unusually bloodshot. "Is Maureen okay?"

Grey kept unnaturally still. "She was puking all night. I don't know."

Tace turned to look at the Merc leader. "She's pregnant. That's normal."

"Maybe," Grey returned. "But she's a pregnant Scorpius

survivor, and to our knowledge, that's a bad thing for the baby and its possible survival."

Jax nodded. "Which is why we need to take the Reno bunker now. We're pretty sure the research is there."

"From the prisoner who used to work there?" Damon asked. "I'd like to talk to him."

"Of course," Jax said. "Figured you'd want to when coming up with your plan. I had him moved here when Tace and Sami came home."

Good. The more complete picture Damon could get before coming up with an approach, the better.

Greyson shook himself out of it. "Raze and I will get you our strategy and sniper positions," he said.

"I'll get you names of the teams I want to use as well as what weapons and vehicles we have," Jax said. "For now, give an update on the Pure church. I've gone through all our documents, and I can't find a guy named Jerome who I don't already know personally."

That was beyond weird. "How can there be a man here we don't know?" Damon asked. "He either got in somehow when we weren't looking, or he's been hiding since the beginning."

"Either way, I don't like it," Jax muttered. "Should we go in?"

Damon sighed. "If you do, you'll scare a bunch of kids and pregnant women." Though it might be necessary anyway. "So far, other than the mysterious Jerome, I haven't found anything wrong. April interviewed everyone, and she believes that they are there willingly. The kids seem healthy and well cared for."

"But?" Greyson asked, knowing him too well.

Damon shrugged. "Can't put my finger on it, but something is just off."

"Maybe you just don't like another man interested in April," Jax offered helpfully.

Could be. Damon didn't answer. The streak of possessiveness he felt toward her was something new and dark. But he planned to roll with it. "I can't recommend taking the apartment building right now." If they infiltrated, what then? Where would they put the people?

Jax eyed a list of what appeared to be weapons. "All right. We focus solely on taking the Reno bunker right now. Damon? That means you're up. We need a plan to start taking the country back from the president."

* * *

THE SUN CAREENED off the buildings in Reno as if fighting Scorpius for dominance in destroying the world. Heat bounced between cement and glass, turning the town into an inferno with no blaze. President Bret Atherton sat back in the black SUV next to a stunning blonde, letting the air conditioning cool him. Someday, they'd be out of coolant as well as gasoline, but not today.

"I don't like your plan," Jerome Blankenship said from the front seat. "Let me shoot my way in, and then we'll reason with whoever is still standing."

"I'm the President of the United States," Bret said, sliding his hand across the blonde's thigh. In deference to the heat, she'd worn linen pants and shirt today, showcasing her perfect body. "What do you think, Georgia?"

The woman tipped up her sunglasses. "I just want to get inside a lab again." Her eyes were the wrong color of green and her voice a tad too low, but she was beautiful and could give a blowjob with the force of a new vacuum cleaner.

Bret squeezed her taut thigh. When Georgia had arrived with Dr. Ramirez, Bret had instantly dumped the grad student he'd pretended to be engaged to.

This woman was at least a doctor, like his Lynne. She'd do for now until Lynne came back home.

Blankenship cleared his throat. "Our scouts say there's been movement between the Century City Bunker and Vanguard territory. That means they're headed this way next. We know that."

Bret nodded. "Agreed. They'll have the intel by now." Sometimes prey just walked right into a good trap. "Let's do what we need to do and get out of here."

"Affirmative," Blankenship said.

Bret opened his door. "I'm tired of waiting. Let's go." He'd been invincible since Scorpius had changed him on a cellular level, no matter what the doctors said. Much more than his brain had been altered by that mysterious bacteria found in a meteorite. He kissed Georgia on her smooth cheek and shut the door.

He'd read her file, and he knew she wanted into her lab to continue her research with Ramirez. On nights when she worked late, after falling into bed, she called out Marcus Knight's name. With fierce anger.

Bret would get to the bottom of that in his own time.

For now, he had a facility to command.

Blankenship motioned three squads of soldiers into formation, all with the directive of protecting Bret at all cost.

Bret didn't bother telling them he was already protected.

They walked through the door of the Thoroughbred Casino and Hotel, which had been a working gambling establishment— as well as a CIA front. Below the casino were five floors that were now a Bunker.

The air was stale and somewhat cool, and silent slot machines stood in every direction. Dirt and poker chips covered the carpet.

The soldiers instantly engaged the flashlights on their vests.

They reached a stairwell behind a bunch of blackjack tables, and the lead soldier opened it easily. Interesting.

Silence met them from below. Bret kept his shoulders straight and followed the two squads down several flights until he reached the bottom. Still...nothing.

He waited as a door was opened.

"Please wait here, sir." Blankenship went in, gun sweeping. In less than two minutes, he returned. "The place is cleared out, and they left a mess. Looks like an explosive was rigged but didn't detonate. My guy is studying it now."

If it didn't go off, then notes would still be here. Bret could finally find the other Bunkers. Just how many were there?

A soldier jogged up. "The bomb is dead. No worries. Come on in, sir."

The silence was eerie. "Get this place running," he ordered. "They wouldn't have had time to take the generators or all of the fuel." The group assembled there must've run after Greyson Storm had infiltrated them and kidnapped Zach Barter. The question was...where did they go?

Bret ignited his own flashlight and strode down the pristine white hallway. The walls glowed and glistened, and soon, he reached what used to be a lab. A soft hum caught his attention.

Walking past file cabinets to another room, he stopped short at seeing the aquarium that took up an entire wall. The generator still worked for it, and luminous jellyfish swam deep into its recesses. Another aquarium housed squid, also floating lazily.

He watched their graceful movements. They were both chock-full of Vitamin B and could restore themselves in life. The cure to Scorpius, if there was one, lay in their DNA.

He didn't care.

A clip-clop of heels caught his attention, and then the scent of pure roses reached him.

Georgia moved up to his side. "They didn't kill the specimens," she murmured.

The bomb would've, no doubt. "Is this like the lab where you worked?" he asked.

She looked around and moved toward the one unblemished wall before striding to the desk. "It has to be here." Ducking low, she pulled a lever.

The door opened, and battery-operated lights instantly ignited down another long and white hallway.

Cell doors were set every few yards, all of them open. The smell of blood, sweat, and urine instantly filled the air.

Satisfaction curved her lips, and she looked like a cat in the dim light. "Yes. This is definitely like the lab where I worked." Her voice was a low purr. "Of course, these specimens are gone." Turning toward him, her eyes lasered through the darkness. "You really must retrieve a couple for me."

He studied her. If he squinted, she almost looked like Lynne Harmony. "Retrieve? I take it you know where you can find one or two?"

"Well, one." She lifted a slim shoulder.

"Marcus Knight?" he guessed.

When she smiled, her canines looked out of proportion in her mouth.

He shook off the fanciful notion. "Georgia?"

"Yes. He could take anything we gave him, and I almost had him turned into the perfect killing machine. I'm not done with him." Her voice deepened to the pitch she used after sex.

Awareness brought Bret up short. He sometimes forgot that everyone had his or her own agenda. His was the most important, but not everyone realized that. Even so, the idea that she had plans to torture Jax Mercury's brother in the future made his dick rock-hard. "I'll get him for you, sweetheart. That's a promise."

Her chin lowered, and she breathed out, her nipples pebbling. "Thank you, darling. Marcus is special." She smiled again. "Every girl needs a lapdog."

39

Sometimes it's easy to forget that kindness takes true strength.

———April Snyder, Journal

APRIL CARRIED warm cups of juice into the younger kids' playroom, fondly remembering the days when she could get ice with a push of a button. Now there was no ice—period. She set the cups down on a bright red table in the middle of the room, and the kids rushed for it.

Little Rory, his blond hair a mess around his face, grasped a cup first and then handed it over to Tina instantly. The girl's brown eyes sparkled, and she smiled at him.

They were the best of friends. How in the world had they found each other and then survived before the Vanguard soldiers came upon them? April rubbed her chest. It was a miracle. Sometimes, even she had to wonder if there was something bigger at play. How had the kids survived?

A shadow filled the doorway, and she partially turned to see Marcus standing there. His gaze was direct, and he shoved his hands into his front jeans pockets as if to show he was no threat. With his size, he was dangerous whether he wanted to be or not. But it was time for her to give him a chance. "Marcus. Come on in."

His expression didn't change, but he strode inside, looking toward where the kids had settled in to play games and drink their too-warm juice. "Penny wanted me to check on you. After the panic attack and then the night of booze." His voice was more hoarse than Jax's. By far.

April arched an eyebrow. "She's sending you on errands now?"

His grin was quick and unexpected. "Yes."

April stared, almost entranced. Marcus Knight had gone from deadly to shockingly handsome with one grin.

He was back to glowering now, however. And eyeing the door.

It was rare to see him away from Penelope. "You're making progress," April said softly.

"So they say," he said, shuffling his feet. "I don't like being away from her, but that obsession has to stop. Scorpius can't rule me."

That was a favorite phrase of Vinnie's. Was Marcus seeing the shrink? Made sense. The bacteria messed with whatever section of the brain held empathy, giving sociopathic tendencies to everyone. Some of those turned obsessive. She'd seen it several times in the past couple of months. One guy had even been obsessed with feet. Couldn't see enough of them. Where was he these days anyway? The guy had been a mechanic.

Lena bounded up and jumped for Marcus before April could intervene.

The man easily caught the girl and swung her up before gently depositing her back on her feet. He dropped to his haunches so they could be eye-to-eye. "Nice jump."

April gaped. Had that just happened?

Lena clapped her hands gently against Marcus's cheeks.

He studied her. "If you don't talk to me, I don't know what you want."

April held her breath. Would the little girl finally speak? Maybe Marcus, as tortured as he was, could be the one to get through to her.

Lena watched him beneath surprisingly dark eyelashes. Then she tweaked his nose.

April's jaw dropped. She stiffened in case Marcus freaked out, but she needn't have bothered.

Marcus chuckled. "You're a feisty one."

Lena snorted and then turned to run back to her friends.

Marcus slowly stood. "Okay. Bye."

April shook her head. "She likes you, Marcus." The girl settled in with Tina and Rory, reaching for a playing card. "I wonder if you can get her to talk." Lena didn't act like she was troubled, but she wouldn't speak. Marcus definitely had a tortured soul. Maybe somehow they recognized something in each other.

Marcus watched the kids play for a minute. "Perhaps she doesn't have anything to say."

A simplistic and yet profound statement. April looked at him, measuring him. "It'd be better for her, a sign of healing if she started communicating."

"She is communicating. You just don't like how she's doing it." Marcus focused back on April, his eyes more green than brown today. "Let her be who she needs to be in this world. If she decides to talk, she will. If not, then...not."

That was more words in one sentence than she'd heard him speak in the last several weeks. And it seemed as if he weren't just talking about little Lena.

How many people had given this new Marcus a chance? It seemed like everyone walked on eggshells around him. She made up her mind right then. "Would you like to help with the kids?"

His eyebrows rose. "Huh?"

Yeah. This was the right decision. "The kids like you and obviously feel safer when you're around. Lena is much freer. So I was wondering if you'd agree to spend some time every day around them. Playing or just hanging out. It'd be good for them." And probably good for Marcus.

His jaw went slack and then firmed again. "I, ah, don't know. I'll have to think about it." He shuffled his large feet. For the first time, Marcus looked surprised. An emotion other than anger, blankness, or amusement. Human.

April smiled. "Thank you. I'll get you a schedule as soon as I can." She really needed to find a new clipboard. It was time.

"Okay. I guess. Maybe." His uncertainty was endearing. He turned for the door and halted when Damon filled it. His shoulders went back, and his chest broadened. "We have a plan yet?" Marcus asked.

Damon walked inside, his gaze raking Marcus. "We?"

Marcus nodded, a muscle now visibly ticking in his jaw. "I'm going on the raid."

Damon pursed his lips, looked as if he were going to argue, and then caught sight of the kids watching avidly. "You should go talk to your brother."

Marcus strode away and out of the room without another word.

Damon studied her. "Why was he here?"

April's stomach flip-flopped. Their night before had been wild, and she was falling deeper with the ex-cop. But it was too late to worry about that. So she forced a smile. "I think Doc Penelope is sending him places so he gets used to being without her. It's time he gave her space."

Damon rubbed a new bruise across his jaw that he must've gotten at the gang house. "Do you think there's something between them?"

"Dunno." If there were, it had to be majorly intense. Not that what April had going on with Damon wasn't. This was beyond intense and miles outside her comfort zone. But she kind of liked it. "I think he'd jump in front of a bus for her."

"Without question," Damon agreed. "I worry about her, though. What kind of pressure is she under?"

April mulled it over. "I don't know, but I think Doc Penelope can handle anything. Whatever they went through in that Bunker definitely bonded them." Though it was sweet for Damon to worry. "I'll make a note to talk to Penelope, though. Just in case."

"You'll keep me updated?"

Always. She nodded. Her chest warmed at his trust and acceptance that she knew what she was talking about. "I'm thinking of finding a clipboard. You know, just to stay more organized."

His eyes flared. "Baby, I would love to see you with a clipboard." His voice deepened even more. "And nothing else."

Her body went all tingly. How did he do that? The sweetness of the moment was overshadowed by the mission coming up. She wanted to act naturally, but her hands shook, and her stomach hurt. How did Lynne Harmony survive being in love with Jax?

Not that April was in love. Nope. She shook her head. No way would she be dumb enough to let that happen. Right?

A soldier entered the room. What was this, Grand Central Station? She turned.

"Hi, ma'am." The kid looked about eighteen but wore a gun on his thigh and the Merc black T-shirt. "I'm supposed to bring you this." He handed over a folded piece of paper. After giving a nod to Damon, he turned sharply and strode out of the room.

"Bet he was ROTC," Damon said thoughtfully.

April shrugged and unfolded the note to read the delicate script. "It's from Sharon. The Pure gang is having Bunko night." She'd played Bunko way back when. Nostalgia swept her.

"No," Damon said. "I can't cover you because we're doing a couple of run-throughs and then taking off. It makes more sense for us to travel at night."

"How far is Reno?" she asked, turning the note around in her hand.

"Eight or so hours...without problems," he said.

Rogue gangs and Rippers still patrolled and set traps on the major highways as well as well-traveled side roads. So there would probably be problems. "What time are you leaving?" she asked, her stomach already starting to hurt.

"Hopefully around ten. I'd like to be in place in Reno for an attack at dawn." His voice remained level, and his body was relaxed, but his gaze was searching.

An attack. At dawn. Her throat constricted, but she kept her voice level. "I heard that the president has probably already taken control of the facility. The Elite Force will be waiting for you." Surely they'd heard of the raids on the Twenty gang houses by now. Vanguard wasn't the only organization with scouts watching everything in the city and reporting back.

Damon rolled his eyes. "This place is worse than a knitting factory. Can't anybody keep their damn mouth shut?"

She turned to fully face him. "Why? We're supposed to share this kind of stuff." She lowered her voice to a tense whisper, oddly hurt. "Even if we are just fucking." A quick glance over her shoulder confirmed that the kids couldn't hear her.

His chin went up, and his eyelids dropped to half-mast, giving him a predatory look. "We're doing more than that, and you know it."

She squirmed beneath his gaze but kept her mouth closed.

"In addition, we are *not* supposed to share mission details. If I do nothing else right, I'm shielding you from that." He cupped her cheek, his palm callused and warm.

"There's no shield in this world." She turned her face and kissed his lifeline.

He tapped her on the nose, the motion playful. Then he dropped his hand and looked at his watch. "I have to go but will meet up with you after dinner."

To say goodbye. She bit her lip.

He took the paper from her and read the script about Bunko again. "Do you want any more discussion on this?"

"You said it can't happen," she said simply. The last thing she was going to do right now was make him worry when he was going off to fight the Elite Force and blow up the entrance to a casino. She wanted him to concentrate and focus, and definitely come back safely. "Okay?"

"Promise me you won't go into that church while I'm gone. I can't explain it—my gut tells me something bad is going on or will soon."

She nodded. "I promise. We can argue about my next step when you get back from Reno."

"Now that's a date." He pressed a hard kiss to her mouth and then walked away.

40

Brothers. Enough said.
　　—Damon Winter, Journal

SINCE NOBODY WAS WATCHING, Damon pressed a hand to his aching ribs as he waited outside Jax's war room in the vestibule that used to be the entry for the whole building. He'd been planning for hours, going over ideas with his squad before heading back to the headquarters. The door was shut, which was rare, so he figured he'd wait a minute.

Raised voices had him lifting his head.

Then something crashed against the wall, shaking paint down his shirt. Releasing his side, he pushed open the door to see Jax and Marcus separated by the ornate table, facing off.

"You are not fucking going," Jax snapped, crimson staining his sharp cheekbones.

"Yes, I am." Marcus was by far the calmer of the two, which served only to show how deadly he'd become. "You can't stop me."

If that didn't sound like a younger brother challenging an older one, Damon didn't know what would. He stepped into the room and shut the door, leaning back against it. While this was no doubt personal, he was in charge of the op. Besides, dealing with brothers was a learned skill, and he had it.

The brothers ignored him.

Jax shook his head. "We just got you back. I'm not letting my brother return to a Bunker. Ever."

"Half-brother," Marcus returned.

Damon winced. Ouch. Strong punch there.

"Bullshit," Jax countered. "Neither one of us knew our fathers, and she made up our last names. We could have the same sperm donor for all you know. She did have repeat clients."

Marcus didn't so much as blink.

It was Jax's turn to go for the jugular. "If you leave here, Penelope is all alone. Sure you can cut the umbilical cord for that much time? And distance?"

Marcus growled.

Yikes. Going dark there. Damon calculated the distance should he need to take one of them down. Arguing was fine, but if they went for broke, he'd have to put a stop to it because he needed Jax in one piece for the attack.

Marcus's fingers folded into a fist.

Damon tensed.

"I am going, whether I'm part of your group or not," Marcus said, his voice a hoarse snarl. "I lived in more than one of those fucking places, and I know my way around."

Good point. Damon studied Jax. Torment burned hot and bright in the man's eyes. "I don't need you for this."

"You don't need me for anything," Marcus countered. "But I'm going. I wasn't alone in those cells, Jax. There were more like me. A lot more. And if we find any of them, I need to be there. Trust me."

Jax lifted his head. "Marcus."

"I'm done. Take me, or I go alone." Marcus turned and strode for the door.

Damon moved out of the way, his gaze on Jax. Then he shut the door, waiting.

Jax stared at the table for two seconds. "Goddamn mother-fucker," he snapped, swinging and arm and swiping a stack of papers off to hurl against the far wall. His chest heaved.

Damon watched the documents cascade gently to the hard floor.

Jax turned toward him, his expression stark. "What would you do?"

"I'd let him come," Damon said, leaning back against the wall. His ribs resettled, and the pain lessened. A little.

"Are you nuts?" Jax turned his formable anger on Damon, his fists clenching.

"Nah." Damon rolled his neck. "I don't think so anyway. Haven't had Scorpius, so I have a better chance of still being sane than the rest of you."

Jax's chin dropped, and he looked as if he were about to charge. "This isn't funny."

"I ain't laughing." Damon hurt for the guy, but they didn't have time for the personal shit right now. The clock was ticking, and he had his op timed perfectly. "I think he needs to face that place."

Jax shook his head. "He doesn't remember his life. None of it. That place, or one like it, destroyed him."

"He's not destroyed," Damon said quietly. "Oh, he's different, and he might have no clue who he is. But he's here, and you're trying too hard to make him be who he was. That is never going to happen. That guy is gone."

Jax dropped into a fighting stance. "I'm not trying to do anything."

"Sure, you are." And it was totally understandable. "But he can't be that person."

"You have all the fucking answers." Jax stood straight again, obviously having decided not to attack. Yet, anyway. "What would you do? If this was your brother?"

"I'd thank God my brother still breathed," Damon shot back instantly. "Then I'd get to know the new version of him, somehow. He's still your brother, Jax. He needs you." When had Damon become the voice of reason for Vanguard as well as for the Mercs? "He's lost, and he's angry. Both of you can't be furious at the same time. Both of you can't be lost."

"I don't know where to start." Jax looked down at the mass of papers and sighed.

"Start with trust." The metal cross Lena had given Damon rested beneath his shirt, somehow grounding him. "Bring Marcus on the raid. Show him you're giving him a chance."

Jax leaned down to gather papers. "It would be nice to get him away from Doc Penelope for that many hours. I'm sure she could use a break from her constant bodyguard."

Curiosity swept Damon, but now wasn't the time to gossip about love lives. If they did have that.

Jax stacked the papers. "All right. Make a place for him in the plan, but make sure he's covered at all times."

Damon already had. "You've got it." He glanced at his watch. "I need to go interview Dr. Zach Barter about the facility just to make sure I've got it right. Any recommendations?"

Jax's nostrils flared. He dug a key out of his pocket and tossed it to Damon. "Yeah. Stay on your toes. He's brilliant and crazy."

Yeah, that's what Damon had heard. He easily caught the key. "Okay." He opened the door.

"Damon?" Jax said.

"Yeah?" Damon partially turned around.

The Vanguard leader met his gaze directly, some of the torment gone. "Thanks."

Damon nodded. Then he turned and strode across the vestibule and unlocked the door. Taking a deep breath, he descended to one of the basements in the main headquarters. This one had been sectioned off by Jax—for good reason. As soon as Damon rounded the landing for the cells, he straightened his body and dropped his hand from his ribs again.

The first cell unlocked with an old-fashioned key, and he walked inside, not bothering to lock the door behind him. The lantern was up high and barely on.

Dr. Zach Barter sat at a metal table across from him. A cot had been pushed over to the side, along with a bucket by the far wall. "Here to hit me?" he asked, apparently unconcerned.

"I'd rather not." Damon pulled out the only remaining chair and sat, studying the man who might've caused the pandemic to spread.

Barter had movie-star good looks. Blond hair, blue eyes, smooth face. Handsome with cunning glittering in those orbs. He'd been a junior doctor, or whatever they were called, to Lynne Harmony at the CDC. He was also the asshole who'd injected her with an experimental concoction and turned her heart blue.

Jax had taken him prisoner not too long ago, and he'd been kept at the Century City Bunker until Tace and Sami returned.

Damon waited patiently. He'd read up on Barter lately, and he knew his mark.

Barter lasted almost five minutes. "All right. You win the silence contest. What do you want?" He had a bruise across his forehead and what looked like fingermarks around his neck.

"I read all the info you gave us on the Reno Bunker and wanted to clarify a couple of things." Damon sat back as if he had all the time in the world.

Barter eyed him and then scratched his arm. The jeans and Metallica T-shirt didn't look right on him. The guy had probably worn button-down shirts all the time before the pandemic. "Sounds like I'm in a position to negotiate a little." His teeth were still a perfect pearly white after being imprisoned.

Damon tsked his tongue. "Not even close. Is there something you think you want?"

Barter leaned forward, clasping his hands together. "A couple of things. First, I want the medical records on Maureen Shadow. She's pregnant after surviving Scorpius, and I'd sure like to tell her when she's going to lose that baby." His eyes nearly glowed in the darkened space.

Damon kept his face nearly bored. There was research in Reno that would help Maureen and other pregnant women. He had to stay focused. "No. Next?"

"An hour with Lynne Harmony." Barter patted his chest. "I turned her heart blue, you know."

Yeah. And then he'd purposefully spread the pandemic throughout the population. Damon smiled. "Counter-offer. Tell me what I want to know, and I won't cut off your balls."

Barter snorted and then sobered as he studied Damon's face.

Damon slowly nodded. "Yeah. Wasn't talking figuratively." He leaned forward now, keeping Barter's gaze. "I know you raped your way across the country, infecting women. The law is gone, so we make up our own for criminals. You need to be neutered."

Barter's mouth opened and then closed. He cleared his throat. "My notes are accurate."

"Have you met the president?" Damon asked.

"No. We kept our Bunker secret. The succession changed so often and so rapidly that the decision was made to keep silent until the world leveled out." Barter sniffed loudly. He looked at the unlocked door and then back at Damon.

"Tempting, right?" Damon smiled. "I'm really hoping you go for it." As a mind-fuck, it was a good one. "With your research, did you find a cure?"

"No, but one of the labs shared information about helping a fetus survive the bacteria that's in the mother's body," Barter said, so helpful now. "But all of that information is in Reno. I don't have it, and they didn't give details."

"Where're the other Bunkers?" Damon pressed.

Barter shook his head. "I don't know. We communicated via encrypted email, and none of us gave our locations." His voice held the ring of truth.

So the computers in Reno were essential. Damon needed a plan to use the explosives and not take out key objectives. "All right." He yanked a notepad out of his back pocket. "We're going to go through the schematics of this place floor by floor, and if you give me any misinformation, I will kill you."

Barter looked up, his eyes guileless. "If you survive, that is."

Yeah. That.

41

He has to come back to me. He just has to.
    —April Snyder, Journal

APRIL HADN'T BEEN able to eat dinner. She checked on the kids, found the teenagers engrossed in writing a screenplay, and the younger kids enthralled with Atticus at his finest storytelling, so she returned to her apartment to clean.

The place might be a dump, but it would be spotless. She had to use the cleansers very sparingly, but when she was finished, the apartment smelled a little bit like lemons and bleach.

She looked at the threadbare sofa and sighed. Yep. Still a dump. But at least it was shelter.

Thunder cracked outside, and she jumped. What the heck? Moving for the window, she looked out. For the first time in a month, clouds rolled across the sky, partially covering the rising moon. The air electrified, charging for a lightning strike.

So not good. They couldn't take another fire.

Then her gaze caught on him. Damon Winter strode toward

her down the street, looking broad and deadly in the oncoming storm.

Her breath snagged.

The moonlight that escaped the clouds cut over his hard expression. His darker skin molded over his angled features, and in the evening light, his eyes were an amber brown. Now that was a beautiful man—in a totally badass way. He wore a black T-shirt over faded jeans with a gun fastened to one thigh, giving him that edge of danger that had called to her from the start.

Her body did a full-on roll from head to toe and back up.

He reached her crappy lawn area and was at the door within seconds.

She opened it, looking up, words totally caught in her throat. Emotion slammed into her even harder than the desire that had taken her earlier, so she moved to the side and let him in, trying to regain control of herself.

He moved inside, and his masculine scent was tinged with the smell of ginger and leather. He must've been wearing a knife sheath somewhere on his body.

She shut the door and cleared her throat, turning to face him. All she wanted to do was barrel into his arms and beg him not to go. "When do you guys leave?"

"Thirty minutes." His voice was a low rumble. "The plan is a good one, April."

It had to be. He was the best, right? "I know." She wrapped her arms around herself in a pathetic attempt to self-soothe. There were so many things she wanted to say, but none of the words came. Her feelings were so jumbled, she'd be speaking gibberish anyway.

His gaze intensified. "I'm not asking for anything from you, but I want you to have something from me."

She blinked.

"Again, just keep this in case, well...in case." He reached into his back pocket and drew out a ring.

She took a step back and hit the door, panic slicing through her.

He chuckled. "Just hold it for me. If something happens, I wanted you to have something to remember me by."

If something happens. Something always happened these days. She sure as hell didn't need a ring to remember Damon Winter. The man was imprinted on her from body to heart. But, a ring?

He sighed and grasped her hand, dropping it into her palm. "This was my mom's, and it's all I have left. You can give it back to me when I return." He leaned in and brushed his mouth against her frozen lips. "It has been my good-luck charm."

"Then you have to take it," she burst out. He couldn't go charmless.

"Lena gave me a new one." He patted his T-shirt at the chest. "I want you to have that one."

She looked down. The ring was white gold with a two-karat diamond surrounded by smaller sparkles. "It's stunning."

"Dad knew his stones," Damon agreed. "I never told you this, but she was the last to go. Handed over the ring and made me promise to give it to somebody worthy. Somebody she'd love."

No, no, no. April couldn't look away from the stunning solitaire. "Damon."

His knuckles brushed beneath her chin, and he lifted her face. "It is what it is, April." His gaze was so gentle it tore her apart. "I won't say the words if you can't hear them. It's okay. I understand."

She couldn't breathe. Her chest hurt. The walls started to close in like last time. "How?" she whispered.

He released her. "How, what?"

She shook her head, and her hair tumbled out of the clip. "How can you even think about the words? You had it all. Your entire life. A family and parents. Real parents who cared. And you lost it all. All of that."

His gaze softened. "Yeah."

"Then how? After you've lost everything, all of them, how can you even think of...more?" She really didn't get it.

"Because I had it all," he murmured. "I know what it feels like, and I want it again, no matter how long I have." His fingers skimmed the side of her face. "It's that foundation that counts. Would you give away any of the minutes you had with Don or Haylee? Any of them, even if you knew you'd end up right here and right now?"

Tears sprang to her eyes, hard and fast. "No. Not a second."

"Exactly. It's those times that matter, not the rest." He leaned in and kissed her nose. "And I know the jury is out on this, but I don't believe we're all done. I think I'll see them again, and I know you'll see your baby again. Someday."

Faith. It was such a rare thing to find in anybody these days. Her body felt like it weighed a thousand pounds. "How can you believe?"

"How can I not?"

She didn't have an answer for that. For anything, really. This was too much, and she wasn't him. Nobody was that strong. Only him.

He leaned down and kissed her, his mouth gentle, and his lips firm. The kiss was a promise. Then he stepped back. "I'm trusting you to stay safe and away from the Pure church while I'm gone."

She swallowed. "I'm trusting you to come back."

With one last, long, searching look at her, he opened the door and stepped outside. The door shut quietly behind him.

She moved to the window and watched Damon Winter walk calmly into the storm, her heart shattering.

* * *

THE STORM BLEW in out of nowhere and impeded their trek north, but at least it kept roving bands of killers and Rippers away. They'd made good time—better than Damon had anticipated. It was already past dawn, but the sky wasn't lightening like he'd hoped.

He jogged across the rooftop of an office building in Reno, the stifling wind slapping against his face. Lightning zigzagged white and hot in the distance, lighting up the nearly purple clouds.

"More fires coming," Greyson said soberly, already stretched out on his gut with his eye to the scope of his deadly-looking rifle. His legs were relaxed, and he'd pushed a lot of the small rocks out of the way to create a nest.

Fires were a concern for another day. Damon nodded at Quincy, who sat next to Grey as a spotter. "See anything?"

"Negative," Greyson said. "Except for Raze on the roof of the office building two clicks north. He's in position and has put me in his scope more than once."

Damon grinned. "Just don't shoot each other."

"Copy that," Greyson said. "Unless we get bored. Then we could play a game of who gets closest."

Quincy snorted.

Man, snipers had weird senses of humor. Damon clenched and unclenched his hands as the adrenaline took him over, preparing for the breach of the building. The feeling was one he was accustomed to...and he used it. Adrenaline sharpened the senses and focused the muscles. "You've been in place for nearly two hours. Shouldn't there be at least one patrol on duty?"

"Yes," Grey said, not moving. "When I infiltrated last time, that's how I got in. They had a rotating schedule."

It didn't make sense for the Bunker soldiers to have altered their protection details because of the infiltration. They should've tripled them. "I don't like this," Damon said.

Quincy pushed his hat back onto his head. "They know we're coming, right? There had to be lookouts on the way with enough radio range to call in a report." He pushed pebbles out of the way and leaned on his hand, stretching his back. "They're waiting."

Yeah. That was a good possibility. But they would always be

waiting, and it was time to strike. "How good is the intel that the president headed this way?" he asked.

"Eyewitnesses," Greyson answered. "But that was days ago. He might be gone. But if he's here..."

Taking the president would be more than Damon could've dreamed. "If he comes out front—and you have to shoot him—don't kill him." It probably went against sniper training to shoot to wound, but Damon didn't care. "We need him."

"Agreed," Greyson said. "Though let's just worry about winning this thing first."

Fair enough. Damon clapped him on the back and then turned around, staying low and clearing the roof before jogging down the stairwell to reach what used to be the lobby. Jax, Marcus, and two squads of soldiers waited for him.

The other squads were approaching the casino from other directions.

Damon took a deep breath and lifted his radio to his mouth. "We are a go." Ducking his head, he turned and ran out into the charged air and down the street until he reached the casino. He opened part of the door, and Jax the other. The explosives team ran inside, their flashlights already lighting their way.

He counted. One. Two. Three. Four.

"Fire in the hole," came over the line.

He and Jax released the doors and hunched over. The explosion rocked the side wall, but the glass remained intact. "Go, go, go," he ordered, turning and running full bore through the defunct casino, his boots smashing poker chips and glass.

The demolition guys had taken their positions, their guns pointed at the gaping hole behind the blackjack tables. An almost glowing white wall showed through next to stairs. He drew his weapon and slid onto the stairwell, pointing down.

Nothing.

Just stairs.

He cut Mercury a look and then started down, his shoulders

relaxed, his focus absolute. He motioned soldiers in on every floor and then kept descending until he reached the very bottom where Zach Barter had said the labs were located.

Marcus was hot on his heels.

Where were the soldiers and scientists?

He kicked open the bottom door and swept in with Marcus and Jax right behind him. Silence. Pure and deep silence. Flicking on his light, he swept the too-white floor and walls. Nothing. Even so, he moved forward, clearing each room until he reached an office and lab with eerie jellyfish and squid floating in thick liquid, their tanks lit from behind.

Marcus stared at a jellyfish for a moment and then ran for the main desk, ducking and pulling some type of lever.

A door opened in the empty wall, and lights flared down a long hallway. Cell doors were open every few yards.

Marcus ran down the hallway, looking inside each cell.

Damon grasped his radio. "Floor four, clear. No combatants."

"Four three, clear," Tace Justice said soberly over the radio before the clear signals came from the other floors.

"What the hell?" Jax asked, sweeping his light around.

The radio crackled. "We have a fully stocked kitchen here," Tace said. "They left a lot of food."

"The weapons lockers are empty." Sami Steel came over the radio next. "Completely."

The president had prioritized weapons over food. Damon couldn't quite blame him. "Why did they give this place up?" Had they been that afraid of fighting a Vanguard-Mercenary alliance?

Silence surrounded him, somehow ominous.

"We have a problem!" Marcus looked up from the very end of the hall, his body still facing the cell.

Damon winced. He really didn't want to deal with dead bodies right now. Keeping his gun in his hand, he moved forward with Jax, their bootsteps echoing loudly on the white tiles.

He saw the bomb first. "Holy fuck."

Jax skidded to a stop. "Oh, God."

Damon didn't work with explosives, but he recognized C-4 when he saw it. A lot of it. Several wires ran from the mass and up a wall, disappearing into a vent.

"This is Sami on floor two," came instantly over the line. "We just found a bomb in one of the food cupboards."

Damon stopped breathing. "When we breached, we probably started a countdown."

Jax's jaw clenched. "We don't know how many there are. Or where they are. Even if we could diffuse them..."

Damon nodded and grabbed the radio. "Vacate the building. Grab whatever is closest to you and run. Now. Everyone vacate, now!" He turned and started running with Marcus and Jax, scooping up a laptop and a stack of papers on his way.

Jax grabbed a hard-drive, and Marcus a box filled with papers near the door.

They ran as fast as they could, through the halls and up the stairs, meeting other soldiers on the way. The air seemed to hold its breath.

Damon cleared the doorway and burst over the poker chips. "Grey. Raze. Get off those buildings," he yelled into the radio. "Explosion imminent." Depending on the blast, their buildings could go down, too.

Two soldiers held the doors open, and he ran through, turning left and lowering his head to increase his speed.

Footsteps surrounded him. They almost made it to the end of the casino building.

The earth paused. The air even stilled.

Then the entire fucking world exploded.

42

I fucking hate bombs.
—Damon Winter, Journal

THE ENERGY RELEASED from the bombs radiated outward, the supersonic blast wave a prelude to the high-velocity shockwaves. Damon flew through the air and smashed into what used to be a parking meter. Pain flowed up his body, and he dropped to the crumbling sidewalk.

Bodies careened by him.

The pain of his body being compressed had barely set in before the depressurization force hit.

He groaned and shut his eyes.

Air rushed in to fill the atmospheric void left by the blast wave. Garbage, bricks, and stones hurtled back toward the explosion. A soldier was hurled above his head to drop several yards away.

He gasped, trying to breathe. A car alarm went off somewhere a block or so away. An actual car alarm.

Silence ruled for a heartbeat.

Then the rumble of falling floors, wood, and objects filled the night as the building imploded.

He scrambled up and looked around to make sure everyone had gotten clear. His radio was gone. Enough moonlight showed through the clouds that he could see the street.

Jax helped Marcus up, and they stumbled toward him, blood covering their faces.

Damon straightened, his body protesting the movement in every joint. He stretched. His ribs hurt like fuck, but he didn't think anything else had broken. His face hurt, and he touched a new cut above his eye that was bleeding like crazy.

Tearing off a piece of his shirt, he pressed it to the wound.

Dirt, dust, and debris floated through the air. He coughed. "We need status on everyone." Then he looked around. Glass had blown out of all the windows and doors on the entire block, and two of the adjacent buildings were now faceless with yawning holes in their fronts.

Quincy rolled off the curb and then stood.

Relief filled Damon. "You're okay," he gasped. "Where's Greyson?"

Rocks were imbedded in Quincy's jaw, and he tugged one out, his eyes watering. A quick glance at his leg confirmed a definite fracture. "Don't know. He'd sent me down to get the other binoculars when the warning came through."

Oh, God.

Damon looked at the main office building, and his legs were moving before his brain caught up. "Grey," he bellowed, jumping over a pile of stones and into thicker dust. The building was destroyed. There hadn't been time between his warning and the explosion for Grey to make it all the way down.

No answer.

He looked wildly around, Jax on his six. "Did anybody see Greyson make it down?"

The roof looked as if it had blown apart on its own, and half of the building was gone.

Jax pointed toward a hole in the stairwell. "He might not have made it out of the stairs."

Panic shook Damon, and he rushed forward, ignoring the raw pain ripping through his body. Rocks and boards blocked his way. He started throwing debris to the side, clearing one step at a time.

Jax and Marcus bent to help him. The rocks scratched their hands, but they kept shoveling.

A soldier jogged up with his radio. "Found this at the corner."

Damon jerked his head toward Jax. "Take over. Find out if everyone made it out and who's injured and how badly. Find Tace Justice. We definitely need a medic."

Jax wiped blood off his cheek and took the radio, heading back to the street.

Damon dug harder, Marcus by his side.

A foot came into view. A Flak boot. "Greyson!" Damon targeted the rocks covering his friend, and Marcus slid next to him, grabbing a board and flinging it behind them. They worked in tandem, releasing Grey's feet, then his legs, then his torso, and finally his head.

Damon held his breath. Grey's head was turned to the side. He definitely wasn't moving. "Grey?" He couldn't lose another brother. He just couldn't.

No movement.

"Greyson?" Damon gingerly placed a hand on Grey's chest to see if it was moving.

Greyson reared up, scattering the remaining rocks. "What the—"

"Grey." Damon grabbed him for a hug. "A building fell on you." He released him, running his hands down Grey's arms. He winced. "This one's broken."

Greyson stared at him, his eyes slowly coming back to comprehension. "Bombs?"

Damon nodded.

"Assholes." Grey winced and then took inventory.

"How bad you hurt?" Damon asked, sitting back on his ankles.

Grey tucked his left arm in and then slowly moved his legs. "Not bad. Broken arm. Head hurts. Probably gonna piss blood for a while."

Damon leaned in and patted his shoulder. "Yeah. We all are." It was a hell of an explosion.

Jax ran up, papers in his hand. "We have a huge-ass problem."

Grey groaned. "When don't we?"

"Sami was tossing these in the truck with all the other stuff we grabbed, and this caught her eye. It ain't good." Jax handed over a perfectly drawn schematic of Vanguard territory. Definitely rendered by somebody on the inside.

Marcus flashed his light over it. "This had to take some time."

And somebody very familiar with the interior of the territory drew it. Even the buildings were listed with who lived or worked where. Labeled with neat and scratchy lines. Damon's gut rolled over. "I know that handwriting."

Jax's eyebrows rose. "Seriously?"

"Yeah. That's Pastor King's handwriting. Psychotic and neat. The *A*s are weird."

Jax's jaw hardened. He looked around and then focused on the map. Fury flashed across his face. "There was nobody here waiting for us, Damon."

The truth hit Damon harder than the blast had.

Holy shit. The bomb had definitely been a trap, but it was more of a diversion. He pulled Greyson to his feet. "They waited for us to leave." Vanguard territory had been attacked before, but this time was different. Very. "Somehow, they're on the inside."

Oh, God. They had to get back in time.

* * *

APRIL HADN'T BEEN able to sleep all night and finally gave up the fight, working all morning with the kids before heading back to her apartment around lunchtime. She rubbed her chilled arms and watched the storm continue unabated outside. There was no rain. Only fierce and jagged lightning strikes followed by furious thunder.

Where was Damon? Was he okay? They should be raiding right at that second after traveling all night.

She sat at her table and planted her face in her hands. Why hadn't she told him how she felt? It wouldn't change whatever happened during the attack on the Bunker, but at least he'd know. She took the exquisite ring out of her pocket and slid it onto her left ring finger. It fit perfectly.

He hadn't asked. But he'd wanted to say the words to her.

And she hadn't let him.

Man, she sucked. What was she so afraid of? Losing everything? She'd already done that, and here she was. Still standing. Or sitting, as it were. Her heart hurt for him, and fear made breathing difficult.

But she should've given him the words.

A knock on the door had her looking up. "Come in."

Sharon opened the door and slid inside, her eyes over-bright and her cheeks the color of ripe tomatoes. "We've been drinking mimosas all morning before the bridge tournament. I made a break for it." She snorted and then hiccupped.

April gaped. It was just past noon. "You've left the church again. That's twice." The woman had seemed like a total germaphobe. Just how drunk was she?

Sharon stumbled inside to draw out a chair. "I know, right?" She giggled.

April would not have pegged the serious Sharon for a giggler. "How did you get out?"

"We're free to come and go if we want, you know. And I was here before." Sharon rolled her eyes.

Oh, yeah. "I don't suppose you've brought any of what you've been drinking?" She could seriously use a snort or two. When was the last time she'd had a mimosa?

"No, but I'm here to bring you back. Janet passed out, and we need somebody in her chair to start the tournament." Sharon grinned. "You missed Bunko last night, and it was fun. I'm sure the kids here are fine for a while. So let's do this."

The invite was a sweet one. April patted Sharon's hand. "I appreciate it, but I'll have to take a raincheck this time. Definitely next time, though."

Sharon wove on the chair and frowned. "Why? Come on. I mean, why?"

Because she'd promised Damon, and her word mattered. April just smiled. "I have a lot to do today. But I definitely want to play next time." And have some of whatever Sharon had been drinking.

Sharon pursed her lips. "I was also hoping you'd take a look at Bobby."

April ran through the kids in her head. "The little, redheaded kid?" He had to be around four years old, maybe five.

"Yeah. He's running a fever, and I don't know what's happening. You have more experience with kids than most of us." Sharon gestured for the door. "What do you say?"

April paused, torn. If there were a sick child, then she wanted to help. But she had made a promise to Damon, and everything inside her wanted to keep that. "If we have an ill child, we need the doctor. Let's go get Doc Penelope and see what she thinks."

"No. Just you. No Penelope," Sharon said, pressing her lips together.

April studied the blonde. If anybody wanted to get her to the Pure, saying there was a sick kid would do it. As well as an invite for fun and alcohol. She didn't want to be suspicious, and she certainly hated skirting the line of paranoia, but something felt off. "I don't think so," she murmured.

Sharon threw up her hands. "Why are you being so difficult?"

April leaned in. "Why are you insisting so hard? What's really going on?"

Sharon huffed and stared at her. "The pastor would really like to see you."

Now they were getting somewhere. "So he sent you out here, in the germ-filled, bacteria-esque world to lie to me?" Anger stirred as well as warning inside April.

"Please. Don't be so dr-dramatic." Sharon hiccupped again. "We have champagne. The good stuff."

"Tempting, but no." April pushed her chair away from the table and stood. "I think you should go back to the pastor and tell him to be honest next time." What in the world was really going on? Man, she wished Damon were there. If nothing else, she was going to keep her word to him until he returned. She'd promised. Plus, something felt off. She was too smart to walk into a trap.

"Fine." Sharon stormed to her feet and stumbled toward the door.

April fought a grin. The woman really was sloshed. She followed and opened the door to help her through as well as point out the right direction to the Pure apartment building.

"Hello." A man shoved inside, pushing April back three steps.

She blinked and then recognized that Jerome guy from inside the Pure. Going on instinct, she turned and started to bolt.

He grabbed her around the waist from behind and slapped a hand over her mouth to keep her from screaming. Fear swamped her, and she kicked, struggling to free herself. He pressed harder, hurting her jaw. She whimpered and tried to scream behind his hold, but he muffled her voice well.

Sharon backed away, her eyes wide. "Jerome? What are you doing?"

April punched back as hard as she could, and he released her, instantly wrapping an arm across both of hers and her waist, partially lifting her off the ground. His body was lean and hard behind her.

She breathed out over his hand, trying to focus. Blood rushed through her head, ringing loudly in her ears.

Sharon held up both hands. Bewilderment crossed her rosy face. "Stop this. I said I'd help get her there, but this is going too far. Let her go." Her voice slurred.

What the hell? April nodded in agreement. She needed to get free.

Jerome sighed, his breath stirring her hair. "Sharon, pull it together, or you're out of the Pure."

Sharon's bloodshot eyes widened. "But—"

"But, nothing," he snapped. "The storm is keeping everybody indoors. We have a small window to get her to the apartment building between patrols." His mouth lowered to April's ear. "They're like clockwork, and this has to be timed perfectly."

She shivered. If they thought she was going quietly, they were freaking crazy.

"Now, I'm going to remove my hand, and if you scream, I'll choke you out." He moved his hand.

Her mind reeled. If she screamed, who would hear? The kids? Atticus was up with the older kids right now and might not hear her. But what were her other options? Before she could make up her mind, Jerome had retrieved a knife from somewhere. He held it up in front of her eyes. "Do I have your attention?"

She stopped struggling against him.

"Good." His hold loosened enough that she could breathe again. "If you fight me, I'm going to gut Sharon like a fish."

Sharon gasped and shrank against the peeling wall.

"Go ahead," April snapped. She was done with these people. Period.

Jerome chuckled. "I like you. Okay, no gutting Sharon. I guess there's only one way to go here." He moved, something shifted, and then pain exploded in April's head.

She went down, unconscious before she hit the floor.

43

Turns out I'm more of a fighter than I realized.
— April Snyder, Journal

APRIL CAME to and instantly recognized Pastor King's basement office. She lay on the sofa, her head on a soft pillow. Gasping, she sat up. Pain blasted through her brain. She cried out and closed her eyes for a second. The world spun, and she quickly opened her eyes again.

She and King were alone in the quiet space.

King turned in his leather chair at his desk and tossed her a bottle. "Aspirin."

She took two and swallowed them without liquid. Ouch. "What's happening?" she croaked.

His eyebrows rose. "Jerome hit you on the head to get you here. I had hoped such measures wouldn't be necessary."

Oh, man. Her gaze caught on the breeding chart still visible. Why did they want her so badly?

King snorted. "Don't be silly."

Relief somewhat calmed her. "Why did you kidnap me?"

"Kidnapping involves transport between state lines, right?" He looked like the boy next door in his jeans and dark T-shirt, his green eyes twinkling. "We have no states any longer."

There had to be some sort of weapon she could use. The guy probably didn't need a letter opener these days. Was there a pen near his hand? "Damon is going to kill you." If April didn't figure out how first.

"Now that might be a problem," King said. "I'm pretty sure Damon was blown up earlier this morning. The Reno Bunker was a trap."

April's head jerked. "How the heck would you even know he was heading to a Bunker?"

King grinned, the sight slightly off. "Do you really think the Twenty gang members had legitimate intel from the president? He's using those morons as fodder, and it worked. Sure, we had to give up some explosives, but they weren't exactly our good stuff."

"How do you know so much about this?" And wait a minute. "Who are you working with? How?"

"Funny you should ask."

They were talking in riddles. "Why am I here?"

Jerome Blankenship moved into the room from the stairwell. "You're here because I want you. Always had a thing for Cherry Valance."

April blinked. Her head hurt again. This guy kept popping up, and now he'd hit her in the head. Payback was going to involve her knee to his balls, whether or not he had a knife. She wished she'd had time to learn to fight. "Who in the world are you?"

"Well, since you asked..." He smiled and moved to one of the long, paneled walls. "I became the vice president very recently."

The VP. Wait a minute. How was that even possible? That was beyond crazy. "The vice president of what?" Was the church now holding elections? None of this made sense. "And why aren't you on any Vanguard member lists?" Her vision kept fuzzing.

He smiled, looking even bigger. "The VP of the country, pretty girl. And I'm not on a list because I didn't come in the front door." He pressed a button, and a panel slid away to reveal about fifty men in a tunnel, all armed. They moved into the room and silently jogged up the stairs.

She couldn't breathe.

Where the hell had those men come from? Everyone had an *EL* on his shirt. The president's Elite Force?

Within a minute, it was just the three of them in the room. She instinctively stood, craning her neck to see down the tunnel. "I don't understand."

King swiveled in his chair. "A lot of people don't know that there are at least eleven miles of tunnels under Los Angles that were used during Prohibition. Rumor has it that the mayor's office at the time ran the hooch for the rich and thirsty."

She blinked. "That's crazy." Yet the passageway was right in front of her. And where had those soldiers gone? She had to get a warning to the remaining Vanguard-Merc soldiers.

Jerome pulled out his knife, and it glinted in the dim light. "There are also abandoned subway and equestrian tunnels. It's amazing what's under this once-imposing city."

King eyed the knife. "I wrote one of my college papers on the tunnels and Prohibition. When I joined Vanguard, I recognized this building. It didn't take much to join the good old church and do some exploring."

"Why?" April asked, her gaze on the blade. "Why find the tunnels and not tell us?"

"The president has promised me a place in his administration," King said calmly. "He has the weapons, the planes, and the troops. Vanguard has held temporary power."

"That's over now," Jerome agreed. "Most of the Vanguard-Merc soldiers were at the Bunker and are most likely dead now.

We rigged the explosives to detonate when they arrived and triggered the bombs. Our strongest force just entered Vanguard territory from the inside, and they're going to clean house. You, my Cherry, get to come with me."

She shivered and turned toward Pastor King. "What about your church?"

He scoffed. "That was a cover. I couldn't care less about the Pure or these people."

The truth dawned on her. "You've had Scorpius."

"Yep." He stood and reached for a gun from the top drawer of his desk. "I'll leave you two so you can discuss your plans." Sauntering with a definite swagger, he moved past Jerome to the stairwell. "Somebody needs to shoot anybody who comes near the building before we leave."

One thing at a time. The Vanguard soldiers knew how to fight. April turned and stared into the darkened tunnel. Moss and bricks made up the sides. How was it possible that the tunnels had existed for so long? "This is how those explosives got into Vanguard."

"Yep. Planted those myself." Jerome leaned against the wall.

She stared harder at a faint outline of a person. Looked like a man. "Who is that?"

Jerome turned, unconcerned. "Oh. That's Joe Bentley. He discovered that King wasn't in this for the church, and there was an altercation. His body will probably start stinking soon."

Oh, poor Joe. The guy really had wanted to create a safe place for the uninfected, and he'd been killed for it. "You didn't have to murder him."

"I enjoyed it." Jerome ran his gaze over her body. "I'm saving your life by bringing you with me to what's now considered the Capitol of the country."

Lake Tahoe? "Please don't kill these people." Emotions churned through her. Most of the Vanguard-Merc folks just wanted to survive and build lives. "You don't need to do that."

He shrugged. "We have our orders. The president wants to make an example here."

How could this be happening? Nobody was that evil. She just couldn't believe that. "What about the civilians? And the kids?" She moved toward him, needing him to understand. "They're innocent."

"This is war." There was no emotion behind his eyes.

"You're right." She kicked him as hard as she could in the balls, and when he leaned over with a startled gasp, she punched him in the nose. Something cracked.

Then she ran.

* * *

THEY MADE the drive home in half the time, mainly because they paid no attention to safety. Damon drove one of the motorcycles, weaving in and out through crashed cars and piles of crap, reaching Vanguard-Merc territory with his men on either side of him.

Gunfire was already shocking through the late afternoon as they approached.

He drove between the tires and overturned trucks. Two Vanguard soldiers lay prone on the ground by the main gate. "Ram it," he yelled back.

Jax nodded and hit the gas of his Humvee, one of the vehicles taken from the Century City Bunker. He hit the fence dead center and careened through.

A firefight was already happening at headquarters, with soldiers firing down from windows to the parking lot where several enemy soldiers fired back, ducking behind displaced vehicles. A quick look at their shirts confirmed that they were Elite Force.

How the hell had they gotten in?

Jax leaped out of the Humvee, already firing.

Damon came up on his right, ditched the bike, and fired at one soldier. The guy went down. Greyson moved up to his side, his arm in a makeshift sling. "Headquarters is barricaded," he yelled.

The inhabitants had put what looked like tables in front of the door.

A bullet winged by his ear.

Grey dropped and fired. A scream of pain came from behind a truck.

"Good." Damon turned as more fire erupted in the inner territory. Where was April? Were she and the kids safe? He moved into a fast run with Greyson by his side. They made it around the building to see two Elite Force guys fighting hand-to-hand with a Vanguard-Merc soldier near the showers. The guy was naked but fighting hard. Two guns sat on the sidewalk across the street, so somehow he'd kicked those out of the way.

Damon lifted his gun and squeezed.

The first Elite Force guy went down fast. Greyson took care of the other one.

Screams came from one of the apartment buildings. His radio crackled. "Yeah."

"Jax here. Headquarters is secured, and we're going through the territory in grid-style. My men have trained for an attack if we're infiltrated." An explosion sounded by the burned-out building. "You and Greyson secure the kids."

"Affirmative." That's exactly where Damon was headed anyway. He ignored the firefights going on all around him and shoved the pain in his body somewhere else. An Elite Force soldier jumped out at him, and he fired quickly.

The guy dropped, dead. Without missing a step, Damon took his weapon and kept going.

Grey yanked him over to the side of a building. "Keep covered, damn it."

For the first time, Damon had trouble keeping his cool. Lightning flashed across the sky, illuminating the weird storm clouds. The smell of ozone competed with the scent of blood and gunfire. Where was April?

They reached her apartment, and he barreled inside. There were two overturned chairs, as if there'd been a fight. She wasn't there. He kept going, Greyson on his six, into the main rec room. Only silence.

"April?" he called, sweeping the kids' rooms. Nothing.

He ran around to the far side and tried to open the door to the basement.

A bigger explosion rocked the territory, and he had to settle his stance. "April?" he bellowed, his chest on fire.

The door opened, and he stared into the barrel of a Sig Sauer. He blinked.

Atticus lowered the gun. "D?"

Relief flowed through Damon so quickly he nearly swayed. "You and the kids okay?"

"Yes," Atticus said, his mouth drawn tight. "All the kids are downstairs, and I'm prepared to shoot anybody who comes through the door. "Is April with you?"

The relief disappeared. "No." He looked frantically around. "All right. Shut the door and keep it locked. I'll be back."

Atticus slammed the door closed.

"Jax?" Damon said into his radio. "Is April at headquarters?"

"Negative. Swept the building. No April," Jax said. "Kids safe?"

The patter of a machine gun ripped through the line. "Yes. Kids are safe."

"Good. We have the north, east, and west cleared. Going south."

Damon looked at Greyson. "Pastor King drew that map." For whatever reason, King was working with the president. How, Damon had no clue. But he'd recognized that writing.

Grey nodded. "Let's go."

Two Merc soldiers rushed in from outside. "This building clear?" the first one asked, blood dripping from his neck.

Damon shook his head. "Just first floor. But I need somebody on this door. Kids are down there."

"Understood." The first soldier took position while the other started clearing rooms.

Damon ran out the back door and down the street, not feeling any pain. There was only April. She wouldn't have gone back to the church willingly, but she wasn't anywhere else in the territory. He knew her. If she could be with the kids, protecting them, that's right where she'd be.

They turned the corner, and Damon caught a flash of her hair. "April," he yelled, running faster and dodging around the side of one of the houses.

She was struggling furiously with a man Damon didn't recognize. The guy had her around the waist and was pulling her backward toward the front door of the church. She clawed and fought, panic on her face.

"April!" he bellowed, running.

The guy lifted a knife to her throat.

Damon stopped. Everything. Running, breathing, thinking.

Grey stopped next to him.

April gasped, tears streaming down her face. The guy pulled her into the apartment building and slammed the door.

Somebody fired at them from a side window. The dirt pinged up all around them.

No! Damon bunched to run.

Greyson grabbed him. "Stop. Just hold on. He has a knife. We need a plan."

Damon always had a plan. He was the calm and deliberate one.

Seeing April with a knife to her throat had changed that. He lost his mind. "No." Shrugging off his friend, he ran full tilt for the front door, bullets spraying the ground around him.

44

He's worth the risk, and I'm taking it.
    —April Snyder, Journal

APRIL TILTED the back of her head against Jerome's front, trying to avoid the knife.

"Do you want to die?" he hissed, dragging her beyond the cement blocks and into the main dining area.

"No." With certain clarity, she knew that for a fact. For the first time in too long, she wanted to live. She *needed* to.

Damon was coming for her. All she had to do was stay alive. That trust meant everything.

She stopped fighting.

Jerome relaxed. "Okay. Good. We're going down the stairs and through the tunnel. If you fight me, I'll knock you out again."

She sucked in air. All she had to do was stay alive. "Okay."

The door flew open and splintered into three pieces. Damon came barreling in, reaching them in a second and grabbing Jerome by the neck.

In all April's life, with whatever time she had left, she'd never forget the look on Damon's face. Determined and fierce. For her.

He lifted Jerome up and slammed him against the wall so hard something in Jerome fissured with a loud crack. His head flew back and forth, and his body jerked in a spasm. He tried to strike out, but Damon punched him square in the jaw. He slumped, unconscious.

"Damon." April leaped for him, and he caught her, holding her tight.

Movement came from the other room. "What the hell?" Pastor King ran into sight, his gun lifting quickly.

Damon pivoted and dropped to the floor, covering April with his body. She struggled to see beyond his arm.

Greyson slid past the cement blocks on his knees, already firing. He hit King beneath the chin, and the bullet exploded brain matter and blood up to the ceiling. King fell forward in death, his legs flying up and then flopping to the ground.

Damon half lifted up. He looked around. Then he stood, taking April with him.

She gulped and shuddered into his side. "I stayed at my apartment. Kept my promise and didn't come here on my own." She gasped out the words, wanting him to know she'd stayed safe. Or had tried to. "Not stupid." She didn't willingly walk into a trap.

He kissed her cheek, his gaze searching the area. "I know, baby. You're fine."

Greyson stood, looking down at the dead man. "I killed a pastor. That probably ain't good."

The room whirled around April, and she tried to focus. "He's not really a pastor, and he's been working with the president. There are tunnels beneath Los Angeles. We're on one."

Grey cut her a look. "Seriously?"

Damon frowned. "That's crazy. But look on the bright side, Grey. You didn't kill a pastor. You and God are still good."

Grey snorted.

April looked at them both. Had they completely lost their minds? This wasn't funny.

Only a wisp of sound warned her. Damon turned and shoved her toward Greyson as Jerome Blankenship jumped to his feet and rushed forward with his knife.

April screamed.

Damon smoothly pivoted, grabbed Jerome's wrist, and twisted it back with a hard shove. The knife shoved up into Jerome's breastbone, and his eyes widened. Blood bubbled on his lips. Damon shoved him to the ground again, and this time, he stayed down.

Her ears started ringing. She shook her head. Now was not the time to freak out. Later. Definitely later.

Damon moved for her, a big, solid form with determination on his face.

She met him halfway and rushed into his arms. "He was the vice president."

Greyson craned his neck. "Ha. You killed this one. Vice presidents aren't safe around us, buddy."

Damon chuckled, the sound still a little angry.

He was there, and he was safe. She needed to touch him. "I should've said it before you left, and I'm sorry I didn't." She gasped for air. "I love you. Am a little scared about it, but it's the truth, so I wanted to say it." Enough with the babbling, but she couldn't stop. "I knew you'd come and get me and—"

"I love you, too." His voice remained strong and steady. No babbling.

She paused. He loved her, too. That meant everything, especially in the world they now lived in. Tears gathered in her eyes.

Jax Mercury strode through the broken doorway before she could completely dissolve into tears. "This place cleared?"

"Not yet," Greyson answered for them all.

Sharon poked her head out from the smaller dining area. She had a black eye and a split lip. "Jerome and I had a fight. The kids are safely barricaded upstairs. I came down to see if I could get word to the Vanguard soldiers about what was happening and then had to hide."

April leaned into Damon's side. "The house is now clear."

He kissed the top of her head. "Everything is."

* * *

APRIL FINISHED SETTLING the kids down after the crazy day and returned to her apartment where Damon stood by her table with a bottle of wine. They both looked absolutely delicious.

"How are you feeling?" he asked, pouring them both a glass.

"Okay. My head is better, but I could use a week of sleep." She reached him, suddenly nervous. "How are you? Sami said you guys got caught in a bombing."

"Darn gossips. I'm just fine." He had new stitches above his eyebrow and a fresh bruise along his collarbone. Both just made him look even more dangerously sexy. "You did a great job fighting Jerome. I'm proud of you."

Actually, she'd sucked. "I think it's time for those self-defense lessons you were talking about."

He nodded. "Agreed."

She accepted the glass and got right to it. "I know tensions and emotions were high earlier today, but I meant what I said. I do love you."

His flash of teeth showed amusement. "Yeah. I meant it, too. Wasn't going to let you go back on it. Trust me."

Well, that was a little arrogant and a lot sweet. "I'm not sure where to go from here." She didn't know how to play coy, so she didn't bother.

"I do. After a nice chat, we're going to bed. I'm going to kiss, lick, or bite every inch of you, and then we're sleeping until we have to get up and eat something." He took a drink of the wine, his gaze intense. "Sound good to you?"

She nodded. Sounded beyond good. Her body flushed hot and then got all tingly. Like it always did with him. "Is the territory secured?" She hadn't seen him for hours after he'd rescued her in the church.

"Yes. We have several dead and wounded, as do the Elite Force. Some of them escaped out the front." Damon took another drink. "Sami is going through all the information that we managed to take from the Reno Bunker. Hopefully, we'll find the location of another one soon."

She took a sip of the wine and let it wash down her throat. It was fairly cool, somehow. "What about the tunnel?"

Damon winced. "We're going to blow it up so it can't be used. Was a hard decision, but too many people probably know about it, so it has to go and it looks like Sharon is in charge of the Pure group from now on. She has no trouble giving us access to the members."

Sounded like a plan. April tightened her hold on the glass, and the ring clinked. Oh yeah. She took it off and handed it over to him. "I said I'd keep this until you got back safely." Maybe sometime in the future she'd get to wear it again.

"I'll always come back safely to you." He set his glass down, and in a surprisingly graceful movement for such a large man, he dropped to one knee. "I've never been in love before, and it took the apocalypse to find you, but you're it for me, April."

Her heart fluttered, and her knees weakened. "Damon."

He looked up, his eyes a fathomless hue. "I don't know how much time we have, but I want to spend it all with you. I love you. Marry me?"

He was the biggest risk she'd ever take. But he was worth it, and she wanted every second she might have. "Yes."

EPILOGUE

APRIL KNOCKED her pen against her bright blue clipboard and gave Jax her sternest look. "I know rebuilding takes time, but the kids are the priority. You haven't signed up to teach any of the classes yet."

Jax looked up from the table in his war-room, surprise on his face. "Why are you still here?"

She barely kept from tapping her foot. "I'm not leaving until you take a slot."

Jax sat back and gave her a look. His tough one. A month ago, it would've had her knees shaking. Now it was just another challenge. "Damon?" he bellowed.

"Yep?" Damon crossed into the room, chewing on a pop-tart with sprinkles. His favorite kind. He wore faded jeans and the Merc T-shirt with a gun at his thigh and a knife at his belt. His bruises were starting to fade, but he still had the badass look.

"Would you please get your woman out of here before I lose my mind?" Jax asked mildly.

His woman. The language was so barbaric and yet, April's breath went all a-fluttery. She turned and gave Damon a level look.

His grin brightened the entire already too hot and over-bright day. "Baby. Nice clipboard."

She tried not to preen. She really did. "Thank you."

He swooped in and pressed a kiss to her forehead. "I found a purple one for you earlier today while scouting to the north."

Purple? Perfect. She eyed the board and her sparkling ring caught her eye, like it had the entire week she'd been wearing it. Happiness caught her, and instead of fighting it, she let herself enjoy the feeling. He'd taught her that. To take the good and let it warm you for as long as possible. "You're too good to me," she murmured.

Jax made gagging noises.

April sighed and focused back on him. "As I was saying, sign up to teach one of these classes, and I'll leave."

Jax lifted an eyebrow. "Winter?"

Damon leaned over. "Jax will teach the first morning class tomorrow on self-defense."

"Perfect." April wrote Jax's name in. "Was that so hard, Mercury?"

Jax looked from her to Damon and then back. "No." He frowned. "Now will you two leave? I'm trying to read through some of this stuff from the Pure church. Sharon is doing a good job of keeping me informed about the members and all the pregnancies."

Damon leaned in, his scent of ginger and man filling April. "Want me to carry you?"

It had been an entire week since he'd tossed her over his shoulder. "Nah." She took his hand and moved from the room, shutting the door behind them. The vestibule of the headquarters building was quiet and somewhat cool. "Thanks for the help."

"Anytime." He smoothed the hair away from her face. "So, I talked to that new preacher. Guy was a minister in Portland."

Her stomach dropped, and her breath quickened. "Yeah?"

Damon's eyes softened. "Yeah. I figure since you said yes, I'd get it made official before you could change your mind. Maybe plan a wedding once it cools down a little."

She chuckled. "You are a planner."

He nodded and leaned down to kiss her, the touch firm and all him. "I truly am. But you know what? I could've never planned you. You're more than I ever imagined."

Sometimes his sweetness stole her breath. She looked up at his handsome face, willing to risk anything for a moment of happiness with him. They both deserved it. "I love you, Damon Winter. No matter what happens."

He kissed her again, this time going deep. Finally, he lifted back up. "I love you, too. And trust me. Only good will happen for us from now on."

Probably unlikely, but so long as they were together, they'd make it. She was sure of it.

COMING SOON...MARCUS AND PENNY'S STORY

More info: www.RebeccaZanetti.com

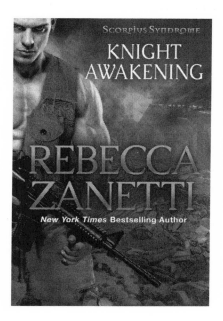

VAMPIRE'S FAITH EXCERPT

We are returning to the world of the Dark Protectors with Vampire's Faith on June 19, 2018! These are all new novels that will feature some of your favorite characters finding their own romances. There will be new villains and fights to wage. It's a great entry point for the series for new readers as well as an exciting place to return for existing fans. Here's the first chapter:

Vampire's Faith - Chapter 1

Dr. Faith Cooper scanned through the medical chart on her tablet while keeping a brisk pace in her dark boots through the hospital hallway, trying to ignore the chill in the air. "The brain scan was normal. What about the respiratory pattern?" she asked, reading the next page.

"Normal. We can't find any neurological damage," Dr. Barclay said, matching his long-legged stride easily to hers. His brown hair was swept back from an angled face with intelligent blue eyes. "The patient is in a coma with no brain activity, but his body is... well..."

"Perfectly healthy," Faith said, scanning the nurse's notes, wondering if Barclay was single. "The lumbar puncture was normal, and there's no evidence of a stroke."

"No. The patient presents as healthy except for the coma. It's an anomaly," Barclay replied, his voice rising.

Interesting. "Any history of drugs?" Sometimes drugs could cause a coma.

"No," Barclay said. "No evidence that we've found."

Lights flickered along the corridor as she passed through the doorway to the intensive- care unit. "What's wrong with the lights?" Faith asked, her attention jerking from the medical notes.

"It's been happening on and off for the last two days. The maintenance department is working on it, as well as on the temperature fluctuations." Barclay swept his hand out. No ring. Might not be married. "This morning we moved all the other patients to the new ICU in the western addition that was completed last week."

That explained the vacant hall and nearly deserted nurses' station. Only one woman monitored the screens spread across the desk. She nodded as Faith and Dr. Barclay passed by, her gaze lingering on the cute man.

The cold was getting worse. It was early April, raining and a little chilly. Not freezing.

Faith shivered. "Why wasn't this patient moved with the others?"

"Your instructions were to leave him exactly in place until you arrived," Barclay said, his face so cleanly shaven he looked like a cologne model. "We'll relocate him after your examination."

Goose bumps rose on her arms. She breathed out, and her breath misted in the air. This was weird. It'd never happen in the hospital across town where she worked. Her hospital was on the other side of Denver, but her expertise with coma patients was often requested across the world. She glanced back down at the tablet. "Where's his Glasgow Coma Scale score?"

"He's at a three," Barclay said grimly.

A three? That was the worst score for a coma patient. Basically, no brain function.

Barclay stopped her. "Dr. Cooper. I just want to say thank you for coming right away." He smiled and twin dimples appeared. The nurses probably loved this guy. "I heard about the little girl in Seattle. You haven't slept in—what? Thirty hours?"

It felt like it. She'd put on a clean shirt, but it was already wrinkled beneath her white lab coat. Faith patted his arm, finding very nice muscle tone. When was the last time she'd been on a date? "I'm fine. The important part is that the girl woke up." It had taken Faith seven hours of doing what she shouldn't be able to do: Communicate somehow with coma patients. This one she'd been able to save, and now a six-year-old girl was eating ice cream with her family in the hospital. Soon she'd go home. "Thank you for calling me."

He nodded, and she noticed his chin had a small divot—Cary Grant style. "Of course. You're legendary. Some say you're magic."

Faith forced a laugh. "Magic. That's funny." Straightening her shoulders, she walked into the ICU and stopped moving, forgetting all about the chart and the doctor's dimples. "What in the world?" she murmured.

Only one standard bed remained in the sprawling room. A massive man overwhelmed it, his shoulders too wide to fit on the mattress. He was at least six-foot-six, his bare feet hanging off the end of the bed. The blankets had been pushed to his waist to make room for the myriad of electrodes set across his broad and muscular chest. Very muscular. "Why is his gown open?"

"It shouldn't be," Barclay said, looking around. "I'll ask the nurse after you do a quick examination. I don't mind admitting that I'm stymied here."

A man who could ask for help. Yep. Barclay was checking all the boxes. "Is this the correct patient?" Faith studied his healthy coloring and phenomenal physique. "There's no way this man has been in a coma for longer than a couple of days."

Barclay came to a halt, his gaze narrowing. He slid a shaking hand through his thick hair. "I understand, but according to the fire marshal, this patient was buried under piles of rocks and cement from the tunnel cave-in below the Third Street bridge that happened nearly seven years ago."

Faith moved closer to the patient, noting the thick dark hair that swept back from a chiseled face. A warrior's face. She blinked. Where the hell had that thought come from? "That's impossible." She straightened. "Anybody caught in that collapse would've died instantly, or shortly thereafter. He's not even bruised."

"What if he was frozen?" Barclay asked, balancing on sneakers.

Faith checked over the still-healthy tone of the patient's skin. "Not a chance." She reached for his wrist to check his pulse.

Electricity zipped up her arm and she coughed. What the heck was *that*? His skin was warm and supple, the strength beneath it obvious. She turned her wrist so her watch face was visible and then started counting. Curiosity swept her as she counted the beats. "When was he brought in?" She'd been called just three hours ago to consult on the case and hadn't had a chance to review the complete file.

"A week ago," Barclay said, relaxing by the door.

Amusement hit Faith full force. Thank goodness. For a moment, with the flickering lights, freezing air, and static electricity, she'd almost traveled to an imaginary and fanciful place. She smiled and released the man's wrist. "All right. Somebody is messing with me." She'd just been named the head of neurology at Northwest Boulder Hospital. Her colleagues must have gone to a lot of trouble—tons, really—to pull this prank. "Did Simons put you up to this?"

Barclay blinked, truly looking bewildered. He was cute. Very much so. Just the type who'd appeal to Faith's best friend, Louise. And he had an excellent reputation. Was this Louise's new beau? "Honestly, Dr. Cooper. This is no joke." He motioned toward the monitor screen that displayed the patient's heart rate, breathing, blood pressure, and intracranial pressure.

It had to be. Faith looked closer at the bandage covering the guy's head and the ICP monitor that was probably just taped beneath the bandage. "I always pay back jokes, Dr. Barclay." It was fair to give warning.

Barclay shook his head. "No joke. After a week of tests, we should see something here that explains his condition, but we have nothing. If he was injured somehow in the caved-in area, there'd be evidence of such. But... nothing." Barclay sighed. "That's why we requested your help."

None of this made any sense. The only logical conclusion was that this was a joke. She leaned over the patient to check the head bandage and look under it.

The screen blipped.

She paused.

Barclay gasped and moved a little closer to her. "What was that?"

Man, this was quite the ruse. She was so going to repay Simons for this. Dr. Louise Simons was always finding the perfect jokes, and it was time for some payback. Playing along, Faith leaned over the patient again.

BLEEP

This close, her fingers tingled with the need to touch the hard angles of this guy's face. Was he some sort of model? Bodybuilder? His muscles were sleek and smooth—natural like a wild animal's. So probably not a bodybuilder. There was something just so male about him that he made Barclay fade into the *meh* zone. Her friends had chosen well. This guy was sexy on a sexy stick of pure melted sexiness. "I'm going to kill Simons," she murmured, not sure if she meant it. As jokes went, this was impressive. This guy wasn't a patient and he wasn't in a coma. So, she indulged herself and smoothed his hair back from his wide forehead.

BLEEP

BLEEP

BLEEP

His skin was warm, although the room was freezing. "This is amazing," she whispered, truly touched. The planning that had to have gone into it. "How long did this take to set up?"

Barclay coughed, no longer appearing quite so perfect or masculine compared to the patient. "Stroke him again."

Well, all righty then. Who wouldn't want to caress a guy like this? Going with the prank, Faith flattened her hand in the middle of the guy's thorax, feeling a very strong heartbeat. "You can stop acting now," she murmured, leaning toward his face. "You've done a terrific job." Would it be totally inappropriate to ask him out for a drink after he stopped pretending to be unconscious? He wasn't really a patient, and man, he was something. Sinewed strength and incredibly long lines. "How about we get you out of here?" Her mouth was just over his.

His eyelids flipped open.

Barclay yelped and windmilled back, hitting an orange guest chair and landing on his butt on the floor.

The patient grabbed Faith's arm in an iron-strong grip. "Faith."

She blinked and then warmth slid through her. "Yeah. That's me." Man, he was hot. All right. The coming out of a coma and saying her name was kind of cool. But it was time to get to the truth. "Who are you?"

He shook his head. "*Gde, chert voz'mi, ya?*"

She blinked. Wow. A Russian model? His eyes were a metallic aqua. Was he wearing contacts? "Okay, buddy. Enough with the joke." She gently tried to pull loose, but he held her in place, his hand large enough to encircle her entire bicep.

He blinked, his eyes somehow hardening. They started to glow an electric blue, sans the green. "Where am I?" His voice was low and gritty. Hoarse to a point that it rasped through the room, winding around them.

The colored contacts were seriously high-tech.

"You speak Russian and English. Extraordinary." She twisted her wrist toward her chest, breaking free. The guy was probably paid by the hour. "The jig is up, handsome." Whatever his rate, he'd earned every dime. "Tell Simons to come out from wherever she's hiding." Faith might have to clap for her best friend. This deserved applause.

The guy ripped the fake bandage off his head and then yanked the EKG wires away from his chest. He shoved himself to a seated position. The bed groaned in protest. "Where am I?" He partially turned his head to stare at the now-silent monitor. "What the hell is that?" His voice still sounded rough and sexy.

Just how far was he going to take this? "The joke is over." Faith glanced at Barclay on the floor, who was staring at the patient with wide eyes. "You're quite the actor, Dr. Barclay." She smiled.

Barclay grabbed a chair and hauled himself to his feet, the muscles in his forearms tightening. "Wh—what's happening?"

Faith snorted and moved past him, looking down the now-darkened hallway. Dim yellow emergency lights ignited along the ceiling. "They've cut the lights." Delight filled her. She lifted her voice. "Simons? Payback is a bitch, but this is amazing. Much better than April fool's." After Faith had filled Louise's car with balloons filled with sparkly confetti—guaranteed to blow if a door opened and changed the pressure in the vehicle—Simons had sworn vengeance.

"Louise?" Faith called again. Nothing. Just silence. Faith sighed. "You win. I bow to your pranking abilities."

Ice started to form on the wall across the doorway. "How are you doing that?" Faith murmured, truly impressed.

A growl came from behind her, and she jumped, turning back to the man on the bed.

He'd just *growled*?

She swallowed and studied him. What the heck? The saline bag appeared genuine. Moving quickly, she reached his arm. "They are actually pumping saline into your blood?" Okay. The joke had officially gone too far.

Something that looked like pain flashed in his eyes. "Who died? I felt their deaths, but who?"

She shook her head. "Come on. Enough." He was an excellent actor. She could almost feel his agony.

The man looked at her, his chin lowering. Sitting up on the bed, he was as tall as she was, even though she was standing in her favorite two-inch heeled boots. Heat poured off him, along with a tension she couldn't ignore.

She shivered again, and this time it wasn't from the cold.

Keeping her gaze, he tore out the IV.

Blood dribbled from his vein. She swallowed and fought the need to step back. "All right. Too far, Simons," she snapped. "*Waaaay* too far."

Barclay edged toward the door. "I don't understand what's happening."

Faith shook her head. "Occam's razor, Dr. Barclay." Either the laws of physics had just changed or this was a joke. The simplest explanation was that Simons had just won the jokester title for all time. "Enough of this, though. Who are you?" she asked the actor.

He slowly turned his head to study Dr. Barclay before focusing back on her. "When did the shield fall?"

The shield? He seemed so serious. Eerily so. Would Simons hire a crazy guy? No. Faith tapped her foot and heat rose to her face, her temper stirring. "Listen. This has been fantastic, but it's getting old. I'm done."

The guy grabbed her arm, his grip unbreakable this time. "Did both shields fail?"

Okay. Her heart started to beat faster. Awareness pricked along her skin. "Let go of me."

"No." The guy pushed from the bed and shrugged out of his gown, keeping hold of her. "What the fuck?" He looked at the Foley catheter inserted into his penis and then down to the long white anti-embolism stockings that were supposed to prevent blood clots.

Faith's breath caught. Holy shit. The catheter and TED hose were genuine. And his penis was huge. She looked up at his face. The TED hose might add a realistic detail to a joke, but no way would any responsible medical personnel insert a catheter for a gag. Simons wouldn't have done that. "What's happening?" Faith tried to yank her arm free, but he held her tight.

Dr. Barclay looked from her to the mostly naked male. "Who are you?" he whispered.

"My name is Ronan," the guy said, reaching for the catheter, which was attached to a urine-collection bag at the end of the bed. "What fresh torture is this?"

"Um," Faith started.

His nostrils flared. "Why would you collect my piss?"

Huh? "We're not," she protested. "You were in a coma. That's just a catheter."

He gripped the end of the tube, his gaze fierce.

"No—" Faith protested just as he pulled it out, grunting and then snarling in what had to be intense pain.

God. Was he on PCP or something? She frantically looked toward Barclay and mouthed the words *security* and *Get the nurse out of here.*

Barclay nodded and turned, running into the hallway.

"Where are we?" Ronan asked, drawing her toward him.

She put out a hand to protest, smashing her palm into his ripped abdomen. "Please. Let me go." She really didn't want to kick him in his already reddening penis. "You could've just damaged your urethra badly."

He started dragging her toward the door, his strength beyond superior. A sprawling tattoo covered his entire back. It looked like...a dark image of his ribs with lighter spaces between? Man, he was huge. "We must go."

Oh, there was no *we*. Whatever was happening right now wasn't good, and she had to get some space to figure this out. "I don't want to hurt you," she said, fighting his hold.

He snorted.

She drew in air and kicked him in the back of the leg, twisting her arm to gain freedom.

Faster than she could imagine, he pivoted, moving right into her. Heat and muscle and strength. He more than towered over her, fierce even though he was naked. She yelped and backpedaled, striking up for his nose.

He blocked her punch with his free hand and growled again, fangs sliding down from his incisors.

She stopped moving and her brain fuzzed. *Fangs?* Okay. This wasn't a joke. Somebody was seriously messing with her, and maybe they wanted her hurt. She couldn't explain the eyes and the fangs, so this had to be bad. This guy was obviously capable of inflicting some real damage. His eyes morphed again to the electric blue, and somehow, he broadened even more, looking more animalistic than human.

"I don't understand," she said, her voice shaking as her mind tried to make sense of what her eyes were seeing. "Who are you? Why were you unconscious in a coma? How did you know my name?"

He breathed out, his broad chest moving with the effort. The fangs slowly slid back up, and his eyes returned to the sizzling aqua. "My name is Ronan Kayrs, and I was unconscious because the shield fell." He eyed her, tugging her even closer. "I know your name because I spent four hundred years seeing your face and feeling your soft touch in my dreams."

"My—my face?" she stuttered.

His jaw hardened even more. "And that was *before* I'd accepted my death."

Vampire's Faith Buy links

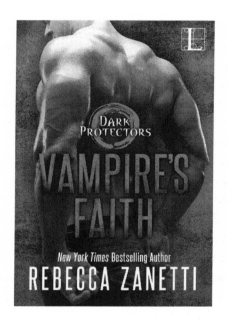

NOW AVAILABLE FROM LEXI BLAKE!

Nobody Does It Better
Masters and Mercenaries, Book 15
By Lexi Blake
February 20, 2018

A spy who specializes in seduction

Kayla Summers was an elite CIA double agent, working inside China's deadly MSS. Now, she works for McKay-Taggart London, but the Agency isn't quite done with her. Spy master Ezra Fain needs her help on a mission that would send her into Hollywood's glamorous and dangerous party scene. Intrigued by the mission and the movie star hunk she will be shadowing, she eagerly agrees. When she finds herself in his bed, she realizes she's not only risking her life, but her heart.

A leading man who doesn't do romance

Joshua Hunt is a legend of the silver screen. As Hollywood's highest paid actor, he's the man everyone wants to be, or be with, but something is missing. After being betrayed more than once, the only romance Josh believes in anymore is on the pages of his scripts. He keeps his relationships transactional, and that's how he likes it, until he meets his new bodyguard. She was supposed to keep him safe, and satisfied when necessary, but now he's realizing he may never be able to get enough of her.

An ending neither could have expected

Protecting Joshua started off as a mission, until it suddenly felt like her calling. When the true reason the CIA wanted her for this assignment is revealed, Kayla will have to choose between serving her country or saving the love of her life.

* * * *

Now available for pre-order!

Amazon: http://amzn.to/2vqfeqd
    iTunes: http://apple.co/2udZAOs
    GooglePlay: http://bit.ly/2v9GLcv
    Barnes & Noble: http://bit.ly/2zDOWPC
    Kobo, and Smashwords coming soon!

"You look beautiful like this."

Kayla didn't respond because they were in the dungeon. She wasn't sure of all the protocols Josh would use. Some Doms preferred their subs remain silent in the dungeon.

A big hand touched her head, palm covering her scalp. "Naturally you have perfect form. Did you learn this at The Garden? I've heard of it, you know. It's so exclusive even I can't get in. I was jealous of Jared when he got a membership to Sanctum. I don't like being left out."

He was an interesting combination of strong Dom and wayward boy. There were major gaps in his history, long periods of time that remained unaccounted for, and that couldn't mean anything good. A good life tended to be documented carefully. What had happened to him between the time he left his foster home and the moment he showed up on Hollywood's radar? What had happened that made him forever need to belong, even if it meant buying his way in?

"You can talk, pet. Unless I give you specific instructions, I never mean to silence your voice."

"If we go to London or Dallas, I can get you into both," she offered. "They're wonderful clubs. Completely different experiences, but both amazing. The Doms in charge are private bastards."

"I belong to a club in Dallas." His hand came off her head and his feet disappeared. "It's very nice."

She knew the one he was talking about. "Well, then if we're in Dallas, you can take me someplace new. I've heard The Club is lovely and that Julian Lodge knows how to treat his clients. It's probably better than Ian Taggart. Ian treats everyone like we're still in the Army and he's the general in charge."

"Lodge is polite, but I still feel like I'm on the outside any place other than The Reef."

She heard the door to the closet open and took a long breath. "It's good to have a place where you belong."

She couldn't see what he was doing. It was part of the glorious mind fuck that got her adrenaline going.

"You seem to belong a lot of places."

"I have a membership to The Garden and Sanctum, but only because of my work status. I feel weird in Sanctum. For a long time I was on the opposite side of Ian Taggart—well, he thought I was on the opposite side. No one was allowed to know my true identity except my handler and his boss. It's the curse of the double agent. Sometimes you feel like no one believes you at all because you've become such a master at lying."

She was surprised that came out as easily as it had. Her former career wasn't something she liked to talk about, but something about being in the dungeon always made her vulnerable. In many ways, the dungeon was the only place she did talk about what had happened to her. It was her confessional, the one place she could be vulnerable because she knew there would be absolution.

"Do you still lie?"

"I try not to. In my daily life, I don't lie at all. I don't care enough to lie. I can be too harsh at times because I gave all my fucks up a long time ago." *Except that I'll lie to you. I'll lie because my job and my friends are all I really care about anymore.*

Yeah, she didn't say that part out loud.

"I like honesty," he said. "No, I require it. I can't stand people blowing sunshine up my ass. I have far too much of that every day. It makes you wonder who to trust. It's why I like Jared. I don't think he's smart enough to lie."

"That feels rough."

"I guess I gave away all my fucks, too. Eyes up."

She brought her eyes to meet his gaze and couldn't help the shiver of desire that went through her body. He'd shed his shirt and every bit of dietary restraint showed in his perfectly cut body. Wearing nothing but a pair of low-slung jeans, he stared down at her. There was no way to miss the bulge in his denims. Joshua Hunt was built on long, lean lines, but that erection was anything but lean. It was a massive beast restrained by denim.

He held a crop in his hand, looking every inch the dark, decadent Dom.

ACKNOWLEDGMENTS

I'm thrilled to bring this next book of the Scorpius Syndrome to readers, and I have many people to thank.

Thank you to my wonderful family, Big Tone, Karlina, and Gabe. I love you very much.

Thanks to Asha Hossain Design for the fabulous cover, Chelle Olson for the fantastic edits, and Michael Pauley for the wonderful audio narrations of the Scorpius Syndrome Books.

Thank you to my agent, Caitlin Blasdell, who gives fantastic advice across the board, and who has been with me through six series. Thanks also to Liza Dawson and the entire Dawson gang for their hard work and support.

Thanks to Jillian Stein, Minga Portillo, Anissa Hammons, Rebecca's Rebels, Writer Space, and Fresh Fiction for getting the word out about the books.

Thanks to my constant support system: Jim and Gail English, Travis and Debbie Smith, Donald and Stephanie West, Jonah and Jessica Namson, and Herb and Kathy Zanetti.

ALSO BY REBECCA ZANETTI

Vampire's Faith (Book 8)

Realm Enforcers (Dark Protector spinoff)

Wicked Ride

Wicked Edge

Wicked Burn

Wicked Kiss

Wicked Bite

Dark Protectors: Reese Family novellas

Teased

Tricked

Tangled

The Sin Brothers series

Forgotten Sins

Sweet Revenge

Blind Faith

Total Surrender

The Blood Brother series

Deadly Silence

Lethal Lies

Twisted Truths

The Maverick Montana series

Against the Wall

Under the Covers

Rising Assets

Over the Top

To keep up to date:

www.RebeccaZanetti.com

https://www.facebook.com/RebeccaZanetti.books

http://rebeccazanetti.com/rebeccas-newsletter/

Made in the USA
Middletown, DE
01 February 2019